## About the Author

Bob was born in Bristol. His career was in the marketing, retailing and distribution of a broad range of technologies, and latterly the event management of technology exhibitions. More recently he has been providing event research for the launches of a number of overseas exhibitions for others.

He has been writing for the last seven years, both fiction and non-fiction.

Bob is married, with two children and five grandchildren, living in rural Oxfordshire.

'Gene Genie' is Bob's second novel and is a sequel to 'Still Water' featuring the same characters facing a brand new challenge. Here it has been revisited and extensively updated.

For more information visit www.BobDenton.co.uk

# GENE GENIE

# Bob Denton

---

# GENE GENIE

© Copyright 2014
Published by Bob Denton

A CIP catalogue record for this title is
available from the British Library.

ISBN 978-0-9569643-6-6

Updated Version 2 - published in 2014
First Published in 2011

# Dedication

To my grandchildren - Daniel, Chloé, Laura, Artie - plus one imminent!

Someone anonymously said, rather poetically, that:
'Grandchildren fill a space in your heart that you never knew was empty.'

Gene Perret more appropriately said: 'An hour with your grandchildren can make you feel young again.
Any longer...'

Perhaps more pertinently to this novel, they are five wonderful, very distinct 'parcels', each wrapped around some of my genes, and I trust this invisible inheritance equips them for the many sorts of challenges that they will surely have to face in their lives, and those of their children and grandchildren...

# Acknowledgements

To Jane for seeking to turn my efforts into correct English grammar, any residual errors of grammar or judgment in the book are mine.
And, all virtues in our grandchildren are entirely Jane's 'fault'!

Apologies to Tyndale Baptist, Bristol, for using the name Tyndale negatively in this story – Jane and I have fond memories of being married there!

**TABLE OF CONTENTS:**

# Chapter 78 - *Double-T R, Morocco*

# PROLOGUE

**Rowan Williams, Archbishop of Canterbury:**

*'We are instantly fascinated by the suggestion of conspiracies and cover-ups; this has become so much the stuff of our imagination these days that it is only natural, it seems, to expect it when we turn to ancient texts, especially biblical texts. We treat them as if they were unconvincing press releases from some official source, whose intention is to conceal the real story; and that the real story waits for the intrepid investigator to uncover it and share it with the waiting world. Anything that looks like the official version is automatically suspect.'*

It was a frightening place, too many shadows, a series of niches concealing threatening gothic forms. She felt that they were ready to leap out at her as she passed.

Her throat was irritated with an unpleasant bitter-sweet taste of damp that pervaded the air in here. Yet the cloying taste was not her overwhelming sensation; that had to be the massive amount of guilt she was experiencing just by being there. She knew this place was out of bounds, that she was strictly forbidden from coming here unsupervised.

The eleven-year-old was not normally disobedient, could not easily have explained why she was breaking their most important rule. It was the stricture most often repeated, the very one they underlined in, what sounded to the girl, to be a most threatening tone.

This powerful sensation of sinfulness was a reaction to the overload of guilt that the Sisters dished out at every opportunity. If she had been pressed to give a reason for this expedition, she would have said honestly that she had not planned it, the opportunity had simply presented itself on this chilly March evening.

The Sisters had been flustered, fluttering all about the place like big black butterflied. They were totally engrossed with what was the convent's main event of each and every year. For today they celebrated their founder's day, their attention was so clearly elsewhere that she had grabbed the chance.

The adults were gathering in the main hall and then would be taking a planned tour around the classrooms. They would later return to the hall for a formal dinner, the centrepiece of this annual celebration of this long-established Catholic school.

All day the Sisters had been engaged in their preparation. Most of the girls were engrossed in preparing to present their term's work to the parents. Those more senior had also been dragooned into becoming guides for the visiting parents, for the many expected church personnel, a whole raft of local dignitaries each invited to this celebration. This of course had required rehearsal time.

Stephanie's parents were not to be among them. Her mother only recently placed in the ground beside the convent's local church. Her father was said to be unavoidably overseas. Though, in truth, he was no Catholic, behaved awkwardly around the nuns, very evidently uncomfortable with their brand of enthusiastic religion.

She knew that he reacted particularly badly to the certainty with which they pursued their faith. He was not prepared to challenge them, but when forced to listen to them his body language expressed his feelings all too clearly.

Today her form teacher had not allocated her any specific task for founder's day, probably because she was still being rather too considerate of the girl's recent loss.

Sister Bernadette was very young and extremely inexperienced both in the Church and particularly in life skills; probably less than ten years older than Stephanie herself.

Bernadette was completely untrained, thoroughly naïve in personal matters. Her gentle nature meant she was poorly equipped to handle this sort of extremely delicate, emotional situation. Fully aware of her shortcomings, the young nun's approach had therefore evolved into a policy of avoiding being left alone with Stephanie at any time.

In class sessions she never called upon the girl to make a comment, never selected her to provide any answer. Outside the classroom she gave Stephanie a wide berth, did anything to avoid being drawn into a conversation, because she just could not imagine what she might say to the girl.

Unfortunately, perhaps predictably, Stephanie's classmates promptly took their lead from their teacher; as a result they had also become very uncomfortable around her. She effectively became isolated, disorientated by her sudden conferred 'island' status. She had become separate, somehow she was now officially 'other'.

This had all happened at precisely the time when she most needed the familiarity and comfort of teachers and school friends around her; the very time when she should have been immersed in the joy and challenge of their classes. In fact she would have benefited by becoming engaged in almost anything that could have helped sweep her past her personal tragedy; but nothing was offered.

Given that she received no useful external stimuli she had therefore little choice but to withdraw into herself. She began to live her life down deep within her own mind, unconsciously building barriers between her thoughts and her surroundings.

By concentrating wholeheartedly on her school books she was avoiding any real awareness of other people's discomfort in her presence. She buried herself in her studies, reading on well ahead of the class sessions. Whenever she had the opportunity she spent long periods alone in the school library, further distancing herself from the chatter of her classmates.

This isolation was expanding her capabilities much more rapidly than lessons alone might have achieved, placing her ahead of her classmates in her knowledge, her understanding and her opinions; this fact didn't help her in building bridges with her peers. While intellectually she was striding ahead, her lack of any personal contact meant her emotional development had completely stalled.

Today's breach of the rules had been originated by one of her library sessions. She had come across an old, well-thumbed book that told the story of the martyred Saint Perpetua whose name had been so proudly adopted and heralded by her convent. Perpetua was the convent's 'founder'.

Stephanie had been enthralled to learn that Perpetua, at the time of her martyrdom, was a young woman, a new mother. The moving account told of one of the oldest surviving stories of a Christian woman, right back in the very earliest days of the Church. Stephanie read all she could find about Saint Perpetua and her canonisation. She learned that Perpetua was one of only seven women, other than the Blessed Virgin, that was named in the early versions of the Canon of the Mass.

In more recent times Perpetua had become marginalised by the modernisers of the Church, but on this annual founder's night her 'Passion' would be recited over dinner, in almost lurid detail, by the head girl.

Stephanie had read Perpetua's own account of her imprisonment, of her father's desperate pleas for her to renounce her Christianity so she would be released from her impending fate. Stephanie knew her own father's preference would be for her to be less committed to the Church, less embroiled in her faith.

Surely this would amount to her renouncing her mother? Her mother had attended St Perpetua's too, had wanted Stephanie to attend the same convent school. Stephanie often thought perhaps all she had left of her mother was this place.

Perpetua had graphically recorded dreams of her forthcoming martyrdom. Stephanie's current dreams were just as gloomy and doom-laden.

The account of the Saint's death while inside an amphitheatre, in the distant year 203 CE, was so very graphic too. First scourged, then wounded by a bull and attacked by other wild animals, finally she had been finished off with a sword. This was of course shocking to a modern young girl, looking back down the years from deep within her middle-class and sheltered existence. But then her loss of her mother at a young age was no less shocking to her.

She realised that when she died her mother was probably only a few years older than Perpetua had been on the day when she calmly entered that Roman stadium to face her fate.

It was with all these thoughts awash in her far-from-developed psyche that she entered the chapel just before twilight. She felt strongly that all this pomp and celebration surrounding their founder's day was completely missing the point of their Saint's life and death. She alone could appreciate the real depth of Perpetua's commitment to her faith. Somehow it reached down the many centuries and touched her so very particularly.

Tonight she realised that she could understand how Perpetua faced her martyrdom with such confidence. Life was just full of pain, of sadness and emptiness. Death within the cocoon of a strong faith would be so glorious, such a welcome departure from a joyless life. It would be so easy, so quick, so satisfying. It would be a reaching out to a more peaceful place; a place where surely her mother would be waiting for her.

During their services in the chapel she sat near the front counting the beams in the roof and the individual pieces of glass in the colourful window while the service droned on. Tonight she went straight to the altar rail and knelt there to pray, her eyes closed tightly.

Thoughts of a glorious suicide were like a maelstrom in her young mind. Suicide she knew absolutely was a mortal sin, though how could it be so wrong to want to be with her mother again? Trying to reach a decision, she thought perhaps tonight might just be a good time. While everyone else was preoccupied she could find the place, the time, the opportunity to end everything. No, not to end it, more the opportunity to make a fresh and exciting start! To be with her mother again.

She suddenly opened her eyes, it was as though they had been opened fully for the very first time. She was completely transported by a beam of light, cast into the chapel as the very last act of the sun's departure from the day.

The light was like a living breathing entity. It did not just shine through the window; it burst through it, cascading through the stained-glass in a torrent. Its Technicolor effect washed across the pale white statue of Perpetua creating an unnatural rainbow, in many more shades than the seven basic colours.

As Stephanie gazed at this kaleidoscope, the statue appeared to turn, the holy face looked down and smiled at her. There could be no doubt, this was a warm and welcoming smile. The lips moved and she heard quite clearly the words *Pax tecum*. When she later thought back over this moment Stephanie found she was confused couldn't recall if it was the face of Perpetua or that of her mother she had seen. Her eventual conclusion was that in her mind the two had clearly become as one within the statue.

But just as suddenly, the last ray of daylight washed over and faded from the statue. Had the whole scene been in her imagination? No, the statue had definitely moved, she had certainly smiled and she had clearly said 'Peace be with you'. Besides Stephanie had not merely heard the words, she had also felt a tangible, bestowed peace that had descended upon her.

At last her faith had been rewarded, she was no longer alone. In that instant she had recovered her hope for a future. Light and colour from the beam had poured back in to her life; thoughts of suicide had been completely washed away by the experience.

Later that evening, when the celebrations were over, she excitedly sought out Sister Bernadette. The young nun still exhibited some reluctance to get into a conversation but as Stephanie enthusiastically related her experience the barrier that the teacher had erected was breached. Bernadette, a simple soul, was delighted that her student had undergone such a change. She was of course, based upon her calling, predisposed to accept the truth of this revelation with evident joy.

Bernadette rushed from their meeting to share the joy with Sister Theresa, her mentor, an older, much more world-weary member of the convent. Theresa had too many years of experience of wilful pupils who had sought to conjure up some act of epiphany so they became the centre of attention or as an excuse for not completing their prep. On a few notable instances it was used to make fun of the more gullible younger sisters, just like Bernadette.

Theresa met with Stephanie the next morning, tried gently yet persistently to shake the girl's story, but in this she completely failed. The girl was convinced she had witnessed a genuine vision, judging by the notable change in her behaviour and attitudes from that of recent weeks, it was clear that she had found it a profound experience. The Sister accepted that there was probably no other agenda for this claimed visitation.

Theresa decided to ask Father Brendan from the local church to investigate the event and to give his view upon its veracity. Father Brendan met with Stephanie many times across the following months.

Having passed the problem to him, the nuns moved on. They failed to ask him for progress reports, showed no evident concern as he progressively managed to undo all the benefits that had come from the vision or dream.

Following the sessions with the old priest the girl became ever more withdrawn. Her subsequent downward spiral was worse than her decline following her mother's death.

These private one-on-one sessions with the old priest certainly left a lasting impression that would affect and shape Stephanie Tasker's mind and soul for the rest of her days.

# BOOK ONE

**Titus Lucretius Carus** (99 – 55 BC)

*'Fear was the first thing on earth to make gods.'*

**Jonathan Swift,** Thoughts on Various Subjects (1706)

*'We have just enough religion to make us hate, but not enough to make us love each other.'*

**Karl Marx** (1843)

*'Religion…is the opium of the people.'*

# Chapter 1 - *Arizona*

Samuel Shepherd leaned forward, pressed the remote and switched on the video. As he swayed back into his chair the plasma screen came to life replacing their view of the back of his head with a larger-than-life, ultra close-up of his face.

Leonine was the first impression he inspired, though one journalist had deliberately transmuted this to vulpine just to allow her to play with his name. The headline she worked so hard to achieve was of course that he was 'a wolf in shepherd's clothing'.

But in truth he was rather more leonine. A mane of grey hair radiated around his big face like a halo. His large green eyes so widely separated they looked as if they were side-mounted. The effect was completed by his broken, flat wide nose and a huge mouthful of bright white teeth above a quite prominent chin.

Yes, definitely leonine, though everything about his demeanour conspired to ensure he looked more 'Uncle Leo' than a threatening predator. But first impressions are usually very perceptive, indeed he was all predator.

Dieter observed as the old man ran his hand through his hair as he saw himself on the screen, almost as though grooming himself. It was clear that, unlike most movie stars, he thoroughly enjoyed watching himself.

Up on the large screen Shepherd was saying, 'I am Alpha and Omega, the beginning and the end. As everyone here should know, those are the words of our Lord Jesus Christ - how he described himself in The Revelation.'

The camera was panning the room in which Shepherd had been preaching. It paused to display each of the various expressive faces of the thirty or more sitting at the heart of the room. A fair proportion of those in the room, perhaps all too aware of the camera, were nodding and smiling at his remarks.

Few in fact needed the additional presence of cameras; their eagerness was as much to get noticed by him, wanting to be seen and recognised by this man. For they had thrown in their lot with him, he was to be their future, their reason for being. This session was their personal Alpha and he was to be the one to define and bring about their Omega.

A long shot showed Shepherd as he surveyed his flock. He had quite a small-framed body, somewhat out of proportion with that large and impressive head. Dieter realised that was the reason he needed the close-ups; he was playing to his strengths.

Shepherd continued. 'Or was it he? Was it Himself, who dictated the Revelation for us? Wasn't it St John putting those words into his mouth?'

Another pause as the camera sought out the audience's faces. The smiles had begun to fade with a degree of incomprehension; was Shepherd questioning the Bible?

'And then, when we talk of The Revelation, just which St John might we mean precisely? Do we mean John the Apostle, or John the Evangelist, or John the Presbyter or was it some other canonised John who happened to be exiled to the Greek island of Patmos?'

Those gathered were now showing their confusion more obviously. This was their much anticipated first direct contact with their spiritual leader. A special gathering of their Order for those who had been freshly admitted to its 'Perfect' status, a closed meeting where they expected their Patriarch would inspire and motivate them; they certainly had not signed up for this challenging of the scriptures!

On the screen it was evident that he had paused deliberately to let these first impressions settle and to develop. He was shown looking out over faces that just a few seconds earlier had been open and eager for his enlightenment. He and the camera watched as the shadow of bewilderment spread to all parts of the room. Some could be seen looking questioningly to the sides of the room to try to catch the attention of their individual mentors, the Level Two Deacons and Level Three Pastors who had developed and supported them to this point.

This was not the man, nor the message, that they had been led to expect. While undoubtedly charismatic in the flesh he might have been a car salesman or a realtor. So far he had shown none of the sparkle that they would have anticipated from the legion of evangelists they had seen on television throughout their lives; this was not the role that they had expected him to adopt, his very first message to them appeared to cast doubt upon the Holy Bible?

Shepherd flicked off the video. Today he was relaxing in his office with three of his recently appointed bishops. 'Look, even with this video you can feel their tangible uncertainty, see that they are not at all sure about me at this stage. As Level One Perfects they cannot be allowed that doubt of course, and you will see how I deal with this shortly.

'You three, now you have been admitted into the Sixth order of Perfects, have become Bishops in the Order, you are permitted extreme access to me. You have direct, insider contact with me and it is perfectly acceptable for you to question me. You must understand I am merely the Patriarch, not some sort of deity; I am truly one of you. In your early days of Perfection it was necessary for me to assume the role of the leader, the teacher - somehow aloof, somehow other, someone to look up to perhaps?

'And, as you will see, I still must play this role with these newly elected Level One Perfects. But you will come to accept that I am just human, with all the desires, needs and temptations that we all share. Leadership can be wearisome. I have to lead the Order. I am expected always to know the way to go, never permitted to have doubts. It's for this reason that I need you, the Fives and Sixes, the deans and bishops of our Order, to keep me on my toes, to criticise my approach, my actions, my direction. You must share the burden with me and ensure that we do lead our people into Salvation.'

He looked around the three. 'So please review this opening of our 'Genesis' session, this is the one I delivered yesterday to the fresh intake of Perfects here in Arizona.'

Hannah had dressed very carefully to try to hide the fact that she was an extremely attractive and shapely brunette, yet all her efforts failed as her beauty still shone through her attempt at dowdiness. In a clipped English accent she was the first to comment. 'Sir, I can see that you have made a powerful start. They would have had all sorts of preconceptions about you. I know that at their stage I had the warnings of my friends and family still ringing in my ears - that this was a cult, that you were a fraudster.'

Dieter was concerned she may have overstepped the line with this, but relaxed when he saw the old goat smiling at her benignly.

Enrique, an open-faced Hispanic American, was keen to move things on too. 'Right at the outset you have shaken their confidence in their past beliefs, even challenged their perceptions of the Bible. I believe that this is what you describe as the first vital step in breaking down their past character to make them more open to the new one. They'll therefore be more receptive to the beliefs that we will instil as we engage them in their upcoming whirlwind of tasks and activities.'

Shepherd started the video. 'Good. Let's look at a little more of the session and see how this course evolves.'

On the screen Shepherd pointed directly at one of the audience whose expression had been too easy to read. 'William, you must not allow those doubts to develop. We are all Perfects here, and none of us questions the divine significance of the fruits of Abraham.'

William's lack of a 'poker face' was evident as he reddened with a mixture of joy, both because he had been recognised and because the Leader actually knew his name. However his expression was also tinged with some concern that evidently he had been displaying his thoughts far too openly.

The screen was scanning the faces as the Leader again freeze-framed it.

'Just look at that sea of open faces. You have to learn how to recognise those who are most needy to be recognised; it is these who should never be chosen. What we need at this stage are those who are still reticent, not showing their thoughts, still guarding their expressions and their minds. These are the ones where we still need to break down the barriers, must shake their confidence.'

He released the pause button.

'Welcome to our first meeting, we call this our 'Genesis' event. But in that title we are not referring directly to the Old Testament book, it's our personal coming together to define what we are and precisely what it is that we believe. Let me be clear that in no manner are we seeking to dismiss the book of Genesis, for Abraham was the vital founding root not just of Christianity but of Judaism and of Islam; he is still revered today by all three of these major world religions.'

Several of the audience were seen to be back to nodding again.

'Who among us here believes a single word of what we read in today's newspapers? I have certainly never seen an article about me or our new religious order that is without error. So then what is it that makes us believe that the Bible, published so haphazardly and so long ago, could be any more accurate? Today's factual errors are published despite our current powerful libel laws and our country's litigious nature; the very weaponry that I might choose to apply to remedy the misreporting of our Order.'

The camera showed that the smiles were coming back. They were starting to relax into the to-and-fro of the Leader's presentation and had recovered some of their joy at being inducted into the priesthood of this new religious movement. For that was what they had each been drilled to think, not cult but 'new religious movement'.

The Leader picked on another of his audience. 'Rose-Marie. You trained as an attorney, so tell me. Should I take advantage of those weapons to correct my reputation?'

Rose-Marie was caught like a rabbit in the headlights, clearly unable to commit herself to a course of action, either way.

He paused long enough to make her feel uncomfortable, 'Difficult choice, isn't it? We all want our reputations to shine, but the world is by its very nature full of lies, deceit and misinformation. We cannot hope to convert this wicked world to see the Light. We have received His message for over 2,000 years and yet still the vast majority does not listen to it.'

He walked up to the girl and sat down on the floor beside her. 'Rose-Marie, you will certainly be able to tell us all what the Israelites did while Moses left them to go up the mountain to receive the Ten Commandments.'

Now Rose-Marie was on safer, well-trodden ground. 'They made a graven image, a golden calf and they worshipped it.'

'Thank you, Rose-Marie. Moses was the great founding leader of the Faith, all three great religions are absolutely sure that this was a man who was selected, sanctified, touched by God. Those with him in the wilderness were his chosen people, they were the converted, and yet Moses was gone for such a short while before they turned their faith towards idols.

'Let's look at the other examples, and there are many. How short a time did Adam and Eve last before they were tempted by the serpent to eat the forbidden fruit? The Ark had to be built, Noah with his family and menagerie needed to be saved from the sinful world that had evolved some years later. Even Christ's closest disciples lost their way, faithful Peter denounced him thrice. We just have to understand and to accept that this is the intrinsic nature of the world outside of our community. People are fickle, wrong-thinking, tempted by the wrong things, seeking out shallow temporal pleasures.'

He stood up effortlessly and looked around at them as he said, 'I don't need to tell you. You have all been out there, you know they'll do anything rather than think. They fill their days with idleness, or they rush to accumulate material things. They worship only the hollowness of celebrity and thrash around loudly in their shallowness. They therefore completely squander the precious gift of life, waste the great potential of their minds. Only here, within this community will you be free to contemplate just who it is that we are, just what we are here for, and together we will establish quite where we are all going.'

He turned his back on the audience, paused, and walked back to the front of the room. Once he reached the stage, he looked up and to the right as if offering up a silent prayer. As he turned his face back to them a light that none had noticed before lit up his face, made him somehow sparkle; then it was gone as quickly as it came.

'Jesus Christ had no such litigious weapons. Anyway, by the time the first three New Testament Gospels were written he had been dead for decades. Now you are a Perfect, you can be shown our innermost secrets.' He walked the centre aisle. 'Perhaps you already know that the Gospel of Mark was the one that came first, it was written in Rome. You may know how those of Matthew and Luke clearly drew from it and other source material to write theirs some time later. Most theologians and researchers believe that this other original source was lost.' He smiled at them meaningfully, clearly indicating that these theologians were misled.

He suddenly burst into a strong and melodic baritone. 'Those things that you're liable to read in the Bible, they ain't necessarily so.'

The video had been paused again.

Dieter looked towards Hannah trying, but failing, to show that he was clearly smitten, always ready to defer to her if she wanted to comment. When he saw that she did not, he asked. 'I guess that your use of their names, and the sitting on the floor, are both mini 'love bombs'?'

Shepherd smiled, 'Yes, and no. Yes I want them to feel at home here and everyone likes to be recognised of course. But I must confess that the kneeling is pure unadulterated TGIF, something I picked up from eating in their restaurants. They train their staff to bend down to the level of the diners; it breaks down any them-and-us barrier, sets the relationship as on a par. This opens up much better channels of communication.

'But don't you see that these are also controlling actions? In the next section you will see that I made clear that I knew them, knew of their past. They will need to come to appreciate that we will know their thoughts and actions in the future too. We want them to know that while they are always being cared for, we are also reviewing their progress at all times. We are watching!'

# Chapter 2 - *London, UK*

Both of them instantly stopped their groping, quickly removed their hands from beneath loosened clothing; there was that strange noise again. And no, it wasn't just their imagination.

No, they couldn't just ignore it and carry on with what had been the increasingly urgent business at hand. The noise could no longer be written off as some woodland creature. They both concluded that there must be somebody out there, stood right outside the van. Yet parked up high on this isolated escarpment they had heard no approaching vehicle. They felt that they had been perfectly concealed and alone; until now.

He belatedly pushed down the front door lock, tried to do it quietly but the noise in the van sounded loud, just like a gunshot. He realised that this action made him somehow less manly, less in charge. Heaven forbid, perhaps it would make him less desirable; he had better go and investigate to make clear that this was not the case.

Zipping up and pulling his shirt back over his shoulders he slowly and awkwardly extricated his limbs inside the rear of the darkened and cluttered van. He could see her lying there awkwardly, embarrassed, trying to cover up parts of her that had been so warm, inviting and compliant just seconds before. God, she looked so beautiful in this pale light.

Perhaps it was some creepy peeping tom, or worse one of those 'dogging' perverts? If it was, then he was about to pay heavily for interrupting them; this dog could expect a whipping!

It was just so frustrating. They were finally here. After over a month of his trying, here she was ready, willing and so desirable! The bastard was really going to pay dearly for this interruption.

There it was again, that weird noise and it was definitely right outside! It was a strange guttural sound that had his hairs tingling on the back of his neck as he wiped off a portion of the steamed-up small rear window to peer out.

In the circle that he cleared, a face appeared. It was startlingly close, right up against the window. He froze with inaction at the sight while his mind raced to process his thoughts. It was evidently a black guy, though he was strange looking. His lips were a shockingly bright pink, and this made him look almost effeminate. With this latter observation his confidence was flooding back, it was some bloody gay wearing lipstick, and he was about to get beaten to a pulp.

There was the noise again. The black guy was clearly excited by finding them, making this guttural noise, eyes sparkling, lips moistened; he was a really bloody creepy looking bloke. Well now he was going to get his!

He reached for the door release, but as he did the black guy opened his mouth. Never before had he seen quite such a mouthful of teeth, and they were large meaningful looking teeth. He grabbed back his hand from the release button.

She had just finished dressing and had not been able to see the face while still lying on the van floor. Now that she was sitting up, she peered over the shoulders of her interrupted lover, looked directly at the weird face looking in at them - and she screamed.

The face at the window reacted to this sudden noise and screamed right back at her. It was at an inhumanly high pitch, and seconds later the face disappeared from the cleared-off panel. The two screams had flushed huge quantities of adrenaline through his body and finally he sprang into action. He swung open the rear door in anger.

He caught a glimpse of a shape bounding off into the bushes. It had a strange and yet strangely familiar gait, almost a scuttling movement. He couldn't quite place what it was, but knew he had some memory of seeing that sort of movement before. Certainly it wasn't very human, just what the bloody hell was he?

It had all been such a shock that neither of them could contemplate trying to resume their amorous intentions and so they drove away from the secluded spot. Rather too fast at first, then once the adrenaline had subsided he slowed and they discussed whether they should report the incident.

It was those who remained unmentioned who won the day.

He didn't want any word getting back to his wife, after all this was just sex. OK, so it was sex that he'd had to work rather too long and too hard for, but it was still just sex. Unconsciously he realized that he had been seeking the confirmation that he still had what it takes. Why should they report it anyway, he had seen the guy off, hadn't he? The unusual, almost bizarre, face and the strange movement as it scampered off, were already being dismissed by his mind. That creep certainly wouldn't hang around any parked cars again in a hurry. He could see absolutely no good reason to screw up the happy home. Besides because of that bastard they'd not managed to do anything anyway!

She couldn't contemplate her father hearing of this. Hadn't he warned her against dating local guys and particularly this sort of older man? Perhaps there really was something behind her father's eagerness to cling on to his Hindu religion from the old country. Maybe that something had arranged this interruption before they'd actually done it?

Certainly the glimpse of that awful face had looked to her a lot like *Hanuman*, her father's monkey God, the one that had fought with the demon king. So was this all some sort of message to bring her back to the beliefs of her family, her people? Perhaps she should now take the arranged husband that they had been proposing from their family village back home?

They mutually concluded that it was best that he drop her a few streets from her home and they agreed they would not mention the whole episode to anyone.

The following evening down the pub he would tell his best mate how he'd finally scored with the little Asian girl who worked at his office. How amazingly experienced and different she'd been as a lover. While he theatrically massaged the small of his back, he would explain how she'd shown him every position in the Kama Sutra in the cramped back of his van,. He would add how he'd beaten a peeping tom to within an inch of his life and then went back to finally satisfy her very demanding appetite.

She wouldn't return to work again. In fact at the same time that he was overblowing his tale, she would be soaring over the North Sea, winging her way back to the old country and to an arranged marriage, looking thoughtfully out over the water.

# Chapter 3 - *Bolivia*

Ah, water. Now this was much more like it! Tom Carter smiled out over the huge lake and felt himself relax for the first time in many days. He had spent the past several weeks deep inside Bolivia, a country which has absolutely no coastline; there he, an oceanographer by profession, had felt very much out of water!

Though by qualification an oceanographer, many years back Tom had managed to shrug off the constraints of his direct discipline. Yet it remained still very much his first love; he was never quite as relaxed as when he looked out over water, or bobbed along on top of it, or plunged down into its depths.

He had wittingly forsaken 'Her' for the greater freedom that he found he could exploit by becoming accepted into the much more general field of the earth sciences; it was here that he had earned his celebrity status.

He was in absolutely no doubt that it was a lot more fun popularizing interesting and selected facets across many scientific persuasions, rather than having to slog it out head-to-head with a back-biting, squabbling peer group in just the one. Looking out over this mass of water, he realised that he was still moved by the subject. It was a lot like returning home after a long trip, just like this one had actually been, and jumping back into his own bed, snuggling down deep beneath the covers.

The water in question was Lake Titicaca; where the small Bolivian Navy managed to keep itself busy. Yes, this land-locked country actually had one! In looking out over it he found it difficult to accept that it was only a very large lake; that it wasn't the sea that it appeared to be. He vaguely recalled the brief joy at some past pub quiz, when he'd dredged from a recess somewhere deep in his mind that Titicaca was the world's highest navigable lake. It had helped his team to win that round, now here he was looking out over it so many years later.

His local host was DINAR, the Department of Archaeology of Bolivia. The body regularly hosted teams from American and British universities to assist with the many archaeological digs it maintained in the area. Apparently it was one such dig team that had made the discovery that had brought him here. Someone within DINAR, catching some of the publicity surrounding Tom's forthcoming book, had invited him to come and inspect those finds.

He had become breathless walking through the shore-side town of Copacabana. But on this occasion it was not the view but the altitude that left him breathless. Disappointingly the town had proven to be absolutely nothing like its Brazilian namesake. No girls from Ipanema were going walking; no keepy-uppy volleyball down on the beach. Mind you it was not unattractive, but it reminded Tom more of one of the small Greek Aegean island ports. Up at this altitude and in this cold, his thoughts of the Brazilian female beach volleyball players might help to raise his body temperature a little, but he realised that they would seem like extra-terrestrials up here.

His main contact was Amaro Paz Bustamante, a dapper little local who worked for DINAR. Amaro had arranged for a boat to take Tom out to one of the lake's larger islands, the Isla del Sol. But he had explained that the captain also had another commission; a higher-paying regular passenger who needed a short stop-off at one of the floating islands in the lake.

Amaro was every bit the tour guide as he described these strange islands. 'There are forty or more of these moveable islands on the lake at any time; we are visiting one of the larger ones. I would imagine that it is probably able to support around twenty extended families of the locals Uros. I thought that you, Mr Carter, would find this interesting because the Uros are an ancient people. They are the direct descendants of a pre-Incan tribe.'

To Tom the island looked substantial enough. It supported a series of buildings and even a high watchtower was visible as they made their approach and moored up; the tower looked something like a lighthouse.

Amaro said, 'It is Mr Berkeley who arranged for our visit here.' He pointed out a large American who was evidently preparing to disembark, leaning down and fussing over a bag at the prow.

Tom's snatched side-view of Berkeley had triggered some sort of memory. He dredged for what had sparked this, then realised that it had been a glimpse of someone whom he had seen when they had taken a side trip, just a few days earlier. It was when he had visited the local *chullpas* or burial towers.

Amaro was still talking as Tom took a double-take, 'These moveable man-made islands are constructed from the *totora* plant, a sort of reed. They bind these reeds together using ropes made out of dried grasses and it's the skilful combination of the reeds and the *totoras* that gives the island its structure and strength. The Uros are of course great fishermen.'

# Chapter 4 - *Arizona*

'Let's look more closely at the Gospel writers and disciples, these fishers of men.' Shepherd had started up the video again. 'Earlier, I mentioned only Matthew, Mark and Luke, but what of the Gospel of St John? It was written in Ephesus in Greece even later, at the end of the first century CE; some of you may recall that Ephesus was one of the seven early churches to which The Revelation was addressed.'

The camera showed the audience was now hanging on his every word. Not just that they knew they would be tested on their memories later, but because they did not want to miss any nuance.

'The Gospel of John was different from the others because it was written more to be used in reaching out to the non-believers; early on the Greeks were a particular target. By this time the early Christian Church was no longer reserved just for the Jew. John's Gospel edits the earlier material and in its content it proves to be much more spiritual than the other three. As a result it has often been in severe danger down the centuries, at risk of being edited out of the Bible; perhaps to be downgraded to an apocrypha included in just a few of the less-circulated versions of the holy book.'

On screen the camera followed the Leader as he walked and looked around the room.

'In your previous life were any of you journalists or editors? Perhaps, edited your college magazine?' Several were prepared to raise a hand following his qualification.

He pointed at one of them. 'Ah, Jon, your name is most appropriate of course to our current discussion! I believe you edited a magazine at your college?'

Jon was impressed that the Leader knew his name and this fact, 'It was just a small political magazine at college.'

'OK, so not so very appropriate after all. I was going to ask how you edited the various journalistic submissions, how you ensured you got to the truth of what it was that they had investigated. But then if yours was a political magazine I guess that was never really an issue of great importance?'

Jon was not going to let the work he had done on his magazine be dealt with quite so lightly. 'I felt that I worked diligently to show our perspective of the truth.'

The Leader let this thought hang out there for a moment, paused looking heavenward, and then repeated it. 'Our perspective of the truth...' He did a circuit of the room simply saying the phrase over and over.

'Jon was dealing in politics, where tactics, strategies and perspectives are of course commonplace; but what of our truth, THE Truth? Should it ever have perspectives or is truth, simply that, the truth?'

He looked around and saw several willing to respond to his question. But he did not need their inputs on this one. He lowered his voice, knowing that the sound system was able to carry his voice clearly to all those present. The light was back illuminating his face. But was it a light? It was almost as if it came from within him as he walked around the stage.

'Today we have had two thousand years of journalists and editors applying their perspectives of the Christian truth, twisting the message to suit their times and their own beliefs, building careers, feathering nests, placating the then current authorities... Let's be charitable and say that they mostly had good intentions in adding their confusion and false ideas to the original story. That's perhaps true of many, but not all. Some, you will come to understand, deliberately set out to make sure that the message is confused. But we will come back to them later.'

The light had gone again. 'So, just who and what should we believe?'

As the video paused, Hannah beamed. 'Brilliant, I love the way you echoed back his own words to make your point, to show his error.'

Dieter was disturbed by her obvious adulation of Shepherd and blurted out, 'Was he a plant, put there to feed you that line?'

Shepherd stood and glared at him. 'Certainly not! It would later become obvious if I stooped to such a cheap trick. It's simply a matter of a skill that we need each of you to develop. You have to work the audience until you get a valuable response, you need to recognise it, seize on it and then use it to the full.

'Otherwise it would be like you setting out to deliver a pre-agreed and fixed patter. You would not be believed no matter how much enthusiasm you might try to apply. It has to be an honest dialogue. You need the individuals that are there to participate, to matter, while of course constantly reminding them that they need to stay within our community for this to have meaning. Let's move on.'

Back up on the screen he was saying, 'We have a whole series of teachings for you to analyse for yourself, to establish what you believe to be true and to conclude what it is that has led away from the truth. Today let me simply suggest to you that a basic time-line of Christianity is very informative.' A gauze screen had reeled down almost unnoticeably behind him and a chart appeared on it.

'Let's look at some of these major branch lines. Following on from the Acts of the Apostles, here in 431CE they held the Council of Ephesus. Decisions they made then led directly to the Assyrian Church parting ways with the main Church. Just twenty years later the Council of Chalcedon effectively split the

Church with the formation of the Oriental Orthodoxy. Then in the 11<sup>th</sup> century power struggles led to the Byzantines splitting with the Roman Church to establish the Eastern Orthodoxy. In the 16<sup>th</sup> century the Reformation saw the coming of the Protestants, driven away by the politics and the pomp, the bureaucracy and the bigotry of the Roman Church. So this chart perhaps best illustrates that there are today so many versions of the Church, each staffed with their own persuasive and active journalists and editors.' He smiled across at Jon, 'Each justifying its very own perspective of the truth.'

'We will teach you that the early Church is the one place where we can find the untrammelled, the unedited Christian truth.' He paused. 'I mentioned a little earlier those who deliberately falsify, who set out to confuse. Don't allow yourselves to become confused. You need to seek out the Truth and grasp it close to you, for we are approaching the End Time. The end time that was prophesised by both the great prophet Daniel and again later within The Revelation; Daniel's four beasts and Revelation's four horses of the Apocalypse, and be assured that the first horse is already loose!'

His audience was on the edge of its seats.

'We will show you over the coming days and weeks that the first of the seven seals of the Revelation has already been opened. There are seven cycles, seven seals; seven of course being the heavenly concept of perfection. The seven seals detailed in the Revelation, those same seven seals that need to be opened before we can reach Salvation.

'It is no accident that there are seven Levels of Enlightenment within our order of Perfects. You join at Level One and your time in the Order will take you on a journey through each of these seven levels.'

# Chapter 5 – *Tiwanaku, Bolivia*

Tom had been invited to Bolivia to investigate some recent finds at the ancient city of Tiwanaku but the outcome of this had fallen a long way short of his expectations. He thrashed around to find something that would rescue this trip, his time and effort, so it was something of an accident that he had taken a side trip to the *chullpas*. He hoped the fact that these intriguing artefacts were conveniently close might just resurrect his journey by casting some new light upon the subject of his current book project.

*Chullpas* are old burial towers, some built to an impressive ten metres in height, each created to house the remains of an Aymaran noble, occasionally constructed large enough to house a whole noble family. The Aymaras were to some extent unfortunates, in that this group did not fare well in history; they were conquered by the Incas, then again later by the Spanish Conquistadores. Yet despite this they still managed to survive right through to modern times.

Their place in history is however not marked in any significant way, except for these intriguing funerary monuments; *Chullpas* are located right across Bolivia and Peru. From his research Tom was aware that there were also some quite similar constructions discovered across on Easter Island. He was all too ready to conclude that surely there must be some form of linkage.

Inside these tombs the remains were not laid out flat, as in the West; instead they were buried in a foetal position. For his book Tom would presume that this must have something to do with rebirth symbology.

Tom had become particularly drawn to these constructions because they were all built to face the rising sun. Surely this must mean they fell within his current interest of archaeo-astronomy? He assumed that this early civilisation must have revered or practised some form of astronomy.

The southern *chullpas* he visited were square in structure, constructed from adobe. Amaro, as he accompanied Tom on the tour, explained those further to the north were more often round in shape and more usually built from stone.

Apparently these burial sites had contained not only the bodily remains but also the possessions, equipment and clothes of the dead. Tom was therefore not at all surprised to find that many of them had been vandalized, their contents plundered down through the years.

He had a further reason for visiting this particular area; he wanted to see for himself the ritual pathways known as the Sajama Lines; these he believed were definitely astronomical relics. The 'lines' had been manually scored into the ground, running right across the landscape connecting up *chullpas* with other shrines and some small villages in the area. The multitude of paths had been created by the locals by simply disturbing the surface soil and rock, this revealed a lighter rock that lay beneath the original surface to create the 'line'. The lines were the accumulation of some 3,000 years of dedicated application. But what Tom hadn't fully appreciated, until he got there, was that this huge volume of work had been completed at such a punishing altitude.

So far no-one could satisfactorily explain the remarkable regularity of the many straight lines, some running for many kilometres, across some pretty rough terrain, without deviation.

These Sajama lines were scored across an area of more than 20,000 square kilometres. Tom believed that the lines were a huge man-made artworks, but the remarkable thing was that it was drawn at so large a scale across the countryside that it was completely impractical to appreciate the outcome from the ground. This of course led to an obvious question from many researchers who queried that given their 'illegibility' at any sort of human or ground level, then for whom had they been intended? Tom presumed they were for their gods.

They were only appreciated when seen from the air. So it is hardly surprising that many have proposed there might be an extra-terrestrial significance to them. Tom had instinctively pooh-poohed the notion that the lines were drawn as some sort of ET landing strip, but he felt sure that they must have serious astrological and religious significance, thus of interest given his current focus.

He had asked a friend to attempt some computer matching of the lines to the movements of the stars and planets at the time they were drawn; so far there had been no real breakthroughs.


Recent finds at Tiwanaku had been the originally reason for Tom to come to this area. He had been publically known to be researching a book on archaeo-astronomy, the study of the astronomical ideas and beliefs of ancient civilizations.

Tom had found this subject to be immediately seductive, he swiftly found that most of these old peoples had left evidence of having developed forms of astrology. He was able to find traces almost anywhere he cared to look, he felt they all appeared to have developed astronomy 'in spades'.

There it was proud and self-evident in ancient Egypt of course, but here in South America the Incas and Mayans were keen astronomers. Wherever he looked, from Stonehenge to Christmas Island, from Native American Indians to Australasian Aborigines, they all had astronomical concepts right at the heart of their thinking, fuelling superstitions and religions.

In preparing his manuscript Tom had shown that it was probably more likely astrological concepts at work, and less to do with its scientific cousin, astronomy. His book would conclude that they were not as interested in the pure science of these celestial bodies, more in divining a suggested influence upon human affairs and society. Certainly this was exhibited within their many long-lived monuments.

Tom felt that he was definitely on to a winner, the plethora of material he had amassed had inspired and urged him to seek out some global concept at work somewhere right in the middle of all this.

If only he could find a common root for these similar beliefs from around the globe, then his latest book would go mega! Ideally he hoped to find some unifying early religion that might be at work here, a deity or deities that had somehow spanned the early globe.

# Chapter 6 - *London, UK*

At this door Bruno was God. His was the only law that mattered. He was the final arbiter of fashion. He was judge and jury, there was no court of appeal.

He had just admitted a large group of chattering young girls. He knew that each one of them was a schoolgirl, and the way they were dressed each fell securely within the category of jail-bait.

He wondered why it was that they had never looked like that while he was at school. But then these English girls were much more curvaceous, they were far more outgoing, put much more out on show, and were very much more available than he could remember from his own schooldays.

However the club was keen for him to let in any good-looking, well turned-out, young girls. It didn't matter if they were under age or not. It was their being here that would bring in all the guys and, of course, they would bring their wallets. It was a tough call when a pretty girl turned up with a 'minger' mate, but heh, that was all part of the job.

As he looked at the last girl disappearing into the club, he couldn't help ogling her low-slung jeans that did absolutely nothing to conceal the lacy T of the top of her thong. But he turned away on hearing a strange noise. This was when he first noticed the little fellow, standing there in the shadows across the street.

Initially he thought he must be there waiting for someone else, but progressively Bruno realised that he was just a little too engrossed in the line that was snaking away from the door of the club. Bruno kept an eye on him and assessed that the little guy was particularly interested in any couples that were slobbering over each other while they waited patiently, and in some cases pointlessly, for Bruno to decide whether he would let them in.

Bruno loved that part of the job, the absolute power he held to make or ruin an evening; and it was all decided completely at his whim. As a migrant Pole with a heavy accent he found he usually got little respect from the locals despite his intimidating size. But it didn't matter how much they pleaded, or offered him bribes, or claimed a friendship with the owners, or suggested that they knew the DJ or one of the bar staff. Here at the door was his realm; who actually got in was his remit. They had no choice, they had to wait on, then accept his decision.

He and Jimmy would often invent special 'rules-du-jour', as Jimmy called them. So one day, and for no good reason, perhaps they'd decide that the girls had to have something red on them to get in. Bruno found it startling how many of them were fully prepared to lift their skirts to show their underwear and prove that they could meet that condition!

Many of the girls were great; they'd all play up to him. If they met him elsewhere or even inside the club he knew that they wouldn't have given him a sideways glance. But out here, on his door, he was God. They would all spark up to him to get in. He had probably been offered more blow jobs than any guy he knew; he'd accepted quite a few of them too!

Jimmy was off tonight so he was short-handed. There'd be no slipping across the street to accept the price of admission tonight; besides, that little guy was hanging around over there.

Yes the girls were great, but on balance he probably preferred it when the guys turned nasty. He'd turn away a group and often one would want to show that he was not going to be put off by Bruno's height and bulk. As the club didn't open until 11 pm, most of those arriving would already be tanked up on booze bought more cheaply elsewhere and would have 'lost their normal critical faculties' - another of Jimmy's expressions that amused Bruno. He was great like that, the smartest bouncer Bruno knew. He would of course have been totally unaware that this was not much of an accolade given the general level of intellect of the others he had met.

When the guys did lose their senses and shape up to him he had to be careful. The business was all licensed now. His SIA, Security Industry Authority, licence was essential for his work; so it was necessary to take their shit for as long as he could.

He could, of course, defend himself against an attack; he just could not be seen to have started anything. But then he had put in lots of ring-time and, as his coach said, he had fast hands. Anyone trying it on would certainly end up regretting it. If some guy really took the piss then Bill would lock the doors from inside, while he and Jimmy escorted the 'subject' over to the lane where, out of sight of any potential 'grass', they could really work him over.

There was no Jimmy tonight. That little guy was still loitering about over there. From across the road he looked a bit of a creep who appeared to be getting off on seeing others snogging and groping along the line-up. He would rock up and down when the 'tongue-tonsil action' got frantic down the queue - yet another of Jimmy's expressions; he was so funny. Bruno nodded to Bill who locked down so that he could go over and see this guy off before he became a real nuisance.

He had to be only around five foot tall and slightly built, with a surprisingly small head compared to his body. Bruno would have to take this one very carefully. Everyone in the queue would naturally root for the little guy if this got at all out of hand.

As he got closer he could see that the guy was black; more warning bells. Bruno knew how PC the Brits were and he must watch his step. He looked like what Jimmy would call a 'nonce'. He seemed to be wearing bright pink lipstick, which hadn't been applied with much skill. Christ, he'd seen old tarts who were too high to get the lipstick on anywhere other than their teeth, but this guy had painted on a ridiculously wide grin. Bruno thought the look he must be trying for was the 'Joker' in Batman.

He had on a hoodie and what looked like military overalls. They weren't British though, somehow they looked more American? The *idiota* was insocks but no shoes, around here with all the discarded needles; that was just not at all smart!

He started gently, 'What're you hanging around here for?'

The guy looked at him and then waved his arms, signing something back.

'Are you deaf?' So he was little, black and deaf. All the alarms were ringing to take this one carefully. He adopted a more conciliatory tone, 'Are you lost or something?'

More frantic signing.

'I'm sorry but I don't do any of that shit. Anyway, look, you can't just hang around here, you're annoying my patrons.'

The guy looked confused and signed a long string of something or other, clearly frustrated that the big bouncer was not understanding him.

Bruno had had enough. He reached out to grab the guy by the scruff of the neck and lead him off away from the queue and down into the lane. But the guy squealed, a strange high-pitched noise; more like that of a woman. Then he swung around and bit him. But this was not just a nip. It was a deep meaningful bite that broke the skin. Bruno distinctly felt the guy's teeth graunch directly against the bones in his hand. Now it was Bruno's turn to yelp as he reached out his left hand to chop the guy's neck and get him to release his hand.

By God this guy was quick. He had wheeled around again and somehow jumped onto Bruno's chest, clinging by his feet around his waist while he pummelled him. He could certainly pack a punch for such a little guy too. Bruno found he couldn't put up his legendary guard for the guy was inside that already. He was relegated to trying for a telling kidney punch but this guy was wiry and it was clear that the bouncer was beginning to lose the battle.

As the weirdo's feet were off the ground, Bruno decided to swing him around and charged towards the wall to smash him against it and spring himself loose. But at the last second, the little guy pulled off an unexpected manoeuvre. Keeping a firm grip with his arms, he released his legs, and then almost gymnastically swung them back to kick against the wall. The kick completely stopped Bruno's momentum and had enough force to topple him, crashing him over on to his back.

The little guy rode him downwards so that he was sitting across Bruno's chest and continued his pummelling. Then the little guy looked up and saw that several of the queue were starting to move towards him. Assuming that they were coming to the bouncer's aid, and seeing others using mobiles, he just leapt off and disappeared down the lane. Those closest noted his strange loping gait.

Bruno was helped to his feet, feeling extremely embarrassed by the outcome. He must have had 45 centimetres in height advantage and was certainly carrying 40 kilos more in weight, yet he'd been completely humbled in front of all these people. Thank God Jimmy hadn't been there to see it.

Bruno insisted he wanted no fuss, but before he could get back into the club an ambulance crew arrived. Typical, when you really needed one they would take all day, when you felt you didn't want one it arrived within five minutes!

The crowd gathered around as the paramedic treated his hand and advised, 'You'll need a tetanus jab and some blood tests, mate. That's definitely an animal bite. I've no idea what, but it's certainly not human. Look at the teeth marks and how deep they've penetrated.'

One of the crowd said, 'Yes, that's it, got it. When he ran off it was just like something out of London Zoo. He ran on his knuckles. I think it must have been some sort of ape or monkey.'

# Chapter 7 - *Bolivia*

The little black, dried and wizened corpse was almost obscene, lying there all hunched up on a pile of rubble, its form bent out of shape. It looked much more like a monkey than the nobleman who had been interred there so long ago.

The remains looked wrong out here in the daylight, they appeared to have been damaged as they had been roughly pulled out of the *chullpa*. Tom thought, surely with so much of their past history tied up within these towers, the locals should see this sort of grave-robbing as sacrilegious?

Tom had by now visited a score or more of the *chullpas,* studying and photographing the outside of the towers. He found that they were indeed all built facing the east where the bodies inside could greet the rising sun each morning. Intriguingly ancient Egyptians chose to locate their necropolises facing west; their symbology for death had been linked to the setting of the sun, not its rise.

During his research he had been much taken with a picture of a Sumerian royal cylinder-seal featuring five figures each wearing hats that most resembled the bowler hats worn here in Bolivia.

At the centre of this Sumerian cylinder-seal was the figure of Shamash, depicted as the rising sun, emerging from a portal set on a mound. Tom found this evocative of the city that he had come here to see, Tiwanaku, and its famous feature, the Gateway of the Sun. Could there be a connection?

Another major figure on the seal was that of Ea, one of the major Sumerian gods that formed part of its major trinity. A number of elements of Ea's story subsequently became applied, or plagiarised, into the later tales of biblical figures of Moses, John the Baptist and even of Jesus himself.

Tom had studied this cylinder closely because, implausibly, this same Middle Eastern god was claimed to have turned up here in Bolivia. An ancient statue at the heart of the capital La Paz bears an image investigated by a number of experts who concluded it could possibly be a depiction of Ea. Was this the link he sought?

Having "discovered" so many Sumerian connections with this part of the world, Tom had hoped that perhaps the *chullpa* carvings might just have borne markings with a Sumerian influence too. When he explained his purpose, Amaro mentioned that the burial towers further to the north often featured carvings of snakes and lizards. But Tom was to be disappointed by this side trip, he failed to find any markings that he might perceive or 'bend' into being anything like any Sumerian cuneiform or imagery.

On his 'tour' he had however been shocked to find that several of the chullpas must have been very freshly vandalised. The latest example had been discovered after they climbed up from the road to discover the adobe of the building had been penetrated. The buried remains had been both moved and damaged, yet other artefacts appeared to have remained untouched. Amaro realised that the tracks were so fresh that it appeared as if their arrival might well have frightened off the vandal while still in the act of plundering.

The area around this site showed deep and distinctive tracks, made by a pair of rubber-soled boots rather than any sort of local native footwear. Looking around Tom caught a glimpse of someone breaking cover and running over a small rise nearby. He gave chase but on reaching the edge of a pile of rocks at the ridge he was forced to pull up, the sudden sprint had left him absolutely exhausted, completely spent.

It had only been a short distance but the high altitude had caught up with him. He just had to stop, the effects of the altitude made him retch, he felt sick to the base of his stomach, but it was this effect that saved his life. As he stooped he heard a ricochet that hit the point where his head would have been if he had not been bending over to spit out bile.

He had no time to consider his good fortune. Dropping to the ground and out of view, he moved his position laterally by ten metres or so and only then, very cautiously, did he feel he could peer over the ridge to see where the grave-robber and erstwhile sniper was hiding.

He was surprised to see a modern 4x4 parked just a few hundred metres away down from the ridge. Somehow, he had expected the likely plunderer to be less sophisticated than this vehicle's presence now indicated; he could see three people up ahead.

The nearest was still making his way back at speed towards the vehicle and did indeed look like a local. He was hunched under a heavy backpack that had quite an array of tools hanging from it.

The second person was not a local, leaning across the roof of the 4x4 holding something. It took another ricochet just in front of Tom for him to recognise it was a rifle. He dropped below the ridge again and hastily edged his way back towards the *chullpa*. Had the shots been intended as a warning? If so both were too close for comfort. Either the shooter was proficient and sought to put the fear of God in him, and in that he had certainly succeeded, or more likely, he had been shooting to kill.

He had caught a glimpse of another person inside the vehicle, he instinctively felt this third person was also not a local, but he was visible more as a presence, a large shadow, rather than anything more obvious.

He heard the 4x4 start up and he prayed that the terrain was too rugged for them to come directly up over the ridge towards him. He ran back towards Amaro and their own vehicle just in case these grave-robbers had a mind to come and finish him off.

Racing back across the rock all ill effects of the altitude were dismissed, for now. Across the shale he ran the risk of falling, breaking something, but somehow a rifle shot was much more terrifying. It galvanised his attention and his balance so that he was as surefooted as a mountain goat.

To his relief he heard the 4x4 speed off in the opposite direction. Clearly its occupants were not of a mind to follow up on their earlier shots.

Much later in the day they were travelling through a small town and he noticed a similar 4x4 approaching from the opposite direction. He couldn't swear it was the same one, but same colour, same look, same vicinity and as it passed them he saw it also had three people inside.

As they drew level the front passenger had turned and bent down to attend to something down in the well of the vehicle. It was this snatched view of that passenger in a suspect vehicle that had rung bells when he saw Berkeley just now.

Tom had learned to trust his inspiration, knew the instinctive power of his mind's pattern recognition. So now he thought it was time to find out a little more about this individual.


He stepped ashore on the floating island and was surprised to feel absolutely nothing to suggest its impermanence. It felt like perfect terra firma. He asked Amaro, 'How long do these fabricated islands last?'

'Usually around thirty years or more, although the base of the island keeps rotting away so needs to be constantly replaced by adding fresh plants at the top.'

Tom questioned, 'If it's floating, how do they stop it from being blown or carried away by the currents in the lake?'

'It's tethered to the lake bottom using the same grass-ropes. Of course it can still be moved if necessary, but that was something only really done as a defensive manouevre, back in the more troubled past, not today.'

Tom could see a small group of locals coming to meet them. Given their scruffy condition he commented, 'While we were in La Paz I read somewhere that the more affluent you are, the deeper you live down in the canyon. Apparently down there both the altitude and the temperature are much more user-friendly. But I guess these guys live here because they wouldn't even be able to afford the highest little shack over there?'

Amaro leapt to their defence, 'Poor they may be, yes, but the Uros are a proud people. They live entirely from the fish and vegetables naturally found in and around the lake. They are one of *the* very earliest prototype green communities in the world. They cook on stones that they lay onto the reeds and they use small detached islets as toilets where the reeds can absorb the waste rather than let it seep directly in to the lake's waters. They might be poor in financial terms but I don't think many of them would wish to change places with any of your city dwellers!'

Amaro had realised that he was just a little too intense, so quickly sought to move the subject on, 'I'm glad you've seen one of these islands, because a few years ago we proved that this floating-island approach could have been used to transport some of the large rocks across to Tiwanaku. Just like your Stonehenge and its massive stones quarried from a distance away, the construction of the structures has been questioned - how were the stones transported? Now you've had the chance to see and feel one of these islands I thought you might see that this approach does offer a practical solution.'

Tom nodded, and took the opportunity to look around the dockside. He was still impressed by the apparent solidity of this temporary island. He walked over and caught up with Berkeley.

'May I ask why you are visiting this particular place?'

It was clear that Dom considered deflecting or perhaps even not answering.

Tom added, 'Not prying. I was just wondering if I could tag along. Wanted to make sure that I wouldn't be getting in your way?'

Dom smiled, 'No problem. We haven't been properly introduced. Hi, I'm Dom Berkeley and I work for Mission.' He shook hands with Tom, 'And, we of course all know who you are, so perhaps it should be me asking you why you are here?'

Dom was managing an affable face, though his eyes appeared a little more unfriendly as they calmly assessed Tom in extreme detail. He correctly placed him in his late thirties, fairish eyed, fairish haired, fair complexioned, an average height Brit. The sort of person who would be very easy to underestimate, but Dom knew better. He instinctively saw that there was more to him than met this cursory assessment. There was obviously some past military service somewhere deep in there. He decided judgment should be reserved for now.

Tom was a little more subtle in making his own appraisal. Dom, a brusque East Coast American, was in his early to mid-fifties with hair that was just a little too black to be plausible. He was well-built with toned muscles, clearly displaying his ex-military status from the string of unit tattoos and in the general way he held himself. Tom had a subconscious feeling that giving this American a wide berth might be quite a sensible approach.

Though he was never one to shy away from a challenge, so he decided he could play the evasive game too, 'You will have to ask our hosts. They invited me to come and see something they've discovered at Tiwanaku. Just what precisely is it that Mission does?'

Dom was clearly uncomfortable with the question, but replied, 'We're working with various bodies in tracing and tracking the ancient migrations of early mankind. We look at communities around the world that have, in modern times at least, tended to stay separate from the general rat race.'

'Why here?' Tom wasn't sure why, but something about Berkeley rankled, made him want to press for more details. While recognising that he was not going to get much from him, he was enjoying the fact that he was irritating him.

'This is just a little favour for a friend. Don't worry I won't hold you up for too long.' Dom had spotted a formal delegation of Uros was approaching and he used the opportunity to close the conversation and move off.

Tom was now fully convinced that there was something about the man that was off, somehow suspicious. It wasn't just the quite different messages coming from his smile and his eyes, Tom detected a strong whiff of deceit in his body language too.

He was now convinced that it was Berkeley whom he had seen up by the *chullpa*. But why would this American be deliberately out there damaging those ancient sites? There would be no truly valuable treasures within, nothing beyond a few worthless personal belongings. Besides the belongings in the one in question had been left behind. Why would he interfere with the human remains while leaving the artefacts?

On the floating island Tom tagged on behind as Dom was led towards a small enclave of huts and shown into a large one. Tom hovered near the doorway and was a tad surprised to see Dom was injecting each of the villagers; he hadn't appeared to be a doctor. What sort of medicine had he prescribed? He watched as Dom followed up by taking a series of swabs from inside the Uros' mouths.

As they travelled on from the floating island Amaro took up the role of tour guide, 'Look, there is the Isla del Sol, birthplace of the very first Inca. You should know that the term Inca properly applies only to the leaders, to the ruling class. It was much later that the term was used for the whole people. Inti, the Inca sun god, sent his son Manco Capac to help mankind and he emerged from the Sacred Rock, Titikala, situated up the backside, on the north of the island.'

Standing at the rail, Dom said in an aside to Tom, 'In my guidebook it talks about a 'Shining Mantle'. This Manco Capac character apparently dressed himself up in sheets of silver with a metallic diadem to suggest that he was descended directly from the sun god. While I'm a pretty religious guy, prepared to take a lot of things on pure faith, in this instance I think I prefer to see this as a simple piece of very human manipulation.'

Amaro ignored this, 'It was in the 12th century Manco Capac created the Inca capital of Cusco and it was from there that the Inca Empire was built. But the Inca rule had lasted for such a short time before the conquistadores arrived.'

As he pondered this passage of time, the steady progress of mankind, it suddenly clicked. DNA! Why else would Berkeley be taking swabs of the Uros? He was taking their DNA! What was it he said his organisation did? Followed the migrations of early civilisations? That might explain why he vandalised the *chullpas* too, to get at the remains inside, to capture their DNA material too – but why?

# Chapter 8 – *London, UK*

**BBC Television Panorama feature:**

'Could someone have stolen Jesus Christ's DNA? Lucy Challoner is in Canada to investigate. Lucy!'

'A laboratory in Canada that was briefly at the centre of a controversial investigation has recently had a break-in and they have only just realised that some vital samples and files had been tampered with during that burglary.

'Lakehead University is located in Thunder Bay, Ontario sitting on the north coast of Lake Superior, around 60 kms from the USA border with Minnesota. Thunder Bay is a city of just a little over 100,000 inhabitants; historically this had been good fur-trapping country. So it is something of a surprise to learn that the university's Paleo-DNA laboratory is one of the global leaders in investigating ancient DNA samples. Forget the fictional CSI television series, this is the real deal.

'It was perhaps then not at all surprising when it was they that were called upon by the film team, its archaeologists, and its documentary team, to investigate DNA traces found on some two-thousand-year-old bones. The bones had been found in two ossuaries within a cave discovered just to the south of Jerusalem; the tomb that has become popularised as the 'Lost Tomb of Jesus'.

'This tomb was uncovered originally by archaeologists back in 1980 when the foundations were being laid for a new apartment block. At the time it sparked no particular interest. However, as is usual in these circumstances their investigation time was limited, the developers keen to complete their building. So the archaeologists had made sketches at the time and the relics were removed to be stored at the Rockefeller Museum. The bones of the dead, removed from the ossuaries, were then respectfully given a religious re-burial.

'As almost a thousand of these sorts of tombs have been found in the same area, it was unsurprising that no particular enthusiasm or significance was noted back in the '80s. It was merely recorded as being of the Second Temple period which is a pretty vague term as this period spans six centuries - from 500 BCE to 70 CE. This was the period after the Romans sieged and then sacked Jerusalem destroying the original temple.

'The so-called 'Jesus' tomb was not reopened until 2005, when the documentary team made their film. But, as they had not obtained all the necessary permits, the tomb was rapidly resealed and is not being made available for further investigation. This of course just serves to add to the mystery and mystique surrounding the tomb, allowing unsubstantiated claims to run rife.

'The ossuaries in this case refer to a series of ten small limestone containers of the bones of a buried family, the burials inside the tomb are said to have spanned several generations of that family. Only four of these ossuaries were originally recorded by the original archaeologist to have had markings or epigraphs scratched onto them, but, during this more recent investigation, markings were found on a further two.

'It also appears that one of the ossuaries, that had been recorded as being unmarked, disappeared from the museum's courtyard. Not too surprising in that there is an enormously lucrative black market in Holy Land religious materials.

'In 2002 a similar limestone ossuary box was discovered and it evocatively bore the inscription 'James, son of Joseph, brother of Jesus'. The documentary filmmakers tested it and suggested that it had precisely the same patina as the other nine found in the 'Jesus' tomb, they concluded that this must be the one that had gone missing.

'However the Israeli Antiquities Authority investigated this and eventually concluded that the inscription on this 'James' box is a modern forgery. This claim appears later to have been disputed by the Royal Ontario Museum, when it put the box on display, and claimed that they could find absolutely nothing that would confirm it as a forgery.

'Where this tomb and the ossuaries became really interesting was when these various markings threw up an intriguing series of names. There was Yeshua bar Yehosef, Jesus son of Joseph; Maria, or Mary; Yose, a nickname for Joseph; Yehuda bar Yeshua, or Judah son of Jesus; Matia, or Matthew.

'The one that caused the most controversy is the one bearing the inscription, 'Maramene e Mara', Maramene can be translated as Mary and the word Mara means Master. The filmmakers claim this could therefore refer to Mary Magdalene, though this is by no means clear or generally accepted.

'In a clear echo of the two books 'The Holy Blood and the Holy Grail' and 'The Da Vinci Code' the filmmakers stress that religious history has much maligned Mary of Magdalene. They cite passages in orthodox Christianity that says she was the 'equal of the apostles'. They make mention of the sects that claim and worship Mary Magdalene as the co-Saviour. What is undisputed is that she certainly appears to have been very significant following Jesus's death. It was of course her that found his body missing. It was also her that cajoled and motivated the Apostles to press on with their ministry when they were at a low point following the Crucifixion of their leader.

'The filmmakers also highlight her 'clash' with Saint Peter and perhaps the jealousy exhibited in him stating in scripture, 'Did He then speak secretly with a woman, in preference to us, and not openly?' Elsewhere in the Bible the disciples are reported to have asked Jesus why he loved Mary more than them. She is in fact mentioned more often than any other woman in the New Testament.

'Gnostic gospels and writings, that were not available or in some cases judged not worthy to be admitted into the official Bible, suggest that she may have been the sister of one of the original apostles, Philip. Some suggest the very fact that her memory has survived down the years must indicate some special significance.

'It appears she is not the fallen woman said to be in the Bible; certainly the holy book does not explicitly say that she is. But if she were established to have been buried with Jesus in his family tomb then this would reignite the speculation of her being his wife, and following on from this would inevitably come the speculation that they may have had children.

'The early Christian Church went through many twists and turns as it expanded outside just the immediate Jewish world and began to appoint bishops and priests to expand their reach. It is clear that the very close family of Jesus, known as the 'Desposyni', did complain about the appointment of Greek Christian bishops to the early major centres of Christianity in Jerusalem, Antioch, Ephesus and Alexandria. They wanted the right to name bishops of their own and pressed for the Church to focus its attention within the traditional practices of Judaism. Their claims were however overruled by the early Church leaders.

'So finding a family tomb for the relatives of Jesus would not of itself be so surprising. But is this particular tomb and its suggestive names likely to be the one? Well, various statistical exercises illustrated that the collection of names found in this tomb was not particularly unusual, as these names were all relatively common for that time and period; though this series of evocative names remains of course extremely thought-provoking.

'The real bombshell is perhaps not the putative marriage to the Magdalene but the shockwaves that would result if these remains of 'Jesus son of Joseph' were established to be those of Jesus Christ; because, how could there be mortal remains if he had ascended to heaven, as witnessed by the Apostles in the Bible?

'The disappearance of his body from the crypt over the weekend and his being reported as surviving death and then his later Ascension are fundamentals, principles that hold a central role at the heart of the Christian faith. These basic beliefs are clearly responsible for both its early growth and its lasting appeal, so if he were found to be a mere mortal...

'Here's where the Thunder Bay university came in, they tested traces of human material that were found in two of the ossuaries. Do recall that the bones found in them had all been removed and re-buried in caches back in the '80s and it would be impossible to re-trace these and establish their provenance today.

'It turns out that it is the DNA from these traces and their investigation file that the Lakehead Uni eventually realised must have been the target of their break-in. They now believe that traces may have been removed and that the files had evidently been copied or referenced during the break-in.

'The reason why Ontario, Canada, should keep finding itself right at the centre of this intriguing story is unclear. But if we look down the years at the esteem within which any sort of religious relic has been held then it can hardly be surprising that these possible traces of Jesus and his family would become a target for theft. But who broke in and what they might want with these traces can only be conjectured.

'This has been Lucy Challoner, BBC TV, Panorama, in Lakehead Ontario, Canada.

# Chapter 9 - *London, UK*

**The Evening Standard headline that evening read:**
"Apeman Attacks - is this the Missing Link?"

The article had included an artist's impression based loosely upon the eyewitness accounts; very loosely, because overnight the 'creature' had grown in both height and bulk, which Bruno for one was delighted to read. Being defeated by some cousin of a Bigfoot or a yeti would allow him to go into work tonight with his head held high, his reputation intact.

However he would still have to wait anxiously for the outcome of his blood tests. And the talk of werewolves and vampires in one of the morning papers was not helping much with his peace of mind.

Sky News had a poor but exclusive video snatch of the creature scampering away taken on a mobile by someone who had been standing in the queue. The fact that it was taken on a darkened street and with a jostled mobile in a chaotic moment meant it was not the greatest piece of material. These flimsy 'facts' just opened the door to the potential for even more exaggeration.

Channel 4 had arranged an interview with a strikingly good-looking witch who talked confidently and expansively of this clearly being one of the many demons wandering the streets of London today.

Eventually a flustered zoologist arrived in the studio. He had already carried out a dizzying round of interviews on most of the other TV and radio stations. He announced that in his opinion, based upon a picture he had been provided of the wound, he was convinced it was definitely the bite of an ape.

A light day for news led to the subject getting major coverage and in turn this resulted in London being alive with sightings and hoaxes. Emergency lines were kept busy with reports of varying degrees of sincerity. However many of the callers were surprised that their calls were not being dealt with by the usual copper in a panda car. Instead two guys dressed in black would arrive in a black 4x4. Many were all too happy to answer questions about the sighting, but those who were prudent enough to ask for some sort of ID were first cajoled into giving up their information or finally just plain intimidated to do so.

Late that night the emergency lines were recording more calls about sightings of these black 4x4s populated by aggressive men in black than of the ape-man itself. Officers attending some of these incidents took descriptions that detailed their black outfits yet nothing of their faces, as they had all been wearing long-peaked black baseball caps. A number did mention noticing a tattoo on the forehead that they reported as being something like a Chinese symbol, though none could give anything like a precise description.

Just when Barry and Paula thought their late shift could not get any weirder, they were proved wrong. They were called to a reported rape in a mansion apartment block on the Finchley Road.

Having inspected their IDs a genteel old lady, well into her seventies, had let them in. She insisted on providing tea for the two members of the Metropolitan Police. It was clear that she would do everything at her pace and in her own good time so they relaxed back into the settee and waited on her.

When she had finally settled she proved quite lucid about what had happened. She explained that she had found him out on the balcony of her apartment. He was obviously scared, very cold, extremely tired and hungry. Her eyesight was not what it was, so she couldn't provide a good description when they prompted.

"He was a darkie," she said.

Today's modern Police Service worked hard to be seen to be politically conscious, almost an overcompensation for the reports that it had become an institutionally racist organisation. The two PCs blanched at the use of this archaic term, but neither felt moved to raise any objection with this particular member of the public.

She went on to explain that he was clearly deaf and could only communicate by signing; she sincerely regretted that she had never had any reason to learn sign language. So she had instead mimed actions and they had managed to get by.

Once he'd been 'fed and watered' he promptly fell asleep in the armchair; she pointed it out.

'So I went off to bed too. Here's where it all gets a little difficult.' She wriggled in the chair but pressed on 'Well, a little later he joined me there. I was just dropping off when he came in and snuggled up beside me. I saw no harm, the poor boy was cold and frightened in a world he can only see and not communicate with. It must be so dreadful. Besides it had been over twenty years since I shared a bed with anyone and it was very nice. God knows I have prayed for someone, but I'd rather given up on Him.'

Paula was leading the interview, 'It sounds like you are suggesting that you had consensual sex with him?'

'I do rather suppose that I did.' She smiled warmly at the thought. 'He was so attentive, so energetic and he blew away many, many years of cobwebs.'

Paula smiled, 'So then why have you reported it as a rape?'

'The thing is, I knew that Grace wouldn't believe me, so I decided to take a picture of him lying in my bed to prove it wasn't all just a dream or make believe. Grace would need proof you see.'

'I still don't understand?'

'I've never been any good with technology. The flash went off and startled the poor dear. He woke, screamed and went out through the balcony and up on to the roof. When I found my glasses and looked at the camera, as you can see it's evidently the ape-man that everyone has been talking about!'

She handed over a small digital camera. The image was indistinct but clearly this was a strange individual, one that was not quite ape or human.

'And the rape report?'

'Well, I thought I'd better suggest that he'd forced himself upon me, or I'll never hear the last of it from Grace.'

Paula tried not to smile. 'OK, if you want us to write this up as a rape then we'd better start again and rework your statement.'

'Yes of course, and you will want to see his clothes I suppose?'

She led them to the bedroom where there was a neat bundle of clothing which turned out to be a pair of overalls with was a small logo on the breast pocket.

It consisted of four interwoven circles bearing the letters Bi, Cog, Na and IT. Paula stared at it and asked, 'Just what the heck is Bicognate?'

Barry laughed, 'It sounds like something my mum used to take for her heartburn. She swore by bicarbonate of soda.'

'Probably it's some sort of medical research company?'

# Chapter 10 - *London, UK*

**Five weeks earlier**

Tom's research had been extensive in pursuit of his current theory. He had accumulated a wealth of material for his latest book in part because he found that he was walking a well-trod path. He was able to identify so many archaeo-astronomic threads, or as he increasingly came to believe it was perhaps more accurately archaeo-astrologic. He had been 'Hoover-ing' up material from right around the globe.

He felt this proliferation must mean that these ancient peoples had somehow derived their thinking from a common base. They surely must once have connected up with each other in some manner? Perhaps their beliefs could have stemmed from a much earlier concept? But just when might that have been? And how could it have been disseminated so widely given communications and travel back then?

Before setting out on his South American trip he could not think of anyone more useful with whom to talk this over than Professor Groves. So five weeks ago he had telephoned his office and learned that the Professor was fulfilling a speaking engagement at Westminster's QEII Conference Centre.

The Centre is located directly opposite the Houses of Parliament and so is well inside the reach of the parliamentary lobby bell - the bell that summons MPs if there is to be a division, a vote. This fact alone encourages many MPs and officials to participate in the regular round of exhibitions and conferences that are held here. Exposure to fresh ideas without being completely disconnected from Westminster was a win-win situation. It was near enough to the corridors of power for them to return and join in with any feeding frenzy should a crisis arise. There was no risk of missing an important division; not one of them wished to earn a tongue-lashing from the whips.

Tom arrived and was met, as arranged, by one of the Professor's aides, a young somewhat aloof guy who introduced himself as Simon Smythson. He was hustled into the rear of the conference room where Professor Groves was winding up his keynote address to the current 'Global Risk Assessment' conference.

'I am delighted to serve this current administration, and particularly this Foreign Secretary. For she has a broad appreciation…'

Tom smiled thinking that her 'broad appreciation' was perhaps as much because she had been the Professor's star pupil and that she still drew regularly upon his help since having taken her high office.

'… a very broad appreciation of the current realities. As a permanent member of the UN Security Council we will always become involved in 'policing' actions around the world. Not with our past style of imperial and colonial gunboat diplomacy, rather more as the Foreign Secretary said only last week, "Today our foreign policy is about us being vigilant, while not becoming vigilante, for our ideas and our way of life".'

Tom enjoyed the clever word-smithing; he thought that this one was almost good enough to be one of his own. It was clear he wouldn't have long to wait because the Professor was evidently building up to his finale, offering the word bites that he expected to be used in the conference proceedings and final press release, and to be quoted directly by those journalists present.

'In that speech she was perhaps subconsciously still taking the perspective of visualising our ideas being sent outwards from Britain, out to the rest of the world. Of course she fully appreciates that in today's global village we have to consider the opposite direction too, all those ideas that are incoming. As Victor Hugo famously wrote, *"On résiste à l'invasion des armées; on ne résiste pas à l'invasion des idées"*.

'Fortunately he's not around to complain at my loose translation. He was remarking that while a stand can be made against an invasion by army, it's a different matter to withstand an invasion from a powerful idea. Particularly an idea that is able to capture the imagination and energies of a disenfranchised or disadvantaged populace.'

The Professor was now up to full pace, forging on to his finish. 'So today, just how do we secure our state and ourselves from what we perceive as the wrong ideas? We live in a world that has porous borders; and with modern technology they are particularly porous to an idea. The world-wide-web for example is a wonderfully liberating tool, a powerful communications device that the world's governments could be using to promote their ideas and using to supply a better understanding of their beliefs, their goals and services. But it also manages to serve all too readily, the dishonest, the depraved and of course the terrorist. Now I want you to pause for thought. Currently which of these do you believe is getting its ideas distributed more successfully via this medium?'

He allowed his audience a few seconds to reach the obvious conclusion.

'So if it is to be a battle of ideas, then what ideas do we, and might we, instill in our youth by using the Internet and our education systems? I detect no idea currently that is anywhere near as powerful as the desire to win the X-Factor, or win in the Voice, or perhaps to become a professional footballer, or a footballer's wife? Few are prepared to take the time out to train in a skill that could provide them with a satisfying role and a contented life. As Freddie Mercury and his band Queen, immortalised "I want it all, and I want it now".' The Professor smiled in a way that confirmed that he was not really on familiar ground here.

'In fact currently tradesmen and retailers are doing a significantly better job than our government. They have long advertised their wares so powerfully that they have created today's extremely materialistic society. Look into our worst sink estates and just examine their footwear, their branded clothing. Watch the scrums each Christmas where pester-powered parents dare not return home until they have acquired the year's latest fad. Examine the trophy wives and 'It-girls'; no longer content with simply being 'ladies-who-lunch', today they also have to 'shop 'til-they-drop'. Consider the overwhelming column inches devoted to 'celebrities' in our newspapers and magazines. It would be perfectly reasonable to suggest that in Britain retailing has very effectively become today's religion; and the shops even open on a Sunday! It's no longer a case of ding-dong summoning us to church; it's bling-bling attracting us to the mall.'

The Professor paused and looked around. 'Let's get back to more serious ideas. I am afraid those ideas that we, the establishment, are seeking to plant are hollow and shallow, and they're doomed to fall upon fallow ground. We are not currently the ones who are planting the ideas that will flourish and prosper. Worse, our political correctness plays right into others' hands. We no longer feel able, or empowered, to name those who do succeed for what they are – they are intolerant bigots, sexual deviants, rampant racists or religious zealots with nothing but conquest on their mind. As a result of current human rights' legislation we are not able to identify them, to discuss them, or even to prosecute them. They will go on winning the hearts and minds of the minorities, the disadvantaged, and the disaffected. And what do we do? We instead concentrate on becoming more obese, filling even more Ikea storage units with current thirty-minute-wonder, must-have acquisitions.

'You may be thinking what does this all have to do with global risk assessment? My keynote message today is that the real threat we have to face is not the terrorist at the gate, not the far-flung despot developing weapons of mass destruction. No, most importantly we have to secure the ideological battle for the hearts and minds among our own population.

'We need to have the better, stronger ideas. We must work to ensure that we spread them more effectively. Only through this effort can we be sure to alleviate our current major risks and in this way we may secure our long-term futures.'

Tom joined the standing ovation but couldn't help thinking that, while these were laudable notions, he couldn't begin to describe how one might set about the task of implementing them.

He had to wait while the gaggle of delegates and journos buttonholed the Professor at the foot of his lectern. Once he had satisfied his audience, they greeted each other and quickly agreed to walk down Victoria Street to find a café.

The Professor quipped, 'If we take a coffee in the venue my assessment is we would risk constant interruption.'

They set off down the noisy and dusty road, accompanied by Simon. As they passed the many government offices Tom commented, 'I felt I saw something of a DICE theme, there lurking at the back of your closing comments?'

DICE was a small group that had been formed and funded by the intelligence service and Tom had taken on the role of managing the operation. He had spent the last few months setting the policies, protocols and processes for this organisation in between dealing with everything else in his currently busy life. They obviously believed the old saying, 'If you want something done, then ask a busy person'.

The name was not so very important, the acronym literally stood for the 'Defence International Corps for the Environment', suitably lofty and laudable while not really defining or constraining its purpose. It was a recent innovation, an organisation formed to evaluate the current global environmental challenges and then set about the professional broadcasting of the established facts of that matter in the face of much disinformation. As Tom had stated in his round of meetings, this all sounded relatively simple but they needed to do this against extremely well-funded pressure groups and 'experts' who sought deliberately to misinform for the benefit of their own products' and organisations' objectives.

Sir Joseph Maudlin, the head of Britain's Secret Service, had set DICE upon its path with two major objectives. First, they needed to capture the imaginations and specifically the column-centimetres of the press and other electronic media and drive them to present the real facts of the case. By doing this he believed that they could then fulfil his second objective which was to capture the hearts and minds of capricious politicians who had routinely shown they were all too ready to be suborned by big-spending pressure groups and corporates.

The Professor had been the current Foreign Secretary's tutor while she was at Cambridge and immediately upon taking up her senior government post she had created a role for him within her advisory team. She had fought off any criticism of his current liberal and past communist tendencies. She found his manner was pure avuncular; everything about him was familiar, comfortable and safe. She knew that while he was tenacious for what he thought was right, he would always find a way of making his point without confrontation and without generating unhelpful emotion.

The Professor replied to Tom's comment about DICE tendencies in his presentation. 'Of course, we must both use every opportunity to remedy the massive amount of disinformation that is out there. One of the benefits of being old and having a little current status is that I am also allowed to step outside the strictures of PC-dom; someone needs to because it's invaded everything. Even the name of that conference is deliberately hiding its true nature. To most of us risk assessment sits right there alongside health & safety, a modern-day nonsense that imposes massive bureaucracy upon procedures that were mostly working pretty well before these new plagues were set upon us.

'But did you see that audience? Most of them are ex-military, many clearly from within the special services. The risk assessment they are talking about is patrolling the Pakistan-Afghanistan border, safeguarding nuclear sites and their by-products, securing oil supertankers from East African piracy and protecting precarious pipelines... When they asked me to give a keynote I thought that I'd give them something just a little more fundamental to think about.'

Simon commented, 'Most military men are only interested in receiving and executing orders and not really encouraged to be too strong on ideas or thinking.'

'Then Simon, let me formally introduce you to Lieutenant Commander Carter!'

Tom smiled and filled the awkward silence by pressing on to describe just what had led to his current investigations into the Sumerians. How he had been intrigued by theories that suggested Sumerian or Phoenician sailors might have swept out of the Middle East and traded with the early South American peoples.

The Professor carefully considered this. 'They were certainly sailors par excellence. They were of course among the first astronomers, mapping the stars and constellations. The five planets visible to the naked eye were given Sumerian names too. Add to that the fact that a number of the major land trade routes of the time passed through their homelands, they would certainly have been fully aware of the potential for trade out towards the east. Perhaps that might indeed have lured them on into the Pacific.'

Tom described the data he had found that suggested they had travelled from the Red Sea eastwards together with a variety of unsubstantiated claims for them reaching as far as South America. The trio finally reached a café with a free table and Simon busied himself with ordering coffees.

Tom settled back into his chair. 'None of this material is particularly convincing or well documented, so this is where the archaeo-astronomy has to earn its spurs. How else would South America have ended up with the same penchant as the Middle East for astronomy, for building pyramids, for erecting stelae bearing glyphs, and for child sacrifice and mummification?'

Simon asked, 'Sorry, but what are stelae?'

Tom guessed that Simon was one of those people that required definitions there and then, rather than nodding and making a mental note to look it up later.

The Professor replied, 'They're stone slabs or columns, often used for funerary purposes, usually with some sort of design or inscription etched into them.'

Tom sipped his coffee and continued. 'I'm keen to go to South America to see for myself whether there are any signs of the Sumerian or Phoenician script. These have been claimed to be found on a number of early South American monuments; but today it's almost impossible to work out what is 'Holy Writ' and what is Wikipedia.

'There's apparently something called Bennett's monolith across there. It's been at the centre of one of the plazas of La Paz for some time. It's said to have some rather surprising carvings. They quite predictably depict the local wildlife like jaguars and condors, but unexpectedly they also include some images of elephants and toxodons.' Before Simon asked, he added, 'It's an ancient beast that looks something like a hippo, they were all wiped out by the Pleistocene Extinction around 11,000 years ago.'

Tom explained that this same monolith apparently had scales on the lower part of the body of the statue. Some thought that this could mean it was a depiction of the Sumerian deity of Ea. The deity was described variously as snake-like or as a sort of man-fish that was said to have brought special knowledge to the early middle-eastern people. The god was credited with accelerating the development of writing, mathematics and agriculture.

Simon suddenly butted in, 'Are you sure they are not feathers rather than scales? If it had feathers then it might have been the depiction of an angel rather than a deity?'

The Professor had taken a large bite into his blueberry muffin and almost spluttered at this. Having to finish his mouthful, there was a pause before he spoke. He gave a long sideways look at Simon and then pointedly ignored the comment.

'Tom, you outlined much of this in your email when you asked for a meeting, and I did get the chance to do a bit of background reading for you. You should be aware that the timing you are discussing and this deity,' he looked at Simon scathingly, 'seem to be heavily tied in with the appearance of a supernova called Vela X. It's located about 800 light years away from us and at some time, around 11,000 to 13,000 years ago, it went nova. At the time it was clearly visible from earth, not quite as bright as a full moon but evidently extremely visible to the naked eye; no polluted atmospheres back then of course. It must have caused a huge stir among the ancient peoples. It wasn't just your Sumerians who noticed it, the Egyptians and the Chinese recorded it too.'

'Your Sumerians did invent one of the earliest written forms of communication. However it was probably its successor, the later Phoenician script, which spread the notion of writing throughout the world, at least the bits of it within which they traded. Its very simplicity led to widespread use.

'The Phoenician script certainly can be shown to have influenced Aramaic and thus Arabic and Hebrew scripts. It was apparently significant in the development of the Ancient Greek script and thus will have shaped Latin, Cyrillic and Coptic. Some suggest that Phoenician was also the basis for India's Brahmi script and Sanskrit, plus its Indic alphabets. If all this is true, then it was certainly the prototype of many of the major writing systems. So if you do find anything Middle Eastern in South America, I would think it more likely therefore to be from this later Phoenician script.'

Tom added, 'Inca records talk of a clan of mysterious bearded men in their past. They knew them as the *suncasapa* or bearded angelic warriors,' he smiled at Simon, 'These angels had apparently appeared in support of one of their deities, but they sound more like mercenaries than priests. Viracocha their god was described as white-skinned, a bearded Caucasian, wearing long white robes and sandals. Surely with that description he had to be a Middle Eastern person?

'It seems to me it was only the Phoenicians who could have been in a position to bring the concepts of mummification, pyramids, cuneiform scripts and other types of Middle-Eastern mythology across to South America. The Incas said that the *suncasapa* later disappeared back across the Pacific – given that direction then they might just have been Phoenicians?'

'Ah, before you run too far with this notion, let's examine the written script viewpoint. Don't forget that China developed its own form of logograms which of course went on to spawn local derivatives like Japanese, Korean, Vietnamese… Then South America, had its own indigenous Mayan glyphs. To my knowledge neither of these has ever been shown to link to the Phoenician.'

'But intriguing isn't it? I do appreciate that mankind generally would have developed the requirement to start with some form of written communication to enable the early trading between peoples. Not surprisingly they would all have started with some form of pictorial script, but why did pyramids spread at the same early time? The answer might just be inscribed on one of the monuments at Tiwanaku.'

The Professor had argued, 'But can you rely just upon monuments? They are after all merely what survived down the years. Who's to say that this was all there was to these people and their lives? If a Martian landed in the UK tomorrow they'd see that there are many churches and perhaps reach the conclusion that therefore we are a very religious people. But if they counted how many people are in them during a weekend service then they would soon achieve a different perspective.'

Simon commented. 'I see what the Professor means. It's like the old tale of the three blind men each feeling an elephant at a different place, each therefore describing a very different whole, each making obvious errors based upon just the small part that they had actually felt. If you go only from the monuments then aren't you working just as blindly?'

Tom nodded at this fair point. 'But any society wanting to leave a heritage builds monuments as the overt concrete sign of their beliefs and values. And these monuments are just so incredible. In their eras they must have taken all the people's time and energy, not to mention all their resources, to build them. Surely they therefore had to be central to their lives and beliefs and therefore highly relevant for us to investigate.'

The Professor disagreed. 'Let me expand upon my analogy then. Any one of our major British cathedrals would have taken hundreds of man-years and became a huge drain on the resources of the surrounding city and countryside. It would have controlled the local populace, most of their energies and thoughts. Yet no-one ever lived in it, arguably nothing useful ever happened because of it, and in fact just how useful a building is it today with its lack of modern facilities? And most importantly would you learn anything of the original builders' lives or of today's modern city by studying its cathedral?'

Simon wriggled in his chair throughout the Professor's comments but decided not to comment.

Tom smiled, 'I had forgotten you are such an atheist. No perhaps I should say that you are agnostic. Weren't you just saying from your 'pulpit' that retailing is the new religion?'

'Touché. Let me loosely quote Carl Sagan. He commented that not a single major religion has ever looked objectively at science and concluded, "Heh, this is all so much better than we imagined! The universe is much bigger than our prophets said, more eloquent, more elegant." It was something like that anyway. So, like him, if religions cannot believe in what science has evolved to show us to be plain and simple fact, then I have little time to waste on them.'

Simon finally became too uncomfortable with the conversation. 'Surely there must be a middle ground between science and religion?'

The Professor sighed. 'I don't expect there to be any time soon. If anything religions are becoming ever more fundamentalist, wanting to stress the soul, mysticism, faith. In effect they seize on almost anything that can't be shown by science.'

From the look on Simon's face he judged there to be no point in pursuing this further and turned to Tom. 'Where did you get with my suggestion of looking at that rather more famous atheist Richard Dawkins? You remember I introduced you to his concept of the 'meme'?'

Dawkins had first proposed the meme as a sort of conceptual mind-based rather than body-fabric-based gene, a type of 'folk-memory' that can be handed on from mind to mind, generation to generation. He included in these memes things like songs and tunes, inventions and architectural styles, fashions in speech as well as dress. One of his proof sources had been that someone had of course to invent the keystone for the construction of an archway; but that once it had been invented it was just accepted by later generations as a known and given fact. It was a handed-down given that needed no further investigation; this then was a meme.

Tom had called for the bill, 'I liked it, found it interesting to consider these early astronomical or astrological beliefs as memes. But surely religion is just as much a 'meme' as any of those that Dawkins and others propose? Just look at how those ideas have been passed down through so many generations.'

The Professor grinned as he made the gesture to pay, but with little conviction as he allowed Tom to take the bill. 'From my perspective I prefer to see religion more like a germ than a meme.'

Simon looked agitated. 'But if a meme is anything like a gene, then surely any worthless memes, just like any unhelpful genes, would have got weeded out and discarded down the years. You need to ask yourself that if these beliefs are memes that have persisted, then perhaps you need to take them just a little more seriously?'

The Professor smiled at this suggestion. As they left the café he continued, 'Look, it's really not at all surprising that these old peoples should look up to the stars. What else would they have had to look at overnight while they huddled down around their fires? There was no pollution to stop the full panoply twinkling away at them, particularly up at the heights that you're planning to visit.'

Tom nodded. 'What really interests me though is how did it get disseminated so globally? Back then communications moved literally at a walking pace!'

# Chapter 11 - *Arizona*

Shepherd was pacing in front of the large screen while the video was being held on a wide shot that looked out over the attendees. He was pointing out particular faces as the new group of Perfects sat completely engrossed in the presentation by their Patriarch. The sea of faces included most ethnicities; they came in all shapes and sizes sporting a wide variety of hairstyles and hair colours.

Enrique commented on this diversity, 'Looking around at this intake it's pretty unlikely that they could each share any similar DNA characteristics, and yet I know that they must. I appreciate that not one of them would have been admitted into the Perfects unless that common feature was present, but when you look at that variety it seems implausible.'

Shepherd smiled. 'As you know we do check and test everyone to make sure that they are completely worthy of Perfect status. But as William Cowper said, "Variety's the spice of life that gives it all its flavour". To become worthy of Perfect status does not mean that we need to lose that variety, in fact it's truly about sustaining it. So please don't be mistaken by our strict admission policies. Our whole approach is very much established to preserve the variety. Let's get back to the session. What else have you noticed about the techniques used?'

Hannah asked, 'Do you recommend that we go to the stage to use those lighting effects whenever we want to underline an important phase or statement?'

'Well noted. Yes that's mostly true, but you do need to use it with care. Make sure it does not become too hackneyed. You are now part of the bishopric and will need to be able to run these sessions on your own. You need to work at it to find a comfortable pace and approach that is best suited to you. Today as you can see the staging worked well for me, but this was preaching to the converted. It was an audience of committed Perfects and I did bring my own well drilled stage management crew. You need to work at it and spend time with your own teams to be sure to make it look so effortless.' He started the video again.

On the screen the Leader was shown in close up looking benevolently out across his new intake. It was clear that by now he had their undivided, in some cases spellbound, attention. Now there was no more grandstanding for his recognition, they were patiently listening to his every word.

'I praise the Lord that I have been very fortunate. I have had the time and the opportunity to study each of the world's great religions and philosophies in detail. Be aware that this is not me exhibiting the sin of pride, but instead I trust that my good fortune and extensive travel can assist you to reach my conclusions much more speedily.'

In the background of the stage a low-key video presentation started up and gently began showing the Leader standing before various places of worship, walking and talking with a number of immediately recognisable religious leaders, and even several famous, some perhaps infamous, political figures.

'I stayed for some months in a *yurt* and I learned directly from enlightened Buddhists about their beliefs and practices. I have been comprehensively coached in the contemplation of the many Kamis of the Shinto faith. I have visited and been guided in worship in a large number of Sikh and Hare Krishna temples. I studied the 7th century Qur'an, trained by a leading Shi'a Imam…

The leader froze the screen. 'Note what I said there, "the 7th century Qur'an". This is a good example of one of the skills you need to develop, in this case the power of word association. By stressing it as a 7th century newcomer we are not disparaging it directly but the implication is self-evident. We should never disrespect other beliefs, but we do need to place them as lesser.

'I learned of word association in my early days when selling photocopiers. Mine were always described as systems or solutions. When I had to mention my competitors then they were described as providing mere equipment or machines. Do you see my point, the emotional context? You will need to coach yourselves. Try out your presentations. Make sure you use all the power available in your choice of words and the juxtaposing of those words.' He flicked the video back on.

'…I have debated theology and studied the Torah with many leading rabbis. I have also made it my mission to seek out every tint and shade of Christianity that I could find. I needed to see for myself what it is that they believe, what it is that they are teaching, where they are going.'

The video at the back of the stage had been speeding up and suddenly now became a cacophony of images, the anarchy of the visuals turned into a virtual kaleidoscope as they turned and whirled.

Standing before the outpouring upon the screen Shepherd spun around and put his hands over his ears. He stopped spinning and shook his head disappointedly until the film had fully stopped.

He looked up and the light caught him. His illuminated and slightly bewildered face slowly took on certainty. He suddenly seemed to become aware of his audience. He started to stride around the room.

'We read in Genesis of the great king Nimrod. Now you are a Perfect you must read the scriptures with your mind, not just your eyes. Nimrod it was who founded the very first great city after the Flood. This city was of course the mighty Babylon. The people led by this great ruler became proud of their city and of civilised lives, so they set about building a huge tower that would reach right up to the heavens. But God saw straight through their motives. He knew that it was being built to the glory of man and its city. It was not, as they suggested, being created in praise of Him. So God destroyed the Tower of Babel and scattered the people.'

The intake of Perfects were swivelling in their chairs to follow him around the room, not wanting to miss anything he might say.

'But here is where so many get confused by the words rather than the intention. God didn't then simply distribute different languages to the various groups as some sort of tactic to stop them uniting again. None of us has any illusion as to how languages and dialects have naturally evolved around the Globe, how they become subsumed and decay. But this was not the purpose or the outcome of the Tower of Babel. What the scriptures mean is that instead He had them go forth to spread different Words, that is words with a capital W. They were dispersed to the corners of the world believing and bearing their different versions of the Word...' The screen showed a close-up of Jon. '...carrying their different perspectives of the Truth. He did not literally make them speak in the words of different languages; they instead departed to develop their own beliefs and customs.

'If you were each to follow in my footsteps you would see all too clearly that these religions and philosophies are each in themselves well-meaning. They are the outcome of many generations of successive interpretations, the sheer cumulative effect of centuries of 'editors and journalists' having their say. The religious leaders have been manipulated by politicians and warmongers, ambitious and venous individuals have had their impact too. Down the years these have served to move us further and further away from an appreciation of the Truth!'

He was back on the stage and his whole body now shimmered with an aura.

'You have just entered the first Perfect level and to you will be revealed the Order's innermost secrets. You must plunge into this learning. We have millennia of accumulated false information that we need to discard before you can begin to catch sight of the Truth. I say again that there is very little time. The first seal of the Revelation has already been opened.

'The first seal is the first horse of the Apocalypse. The white horse and its rider, and they were set loose upon the world at Babel. Many will have told you that this horse's name is Conquest, for the scripture says "...he went forth conquering, and to conquer..." But I assure you that this is not about the word conquest in the traditional sense of that word. This is instead a conquest by false witness; false prophets seeking to conquer your mind and soul by their guile and their testimony.

'They will use every means to reach you and turn you from your chosen path. Don't be confused for they may come to you in the guise of family and friends from your past. They will be very convincing, for they have all the mighty power of Evil on their side. Their words will often be seductive. They will use every trick in trying to lure you from the path. When you show them your strength of character and don't turn, only then will they become aggressive and threatening, seeking forcibly to carry you away from our community.'

His voice was low. Even with the sound system they all had to lean forward and listen intently. 'But don't be afraid. We are here to shield you. Fear is simply your mind and body's natural defence to the unknown and to real and present dangers; it is a perfectly healthy reaction. But we will help you to control that fear. We will surround it with the confidence that you have found the right direction. Be assured that your colleagues and mentors within the Order are here to give you any added strength and provide any support that you may require.' He dropped to his knees and clasped his hands high over his head. 'For together we can and will reach Salvation.'

As the video paused, Hannah caught the Leader's desire for their approbation and was the first to speak, 'I fully appreciate how you achieved our two main objectives. You made supremely clear the exclusivity that we have on the Truth and hinted at the secret books that we have to fortify and to guide us. You made very clear that they must mistrust the outside, even their past friends and family, and look only within the community for guidance.'

Samuel replied. 'Thank you, my dear.' Dieter watched the exchange with disgust because the Leader's look towards Hannah was so openly lustful.

'However you have to appreciate that these presentation have a real mechanical problem, even with that committed audience, it is in how to get off the stage. We need the set and stage to remain minimalistic so that the message and the effects are more powerful. Our goal has to be that fewer will recognise them as effects because of that very simplicity. But once you've hit the crescendo anything you might do thereafter can only subtract from the emotional pitch you have created. Here I used a large team to usher the audience away speedily or else that pose I held at the end becomes too embarrassing, not to say darned uncomfortable,'

Dieter had been involved in a prior discussion on this matter, still bothered by Shepherd's lascivious leer, he couldn't help delivering his comment in a flat tone, not trusting himself to inject the emotion running through him. 'We've looked at using curtains, trapdoors, even turntables but they're all just too obvious, far too artificial. We have one or two more concepts we are working through.'

'So my colleagues, do please go through this video and review the content time and time again to see if you can spot all the stages of the induction process - how to use threat, when to use motivation, when to recognise and encourage comment, when to deliver your messages. We will meet again later to have you try to present your own sessions.'

As they got up to leave he looked across at the girl.

'Hannah, will you stay back please. I need your particular skills to assist me with some other matters?' She smiled back her acquiescence.

Dieter hated that he had to leave her with this manipulative old man. His emotions were in turmoil. His original zeal for the Order and its community was beginning to clash with his personal passion for the woman, albeit that this was apparently unrequited.

# Chapter 12 - *Tiwanaku, Bolivia*

For now Tom decided he must cast aside his interest in this Berkeley character. Instead he urgently needed to concentrate on a review of what it was that he had learned while at Tiwanaku; he desperately needed to start to get these chapters and the general flow of this part of his book fleshed out.

Tiwanaku was one of the oldest cities that has so far been found anywhere in the America, regularly in use from around 1,200 BCE. At its peak it appears to have been able to sustain somewhere between a half million to one million inhabitants, based on its capacity for irrigation and its agricultural innovations and ingenuity.

Tom believed this process was all too reminiscent of the way that Mesopotamia had developed its civilisation based on its own strength in agriculture. Mesopotamia literally means 'between the rivers', the rivers in this case being the Tigris and Euphrates. It was here that early cities like Ur and Babylon were founded based upon their populations' creativity in irrigation and agriculture.

In Tiwanaku all this had fallen into disrepair at some stage and by 1,000 CE it was derelict. Originally the South American city was located directly on Titicaca's shoreline, but the lake's levels have receded down the centuries. So it is now quite a distance away from the lakeside, around seventy kilometres west of Bolivia's capital La Paz, close to the country's border with Peru.

Teams from the States and Europe were regularly attracted by Tom's hosts DINAR to visit this ancient city. An undeniable part of its attraction is that it has often been referred to as the 'American Stonehenge'.

Just as with Stonehenge this city used some extremely large stones in constructing its many monuments. Huge stones that needed to be transported across great distances and man-handled into place, all by human muscle power alone. Like its English 'sister', many of the stones have been identified as coming from quarries located at anything up to one hundred kilometres away from the city. But the truly remarkable thing at Tiwanaku is that all this building work had not only been achieved in the very early centuries, but that all this extreme effort was carried out at a giddy 3,800 metres above sea level!

The lack of any really hard data on Tiwanaku or its inhabitants automatically imbues it with mystery, gives it an enigmatic feel. In some other locations this implied mystery is disappointing in reality but Tom had not been disappointed with Tiwanaku. He found its arcane reputation was fully realised as he walked around its plethora of cryptic sites.

One of these was the *Akapana*, the biggest platform found at the site constructed from sandstone and andesite blocks, some of these weighing over 100 tonnes. It was incredible that these huge stones could have been moved such a distance up here and then manipulated into position. It was deep within the *Akapana* that a recent ground-radar investigation had uncovered a series of seven small stelae.

While the original people of Tiwanaku appeared not to have used any written form, these stelae were found to have markings or '*petroglyphs*' etched onto them. It was these markings that Tom had been asked to come and see. While there he had taken photographs and rubbings of all seven for later analysis back in the UK. Carbon dating of the stelae he had left with the locals.

Tom knew that petroglyphs, literally stone carvings, had been found in recent years across five continents with a surprising commonality of symbology. They had been found close to major ancient civilisations in Egypt, and in India, they had been drawn by Native Americans and Australian Aborigines.

The similarities in images are usually cited as based upon Jungian theories of the collective unconscious, our common brain structure and in-built archetypes at work. Or as Tom had concluded perhaps these were Dawkins' memes at work.

The Inca's had come to Tiwanaku several hundred years after it had been abandoned and could not help but be inspired by its architecture. They had drawn upon what they learned of this city to create the style and the approach for building their own capital at Cusco a little to the north. But, a proud people, they also sought to subsume the history and mythology of the city, to annexe it within their own, to make clear that they were the first and foremost civilisation. This hubris drove them to ensure that no-one could ever believe that anything more significant had ever existed prior to the Incas.

Tom found that the precise provenance of these freshly discovered stelae was therefore extremely confused. The Incas had built their own settlement here and cavalierly plundered and re-used the large stones from the pre-existing monuments to do so. The site had fared no better during Spanish colonial, and even more recent times, with a local church and a nearby railway bridge both having been built from stolen Tiwanaku materials.

Even the 1960s attempt at a scientific reconstruction of part of the site had been ill-judged. It had been poorly researched and had as a result done no favours to those trying to understand something of its past and its original state.

It was their sophisticated form of agriculture that was most intriguing to Tom for his current project. The city had established a system of terraced fields, using raised planting mounds and a network of small lakes for their irrigation. These had formed the very roots of their civilization and provided the basis of their community wealth, able to attract and sustain its population.

The lakes were connected by canals that not only provided irrigation but apparently acted to absorb solar radiation during the day. They could then give out heat overnight to combat the cold temperatures encountered at this high altitude. How did this complex technology emerge?

It all seemed so sophisticated, rather too rounded given that there had been no signs elsewhere of its evolution in the region. The best conclusion Tom, and others before him, could reach was that it must have been learnt from others, somehow implanted with the meme that enabled them to implement it full-grown. But at this early stage of human development where might they have learnt about this form of agriculture, if not from the Middle East?

Tom had tried to focus his interest upon those who had built the city, and not be diverted by the many who had come along and plundered it later. He lit on the tale of Viracocha, a god that the Inca's had inherited from Tiwanaku to become their prime deity, their sun and storm god.

The story of Viracocha was tantalising for Tom's theories. The god was said to have created the original humans using the rock or clay at Tiwanaku, echoing precisely the creation story of the Sumerian religion and its later plagiariser, the Bible.

The local legends go on to explain that each of the ethnic varieties found in the Andes was created right there in the city and then dispatched away from Tiwanaku in different directions to found its own tribe. Tom felt that while this South American version was a tad less traumatic, certainly a lot less smiting going on. Yet it was still far too similar to the Tower of Babel story to be a coincidence; that ill-fated biblical tower is assumed to have been a Sumerian ziggurat.

Some time later Viracocha had become disenchanted by the way that his people were developing and decided to punish them for their wrong-thinking by creating a flood. Tom was bemused, a flood? Up here? How would that work at these heights?

Surely these were both stories that must have been brought here from the Middle East?

A version of Viracocha is carved onto Tiwanaku's iconic 'Gateway of the Sun'. But this gateway had been moved from its original site by the reconstruction. He had to keep reminding himself that absolutely nothing here could be taken at face value.

He had tromped around the various sites talking to those working there to seek out anything that looked vaguely Sumerian or Phoenician. He had accumulated many pictures and all sorts of theories. Admittedly most of these would require him to take a leap of faith but he could now prepare something that would be at least entertaining. He also had those stelae rubbings with a promised carbon-dating following along soon.

In writing his book he believed that he would need to ensure he put some distance between himself and some of the more bizarre conclusions of others, even when he was inclined to them. But how else could a sophisticated society emerge full-grown up here? He decided perhaps it would be best to sprinkle a little humour here, some healthy cynicism there, underline that he was just being the objective author in mentioning them.

As he worked through these thoughts he could imagine vividly the Professor giving him a despairing, yet at the same time clearly good-natured grimace as he said something like, 'What price celebrity? So it's going to be sound bites and good television put before the facts! Again!'

He had to concede that this sort of 'stretch' had very much become a feature of his recent career. Odd then that his work with DICE was planned for him to manipulate the mass media and reverse the very trend he espoused. He shrugged this off, he was confident he would be able to make sure the facts could be presented to his public to replace and expunge all the misinformation out there. At least he did appreciate the difference!

Yet currently it was his publisher who frightened him most, so for his writing he wasn't ready to stick just with the truth. He concluded. 'Anyway, why beat yourself up and ruin a good book?'

# Chapter 13 - *London, UK*

WPC Paula closed her notebook. She and her partner had just finalised their arrangements, packed off a rather confused, yet contented, old lady by ambulance to hospital for a thorough check over, when they received their next call.

They got the shout because it was located just three streets away from the old woman's mansion block. Only three streets away but the new location was a run-down terrace of houses overlooking a small scruffy patch of open land. Paula read a sign at its edge and thought that to call this scruffy little patch a park was a real stretch of the imagination.

Again the two police personnel realised that they had to be patient as the old man explained the background to his call on his own terms. But no refreshments were offered this time! He rambled on about his insomnia and how he enjoyed looking out over London and the small 'park', as he clearly considered it to be.

The old man's bedroom overlooked this waste ground and he explained he had been looking out when the small creature arrived. He watched as it competently climbed up into a tree and settled down, resting on a large bough. The man had been watching the day's news earlier and immediately knew exactly what or who this was. He felt from his vantage point that its movements made it look somehow sad. He empathised with the poor little guy who was seeking sanctuary in the tree, but he still accepted that he had his civic duty to perform.

He had called the emergency services reporting his sighting of the ape-man and stressed that the creature was still there!

'Of course when I called your lot they treated me as if I was a nutter. Pretty patronizing on the phone as a matter of fact and of course no-one from your lot even bothered to turn up that time.'

He said he had kept a careful watch to ensure that the ape-man didn't leave before someone finally decided to show up. Well someone had to have some civic spirit even if the Met Police couldn't be bothered. He glowered at them from under the huge foliage that conspired to give him just the one large eyebrow. He went on at length to explain that it had been he who set up the Neighbourhood Watch scheme for the area.

'No thanks from anyone. They all just think of me as a sad old git, a grumpy old man with nothing better to do. A 'nosy old bugger' one teenager called me. To my face! There's no respect for age and experience these days! But if no-one cared then where would we all be?'

He finally went on to explain that two 4x4s eventually arrived and four black-clad individuals had approached the open area cautiously and quietly.

'Whoever they were they must have been monitoring the police frequencies or something. They certainly weren't official. Looked to me more like something out of CTU - far too slick and capable to be plodding coppers.' He suddenly caught Paula's eye and hastily added, 'Present company excepted of course.

'Well I watched as they stalked up to him, then blow me if they didn't just pull out a rifle and shoot him out of the tree. Poor little thing hadn't a chance. He just dropped to the floor like a stone. I wasn't sure if they killed him or just doped him. Whatever, he fell to the ground and they bundled him into the back of one of their vehicles.

'It was just like an episode of 24. They acted brutally, just like Jack Bauer. He's the one that never cares about using torture or even murder to achieve his objective. Bloody Yanks always gung-ho, always right! That Jack knows that he's on the right side, on the side of right and so he goes out there and does whatever it takes. Bit like me and my Neighbourhood Watch duties really, even if the Neighbourhood doesn't particularly care. I know what's right and I make sure that I see it through.'

# Chapter 14 - *London, UK*

Sir Joseph Maudlin was a through and through patrician. He had been born, bred, boarded, Balliol-ed and briefed to make sure that he would become someone senior in high government. In another age he might have sought a Governor-Generalship in some far-flung colony. But who wanted to live out their days on the few dots that were left, not Ascension, or the Pitcairns, or the Falklands; perhaps Bermuda, the Turks & Caicos, the Caymans or the Virgin Islands might be a tad more appealing, but all of them are literal backwaters.

He had concluded in today's world he much preferred his current fiefdom in the intelligence community. But in this secret world, perhaps his twinkling eyes were not his best asset. They did absolutely nothing to hide his mischievous nature and they couldn't conceal a sharp intellect that was constantly at work right there behind them.

Sir Joseph had summoned Mark Elliott to attend this meeting and had also invited Brain, one of his key field agents. Brain was one of those people who you would pass in the street without ever noticing, unless you happened to catch a glimpse of the jagged scar at his neck. Something about the scar said it couldn't have been caused merely by accident. It was of course his unobtrusive quality that was the major asset in his covert role.

Sir Joseph had wanted to meet with Mark as he had proven quite useful to him before and appeared completely open-minded about participating in 'joint ventures'. He had certainly worked well with Brain last year while displaying absolutely no sign of any undue ego, and no sign of the usual agency demarcations, the usual nauseating mistrust, or worse, the personal one-upmanship. Mark had been revealed as a CIA operative in that 'still water' matter. He was well connected directly into the US politicos as well as his own Service; so he should be perfect for Sir Joseph's current purpose.

He also appeared to still be young and impressionable; hopefully pliable enough that just the fact it was Sir Joseph who was asking for assistance would prove of significance for him. Sir Joseph believed his youth also meant he had not yet become case-hardened or cynical; thus it was unlikely the proposed operation would ring any warning bells for him.

Mark arrived promptly and had clearly dressed carefully for the meeting, but despite the evident care he still managed to look a tad scruffy. He was just one of those destined to be a jeans-and-trainers kind of person. After fussing around to get him settled and furnished with a pot of tea, Sir Joseph wasted no time explaining what he had in mind, in his own inimitable style.

'You can imagine that we are none too impressed when mysterious vehicles bearing young fit Americans, clad in black, start cropping up all over London. Evidently they must have been monitoring our emergency frequencies and turning up well before our boys in blue deigned to do so. I'm sure you can appreciate that we can't have the 'man on top of the Clapham omnibus' or 'Disgusted of Tunbridge Wells' getting annoyed by these Hollywood antics.'

Brain smiled as he saw the mystified look pass across Mark's face. 'What Sir Joseph means is that nothing gets up the nose of Joe Public more than a failure of our emergency services; particularly when these mysterious men-in-black proved not to be some sort of promotion for Will Smith's latest movie.'

Sir Joseph continued. 'Indeed, wasn't that what I just said? So these ape-man sightings created such a furore that the Fleet Street hounds are still sniffing around. Make no mistake; some of their investigative skills are certainly the equal of Scotland Yard. It turns out the vehicles were hired by an American security organisation called gNOS, which apparently has the presumption to stand for Global New Order Security. Indeed! Therefore presumably these peripatetic men-in-black are gNOS operatives.' He flicked some papers, 'And they do not have any licence to operate here in the UK at all, let alone in the cavalier manner they chose to adopt.'

Mark took the prompt and pulled out a file. 'Following your telecon I did look to see what we have on these gNOS folk. It's precious little I'm afraid. Formed just five years ago as an LLC. Their accounts and taxes are all in order, they have four directors. I looked them up but we have no real data.'

'No real data. Doesn't that automatically set off a concern with your people?'

'Of course it would have done if we had found absolutely nothing at all on record about them. But they seem to be plain Joe Schmos who have each led a blameless and unremarkable life. All four are executive directors. Ethnically and geographically they are quite a mixture, a Hispanic CEO from Texas, a New England Wasp financial VP, a West Coast African-American sales and marketing VP and a Philadelphian with an eastern European name who works as their Operations VP. Nothing suspicious at all. They each grew up, were educated and worked in the US of A. All cool from our perspective.'

Sir Joseph raised his eyebrows. 'How very democratic and PC they sound as a board of directors.'

Mark ignored the comment and continued to read from his documents. 'They are based in northern Florida and they do have all the requisite licences to operate within the States. They don't appear to be strapped for cash, but equally don't have any major blue-chip clients or any great turnover either. But then it's one of those security organisations that is pretty tight-lipped about their clients and what they do for them.'

'Perhaps someone in your headquarters might have a gentle word with them about clearing in advance any major operations that they might plan in the future upon old Blighty's soil?'

'Do you have any significant material that we can use to show them that we are aware of what they were doing last week?'

Sir Joseph nodded to Brain. 'I dare say Brain here can furnish you with some stills and videos that we have collected from traffic and other cameras. So let's move on to what this meeting is really about. This other American organisation,' he flicked through his papers, 'here's the name, BiCogNaIT.'

Brain volunteered, 'Yes, on them we do have information about their UK operations and from their website we see that they have some major contracts with your Department of Defense, but do you have any more information on this organisation?'

'Thankfully we can assist a lot more on this one. Apparently from their blurb BiCogNaIT is an organisation "set up to exploit the ongoing and fruitful convergence of BIotechnology, COGnitive technology, NAnotechnology and Information Technology". That's what it stands for, but don't begin to ask me what it means. However we do know that it is the corporate entity that handles all the work of an absolutely remarkable and brilliant US biologist and geneticist called Dr Marsha Davenport. She is mega-bright and has become mega-rich as a result. Apparently she's a Creole.'

Brain asked, 'I thought that was a style of cooking, seafood or something?'

'No it's the name given to those of mixed European and black heritage. In her case she's from the Deep South, not the Caribbean. Her family hails out of New Orleans.'

'So a product of those steamy hot afternoons down on the plantation?'

Mark smiled, 'Precisely, and a pretty damned remarkable product she is too. Creole women were always very capable. They often ran businesses and plantations long before we 'civilised' people thought of giving women the vote or any credit for their intellect. Ostensibly she is termed the Research Director, but our information is that she is in fact BiCogNaIT, and it would frankly be irrelevant without her ideas and her research, apparently she's nothing short of a genius.

'She was a child prodigy identified very early as remarkable. Shamefully she was extensively prodded and tested from the age of ten to twelve years old. By then she had already passed a medical degree and was studying for her law finals. Her early form of MRI scans showed that she could naturally deliver more than five times the amount of blood to areas of her brain than is normal; experimental PET scans showed her using some areas of her brain that we mere mortals seldom bother to energise. But as soon as she finished her law qualification she immediately used it to stop anyone running any research on her ever again. She was just twelve!'

Sir Joseph commented, 'Sounds something of a little madam?'

'Yes, a good description, because according to our reports she may be brilliant in many fields but her interpersonal skills did originally leave quite a lot to be desired. Though I believe she has worked on them since.'

Brain offered, 'Well, if she was obviously so much smarter than them, I don't suppose she bothered to talk much with her school friends and they would tend to ostracise her and begin the name-calling.'

'Yes as a child and teenager she was something of a loner. Now in her late 30s, unmarried, but she seems more than fulfilled by her work.'

'And what, dear boy, might that be?'

'Her organisation is one of the leaders in the research of many genetic and biological developments, for example she is heavily involved in ageing…'

Sir Joseph smiled, 'Aren't we all!'

'I mean she is looking at how to combat it.'

Sir Joseph interrupted. 'So she's a perfectly normal late-thirty-something woman in that respect!'

'I don't just mean anti-wrinkle creams, not just simply hiding the effects of ageing. She and her team are looking at the ways she could stop the process of ageing altogether!'

Sir Joseph twinkled, 'When will people simply learn that they should grow old disgracefully and not worry about the odd grey hairs and wrinkles? But surely that's not what she's doing for the Department of Defense?'

'I've identified a number of strands in her work for the DoD but the one that shouts out from the list is her pioneering work with bonobos.'

Sir Joseph asked, 'What on this good earth is a bonobo when it's at home?'

Mark explained. 'Brain and I might have bumped into one when we were down in the Democratic Republic of the Congo last year; that's its original home, the only place that it exists naturally. It's an interesting variant of the chimpanzee, an endangered species that has a few quite key differences from the common chimp. The Congo river has apparently always remained a significant barrier right across the heart of Africa and it has effectively kept the two strains separated. A bonobo is more inclined than the standard chimp to walk upright and its slightly different shape makes it look much more human. Don't forget that the genes in the human and both sorts of chimp vary by less than 5%. I'm not sure but the one she has developed might be even closer than that.'

'So that's what was running around last week in London? A boney-oboe did you say?'

'Bo-no-bo. I thought initially that this was unlikely because they have another name, the Pygmy or Dwarf chimp. Your ape-man reports show that it was far too tall to be a straight bonobo.'

'It was wearing a BiCogNaIT outfit.'

'Yes. After a bit of delving I was able to establish that one of Davenport's more secret DoD undertakings is the development of a 'humanzee'.'

Sir Joseph wrinkled his brow, 'Is that what the name suggests? Some sort of cross-breed between a human and a chimpanzee?'

'Well, to be more precise, a cross between a human and a bonobo.'

Brain was confused. 'What on earth would the DoD need with that?'

'Just think about it. The chimpanzee has extraordinary strength pound-for-pound compared with us; its climbing skills are far superior too. Mix an amalgam of our skills with theirs and you create a new and more powerful sort of soldier. In this way our politicians would no longer need to send our own sons and daughters in to combat. I got hold of a copy of the original prospectus that she presented in order to receive the initial funding, Davenport called it the opportunity for 'strife without grief'.'

Sir Joseph commented, 'She sounds to me like a very cold fish.'

Brain shook his head in disbelief. 'That's no grief unless you just happen to be that humanzee's proud parent. What about the animal rights people, they'll be up in arms?'

Sir Joseph corrected him, 'But if this Davenport woman truly has changed them so that they are even closer to becoming a human being, then mightn't they expect to deserve human rights for themselves?'

Brain muttered, 'By all accounts the men in black certainly didn't show it any courtesies.'

Mark smiled, 'Didn't sound like it was given much of a welcome by the human race!'

# Chapter 15 - *Isla del Sol, Bolivia*

The only sign of life was this jetty, looking rather incongruous on an otherwise pretty featureless piece of shoreline. They had travelled from the floating island up along the west coast of the Isla del Sol. All along this coast a stark spine of rocks showed no sign of an inviting harbour.

Tom had studied the charts and saw they were turning around a headland before they would reach another small island; one that on the chart resembled the side view of a scampering iguana. But all he saw as they rounded the headland were a few clouds in the distance where the iguana island must have been located.

Around the head they came to a squarish secluded bay where the jetty stuck out like a sore thumb, so new and somehow so technically current, it looked completely out of place.

As they approached this modern landing point Tom could discern a series of creeks harbouring small boats and signs of agriculture along the foreshore. The landing place was between two of these creeks and extended out far enough to allow the mooring of boats with a much deeper draught than the one that they were using that day.

Tom had been advised to stay aboard. This would be where Berkeley and his group were leaving them. As they got closer a white people-carrier came barrelling towards the land-end of the pier, it stopped with its engine running, obviously waiting on Berkeley. He and his team quickly removed all their equipment and baggage and moved off across to the vehicle. There were no farewells, no thankyou as they left. Tom watched as his boat pulled off, the vehicle turned and chased directly away from the shoreline along what looked like a well-used track.

The boat's course took them back along the headland until they struck across the bay to another beach; his iguana island still remained too distant to be properly visible. This new beach had no foreshore, instead the island shelved steeply up and away from a thin strip of beach. Amaro pointed out their destination located up on top of the cliffs. It looked a steep climb at sea level, but add to this the impact of the altitude and it took its toll upon Tom.

Along the beach from where they moored Tom saw a fascinating boat, presumably made from the same reeds that were used to fabricate the floating islands. As they approached, it reminded him of a Viking longboat, with a high prow and stern. His first impression was that the prow was built to look like a dragon, but as he got closer it became more lizard-like. Though as they drew alongside it he realised that there were also some catlike features, presumably a jaguar?

They made the breathtaking climb to find some desultory ruins that Tom found extremely disappointing. The same pile of bricks could have been seen anywhere in the world. And with much less effort! It was only the heavy breathing from the effort of his climb and the two llamas, that some enterprising local had tethered there as a photo opportunity, that made clear the locality. Tom admitted that perhaps he had begun to lose interest in these monuments. It was now this Berkeley character and what he was up to that was exercising his mind.

They hiked across to a small Inca temple that featured a central raised altar; Tom assumed it to be so anyway. It was surrounded by two circles of stones of a reasonable size that would have been easily transported, certainly more easily than those at Tiwanaku; though his current gasping might argue otherwise. He established that no inscriptions could be found on them so they pressed on. His mind was still picking over what he had learned of Berkeley, and just what might be Mission's mission?

Amaro urged him on to view the sacred rock from which the original Inca was said to have emerged. It too was pretty unremarkable with a small wall built before it. It was not even particularly photogenic, though he dutifully clicked away. Tom went through the motions of expressing his appreciation, but so far today's side trip had added absolutely nothing for his book - not even a petroglyph that he could weave into his tale.

On the way back to the boat Tom pressed Amaro for more information about the jetty and whether he knew what was beyond the track that Berkeley had taken? All his guide could add was that some foreign organisation had bought a large area of land located just a few kilometres back from the beach. He knew that they had been freighting in regular and large shipments to La Paz, then trucking them across to Copacabana and ferrying them across to the jetty for several months. He also volunteered that several locals had become extremely rich from handling the organisation's many shipments.

Tom pressed for more details but Amaro could only come up with a name for the organisation. Tom was surprised to learn that it was 'Tyndale' and not Mission. Tyndale sounded far too pastoral, extremely English for something that was located out here in the middle of Lake Titicaca. Tom had presumed that Mission was a rather more American name in its tone, more forceful, more like Berkeley himself.

He made some feeble excuse that he needed to pass some information on to Dom Berkeley and urged that they call back at the jetty. Amaro looked dubious but he had been charged by DINAR to take this celebrity anywhere he pleased, so he reluctantly complied.

They made the reverse crossing to find the jetty and its approach unoccupied. Other than a few small boats visible in one of the nearby creeks and the few traces of agriculture, the whole area looked pretty much uninhabited.

Tom asked Amaro, 'Two kilometres you said?'

Amaro confirmed this as just approximate and was clearly confused that a breathless and sweaty Tom, who had quite evidently been unhappy with the climb up to the ruins and the sacred rock, was now keenly preparing to set off on this much longer and apparently pointless journey.

It was late afternoon and the temperature and humidity was dropping speedily. There was cloud cover that looked none too threatening so Tom set off at a slow steady pace that would not leave him too breathless. On either side of the track there were increasing signs of care having been taken with the fields, each growing a variety of crops that he realized that he had no hope of identifying.

Around a thousand metres along the track he found signs of terracing located off to his right. These looked as if they had been there a long time, yet unlike the ones he had seen abandoned in southern Spain they were still very much in use. In Spain Tom had been advised that similar terraces had been extremely functional in past times when tended by a man and his donkey. They had however proven completely unworkable when tractors were introduced; tractors could not clamber up to the next tier like the old beast of burden had so readily managed. Here they must be maintaining the traditional approach; with llamas he pondered?

He reached the top of a small rise and unexpectedly was able to look out across a broad valley. Spread before him was a surprisingly large community. Arrayed in the distance were a large number of low pre-fabricated dwellings gathered around a sprinkling of much larger buildings. But the big surprise was to suddenly be confronted by hordes of people working the fields and others about their business bustling along a grid of roads and tracks. After the empty countryside this came as a complete shock to the senses; the sheer industry and size of it all. Here was a busy and thriving agricultural village. It was hard to rationalise all this manual effort being applied at this fatiguing altitude.

Tom set off down the road into the village and noted there were no vehicles other than the white people-carrier which was parked at a distance up near one of the larger buildings. There was absolutely no sign of any agricultural mechanisation, just oxen and donkeys, not llamas, assisting with the work in the fields. He could also see several horse-drawn carriages, all fully-functional. But they were drab working vehicles, not a single surrey with a fringe on top anywhere to be seen.

As he descended into the valley he began to see the clothing of the workers much more clearly. It did not look at all like any he had seen locally, more like what he'd expect from say an Amish community. And this would fit right in to this no-nonsense vista that was spread before him. As he got even closer he confirmed that these inhabitants did not have any South American characteristics. In fact they appeared to be from all sorts of racial backgrounds rather than South American.

He approached to greet one of the workers at the side of the road. The individual completely ignored him. At first Tom assumed that he might have been deaf or perhaps not understood English, but then he seemed to deliberately move away from any encounter. The man definitely did not want to acknowledge Tom's presence. He moved twenty paces away and then set to work again. He was thin and wan with something of a persecuted look on his face. Perhaps it was just that Tom had the misfortune of approaching the village idiot?

He pressed on becoming increasingly spooked by the people working in the fields and their lack of courtesy to a visitor to their remote community. But perhaps worse than this was their complete lack of curiosity; not one of them was prepared to acknowledge his presence.

He had by now come closer to the buildings and could hear the drone of some large diesel generators at work. So they had not completely dispensed with modern technology here.

On reaching the first large building he found he could freely pass through two sets of entrance doors. Disappointed at finding no reception area, no receptionist, he walked straight in to a large modern laboratory. White-coated technicians and scientists were busy at benches laden with high-tech equipment.

All those working here worked hard not to notice his entry! Though he did spot someone at the rear quickly raise a telephone handset and begin a conversation. The individual was studiously looking elsewhere as he did it, trying to suggest that the call was unrelated to Tom's sudden appearance.

Ignored as he was, he approached several of the workstations and tried to assess what they were working on here. He could detect the distinctive smell of lab animals coming from somewhere and a row of sophisticated refrigerators filled one wall, but on the work surfaces there was nothing to give him a clue.

Without warning he heard the doors open behind him and two large individuals rushed towards him. They were dressed completely in black, in some sort of uniform. The two 'guards' grabbed him and forced him back out of the lab, all without saying a word.

He did ask why they were being so hostile, but they offered no response, just pressed him across to a smaller building. He argued but made no real attempt to stop them; they were clearly under instructions to take him to their leader. In their hurry, one who had been wearing a baseball cap had it dislodged revealing a distinctive tattoo on his forehead. It was probably some sort of Asian pictograph. He noticed disappointedly that is was not a Sumerian or a Phoenician one!

Both individuals had the letters gNOS sewn on to their shirt pocket. Tom's first thought seeing these letters was the word Gnostic? But he dismissed this. Their manner and their outfits suggested it was more likely some sort of corporate logo.

He was marched into what appeared to be a military security facility and then pressed on directly through to the rear where, as he expected, he saw a series of cells. He was pushed into one of these and the door was summarily slammed in his face. He had complained all the way from the lab that he was here to see Dom Berkeley, yet neither of his minders had made even an involuntary noise; what was this, a community of deaf mutes?

The cell had no windows, not even an evident hatch in the door. In fact the door itself was difficult to discern from the rest of the walls. There was absolutely no furniture or plumbing. All the surfaces were coated in a highly reflective white material. Something like the material in the white lines of a road marking or on a road sign, it had a multitude of tiny reflective elements which cascaded the light back in all directions. The large bank of lamps were far too bright, even when he scrunched up his eyes tight he could still feel the brightness burning through his every pore. But the tubes were set high, beyond reach, and set behind a security grille so nothing could be done to avoid their glare.

As if this was not disconcerting enough, he became aware of a constant whining noise that worked away at his skull, audible even when he clapped his hands over his ears or rammed his fingers deep in to his ears. It was unbearable. It was torture of the most intrusive kind. He found he could not think of anything else. His mind was completely overwhelmed by these two assaults upon his senses.

He had no idea of the passage of time, but after what felt like hours the room was suddenly plunged into darkness and the noise was gone. The dark was Stygian, the silence as stultifying as the noise had been. Tom had only once experienced this complete lack of light before, when he was in a submersible deep below the Pacific. In sudden darkness after his long period of sensory assault, he felt again the pressure of that previous event. He vividly remembered being back down at the depths with water pressing to get in, threatening to overwhelm him. He was breathless, just as he'd been in that submersible that was not circulating any air.

He managed somehow to summon up the mental energy to cast this memory from his mind, to reassert that his breathlessness was because he was in fact way up above sea level at this Tyndale place. From this first step he started to rebuild his internal models and to shake off the disorientation that the cell had created.

More time passed in this dark place until finally the door opened and someone entered. Tom could not take even the low light from outside and could only barely make out that the individual was not one of the guards. The man was in the 'Amish' clothing he had seen earlier. He handed him a coffee and a small plate.

Tom found he was dry and hungry from his experiences and gratefully accepted it. As he took the plate he felt a small piece of paper beneath it and caught the look of warning from the individual not to react. At last someone looked him in the eyes and acknowledged his presence.

The man left, the door slammed to eclipse the external lights, and restore the Cimmerian darkness.

More time passed in the dark, he had no idea how long. But he could deal with this much better than the assault by light and sound. He was able to sit calmly and concentrate on planning his book, fleshing out several of his themes. It was working so well that he thought perhaps this would be a good tactic to employ by choice. Remove all external stimuli and establish this supreme focus on the subject at hand.

Once again the door opened without any warning. This time a guard entered and pulled Tom to his feet thrusting him out into the light and across to a small office. Tom was still struggling with the light overload and could not get a clear picture of the individual behind the desk.

The man said with an evident English accent, 'Now Mr Carter, just what is it we can do for you?'

Tom still couldn't focus, 'I came to talk with Dom Berkeley.'

'Indeed, what might you need to say to him that you could not have discussed earlier today?' The tone was arrogant and somehow world-weary. Tom instantly recognised the tone, only an English public school imbued this sort of style and delivery of speech.

Tom was not going to be put off that easily. 'I realised I had seen him earlier in my trip when I visited some *chullpas*, and wanted to ask him something about them.'

'I regret to say that Mr Berkeley has already left.' When he saw Tom's quizzical look he added. 'He left us by helicopter. Let us give you a ride to the jetty where you will find your guides are getting restless.'

'What is this place? On what basis did you feel you had the right to lock me up without reason?'

The man did not reply. Instead two younger men pushed him outside and towards the vehicle. He could see no point in resisting because it was clear they would use force if necessary, so he calmly climbed in.

'What sort of community do you have here? It looks sort of Amish?'

Neither of them deigned to reply.

As they approached the jetty he tried one more time, 'I thought my guide said you were called Tyndale? What sort of organisation is that? And what does gNOS stand for?'

No response. He was just ushered from the vehicle, his backpack was thrown to the floor, the van quickly turned round and sped back the way that they had come. Tom looked at the backpack. He had not taken it with him, the extra effort would have been unnecessary. They must have come and taken it from the boat while he was locked up?

He had been dumped short of the jetty, presumably to ensure they did not come into contact with Tom's guide or the crew of the boat. He quickly checked his bag but did not notice until much later that the stelae rubbings had been removed.

Tom extracted from his pocket the piece of paper that he had been passed to him in the cell. It read, 'Help! Held against my will at TIDS! Please call my family…' and it gave a US telephone number.

Easy enough to work out that TIDS must mean Tyndale Isla del Sol, but his foray there had provided him with no information. Other than it did not seem a happy place.

# Chapter 16 - *London, UK*

Brain was delighted. In just a few minutes he had disabled the alarm system and then he and Mark Elliott were able to safely enter the small BiCogNaIT laboratory in Central London. They quickly dismissed the front office and reception area as unlikely to hold anything of interest. Instead they turned left and passed through a door that led into a large storage or warehouse area.

The warehouse racking appeared to disappear off into infinity and there was a faintly unpleasant smell. It reminded Brain of the pong when he recently visited the menagerie at the rear of a travelling circus with his nephew.

They had assumed their available time would be limited so they turned back to the reception and went right. Here they found themselves on a short corridor with five other routes leading from it.

Sir Joseph had convinced Mark that he should be involved in the break-in so that any USA Department of Defense interests would be fully safeguarded. Mark did not need too much convincing. He was intrigued by this area of research, sharing Brain's reservations about its very morality. Besides he had come to realise that he liked to hang out over the edge of a precipice just to see how it might feel. He took no time in agreeing to participate.

They did not waste effort on the first two side rooms after they proved to be merely offices that were probably being used as hot-desks cum meeting rooms by travelling BiCogNaIT personnel. There were no signs of any files or communications. They assumed that these would be held on the computers' server and neither of them was skilled enough or even equipped to try and get past the inevitable passwords.

The next two side doors opened onto small laboratories. In the first was a whole series of trolleys each bearing racks of small packets, clearly they were all queued up to be tested in some manner by the lab.

A quick look showed that each tray was labelled with the name of a particular town or city together with a suffix code number. There was a logo on the containers of the items - two interlocking Gs. Brain picked one of these up and pocketed it. GG? He hoped that it didn't contain horse semen!

The final side door revealed another much larger lab with a series of work surfaces holding various arrays of equipment. The far wall was completely racked with small doors. The plant noise in here was so loud. They must be fridges? Brain thought it reminded him far too much of a morgue. This impression was supported by the doors bearing a small label saying 'CryoVat' and a warning to wear protective gloves before opening one. He took a picture and finding no obvious signs of any gloves decided that he would like to keep all his fingers intact for now.

Mark whispered, 'Shouldn't we be going for the last door? Surely any silent alarms they've installed should have someone heading this way fast?'

Brain shared his fears and moved quickly to the door at the end of the corridor. He found it had a simple Yale lock which he was able to spring in seconds with a piece of plastic he removed from his pocket.

Mark smiled, 'You are one very scary guy. Thank God I've never been entrusted with any secrets or treasures. I'd become completely paranoid about how to secure it from guys like you.'

Brain smiled and moved on into the laboratory where he was delighted to see that several lights had been left on overnight. He looked around the impressive array of test equipment, but was disappointed to see mostly featureless boxes of electronics. There were no Bunsens, or retort vessels, or burbling and dripping coloured liquids that he normally associated with the lair of a mad scientist.

They moved down past these workstations to the rear wall with its three solid looking doors, each with a small in-built window and a vent panel above. There was a faint musty smell at this end of the room. Brain looked in through the first door and rapidly took a pace backwards.

Looking back at him through the window was what he realised must be this humanzee that they had heard about. But even having seen all the ape-man reports and being pre-warned of the concept it was still quite a shock when up close and personal.

The humanzee looked to Brain like a slightly effeminate black guy, the effeminate impression being prompted by the bizarrely pink lips and the slight and delicately shaped head. Perhaps the forehead was not very human, but there were none of the prominent brows that he associated with chimpanzees and there was little facial hair. The hair on the crown of its head was cut and arranged in a standard human style, but the ears were just a little too small to be human and the nostrils just a little too large and flat. Notwithstanding these various differences this was just like looking into another human being's eyes.

Mark called him over to another door. Behind this one was a female and the very evident feature here was a large fleshy bust. Brain tried to think back, and could not be certain, but he was pretty sure that chimp boobs he had seen had never been this large; certainly not full blown bazookas like these coming together to form a deep cleavage at the top of her dress. He tore his eyes away having noticed a look in the eyes of the female that was both coy and yet strangely he got the impression that it, or she, was pleased that he had been appraising her assets.

She, for he had concluded to even think of her as an 'it' was just plain rude, was signing to him but he had no idea what she was trying to communicate. 'Mark, did you ever learn how to sign?'

'There's nothing in the third cell.' Mark came back to the small window. 'Yes, there was a deaf kid at my school who we were all taught to sign to. But that was quite a while ago.'

He studied the female's signing. 'No, I don't think this is the ASL signing that I learned. Tell you what it does look like though. Several of the signs look a lot like the baby sign language my sister insisted on using with her first. I never really bothered to learn that, assumed it was just another of her short-term fads, like her birthing pool!'

Mark went back to look at the male and Brain turned his skills to the lock on the female's cell. Brain had released the door and stood at the threshold. He briefly looked around the room which he saw was furnished like an apartment, not plush but still too comfortable to be considered a jail cell. But before he could take in too much the female had grabbed him, propelled him on to the bed and lay on top of him.

Her sheer strength had taken him completely by surprise. She started rubbing her groin firmly and slowly against his. She took his hand and pressed it against her breasts, then clamped her wide mouth over his and penetrated his mouth with her large and lively tongue.

Mark stood at the door in fits of laughter, 'Oh, I meant to say that the other thing I read about bonobos is that they are heavily into sex. They have a matriarchal society and sex plays an extremely prominent part in their culture. Clearly that feature of the species was not programmed out during their transgenic procedures.'

'Help me get her off. Please!' The two only managed to remove her because she had become rapidly disenchanted by his lack of response to her advances.

Outside the door and with the female safely inside Brain commented. 'Yuk, I can't shake the feel and taste of her tongue. Just imagine an army of these humanzees taking over a town or a village. Rape and pillage has always been a feature in some manuals of war, but this would write a whole new chapter!'

Before they could ponder what they might do next there was a noise from the front office. Brain sprinted to the door that, unfortunately, was not equipped with any viewing window and so he was forced to listen. He thought there were two people and it was evident that they were trying to be a little stealthy in their approach. They were trying each of the doors, obviously they couldn't fail to check each of them, so he realised that they had a little time.

He told Mark to stand behind a piece of particularly bulky lab equipment while he flicked off the lights. The effect was better than he'd hoped. The lights also darkened the humanzee rooms, they immediately became agitated, starting to whimper and to bang against the doors.

The two outside abandoned their search of the offices and approached the laboratory door which they opened carefully. Brain standing on the open side of the door lobbed a piece of small equipment over the doorway and past the open door, so that it crashed on the other side.

The lead person now abandoned any stealth and slammed the door back against the wall. As a result, as expected, he had turned his back on Brain. Brain immediately lashed out and kicked viciously at the side of the man's knee which he felt bend unnaturally as the man went down with a scream.

Brain quickly leapt up and over a workbench to distance himself from the second person who was now of course fully pre-warned. He caught a glimpse of the man who was evidently one of the notorious men in black.

The first security man was writhing in agony on the floor. The second had pulled a gun and dropped into a stoop. He called out, 'Was it the TG?'

'I didn't see.'

'Where did he go?'

'The noise came from back there.'

The second guard started to edge forward and Brain watched as the two exchanged hand signals; he wondered if they were the same signs the humanzees used. The able guard moved on into the laboratory while the first, now showing signs of recovery, went for the light switch.

As the lights flickered on the whimpering from the humanzees stopped. The second guard was stalking the room cautiously and in the lights caught a reflection of Mark in the glass panel of an adjacent piece of equipment.

He called out, 'Come on out, with your hands up. I can see you clearly. The blue of your jacket is like a beacon.'

Mark dropped to the floor and slid under a bench, cursing that while here in the UK he was not permitted to carry a gun. At home he would have just blown him away.

Brain made a bolt for the first guard who was still tending his damaged knee. Stick to first principles he thought as he slammed an elbow right across the security man's nose. Break his nose for lots of blood and pain. However the man was good. He didn't just grab his nose but instead tried to counter. Fortunately he could not pivot adequately on his damaged knee and the move was easily met by Brain. A kick landed directly on the wounded knee and the man went down with a double-handed clubbing on the back of his neck. That stopped any resistance - for now.

The second guy hearing the commotion from behind him realised he had a limited opportunity and quickly rushed to where Mark had disappeared. Finding him sprawled awkwardly underneath a workstation he wasted no time and calmly put a shot straight into his chest.

Brain had seen what was about to happen, had been sprinting to reach the guard but arrived just a little too late. Mere seconds after the shot had been fired he reached him, angrily slammed him against some heavy equipment, then grabbed his head and smashed it repeatedly against the same piece of equipment until any resistance was halted.

He went straight over to Mark to see what he could do for him. He pulled open the jacket and tore at his shirt and was surprised to find no signs of any blood, just a single big puncture mark. On a hunch he searched around on the floor until close beside him he found a small dart. The men had come expecting trouble with the humanzees, so Mark had only been tranquilised, not killed!

The guards were not going to be out of action for long and more might already be on their way. Brain used his camera-phone to take shots of the gNOS logo on their shirts and the distinctive tattoos he'd noticed on both guards' heads. He quickly frisked them but found nothing; not even a wallet. He looked to the rear of the room to the humanzee doors. He couldn't shake the memory and the taste of her assault. There was nothing he could safely achieve down there, no samples or records to grab. He hoisted Mark up onto his shoulder and got the hell out of the laboratory while he still could.

## Chapter 17 - *Lima to Buenos Aires*

Tom was trying to relax on his journey that was taking him right across the heart of South America. Having set off early from La Paz he found to his consternation that the flight his travel agent had recommended as being direct to the UK turned out in fact to be a two-legger. He cursed himself for not having checked this more thoroughly. It would have been so simple to have looked on the Internet, but no, he had just picked up his tickets and followed the itinerary like some damned sheep.

The national carrier used must have had a sub-contract relationship with a low-cost economy airline for this first leg. All announcements were only in Spanish; fair enough as he looked to be the only non-Hispanic aboard.

He ran his hands over the note he had been given at that Tyndale place, and decided he would call the number once safely back in the UK. He would also have the opportunity to do some research on this Tyndale camp and its team. They had arrogantly locked him up, refused any form of dialogue with him, and finally bundled him back to his boat.

There had been no sign of an apology and on top of all that he later realised they must have stolen his invaluable rubbings. He would have to ask DINAR to supply new ones; after all their representative had been the one who had handed over his backpack to those Tyndale people.

He refused the offer of a headset and sat instead with his laptop open going over the notes for his book, but he could not shake the feeling that something was clearly not right about this Berkeley character or that settlement on the Isla del Sol.

He was trying to write his piece on how the Sumerians or the Phoenicians must have reached this continent to spread their very particular brand of astronomy and beliefs. But he kept wondering about what the beliefs might have been at that campsite. Wasn't it somewhere in South America that Jim Jones had set up his cult headquarters and all those people had ended up killing themselves?

Something caught his eye on the A320's screens. He could see a distinctive aerial view of one of the Titicaca floating islands. This initial clip was obviously some sort of archive shot of the island but the picture then switched to a panned shot that must have been taken from a hovering helicopter. It was the sort of footage that the BBC would never have been allowed to use. Uro islanders were lying along the shoreline like dead fish that had been washed up on the shore.

He tried to ask those sitting near him what had happened. From his little Spanish and their miming he assumed they were trying to tell him that the Uros had been victim to some rare flesh-eating disease. It sounded pretty awful in any language.

# BOOK TWO

**Mihail C Roco and William S Bainbridge** of the National Science Foundation, Arlington, Virginia, Executive Summary of paper 'Converging Technologies for Improving Human Performance'.

*'In the early decades of the 21ˢᵗ century, concentrated efforts can unify science based on the unity of nature, thereby advancing the combination of nanotechnology, biotechnology, information technology and new technologies based in cognitive science. With proper attention to ethical issues and societal needs, converging technologies could achieve a tremendous improvement in human abilities, societal outcomes, the nation's productivity and the quality of life.'*

**Charles Darwin**:

*'We must, however, acknowledge, as it seems to me that man with all his noble qualities...*
*...still bears in his bodily frame the indelible stamp of his lowly origin.'*

**Carl Sagan**:

*'They laughed at Galileo.*
*They laughed at Newton.*
*But they also laughed at Bozo the Clown.'*

# Chapter 18 - *London, UK*

The mother turned to the young woman sitting beside her. 'I've never been very good with computers. Brighton usually handles this sort of thing for me, but she's in a right strop this morning.' She nodded towards a teenage girl lounging awkwardly on one of the side chairs.

'Don't worry, it's all pretty straightforward. You don't need to do too much. After you enter your name a question comes up and then after a pause several possible answers. You just have to use the mouse. Point at the one you most agree with and click.'

Avril was in her late twenties although something in the way she dressed and presented herself made her look older. Many would have placed her around the same age as the woman she was assisting, in her mid to late thirties.

She was normally very shy with strangers but the shared situation helped overcome her reticence. 'What is it that you're checking for?'

'It's Brighton's Dad. Suddenly he's denying all knowledge of her. He's just got himself hitched up with a new woman. A right piece of works she is - seen he's starting to make some money in his chauffeur car business and now she wants it all. I helped him through the tough years that it took to build it up; did all his accounts and VAT, didn't I? Now she comes along, skirt up round her backside, and he's denying everything.'

Avril was now realising that shyness had its benefits. In showing friendliness and interest she had released this tirade and now she would have to live with the consequences.

'Six years he'd paid his maintenance without a problem, good as gold. But she made him take blood tests and what-have-you before she'd screw him; how cold-blooded is that? But men can't ever seem to see through these gold-diggers can they?'

Avril tried to turn back to her screen and continue to complete her questionnaire but the woman didn't stop.

'Now she's saying the tests mean that he can't have been Brighton's Dad. I'm no Virgin Mary. Who else could have been her Dad if not him? Honest, I never slept around while I was with him. Next she'll have him dressing up like Batman and hanging off some bloody scaffolding somewhere. What're they called 'Fathers for Justice' or summat? Fathers avoiding their responsibilities is more like it. No wonder our Bree's so confused.'

Avril looked over at the girl and thought she might be confused whatever her parental situation had been. Then, on second thoughts, Avril was confused too. Why would he need to dress as a superhero and join the protests against the Child Support Agency if he was denying his parenthood?

'What does this one here mean? "Have you all the necessary consents?".'

'I suppose it means that you need her father's agreement to take his test too. Without his samples there would be no point in doing it. They need to compare the two DNAs to see if there is a match.'

'Why didn't they just ask that then?'

Avril completed the last question on her list and was relieved to be able to get up and move across to the receptionist. She had to wait while Brighton reluctantly removed her legs from the chair across the aisle. Her large feet were clad in heavy boots that looked like they were only available on prescription.

Avril was seeking a paternity test too, thanks to her mother's bombshell delivered from beyond the grave. Her mother had made the confession in her will. It was just like her to make sure she avoided any embarrassment that might be coming her way. The dry old solicitor had explained that there was some doubt as to whether it was her father or her uncle who had been her genetic father.

So far as Avril was concerned her father was her father. He had brought her up and been there for her at every stage of her life. He had shaped her views, had both consciously and unconsciously directed her development, he had been there when her mother had fallen ill, and had nursed her until she had been taken from them so very quickly.

The reading of the will had been the lowest point of her life. Sitting in that drab little office, they were stunned as without warning he had read out the sentence that had brought her to this testing centre.

The solicitor intoned without any sign of emotion, what proved to be probably the most emotional statement she had heard in her life. Her mother had stated, "It has always been of great concern to me and has caused me much turmoil down the years. I was never sure if my daughter Avril Rose was born of my husband Phillip Stanley Cooper or his brother Christopher Martin Cooper."

That was it, one simple sentence that had condemned Avril, her father and her uncle to more turmoil than her mother had ever borne in her life. Her father had got up and walked out of the office. He still refused to speak with his brother. He was adamant that he did not want the test performed so it was her uncle who would provide the sample to be tested against hers. Avril really needed to know. She dearly hoped that it would prove her father was indeed her father. That was what had brought her to this centre, to reinstate her father in his rightful place!

The receptionist directed Avril to a small room behind the desk where a technician settled her in a chair and made sure that she was at her ease. In front of her was a large black box with a viewing location fitted with some sort of rubber cradle. She assumed, correctly, that it was for her to rest her head.

The technician advised that the 'T-scope', as he called it, was to test her eyesight. This was a completely free service that the centre offered to its clients while they waited for their DNA tests. He went on to say they believed too few people visited their opticians regularly enough. This free test could give early warning not only of deteriorating eyesight problems but also of other conditions.

'Through your eyes we can see so much'

Avril struggled to remember if she knew who had said that the "eyes are the window to the soul". She found she was extremely uncomfortable with the idea of anyone looking into her soul!

# Chapter 19 - *Oxfordshire, UK*

Dr Marsha Davenport was clearly a driven soul, her regular daily schedule was intense, exhausting and long.

She was already there when Stevie Tasker arrived at the Culham office. Stevie was well known at the laboratories as being something of an early bird but when she arrived just before seven, Marsha was well in to her day.

Tom was currently away in South America so Stevie had no current commitments. She was prepared to match Marsha's working day as she felt instinctively that this woman really had something about her. She was inspiring, certainly very bright and Stevie really wanted to work with her.

She watched as a hyperactive Marsha wielded two mobile phones both of which seemed to be in constant use. Invariably she had one or the other up to her ear, apparently talking with one of her many assistants that were located all around the world.

Stevie Tasker was a pretty blonde 30-something, the reason that she was often overlooked, pigeon-holed on the basis of the widespread prejudice surrounding her natural hair colour. This assumption was not helped by the fact that when thinking she often exhibited somewhat disconcerting rapid eye movements. But those who spent time with her learned this was because her very competent mind was running at such a high speed; and she always came up with something valid and valuable following these REM episodes.

Stevie had been put forward by the Culham secretariat as a potential branch manager for Marsha who was planning to establish a new BiCogNaIT research facility right here at the labs. Stevie had already had a full medical and a complete set of psychological tests before being considered. Now she was reading through some prepared material while she waited upon Marsha's availability for her personal interview.

The notes provided to Stevie indicated that Marsha was pushing hard on many fronts in researching the processes and effects of ageing. It explained that she planned to establish a BiCogNaIT facility at the Culham site to take advantage of the synergy she expected to find by working with other researchers and businesses that were already operating there. In particular the notes explained that the cryogenics and microwave expertise had specifically attracted her to the site.

As part of her application process Stevie had been required to sign a very detailed and restrictive non-disclosure agreement. Now she sat patiently waiting to establish some sort of rapport, the basis for a working relationship with this remarkable woman.

Stevie was pleasantly surprised when Marsha suddenly proposed that they walk and talk around the Culham site so that their meeting would have no interruptions - no mobiles, no emails.

As they left the unit in the Culham Science Centre the sun had burnt off the cloud and this was as good a day as rural Oxfordshire ever managed to achieve. A light breeze rippled the grass which was quite long, now well into the autumnal phase when it could be left for a fortnight between mowings.

Marsha breathed in the fresh air and pointed out one of the trees. 'Look, there are the first signs of the leaves fading and dying; part of the inevitable annual cycle. Human life usually has an autumn too, but what I'm questioning is whether that is an immutable fact. Must we age, become enfeebled and die from the ageing process? I hope you enjoyed the reading matter I prepared and that it showed there are quite a number of current promising avenues for us to research with the aim of delaying and eventually halting ageing.'

Stevie was keen to impress. 'And there's an awful lot of nonsense out there too! I can't believe the range of new products that every woman 'must have' - hyper peptides, collagen, anti-oxides. It's bewildering and mostly pretty ineffectual. The leaves still fall; the creases still creep across our faces.'

Marsha smiled, 'A pretty young woman like you can't possibly be resorting to those types of products already?'

'That doesn't stop me wanting to stay this way!' Then her neck reddened as she realised the basic assumption at the heart of her comment.

Marsha ignored her embarrassment. 'In looking into ageing scientifically you first have to appreciate that all of our cells get damaged by the processes of living. They also become chemically damaged during their many replications. These are currently considered the inescapable facts of life and death.

'Cells have all sorts of environmental stresses, most of these we just have to grin and bear. Of course the most significant is the damage caused by the seemingly pleasant ultraviolet rays that are washing across our faces right now. Then there's the damage caused by smoking, either active smoking or passive smoking from others.' She pointed to a distant chimney issuing a steady stream of white smoke. 'And of course our cells are routinely damaged by carbon emissions from vehicles and industry.'

Marsha turned the corner of a building, paused and looked directly at Stevie and took a new direction for their conversation. 'Are you a religious person?'

Stevie returned her direct look and without hesitation said, 'Yes, I am.' But she was still considering Marsha's point about carbon emissions. 'We are a global village, even if we move away from the worst polluting industries, that won't stop pollution reaching us through the air and via the water cycle.'

Marsha appeared to be going to say something but checked herself. Instead she got back to the subject at hand. 'There are still the things we do to ourselves. By that I mean our eating and exercise regimes. The effects of the terrible foodstuffs, like burgers and pizzas, and the very volume of it that we choose to eat, backed up by an over-consumption of alcohol and a general lack of any form of exercise. This completely avoidable self-abuse damages our cells considerably.'

Stevie grimaced. 'I guess it is down to the individuals themselves. Surely they must take their own responsibility for these factors?'

'Agreed again. You can lead a horse to water, but...'

Marsha led them into the Costa coffee shop. 'So let's get back to ageing, as if we could ever stop! While these environmental effects deliver the macro cellular damage, food and exercise could be said to provide the individual or micro effects. And, somewhere in the middle of all this, while we are living and ageing we suffer various forms of stress that only serve to hasten the process. Stress in itself damages our cells too, but that's a whole different ball game.'

They each had a carry-out coffee and continued their walk around the site.

'Let me ask you another question? What is your attitude regarding gene research given your religious beliefs?'

'I see no conflict. God created all life and genes are a very fundamental part of that. I feel that just as we have developed approaches to deal with cuts and bruises, fractures and diseases, we need to be just as interested and involved in the mechanisms of our genes and our DNA.'

'Good. Because where I start to get interested is when we look at the gene-based features that may or may not be at the very heart of senescence or ageing. Some suggest that our cells, as part of their very structure, bear an inherent sell-by date. By our middle age the series of cell divisions start to introduce errors. For example four-fifths of cancers are diagnosed after the age of fifty-five.'

Stevie was not convinced. 'Some people seem to naturally have much longer lifespans. Surely we could find ways of synthesising what it is that gives them this longevity and pass it on to the rest of us?'

Marsha finished the last of her coffee and tossed the cup into a nearby bin. 'That's one obvious goal. But some findings suggest we may yet be defeated in this. There's a gene called daf-2 found in the humble roundworm. It seems that this gene acts like a controller of the other genes, and it shuts down their internal repairing mechanism over time. If we too have something like this daf-2 then perhaps we may just have to accept our mortality?'

Stevie thought about this, 'I guess it wouldn't bother me too much if it was proved there is a principle that God has embedded deep within us that limits our time here. It has always been accepted as a fact; perhaps it is just that, mortality the ultimate fact.'

Marsha turned to look at her again in her rather penetrating way. 'But surely we have to test this to the full? If we can extend our life, we can extend the time available for our work and use that extra time to achieve more understanding. Surely that cannot be wrong?'

Stevie held her look while she considered her answer. It was evidently a question that was personally important to Marsha. 'I am convinced that we always have to extend ourselves, reach beyond our current limits. Look at where we are standing, it's a global centre of excellence for physics. Just over there scientists are essentially creating stars. Yes, of course you must strive to find your answers.'

'Thank you. Though now I'm not sure just who's doing the interviewing here? I thought I set out to evaluate whether you were the right person for my team and then I end up asking you to approve my avenues of research! It's very obvious that you have a quick mind that retains a broad understanding of many fields and issues, clearly a very powerful individual. Sometime I'd like to know what brought you here, but for now I just thank God that you are.'

Stevie had always been uncomfortable with praise and this all sounded far too American for her to know how to respond. She decided to deflect and get back to their subject. 'Didn't I read somewhere that there is promising progress in looking at telomeres?'

Marsha quickly realised that she had embarrassed Stevie with her comments and followed her lead. 'Certainly a huge amount of work has gone in to investigating telomeres. Telomeres are little DNA sequences located at the end of our chromosomes. They seem to be there to protect the cell; to stop them forming into rings or connecting unhelpfully to other parts of our DNA. We start out with hundreds or thousands of these; they act like the end of a software programme marker, a 'stop-here' sub-routine for our DNA.

'As our cells divide time and time again we lose some of these telomeres, many theorise that it is this progressive loss that is the essential essence of ageing. As a cell sequentially divides these telomeres get shorter and shorter. After shedding its telomeres, progressively this ageing cell is less controlled in its division and more readily replicates itself with faults. Eventually these telomeres become so depleted that the cell can no longer replicate itself at all.'

Stevie asked, 'So you just need to either secure these telomeres, or extend their life, to extend ours?'

Marsha smiled. 'Wish that it were as easy as you make it sound. It turns out that there is a chemical called telomerase that is one of the systems our bodies has adopted to prolong and replace our telomeres. Though most of our cells have this telomerase, it is used mainly during foetal development and then switched off for much of the rest of our life. Some suggested we should flood our bodies with this telomerase to 'stop the rot' and QED we could live forever. But that proved a poor conclusion spelled with a large C, C for cancer. It turns out that tumours and cancerous cells are usually most easily distinguishable from normal cells by a significant presence of telomerase!

'It would appear the telomeres and their possibly inevitable decline is there to halt any cell mutations; to avoid the tumours and cancers. So in playing with them and the enzyme telomerase we have to be cautious. Potentially there lies dragons!'

Stevie looked confused. 'But as I understood it we at BiCogNaIT are still planning to look at telomerase?'

Marsha noticed and approved of the use of the 'we'. She replied, 'Yes, it's one of them. By the way, remember I mentioned stress? Well be warned that chronic stress can reduce your telomeres too! Avoid stress at all costs. Do you meditate?'

'I've tried yoga but never meditation.'

'You must let me take you along to my class. You'd find it very valuable. It helps to keep those signs of ageing at bay by relieving stress, provided you combine it with regular exercise.'

Stevie nodded. Surely she wouldn't be invited to her class if she was going to turn down her application. She smiled, 'I'd like that very much.'

They walked on for a while enjoying the day. Apart from a voluble blackbird the only other noise came from a distant tractor. Stevie found it strange that so many people were striving to develop earth-shattering ideas and concepts at this site, yet making so little noise about it.

Stevie started up the conversation again. 'I see the other approach that your notes focus on is the subject of 'free radicals'?'

'You obviously read through it all very thoroughly. Free radicals damage our cells, by playing havoc with fats and proteins, with our RNA and DNA.'

'So what are you planning to do about them?'

Marsha paused as they'd come full circle and were about to enter their unit. 'Free radicals are often created by those environmental, dietary and exercise factors that I mentioned earlier. What is important is that they are particularly harsh on the genes that we use in learning and memory. It's the remorseless attacks from the free radicals, spread right across the years of our life, that progressively depletes our defences. One hopeful approach therefore is to find some way to combat them.'

'So we have telomeres and free radicals. What else will we be investigating?'

Marsha smiled at her eagerness. 'Other research shows that mitochondrial cells tend to mutate. Control that and you can perhaps at least control the skin-deep effects of ageing.'

'I didn't find anything in your package about stem cells?'

Marsha gave her that penetrating look again. 'I can see that I need to set aside a lot more time for this briefing! For now I have to get back on the grid and see what's happening. And I think you need to come along to my class so we can develop your skills in meditation. With an active mind like yours you do need to be able to park it up from time to time and get yourself some 'me time'.'

# Chapter 20 - *London, UK*

Avril settled in to using the T-scope very easily. She had expected to see the familiar rows of letters set at a declining size, or the rapidly appearing and disappearing spots. Instead she was surprised to see a series of still images.

The early images were warm and cosy - family life, small animals, that sort of thing - and all delivered at a steady and reassuring pace. She assumed it was a subject matter to relax her. Sure enough, it did then proceed to letters and spots in small sessions punctuating the kaleidoscope of images; the technician prompted the necessary responses from her.

Unexpectedly the images speeded up and became rather less pleasant. Initially they were just a little disturbing but gradually they became positively threatening. As she was considering sitting back from the viewer the pace slowed and the images reverted to a more agreeable subject matter.

The technician switched off the device and thanked her for her time.

Avril asked, 'Not at all what I expected. So, how were my eyes?'

The technician was a little evasive as he explained that she would get a full report from the counsellor at the end of her tests.

The use of the word 'counsellor' jarred with her. She had not come into this shop unit for counselling. She wanted a paternity test, plain and simple.

The technician had noted her reaction; Avril assumed he was probably used to it from previous clients. 'You shouldn't react to the term. You have to appreciate that a DNA test is a little like Pandora's Box, we have established that the background to the test is as vital as the test itself. Many of our clients are just not emotionally equipped for the outcome of the test. We have decided therefore that the person delivering the result needs to be more than a simple administrator.'

Three days later she was back at the centre with its distinctive double-G logo. She waited for her session with the 'counsellor' with mixed emotions. God, she hoped that it would prove to be her father who was identified as her biological father!

What would she do if it turned out to be her uncle? She'd had nothing much to do with him, only met him at odd family get-togethers. They hadn't been what you would call a close family. Though at least at weddings he hadn't been the sort of embarrassing uncle who tried to pull you up on to the dance floor and jig around ridiculously.

Just what had her mother seen in him? Avril thought him much the less attractive of the two brothers; certainly he was by far the less successful. Thinking about him now she guessed he had a sort of vulnerability about him; she assumed that was probably what had started it. And what was it that they'd had? Was it a one-night-stand or a full-blown affair? God, what a mess! Her mother may now be resting in peace; but she certainly hadn't granted any peace for the rest of them!

The door opened and the woman whom she recalled from three days earlier thrust her awkward teenager in ahead of her. What was her name? Brighton. That was it. Avril wondered if this was because she was the product of a drunken dirty weekend at the seaside. Or, she smiled, an accurate forecast of the 'rocky' times she faced ahead?

Unfortunately the woman recognised her too and came over. 'I hope you get on better in there than we did. They've said that Bree is not her father's. But that can't be true. I swear on my sainted mother's grave that I never slept with anyone else!'

To Avril's surprise the teenager could actually speak. 'Nan's not dead. She's still alive and kicking, lives out in Penge!'

'It's just a what's-it, you know, a thingamee. Anyhow, you know what I mean you awkward little cow. Anyways, I kicked up a stink in there, said their system must be wrong or summat.'

Avril was obviously not required or expected to respond as the woman ranted on.

'At first they just stuck to their guns. But in the end they pulls out this piece of paper.' She handed over a single sheet of densely printed A4.

'Anyways, it says here that it can't be foolproof. Somethin' about a chee-meer-a or summat. Any ideas what that means?'

Avril read the note to see that the word the woman had struggled over was chimera. Her recollection of the word was from Greek mythology, a fire-breathing monster she thought, a mixture of lion and snake. She had no idea what it could mean in this context. But it certainly made her take another look at the child.

She probably stood at over six foot in her very high-heeled thigh-length boots. To Avril they looked a little more attractive than the surgical boots she had worn before. She probably scaled in at well over 17 stones, that was being charitable. She was dressed in the standard doom-and-gloom Goth uniform, her face hardly distinguishable under heavy black and purple make-up. She was certainly a pretty monstrous sight!

As the mother carried on berating the service she skimmed the note to see what they meant. This was difficult with the mother's tirade going on and the regular need to nod to suggest that she was listening. From what she could glean from the sheet there had been a number of cases where a child initially tested, and said not to be related to a parent, proved in fact to be a chimera. In these cases some abnormality in development had placed different DNA within different tissues and parts of their body.

Avril decided just to shake her head and keep her pretty distant mythological memories to herself. But what if her own results were skewed in this way too? She had only been tested against her uncle; her father had pointedly refused to participate. She had believed that this test would resolve the matter. Now she realised that there was a whole raft of other possible outcomes!

.

It was a relief when she heard her name called to enter the counsellor's room.

The counsellor was a young American, smartly dressed in a suit and collar-and-tie. Avril thought it quite sad that so few people wore ties these days. He was cleanly-shaven with well-groomed hair and wore a warm smile that revealed the readily distinguishable results of the best in American orthodontics. He wore no jewellery. With a firm handshake he introduced himself as Malcolm.

She couldn't resist looking around for a Bible because he reminded her of the young Mormons who often canvas door-to-door; surely no-one else she had met in some years was quite as clean-cut, neat and tidy as this Malcolm. He was the sort you could safely take home to your mother; though she realised in this case it was her mother who'd brought Avril to see him.

'So Avril, how are you feeling today?'

'Honestly? I am extremely nervous about the outcome of the tests.'

'That's natural of course. But the outcome shouldn't change you at all. You are as you were before you undertook the test. There is no reason for you to change, no matter what its outcome.'

'Now you're making me really nervous. Are you confirming my worst fears, that my father is my uncle?' She grimaced at the awkwardness of her comment.

'I see from your questionnaire that you have no-one who you can share this with, no-one you can talk over the results with. Your only confidante has been your father. You have no husband or significant other, no groups to which you belong. Is there anyone you might turn to?'

'Now I'm terrified. Why might I need to talk it over with anyone?'

'Sorry, I am not handling this very well. Perhaps you would rather have another counsellor?'

'No, no, you're absolutely fine. Just please get it over with. Who is my father?'

'Based upon your questionnaire responses, I am happy to confirm that your father is the man you have always called your father.' Malcolm saw her glare and raised his hands in defence, 'But your biological father is your uncle.'

Avril had prepared herself for this outcome for several weeks but it still took her breath away. Everything she thought she was, she had ever been, was founded on a lie. Betrayed by both her mother and her uncle for all these years! How could she ever look her father in the face again? Could she bear to meet up with her uncle?

Presumably he would now want to create a new relationship with her. But how could she do that. It would be such a betrayal of her father? Just like her mother had done thirty years ago!

Malcolm let her whirlwind of thoughts subside and then commented, 'It's quite a shock, I know. You will be feeling the whole fabric of your life has been torn apart. Everything you believed in twisted, out of kilter, somehow wrong.'

His delivery was so gentle, so reassuring. It gave her the same feeling as the first pictures on that T-scope thing. She found herself relaxing, carried along on his words and not wanting him to stop talking.

'You will come through this stronger, thinking more clearly. You will have been tested, but you will overcome this and move on. The shackles of your childhood are released. The constraints of your family have gone. You are ready to seek out your own place in the world. You will no longer do things just to please others. You will no longer worry about how you look in the eyes of others. From here it will all be about you. I don't mean that you will become selfish, but that you will seek out the things that will help to develop you, yourself. Help you to set and achieve your own new goals, your own role in this world.'

One deep part of her mind was thinking that he must be a Mormon because all this started to sound like some sort of sermon. Yet at the same time, most of her mind was welcoming these thoughts, the comfort of his voice, the warmth of his imagery.

She gradually, and regretfully, became aware that the session was coming to an end. She looked down and saw she already had her results pack in her hand. How did they get there? Glancing at her watch, she was shocked to see that she had been in the session for close on an hour.

As Malcolm passed her a piece of paper he said, 'So we will look forward to seeing you tonight at our little group.' It wasn't a question more an assumption.

She took the note, slightly confused and bothered by this man's assumption. What group? Tonight? Regrettably she had other plans for tonight. She would need to go and see her father; no matter how painful that would prove. Oh gosh, it would be so horrible!

When she looked down at the note, with its complex design and artwork, she nodded calmly and instantly said, 'Yes, I shall be there'.

# Chapter 21 - *Oxfordshire, UK*

Switched off from the relative calm of their walkabout, Marsha quickly settled down to deal with her email backlog, and prompted by one of these she made a mobile call.

Collecting together her things Stevie was stopped short. To her surprise Marsha was using the sort of silly little girl voice that she had heard and disliked in many American women, and she had noticed it in a few English women too, usually large ladies at that. It was a simpering, flirting tone. No, worse, it was somehow a subservient voice. To Stevie it grated and was so completely out of place coming from Marsha who earlier had seemed far too sensible and much more together than this voice would indicate.

Stevie thought she had to be speaking to a very special man-friend to generate this; only sex could create such a complete change in Marsha. Her assumption was confirmed when Marsha bustled out of their unit obviously seeking some privacy for the call.

Safely outside Marsha continued. 'Samuel, it's so-oh very nice to hear from you. I trust that our paths will cross again real soon?'

Samuel Shepherd clearly was not wanting to waste too much time on pleasantries, 'I'll see to it that we do. But first, I understand from Trajan that you had a little local difficulty over there?'

She took his lead and was all business again. 'Yes, it was very annoying. But I had no choice. The Ministry of Defence over here wanted to see the TGs for themselves. In fact they are much more open to the notion than our own DoD. The DoD is content to hide behind its laundered terminology like 'collateral damage', hailing lost military personnel as 'heroes'; and the US public are content to be led along by their noses.

'The Brit's MoD is very clear that what they are dealing with is unacceptable servicemen losses. And the UK press and public see them clearly for what they are too - deaths. They used to line the street of some village here to welcome back the bodies of their victims, not heroes. I believed therefore that my trans-genics might be much more readily accepted here.'

The satellite phone line and its scrambling system produced a loss of quality in Samuel Shepherd's voice. She normally appreciated its rich mellow tones, but on this line it sounded almost machine-generated.

He asked, 'So how did the male manage to escape?'

'It was down to slack procedures within a hastily assembled facility at our central London labs. We shipped them over early and were settling them in for a week or so before the presentation was scheduled. Unfortunately one of the local female technicians got far too close to the TG; she started to think of it as some sort of pet or companion.'

Samuel was not letting her off that easily. 'Farmers manage this sort of thing every day. Stock is kept quite separate, deliberately not named. When it comes to sending them off to market or the slaughterhouse there's no issue.'

Marsha was annoyed by the brusqueness of the comment. 'But you have to appreciate that they are not at all like some dull lambs or cows, no matter how charming some may find those particular creatures. You see the way they are, their behaviour, so human-like, it could drag at the maternal instincts from any woman. And, of course, theirs is such a maternal society too. The TGs inherently have their own drive to seek out their mothers or their aunts; there is huge pressure being applied from both sides.'

Samuel snapped, 'Do I detect that you too may be having this same reaction?'

Marsha paused and bit back her instinctive angry riposte. She replied calmly but firmly. 'No, certainly not. Not in any way. They certainly don't trigger any sort of maternal instinct in me. They're no more significant than a lab rat in my mind.' Then she decided to change tack. The simpering voice was back. 'However, since you mention it, I do have maternal requirements that I will need to address some time very soon. I don't want to leave it until it's too late.'

Samuel chose to deflect the issue. 'Marsha, together we have so many children who we need to guide and develop.' But then he relented. 'You do know that our time is coming, and it will be so very soon. We can be together for all of time when these next few phases are completed. All is very much on track. Everything is running smoothly.'

Marsha wasn't ready to move on. 'I know. I do fully appreciate that we have so much to do and so little time. I really miss spending time with you. We used to have such great times. It felt like an infinity for us when we were working through everything, planning this whole operation. Those were truly wonderful times, and I miss them much more than I had expected.'

'We are at the vital execution phase. Rest assured that those good times will be back before too long. But let's get back to this break-in of yours. Who do you think was behind that?'

'The gNOS team is still trying to trace precisely who it was. We must assume that someone found the TG's shirt as it was not recovered when they recaptured it; and of course the shirt had BiCogNaIT printed on it.'

'Did they take anything in the break-in?'

'Nothing was there for them to take. Relax. If it's anyone official they will come up against the DoD and MoD projects and be forced to back off. This military contract is such a strong cover for our real activity. I don't believe anyone will come to appreciate or uncover what that is before it is too late. I have had to terminate the TGs here, just to be safe. They are not being wasted however. We can re-use all their tissues and major organs.'

Samuel was quiet. Marsha pressed on. 'By the way, finally I have found her. I have discovered a wonderful person for both of us. She's called Stevie. Sadly, she would have been just right to run the new BiCogNaIT facility at Culham. But our requirement takes priority.'

Samuel was now relaxed, 'How's your Culham thing going?'

'Still at a very early phase. I'm in the process of establishing the facility and the team right now. This morning I took a stroll around the site and there is pretty limited security inside here. I could just walk right up to various buildings without ever being challenged at all. Getting inside them could be something more of a problem of course, but once the gNOS team is settled in here and there is regular liaison with the local security team then we should be able to resolve an approach.'

Samuel responded. 'OK. Well, I can report that we have already successfully introduced your new regime into the South American community, it would seem to be working very well. Thanks to you our control has certainly been radically improved. Your programme combining rigorous exercise with meditation and medication keeps them all gainfully employed, and contented.

'Some of it, of course, may be down to the fact that they're just too tired to be worried about what's happening in the outside world. The technology we have in the surveillance centre ensures we know everything that is said and done; we've found our use of this intelligence allows us to keep them off balance. It's all coming together to maintain a good healthy state of paranoia. Our latest video programmes are strong too and these will help to underpin your control.'

'How many have you got there so far?'

'Currently a little less than half of the planned 12,000 have been moved there. Our recruitment and assessment programme will be delivering the rest very soon though.'

Marsha asked, 'So, where's next?'

'We'll put it all into place at the new North African retreat. The early teams are assembled there already. I will email you my schedule once it's been agreed and booked.'

'Then I think perhaps that's where we should arrange to meet next. I'd be interested in seeing a retreat in its early phases.'

# Chapter 22 - *Hebron, the West Bank*

In its formative stages Hebron was a Canaanite city. Tom would therefore have been very interested in visiting the city, because 'his' Phoenicians had originated from Canaan too.

A great deal of history, emotion and bloodshed had shaped the city down through the centuries. But it was probably an immigrant from Iraq, some 3,700 years ago, who had attracted much of this attention with the simple purchase of a small plot of land and a cave from a local Hittite. He bought the parcel of land to have somewhere he could bury his wife.

The fact that made this significant was that the ancient land purchaser was the biblical and Qur'an figure of Abraham. He made the acquisition following the death of his wife Sarah. He and she both have tombs on the site; as do their son Isaac and his wife Rebecca, and their grandson Jacob with his wife Leah. These six significant burials and their location are all faithfully recorded in the Bible in the book of Genesis.

There are those who suggest that this plot of land is also where Adam, the fourth Patriarch, and his wife Eve were buried. But others consider the story of these two individuals to be more of a fictional device than the history of real individuals.

Dom Berkeley of Mission always liked a good story so was completely open-minded. At one meeting he had used an appalling cockney accent to say that he for one was fully prepared to 'Adam & Eve' it until the facts showed otherwise.

Dom could not believe his luck that they had so conveniently arranged for the vast majority of the Patriarchs and the Matriarchs of the Jewish people to be so neatly laid out in two rows of three; only Rachel was missing. He learned that she died in childbirth and was buried somewhere near Bethlehem.

No surprise then that this was one of their earliest defined targets. The double cave of Machpelah was after all the second most sacred site in the Holy Land for both Judaism and Christianity.

Known as Ibrahim, Ishāq and Yakub, these historic figures are also central in the Qur'an, the same six tombs therefore are just as revered by Muslims; but it was this fact that meant they came up against something of a problem.

The Prophet Muhammad granted Hebron, among other lands, to Tamim al-Dari. He was not permitted to enslave the local inhabitants but he was allowed to tax them. He was also awarded a *waqf*, an inalienable religious endowment, to protect and preserve the tombs at the site the Muslims term the 'Ibrahim mosque'.

Dom and his team felt that Hebron's story was a who's who of Holy Land figures. The Virgin Mary's sister Elizabeth was said to have lived there, John the Baptist to have been born there. Saladin captured the city only to have it wrested away later by Richard the Lionheart. The Templars and the Hospitallers vied for many years over control of the city. There had been a Byzantine and a Crusader church established, an Augustinian chapter too, together with a series of mosques. One account also claims that a synagogue was once located in Hebron. The Egyptians, the British, the Jordanians and the Israelis have all tried to impose their will upon the place; none of them achieved any great credit or success.

Dom Berkeley had no time to dwell on all this history. The place had been very high on his list of targets since the very formation of Mission. Every time they had considered it before they had concluded it was an impossibility. Now finally he thought they had found an angle; a superb window of opportunity had presented itself.

He obviously wanted to get in and out of it as fast as possible. He knew this was currently one of the most dangerous places on earth and he certainly didn't want to be there any longer than was absolutely necessary.

While the six had been left to rest in peace for millennia, the city above their heads had been the focus of many centuries of strife. Today its location is within the disputed West Bank area, with the city divided into two zones - H1 and H2.

H2 is the area where fewer than a hundred Jewish families have settled. Their presence is secured by the Israeli Defence Force, with a heavy-handed use of check-points, curfews and roads that only they may travel.

These settlers were originally heralded by their fellow Israelis for their pioneering bravery, but with time they became discredited, identified as hard-liners and vilified for their aggression. International law is quite clear. It declares these settlements illegal. Yet there are almost half a million Jewish settlers in the West Bank and east Jerusalem, and the number is growing with no signs of any move to respect these laws.

Dom stood outside the building that housed the tombs, trying to visualise just what was happening inside those very solid walls right now, walls that had been burnished by the sun down all the years so they looked as if made of bronze.

The caves had been revered since well before 1,000 BCE. The shrine complex built above the cave is most often accredited to Herod, thus from the 1st century BCE, but others claim it for earlier rulers. Perhaps King David who had begun his reign from Hebron, he built his nation from here, expanding it from a mere vassal of the Philistines finally to establish his place in history when he took Jerusalem; taking back control of Saul's old kingdom.

Dom was scanning what was a very substantial building; sixty metres long by thirty five metres wide and built to a height of around fifteen metres. He ran his mind over the plans of the place that he had acquired at considerable expense. In his mind he retraced the recce he had made through the parts that the

Muslim *Waqf* permitted non-believers to access. From the plans he tried to imagine the section where his team must be right now. They would be deep inside the area strictly closed to all non-Muslims.

Dom was concerned that their research was by no means conclusive in indicating what they might find; if anything! In the 12th century CE, Ali of Herat had reported that the intact bodies of the Patriarchs had been discovered lying propped up against the wall of the cave. Their shrouds had fallen to pieces and these were replaced by the then King before the cave was resealed.

However it was evident later, at the time of the Crusades, that many relics had been looted and shipped westward to satisfy the many demanding monasteries, cathedrals and churches of Christendom; their huge appetite for relics that could in turn attract pilgrims and patronage.

Much later, during the building of the domes and minarets for the mosque at the site, two of the sepulchres had needed to be moved to facilitate the construction. Any residual bones were reported to have then been placed in reliquaries and buried in the caves located beneath the shrine.

From the 13th century CE, Jews and Christians were forbidden to enter the shrine at all; Jews were permitted to climb up only to the seventh step leading to the shrine. With just a few notable celebrity exceptions this ban had continued right up until after the 1967 Six-Day War.

The then Chief Rabbi of the Israeli Defence Force, Major-General Rabbi Shlomo Goren, was reputedly then the first Jew for over 1,000 years to have entered the caves. It was that war that ceded 45% of the West Bank to Israel, and David Ben-Gurion, Israel's first Prime Minister, had insisted Hebron must remain under Jewish control. He based this claim upon the fact that it had formally become Jewish some four thousand years earlier by virtue of Abraham's land purchase!

What was a little worrisome for the Mission team was that Israeli archaeologists had investigated the caves after that war and reported that only Iron Age and crusader artefacts had been found. Had they been negligent in their excavations? Or had they withheld the truth of their finds? Or worse had they removed anything they had found?

Dom's team's attention had first been focused upon a small *baldachino* or canopy that was set beside an 11th century pulpit, the *minbar*. This had the distinction that it was within the part of the shrine that Dom was permitted to visit as a Christian. It was through this route that the crusaders had reportedly accessed the caves. He had no idea how deep they would have to burrow to unblock this route and the location would be in full view of the huge tourist crowds that flooded the shrine each day; the site attrcated some 300,000 visitors each year. They could not hope to gain access and then reconstitute it satisfactorily in the time that was available to them.

Another sealed entrance to the caves existed through a small opening set in the floor between the tombs of Isaac and Rebecca. Frustratingly these two tombs were inside the area still closed off to any access by Jews or Christians. Nonetheless it was from here that Dom had concluded they should make their entry.

Following on from that decision the team had amassed everything they might need. This all had to be capable of being carried into the shrine and then inserted down through this relatively small hole. This meant a great deal of organisation, customisation and ingenuity. This was the bit that Dom had enjoyed most.

It also led to something of a selection problem for the team. Dom would not be physically capable of getting through the hole; in truth he was perfectly relieved to be excused from participation in the break-in.

His 'local knowledge' was a Jordanian antiquarian dealer with the reputation of being easily blinded by a large fee. He had routinely sailed close to the wind right across the Middle East, spiriting away relics and historic items from the authorities, museums and from many properly constituted archaeological teams. There had been a big fee and it had purchased all this man's guile; any religious beliefs he might hold were readily and completely suspended.

The local team had gone in late on Thursday and been concealed inside as the shrine closed at 17:00. It would not be open to the public again until Sunday at 07:30. They had bought themselves just over sixty hours in which they might achieve their objective and this had been judged as ample.

Now it was Saturday morning. Half the allotted time had passed and Dom had to stand outside wondering just what was happening down deep beneath the shrine.

That damned Jordanian had not permitted any mobile phones to be taken into the shrine. Dom just had to wait it out. His frustration was building. He felt the need to run over and rip down some of those large stones in the wall with his bare hands so he could get in and see precisely what was happening. He couldn't quite accept that the outcome was completely outside his control. He could only walk off the adrenaline and frustration by pacing the streets.

What a huge coup if he really did find the remains of these historic figures. For him and Mission acquiring the DNA would be something akin to the philosopher's stone. Not just any DNA from 4,000 years ago but material from perhaps the most significant group of holy people imaginable! He guessed he could wait another day for that!

His pacing and his clearly stressed body language had not gone unnoticed. Surveillance of Hebron was intense and images of this strange individual loitering around close to the holy place had caught their attention. He was clearly not a local, yet the signage and tourist information could not have led to any confusion about the opening times of the monument. Why did he keep coming back to stare at its walls?

There he was again early on Sunday morning, pacing around and staring at the walls. Then the surveillance had to switch from him as a small pitch battle unfolded. The monument had been opened as usual and to the surprise of the observer a file of people emerged from inside. Not literally a file, but one by one, around forty seconds apart, a sizeable group was recorded leaving the building.

Each was laden down with some form of backpack or carrying case, all of them looked heavy. The watcher raised the alarm. She called over her supervisor and succinctly explained what she had noticed. The individuals were forming into a huddle off to one side. They must be waiting on transportation.

When what appeared to be the final pair of individuals emerged, with a heavy canvas bag held between them, all hell broke loose. Two small jeeps then arrived at the location, these were clearly not the vehicles they had been expecting. The canvas over the rear was thrown open and eight armed men leapt out and sprayed the waiting men with automatic weapons. One of the assailants did not join in with the slaughter. Instead he shot out the camera that had been recording all the action.

The watcher and the rest of her team desperately tried to access any cameras that would film anyone leaving the site as air resources were scrambled to get them aerial coverage. When officers eventually reached the shrine it was to find the bodies of those who had emerged from the holy place and the two stolen jeeps; the bags and the assailants were gone and no record of the attack or the escape could be found on the many cameras in Hebron.

Dom had been watching all this. He did nothing to interfere. He had no idea if they had recovered anything from down in the caves, his plan for the attack as they emerged was inspired. Mission's part in this was pretty much invisible, and by eliminating the entry crew he had muddied the waters even further.

As he made his way back to his hotel he felt content. It had been easy to find a rival crew to the Jordanian team. He made sure that the authorities would believe that one of the Jordanian's team had become loose-lipped and boastful, talking of his expected big bonus from the raid. The rivals needed little encouragement to reap the harvest of the others' toil, particularly as so little was expected of them. Once he had his samples he could spirit himself away from this Middle East hot spot.

The report of the incident and its tapes were forwarded first to *Aman*, the IDF's Directorate of Military Intelligence. At its next meeting this was all shared with *Shin Bet*, the internal security service, and the *Institute for Intelligence and Special Operations,* more popularly known as Mossad.

Mossad has a worldwide reputation for a brutal effectiveness. The paramilitary intelligence arm is responsible for counter-terrorism and is the organisation that mounts covert operations such as political assassinations. It could find no reference in its files to the individual captured on camera hanging around outside the shrine. A painstaking cross referencing came up with the most probable match as some journalist with genuine credentials working for an American satellite television channel. On contacting the channel it was found they had no knowledge of the individual and had no crew in Hebron.

Investigations found no evidence of anything having been taken from the tombs. The *Waqf* had refused entry to the caves so it was impossible to establish what had been their target; though this was the conclusion that the Israelis reached. A number of the dead crew were identified as known associates of the notorious Jordanian antiquarian dealer, accepted locally as another term for grave-robber. The Jordanian had disappeared, either eliminated or gone to ground. Of the attackers and what they might have taken there had been no leads.

There was only circumstantial evidence that the foreigner had been involved in what had happened here, whatever that had been. However using false identity and odd behaviour at the site was highly suggestive. His details and images were tagged in the investigator's files and there was a limited sharing of information with other international agencies in an effort to assist in his identification.

# Chapter 23 - *London, UK*

Avril looked around her trying to pick out anyone she might know.

They were in an ante-room being offered coffee and soft drinks. The room was dominated by a statue viewed through glass and bathed in a blue light. Avril thought the statue looked like something straight out of the Russian Soviet past; not too surprising as this was the Congress Centre, run by the Trades Union Congress.

Avril had arrived clutching her invitation, still unclear quite why she was there. She should have been with her father giving him her awful news? She really had to get to him before her uncle found out and told him first. But somehow the pressing need to do that was overwhelmed by her desire to come here. This fact made her feel uncomfortable, somewhat out of control; not a feeling that she ever much enjoyed.

She noticed a girl arriving, who looked more her type than the others. She was around the same age and dressed in some sort of exercise gear. She looked just as uncomfortable and out of place here as Avril felt. In fact she looked quite flustered.

'You look a bit upset?'

'It was just something that happened down on the tube platform just now. Some young bloke just went crazy for no particular reason. He sort of berserked I suppose, and struck out at anyone and everyone. It took about four of them sitting right on top of him to stop it. It was just so sudden and so violent that I must admit it's made me sick to my stomach.'

'How awful!' Avril paused at the thought of this, helped her find a soft drink and then asked, 'Are you new here too?'

Stevie smiled back. 'Yes, I wasn't quite sure what to expect. My new boss invited me to attend what she'd called a class. She indicated that it was a new form of meditation and exercise, hence the jogging kit. But if I felt a bit of a fool sitting on the tube, I certainly feel a wee bit underdressed here.'

'The crowd looks like a pretty varied bunch. None of them appear to know each other. Perhaps they're all new?'

Stevie smiled. 'Why are you here?'

'That's the thing. I really don't know. I have so many other important matters I should be taking care of but I got invited and well I sort of turned up. I have to admit that I've absolutely no idea why I'm here.'

Before they could talk further they found themselves being ushered down stairs and through glass doors into a modern conference room. The stage set was washed in an ever-changing series of pastel colours. They took adjacent comfortable chairs towards the rear and off to one side where they could see that there were perhaps two hundred or more other people; a much larger audience than they had appreciated from their room upstairs. These others appeared to have come from a whole series of ante rooms.

Stevie looked around. The audience certainly contained a very broad ethnic variety, and if their appearance was anything to go by it was a broad spread of socio-economics too. But the age of the group she would have guessed was contained within quite a small spread, probably no younger than twenty-five and no older than forty.

The technicians who they had filed past , towards the rear of the room, suddenly dimmed the lights and a screen lit up just as the meaningful-looking series of speakers sprung into life. There was no preamble, no intro, and no title screen for what came next.

To Avril the opening sequence was very reminiscent of the T-scope material. It was quite chaotic initially and then became somehow warm and comfortable. She visibly relaxed in her chair welcoming the return of that same relaxed feeling she had experienced in the GG centre.

To Stevie this was a pretty strange movie reminding her of some of the art films that she had been subjected to by a very early boyfriend. He was long forgotten, but the initial jarring images reminded her of the many avant-garde, or in her own words pretentious, statements that she had been subjected to as part of the price of that ill-judged romance.

Then the rapid pace of the images made her think about subliminal messages. She has read of advertising messages buried deep among images like these. She started to blink very fast to try to freeze the image and see if she noticed anything concealed within the visible montage of shots. She could detect nothing, but then her approach had hardly been scientific or conclusive.

The early jarring and frankly disturbing images were then replaced with a slower sequence of rather warmer imagery and the sound track had become more soothing too.

In the light of the film Stevie looked around at the rest of the audience and most of them were fully engrossed in the material. She was the only one who was looking around. The helpers, those who had ushered them to their seats, were standing in the side aisles and they too were concentrating intently on the screen. Was this intended to provide the meditation that Marsha had discussed? If so, then it wasn't working for her. And, just where was Marsha by the way?

The screening came to a calm ending and was replaced with a large head and shoulders shot of an attractive young man. It was not clear to Stevie if this was a real person or a piece of computer generated imagery. Something about the flesh tones suggested that it was the latter. This was then confirmed when the face slowly morphed into a female. The basic face shape and colouration were unaltered. Just the hairline, hairstyle and some minor cosmetics changed.

The morphing happened again and again, the pace of these changes becoming ever more rapid. It became difficult to fix upon any particular face as the shape, the features on it, the hair style and colour, the gender and the racial characteristics were all blending and changing far too quickly.

A voice-over started. It was a deep and melodious male voice, the sort that would never be short of work in advertising. Stevie could detect no trace of an accent or dialect; she assumed perhaps the speaker was Dutch. To her the Dutch always seemed to speak with a crisp English, more Queen's English than the English who were often suffused by regional accents.

'The Human Race.' The shifting faces on the screen coalesced into individual faces as the voice intoned each word. Then the features shuffled again until selecting a series of three or four suitable images to fit each next word. 'Beauty. Nobility. Simplicity. Intelligence. Resolution. Confidence. Fatigue. Fear. Reassurance. Relief. Disappointment. Frustration. Love. Anger.'

Stevie thought the producer had been very PC; the ethnicity mix was very much the same as that currently used in TV advertising. In her opinion this slightly disproportionately favoured the minorities in order to avoid any claims of not being inclusive. Stevie felt the only group that might complain about the proportions was the under-represented British majority; but then she knew they never would. Or was it more that they never could, for fear of being declared non-PC?

'The Human Race.' The pace of the facial changes was running at its fastest rate yet. 'But just what is all the hurry?'

A long pause as the image-changing slowed. 'And just what is the goal?'

Without warning the images were being made up from this evening's audience themselves, pictured as they arrived here earlier. Stevie spotted Avril among them. 'And, where are we all going?'

The screen faded, the room lights came up and a young man stepped onto the stage. Avril recognised him as Malcolm from the GG centre. Stevie took the opportunity to look around again and thought the majority of the audience looked strangely open-faced, as if they were a bit out of it somehow. Avril too looked as if she was in some sort of trance. She was fixated upon the stage.

'We have a really huge treat for you tonight. Dr Marsha Davenport, the scientist, philanthropist and meditation guru is here for just a short time in the UK. Some of you will know that we have been using her meditation programme for some months. We are delighted she agreed to spare the time from her busy programme to give us a real insight into some of the background to her meditation technique.'

Marsha stepped out on to the stage. She seemed to seek out and smiled directly at Stevie before she addressed the room. 'Good evening and thank you so much for coming this evening.'

She spoke without any apparent notes, not even one of the transparent autocues that so many politicians and presenters rely upon. There was no lectern and she exuded supreme confidence in a situation within which many would look awkward. In Marsha's presentation, Stevie was reminded of the recent fad for British TV newscasters to stand and walk around, waving their arms about in a very European way. Sadly, very few of them were able to pull it off and look natural.

'Various forms of meditation have been recorded down the years. It is a fact that meditation has been practised for over five millennia. This means that throughout humanity's civilised period meditation has been there in some form. Perhaps that's significant? Did civilisation introduce the very pressures that mean we need to meditate to deal with them? Few other practices could be said to have such a comprehensive claim. Just pause and consider that most of our religions are much shorter-lived than that and only a very small number of today's nation states have been around for as long as a single millennium.'

Stevie was thinking that she had never stopped to think that religions and nations were so ephemeral. She had always instinctively respected authority and that concepts of nationality and faith were such a big part of that fabric. The notion that either of these were not constant was just too big a thought.

'As a scientist I know the cells in our brains act differently from all our other cells. They alone do not retain a reserve of nutrients. This is because these cells burn up any energy that they get virtually as soon as it is made available to them, this is to maintain the vital uninterrupted flow of oxygen. The reason I believe meditation has been so successful is that its techniques give what Hercule Poirot would call your 'leetle grey cells' a chance to pause, an opportunity to repair any damage and to flush out any waste.

'Meditation has therefore been used by many simply at the level of a form of relaxation. Others find that meditation assists in developing better skills of concentration. While I too was drawn to meditation for these benefits, I also sought a rather more important reason. Meditation assists me in the development of my personal self-knowledge.

'For I really didn't know which me, was truly me. In my early years I played many roles. I was the daughter, the sister, the friend and the student. Then a little later I was the girlfriend, the lover, the wife and, I am extremely ashamed to admit to you today, the mistress. I have also been the employee, a colleague, a manager, a customer, a supplier, a debtor and a creditor. While performing all these various roles I realised that I spent very little time trying to work out what actually made me, me; I just played the required role.'

Well, Stevie could certainly empathise with that. She too often found a strain in distinguishing between her various selves.

'In fact, I often bent myself inside out to perform all those various and often conflicting roles. How to be the diligent student and yet maintain friendships with classmates, how to balance being the wife and the mistress, just when to be the colleague, when the manager. Some of these roles quite clearly lead to conflict with others, and yet I found I could cope with these readily. But if I was able to play these roles from both sides, then which role actually reflected the real me, or at least which was the one that was closest to me? The most frightening conclusion I reached was whether there was in fact ever a true me!'

Absolutely, thought Stevie. She too often asked herself to pause while she tried to fathom why she was doing things, to try to work out what she really wanted to do, rather than what she thought she ought to do. And just who was it that fed her these 'ought to dos'. Surely that *ought* to be coming from the kernel of her, or was it simply from layers of conditioning ordained by others?

'Also, I have to confess that beyond these natural conflicts I added yet another layer of issues all by myself. I found that I betrayed many of the things I would have claimed were the real me. I acted directly against the very things I believed that I believe in. I have been unfaithful, betrayed loyalty, cajoled and bullied, lied, cheated and stolen. So why did I do those things which I would criticise in others – things which I would deny had any part in the belief system of the true me?'

She paused and looked around the room. 'Please raise your hand if you believe that stealing is completely and utterly wrong and extremely reprehensible.' Some complied reluctantly but eventually the whole audience had raised an arm.

'Do please keep your hands up for a moment or two. Now think, have you ever taken home stationery items or office products, say like a pen, from your place of work? Keep your arm aloft. Ever taken something from a shop without fully paying for it? Keep your arm up. Borrowed something and not returned it? Keep stretching there. Found something on the road and not handed it in to the police? Keep 'em up. These are of course all forms of stealing. So if you can honestly say that you have never done this sort of thing, or perhaps worse things than these, if you have never stolen, then please lower your arms now.'

Stevie noticed that just one or two hands dropped. Hers was still held aloft, not because she felt she had ever stolen in a damaging way, but of course she had to admit that she had done some of the minor things that Marsha had listed.

'So look around you. Those with your hands still raised are therefore proudly displaying your ability both to lie and to steal. Please feel free to put them down now. So, how do you rationalise your two responses? Almost all of you have done something that you said you believe is utterly wrong and reprehensible. So that's a lie. You can't really believe stealing is so reprehensible if you have in fact stolen. And, in my book, that's absolutely the worst form of lie – for you lied to yourselves.'

She was trying for eye contact with as many of them as would catch her eye. 'Ah, but I can already hear you compounding the lie, misleading yourselves yet again. You are thinking that it was just a little thing, not important in the big scheme of things, just a little white lie, just a little victimless theft. Am I right?'

There was a buzz of general agreement from around the group.

'Then let's all pause. Make yourself comfortable in your chairs. Just relax your neck, your arms and legs. There's absolutely no need for any special posture. Now please take a few minutes and I want you to focus upon two things. Close your eyes and try to analyse the following thoughts fully and carefully. Do you really believe that all forms of stealing are wrong? Of course if you can honestly conclude that for you they are not, then I have perhaps started you upon a new career path that may be very lucrative, but hopefully for the rest of us this will only be in the short term.

'But do focus a little on the subject of theft. This always, always without fail has two sides, a winner and a loser. Is it right to subject the loser to the loss? I trust you will conclude that this is therefore always a wrong.

'Now for the second part of this exercise. Why then have you stolen? Is there some way that you can change your approach for the future so that you will not put yourself into this sort of conflict? Please, close your eyes. We will play you some music while you think through these two aspects of this extremely simple and yet fundamental issue.'

Stevie could appreciate Marsha's point. She thought it was crazy that you have these beliefs but then lack any staying power to see them through in each and every situation. Even down to when she last used this jogging outfit. She recalled that she would see a target like a tree up ahead, she would tell herself she would sprint all the way up to it. But some flaw inside her would usually allow her to stop sprinting a little way short of that target. It was only a little way short of it, and it wasn't that she couldn't physically make it there.

It was as though some other self would say it was OK not to complete the goal that she had set for herself. No-one had told her she must. It was a personal goal, yet she had personally allowed herself to fail without any self-criticism of this wishy-washy thinking. So who was it that was really in charge of her? How could she set herself such a simple target and yet at the same time then choose, herself, to fail it? Just what was it that could intervene and override her goal and, worse, confirm internally that it was perfectly OK to fail?

The few minutes passed quickly. The music faded and Marsha took to the stage asking everyone to open their eyes and relax.

'This was just a very simple example of what I mean about seeking better self-knowledge. We are all too ready to declare, even shout out, our principles and yet at the heart of us we are often not principled enough to stick to them. I feel sure you all concluded that it is not a nice thought that you are so malleable that you can believe in something and then not see it through. How pathetic am I that I cannot complete my own simple aims without wandering from my chosen route?

'And that's with very simple, small aims. What about our big goals and dreams? How often do these many roles that we have to play, get in the way of us ever setting ourselves any big goals at all. If you cannot take care of your own internal aims, if you are buffeted by the roles you have to play, can you be trusted to have any goals or dreams of your own? And if you do, as we just saw, will you ever see them through?'

Stevie found herself nodding and realised that she was certainly not alone. Marsha had them all in the palm of her outstretched hands.

'What my meditation technique is all about is to get us to accept that we really do not know ourselves at all and to help us at this low level to start to recognise our inbuilt hypocrisy, our inbuilt capacity to fail. But I have found in my work and in my life that we can overcome these failings if we set out a clear and precise goal. Let me show you a small film that will show you one organisation that is creating a valuable goal for many on their paths to this self-enlightenment.'

This film was very different and, if Stevie had been slightly removed from the first, this one grabbed her from the very first frame. The opening sequence showed the text 'Perpetua – a new Order.'

Stevie was momentarily dazed. She hadn't thought about the martyred saint for twenty years. Now a floodgate opened inside her, her memory of the visitation with all the subsequent guilt and shame that she had wrapped around it for too many years. She had walled all this up, now it came flowing out and inundated her.

She missed the opening minute or so of the film as she collected herself. She saw enough to understand that this Perpetua was an organisation planning to build communities that would set out to make a real difference in the world. The film showed a young community working and having fun together. In one sequence Marsha was clearly leading a meditation session.

It looked and sounded to Stevie something like a kibbutz. In the film they talked of using hard work to create personal development, to form fast friendships and to be part of a community that could and would make a difference. There were signs of some religious background to the organisation. Why else would it be named after Perpetua? But this was all down-played in the film.

The final frame said, 'Join us. Learn what the human existence really means, why we are here, where we are headed. Help us to make a difference!'

She wanted to know much more. She needed to know everything. Hadn't Saint Perpetua appeared to her personally? It couldn't just be chance that this organisation came along bearing her name at this very stage of her life which she had recognised as another major turning point.

All this just as she was confused as to what should be her next steps with Tom. Was it to be marriage, children and all this entailed? She wasn't getting any younger and wanted children of course. But what of her career if she went down that path? Surely there was much more to life than all these things, this new collection of roles?

# Chapter 24 - *London, UK*

Tom was trying to balance his roles as he prepared. Normally in this environment he was the celebrity scientist but today at the request of Sir Joseph he was using his status to talk on behalf of DICE; though the name would not be divulged.

He was directed towards a chair behind the studio's over-sized desk while the programme was still being cued up. The screens in the studio were relaying the station's top-of-the-hour news-in-brief.

A disembodied voice was saying, 'The Metropolitan Police and a number of minority group leaders are to meet with the Mayor of London in the morning to discuss the disturbing rise of hate crime in the capital. The, by now familiar, spate of knife and gun crimes are being eclipsed by the huge increase in brutal physical attacks on the person...'

The end of the live feed was blocked out by the production team advising that there were five minutes to go. The news broadcast over, the station went to a commercial break, coming back directly into the opening credits for this popular current affairs programme.

The programme started with a grainy old VT to air. Tom could see from the monitors that it was a pop video of David Bowie from his early period. He was dressed at his androgynous best, a tight-fitting suit overlaid with stretched cobweb lace and a pair of green sparkly false hands clasped over his 'breasts'. His sleek red haircut maintained a line somewhere between male and female, as he completed the verse 'Jean Genie, let yourself go!'

A voice-over set up Tom's piece while the caption at the bottom of the screen was showed a different spelling, 'Gene Genie'. As soon as the refrain ended the caption changed to read 'Tom Carter, Life Sciences Expert'. It appeared just a little before his head and shoulders filled the screens.

Tom, always calm on screen, had the time and compartmentalisation silently to bemoan the lack of the apostrophe in *Sciences'* while he was still able to listen fully to the interviewer's question.

He also took in that, while the video clip was probably some forty years old, bizarrely the presenter had blond hair that was cut not so very differently from the style that Bowie sported in the video, now playing quietly as their background.

'Welcome Mr Carter, or can I call you Tom?' She hardly waited for his nod of agreement. 'Tom, what do you think about this latest trend on our high streets, this Gene Genie franchise?'

'I think that the individuals who invest in the franchise will do very well. There is an endless series of reasons why individuals will want to use their services. But will those who use the services profit or be happy with the outcome? That I sincerely doubt.'

While the interviewer voiced over, the screens changed to show a series of Gene Genie outlets, each showing its distinctive double-G logo. 'These units are popping up everywhere, usually in quite small spaces. The size and the pace of their emergence is very reminiscent of the Tie Rack and Knickerbox chains. They are everywhere, cheek-by-jowl with the more familiar high street names, taking advantage of prime locations that have been vacated by companies that fell victim to the credit crunch.'

Tom chose to fill the silence that followed, 'They only need a small footprint on the high street to get noticed. There are no products to stock, their services are provided in laboratories well away from the shop unit, so all that is necessary is a small but noticeable shop frontage. But it's what the company does that really concerns me.'

The cameras went in for an extreme close up of the presenter as she asked. 'Tom, just what are your concerns?'

'Let's look at their brochures. First they offer what they term as a fast turnaround parentage confirmation service. This is perfectly conventional in that a simple mouth swab is DNA-tested. The Gene Genie appeal would appear to be that it has set up the back-office facilities to provide the results far more speedily than was previously the case. It's offered at a super low cost too, so all good so far. But my concern is the outcome of these tests. I believe that this mass-market approach will cause much consternation and pain to the thousands of parents, and particularly to any affected children.'

'How is this parental confirmation made? And Tom, is it accurate?' Her constant use of his name began to irritate, but he had provided the broadcaster with some simple illustrations and was able to shake off his annoyance by talking through the science.

'Kay, you asked me to prepare a little background piece on DNA. The letters stand for Deoxyribo-Nucleic Acid and what's important is that it carries the genetic instructions that are held deep within our cells. DNA usually consists of a double molecule which is arranged into the well-known double helix shape.

'DNA consists of a series of chromosomes. In the case of humans we have 23 pairs or 46 chromosomes in total. These individual chromosomes contain the hundreds of genes that define our many inherited characteristics.

'As every schoolchild should know, our current PCs and laptops operate using a binary system. This uses two conditions, power-on being 1 and power-off being 0. Given these two opposites and by using a whole host of 1s and 0s, we have been able to develop some pretty amazing capabilities. Of course getting man to the moon was just one of the early successes. Today there are few things we use that do not have a microprocessor at the core processing its specific crop of 1s and 0s.

'Well, *our* DNA operates on a base of four. Not 1 and 0, on and off, but instead the four letters A, C, G and T. These are based on the initial letter of four important hydrogen bonds - adenine, cytosine, guanine and thymine. Our 46 chromosomes consist of around 3 billion pairs of these letter sequences. All of those expressed in our binary computer software terms would add up to being just a little too much data to fit onto a single DVD. But in our cells the DNA is able to hold all of this compressed down into around 2.5 nanometres; a nanometre is a billionth of a metre!'

The presenter's 'noddy' to camera was designed to show that she was interested and following his every word. To Tom it looked more like she was trying to remove something caught between her rather full mouthful of teeth.

'You might think of these A, C, G and Ts arranged in the chromosome like a sort of barcode. This genetic 'barcode' is read when our cells are reproduced. It's perhaps easiest to imagine that your DNA acts like a chemical hard disk that holds a vast series of software programmes. Our genes and chromosomes are the subroutines that tell our body how to create and sustain us at the chemical level.'

'Yes, Tom, but how do they use this to check for parent-child relationships?'

'Let's be clear, Kay, that it's usually paternity tests that are undertaken.' He smiled to camera, 'As the presence of the mother at the birth is something of a give-away.'

The interviewer gave one of her signature sideways head-tilts with a serious look into her camera, 'That is, apart from those mix-ups in hospitals where babies get switched through nursing incompetence.'

Tom pressed on, 'When a baby is created it is of course the product, a mixture, of the DNA of both parents. In a unique fashion these get intermingled each time we procreate. For these tests we have to seek out the areas that are not quite so muddled. The mitochondria are little batteries within each of our cells that provide chemical energy to the cell and control the cell's growth and its life cycle. Fortuitously these mitochondria pass directly to the child from the mother without any sort of shuffling. Thus maternity is easy to test just by comparing the mitochondria of mother and child. So where there is a demand for a maternity check, it is pretty straightforward.

'For paternity checks it's necessary to look elsewhere. If checking a son we can use the smallest and final, or 23rd, chromosome. This Y-chromosome is the simplest approach as this is passed directly from father to male child. It's more complex where the paternity of a female is being tested. A blood test can assist at a macro level; the rest is down to a series of painstaking comparisons of the DNA of the parents and the child.'

'But, Tom, if I understand the basis of your concern here. It's that the truth can often hurt those being tested? Not physically but mentally and in their future lives? A father learning that the child he has raised is not his own, a child finding its parentage is based upon a lie.'

'Yes that's my point. But it's not just parentage tests that Gene Genie is offering. They also offer to analyse the tens of thousands of genes in your DNA against their databases and advise you of any genetic disorders or of propensities that might be present. Your chances of getting breast cancer for example, or your chances of passing on some genetic disorder to your children. But these are just propensities and probabilities, they are definitely not certainties. Just imagine the amount of mostly unnecessary concern and anguish that this could cause. So you learn that you have a heightened chance of getting breast cancer; it does not mean that it necessary will happen.'

'Tom, surely if you know that you might be at risk you can take precautions and have regular tests to be sure.'

'Yes, but what other problems might your heightened fears and anguish then cause you? We aren't just a bundle of physical symptoms, our mind has a part to play too. So what mental turmoil might the discovery that you have a higher propensity towards contracting a disease cause you mentally? Not to mention the fact that once you are aware of something, are you then legally obliged to reveal it to your medical insurance company, or your potential employer?'

She arranged her features while waiting for the camera to come in for a close-up, before saying, 'I see. So Tom, what you are saying is you could not only be stressed but uninsured and unable to get a job!'

He summed up, 'Once you've let the Gene Genie out of the bottle, who knows where it might lead. Kay, as always with genies, you have to be very careful quite what you wish for!'

# Chapter 25 - *Atlas Mountains, Morocco*

The team wished for complete privacy during their meeting. The hotel staff was tipped lavishly to ensure that they reserved, and kept reserved, a large area of the garden for their use. Reassured by a nod from one of his people, Dom Berkeley swept 'presidentially' into the hotel garden, his small retinue bustling to keep up with his long strides.

This group was not just a collection of toadies or functionaries; these were from the inner sanctum of the Mission organisation. Each was party to the details of the overall task and knew what part he was to play in it. Each was a male and each had been selected and charged with bringing about his goals smoothly, expeditiously and to feel free to do whatever it took to achieve that individual mission.

Each also had regular experience of the inner steel that Dom would apply to ensure their goals were attained. Every individual was proud to have fought his way, often literally, to earn his place within this team; having got there each was ruthlessly ready to retain their status. Perhaps there might even be a shot at the top job some day as well?

They went en masse to a buffet table and milled around it selecting their lunch before settling back into comfortable chairs waiting on Dom to start the meeting.

Dom had by that time dismissed the Hebron outcome as just one of those things. They had developed a plan, they had executed it and it hadn't worked out; life was like that. But this hadn't been the response from his superiors. They believed he should have been inside directing the entry team and making sure they obtained the vital prize, but he had left it to others and subsequent tests showed they had failed to come back with anything of value. Worse his brutal attack to cover his tracks had provoked some interest by the authorities and there could now be no going back to the caves.

Dom was still sore from his dressing down, though he would never show it to this group. His first comments were chosen to try to lighten his own mood. In this group he had no superiors.

'I guess you have all taken the opportunity to get a snapshot of the famous sign near here. What does it say? *Tombouctou cinquante-deux jours*, 52 days to Timbuktu.'

A pause, a smile, and then a fist abruptly slapped hard onto a side table to make them all jump.

'By the time that freshly-informed traveller could journey by camel and reach those fabled riches of Timbuktu we should have completed our mission here.'

Only one member of the team had not flinched at the sudden noise; this was Will Patterson. Dom knew they would all step up into his shoes given half a chance. He was committed to ensuring they never sniffed any sort of opportunity. Dom's insecurities immediately drew his attention to Will and his lack of a reaction, 'So Will, perhaps you can tell us what news you bring from Tamegroute?'

The small village of Tamegroute was situated just a few kilometres south of Zagora where they were meeting right now. While to the casual observer this was apparently a small and unremarkable village, it had at one time sought to become the equal of the mighty cities of Mecca and Medina. This seemingly implausible claim was based upon its powerful Sufi credentials.

Will was quiet, yet supremely confident. He always appeared fully at peace with his role. Dom considered that he was just a bit too cool, far too content with himself. He was not a big guy like Dom, yet still it was obvious one should not mess with him. He was known by his peers as a very determined individual, certainly not someone to upset. Not that he would ever show that he was disturbed, he would just deal with any irritant quietly and assuredly. Reputedly his response could be both quick and extremely vicious; he had never been accused of taking any prisoners.

Will explained. 'For the rest of our colleagues let me describe Tamegroute. For a very long time it has been one of the key centres of learning for the Sufis. For those who are unaware, Sufism is the part of Islam that focuses upon the development of the more mystic side of the Islam faith. Yet Tamegroute is not known just for its school; it has also assembled an important library of thousands of important texts, many dating back to the 13th century and beyond.'

Will was not a bit surprised or concerned when Dom interrupted him. He thought Dom so comprehensively stupid, mostly because he always wanted to show off the meagre knowledge that he did possess. He had obviously not become head of Mission through his intellect; no, he had belligerently bullied and blustered his way there.

Dom prattled, 'Many suggest that Sufi, the origin of the word itself, has two possible Arabic roots. Derived either from the word *sūf*, meaning wool, clearly a reference to the simple woollen cloaks worn by early followers. Or it could be from the word *safā* meaning purity. The two possible interpretations were neatly unified by one of their gurus who concluded that, "The Sufi is the one who wears wool on top of his purity".' He looked around the team. Will thought to himself whether Dom was expecting applause for his erudition.

Will pointedly looked at Dom, noticeably paused to be sure that he had finished, then resignedly pressed on. 'Whatever! The Sufis' purpose is to show ways in which mere humans can reach out towards the Divine. Their thinking has to be admired for its purity, its purpose and its piety.'

'Though, of course, they are completely deluded.' While saying this Dom thrust himself up from his chair and went to the table for a second heaped plateful of food.

Will ignored his comment. 'Tactically our best opportunity comes up later this week; hence the reason we are all here. It's just over a month after Eïd, the Sufis always hold a *moussem* festival in Tamegroute to celebrate one of their major saints.'

On his way back to his chair Dom interrupted again, 'Eïd is one of their prime festivals. It celebrates Abraham's willingness to sacrifice his son Isaac when God requested it. Christianity and Islam, not of course to forget Judaism, all share Abraham in their history. The Islamists believe that Mohammed descended directly from the other son of Abraham, Ishmael.'

Will was getting his seconds and commented back towards the table. 'Then it's just such a shame that we weren't able to bring them some relics of Abraham or Ishmael back from Hebron!'

Dom was suddenly short of words. No way was he going to try to defend his actions with this group. He was still fresh from not succeeding. He ducked his head and feigned interest in his food.

Will came back to the table. 'Eïd is the time for families to make a sacrifice. Not a child these days, usually just a sheep. But it's also a time that I assume to be a lot like our Christmas, a time for giving gifts, for visiting with friends and family.

'This upcoming local festival in Tamegroute is to celebrate the life of a Moroccan saint, the one who founded the library here. It houses all the material that he collected from his six Hajj pilgrimages to Mecca. He also travelled very extensively through Egypt, Iraq and Iran and amassed an amazing collection of early works. Again we have to admire the single-mindedness, the sacrifice, the scholarly endeavour...'

Dom had a mouth full of food but couldn't help but chime in. 'Even though it's all founded upon sand of course.' Then realising quite what he'd said, spraying bits of food in all directions, he spluttered, 'In fact that's literally!'

Will hardly acknowledged the comment as he continued. 'So this festival will pull in crowds from all over the region and from much further afield too. The basic village population will be swelled to many times its normal size. I concluded that, because of the general confusion in the town, this will be our best moment to strike.'

'You have already received your UNHCR accreditation?' Will nodded, but Dom still felt the need to explain to the others. 'The Office of the UN High Commissioner for Refugees is already very active in this region. It's here to identify and control the massive flow of AIDS carriers who travel up into northern Africa and beyond. It's a major local issue, and it provides us with the perfect cover. Nobody will suspect your proposed blood and other tests here. As a minimum they will be tolerated, and they may even be positively encouraged by the locals.'

Will was determined to finish his contribution to the meeting. 'Everything's in hand. We've assembled volunteers from several US universities and medical colleges who have the requisite skills to do the work, but they'll have no idea why they are doing it.'

Dom pointed at another of the team. 'Next, Buck. Where are you with your plans?'

'My task, as I trust you all know, is to handle the aftermath of Will's "tests". We decided we could continue using the UN theme. The death of most of those who will be tested is completely assured. But a few will survive and we believe that this will confuse matters enough to conceal any connection of the deaths with the tests. But we will invoke a UN quarantine area, claiming it is perhaps an Ebola or a Marburg outbreak. We already have the CDC covered off.'

Will watched, knowing that Dom would be eager to show off his knowledge again. Just when would he accept that he was the boss and didn't need to do this?

Dom couldn't help himself. 'The Centre for Disease Control and Prevention is based of course in Atlanta, Georgia but with offices and connections all over the world. If something like Ebola or Marburg fever gets mentioned anywhere they will immediately respond and descend upon the site. We've placed people in the local office here who'll alert us of any incoming team and there are detailed plans as to how we can keep them all busy and confused until it's far too late.'

Buck continued. 'There are a lot of outbreaks about; recently they've been reported in Uganda, the Democratic Republic of the Congo, Sudan, Gabon and the Ivory Coast. There's such a general northward flow of migrants, all trying to reach Europe of course, that any outbreak would be perfectly credible.'

Dom needlessly added. 'The usual way of catching these fevers is through eating bushmeat, or from contact with infected primates. It can be caught from the blood or fluids from others who've got the disease. So we've invested heavily in a troop of chimpanzees that we'll stage manage to be seen escaping from a truck during this festival of theirs. We've prepared the chimps so they're pretty mangy with all manner of cuts and open sores. That should put the fear of Allah into the locals. Those that die will be burned, the remains buried without any concerns, because of course they don't have those diseases. We'll bring in lots of people in protective gear, masks, gloves etc. Rest assured no one who manages to survive will want to be anywhere near here.'

Buck took up the report again. 'We have also recruited a team of previously Coptic, or Christian, Arabs who've joined up with us. They'll be scattered around the crowds attending the festival and they can help to feed the panic and spread the misinformation too. But most importantly they'll seize and hold the library to protect its artefacts.'

Dom explained, 'We understand there are items that we need within the collection.'

Will commented. 'It's a shame that we can't have more time to work with these particular Islamists.'

He knew Dom could not allow this comment to go unchallenged, 'But we just don't have that time, and don't forget the terrorism that they've allowed to ferment right within their midst? We need to put an end to that.'

Will wasn't ready to capitulate fully. 'Do try to see it from their viewpoint. Look how corrupt and profane we have become in the West, how awful we must seem to them. We're only gathered here today because we too have recognised the horror of our own condition, and now finally plan to do something about it!'

Dom smiled, 'Don't you love it when a plan comes together. We can solve both our problem and theirs, at the very same time!'

# Chapter 26 - *London, UK*

The plan had been amended so that they could watch a video of Tom's recent TV appearance to set the scene for their meeting; not everyone had caught the daytime broadcast.

Sir Joseph Maudlin reached for the remote and muted the TV set, 'Well done, my lad. Sorry we had to dragoon you into doing this for us. But we needed to intervene. Hopefully that last comment of yours, "be careful what you wish for", becomes the sound bite that the newshounds will use. We might just be able to slow down the headlong rush with a few more well managed interviews like this one.'

Tom had come directly from the studios to chair this DICE session which was looking at what they might do to follow through on this somewhat worrisome new retail phenomenon.

He smiled to himself. Just as he had reinvented himself from oceanographer and geologist into a celebrity life-scientist, so too it appeared was DICE able to stretch its remit if it was now being used to investigate and investigate this Gene Genie organisation. He had helped to define the remit of the organisation but was realist enough to know that this would be routinely manipulated by the cold war warrior who held its purse strings.

Professor Groves had finished his coffee and mused aloud, 'These direct-to-consumer genetic tests are actually nothing particularly new. In themselves they should not be too much of a concern. It's just that this, I presume American, organisation has suddenly made it into a very large business. They have brought it right out onto the High Street, introduced affordable prices, and are delivering some impressively fast turnarounds. Should we be worried that now, suddenly, it's no longer just the province of the legal professionals and police forces? What they have achieved is that today a test can be taken by anyone, on the merest of whims. Right in between buying a baguette and choosing some new brassiere!'

Sir Joseph stood, then paced. As the head of the Secret Services he was bemused by the sorts of things he now had to involve his people in investigating; baps and bras for goodness sake. It was so much simpler when it was just about double-guessing and outwitting the Eastern bloc. If he was honest he understood them a lot better than these entrepreneurial types who seemed to have absolutely no code at all, no form of moral compass.

Sir Joseph commented. 'The real issue is that there is little or no framework of legislation here. This is a commercial enterprise meddling with something that's so, well uh, so fundamental. What's in it for them? Certainly it's not profit, as yet. I suppose no-one can really say whether the meddling is a good or a bad thing; though of course my suspicion is that it may prove in some manner to be bad. Don't forget that not so long ago it was the Americans who were seeking to patent the human genome itself!'

The Professor responded, 'But here in the UK, the modification of our Human Tissue Act currently allows any consenting parties to give up material for testing to such an agency without any sort of check. In the USA the Senate unanimously passed a Genetic Information Non-discrimination Act which means that the fears that Tom mentioned in his interview could not in theory happen in the USA. Employers learning of any propensities to illness would not be allowed to reject a job application, and insurance companies could not refuse cover or unduly raise premiums. But that's not yet true here!'

Tom asked, 'I discovered that currently there's no legislation in place or even proposed for the UK, or, in point of fact, anywhere else in Europe?'

The Professor took this thought further, 'I guess where these shops are being rather clever is in their complete avoidance of the medical professionals at every stage of the process. This Gene Genie organisation therefore circumvents the usual form of control that the UK would impose on such matters by using NICE, our National Institute for Clinical Excellence. Normally NICE sets the medical guidelines, approves all and any forms of drug use for example, and most often this is shown to be operating for the general good.'

Sir Joseph slumped back into his chair. 'But the Government is trying to rush in some regulations. And that's the reason I mobilised DICE on this matter. It became clear that the people behind Gene Genie were spending heavily on lobbyists across all of the parties. Anyone who is seeking to control governmental thinking in this way is immediately suspect in my book. Perhaps it's the result of their lobbying, but there is apparently little current confidence that any legislation would get a majority. Lobbyists are citing Open Government, Human Rights. In fact they are pulling out all the stops by tugging on the MPs', albeit skin-deep, politically-correct credentials.'

Sir Joseph had been spending heavily too, trying to fathom out just who was behind this organisation. It had come out of the States with such unprecedented speed and reach and appeared to know how to work along the UK's corridors of power so very effectively. Worse from his perspective, it was currently unclear where its initial funding had come from. This always bothered him, for he knew that following the money was usually very illuminating.

At the same time that these Gene Genie people were proliferating he also had the gNOS team and also this BiCogNaIT operation being investigated. He was beginning to conclude that they were all somehow inter-connected. Certainly BiCogNaIT was providing the laboratories that were doing the tests for the new retailer. If so, then just who was behind all of this? What were they after? But he cautioned himself, for the purposes of this meeting he needed to keep the focus securely upon the Gene Genie operation.

Sir Joseph explained to the meeting that the stores' initial funding was not the only mystery. His intelligence reports indicated that the traffic through a sample of monitored Gene Genie outlets could not yet be showing anything like a profitable performance. His analysts had provided an estimate of the costs of acquisition and then of outfitting the shops, the costs of staff recruitment, training and salaries. Then there were the fees paid to the network of supporting laboratories, not to forget its massive marketing and advertising campaigns.

Everything was growing far too steeply for the stores yet to show enough return on this ongoing major investment. Nevertheless, there was no slow-down in store openings. He estimated that there were already at least four hundred in the UK, with new ones opening daily.

Sir Joseph added, 'Today my team has established that they are about to offer small village stores and post offices, the very few that we have left of course, a collection service. It will be similar to how they operate with a laundry or dry cleaning company. They will train the shop staff to take the swabs, provide them with cooler units and collect the samples daily.'

Tom asked, 'At their growth rate I wonder how long it will be before they have every single UK citizen on their database?'

Sir Joseph nodded then added, 'Interesting. But it's not only the UK. This is progressively happening globally. To be honest, this has all the signs of a military campaign, a full assault, but I just cannot see who it is that stands to gain from it. Well, not yet I can't!'

Tom had been concerned upon his return from South America as he couldn't find any trace of Stevie. She had not recently been at his place or hers. When he had called Culham they were none the wiser either. They explained she had been looking at a new role there and they assumed she was off being trained by her new employer, BiCogNaIT. As this name had not been mentioned by Sir Joseph in the DICE meeting, Tom could make no immediate connection; many governmental operations had this sort of lengthy acronym. It meant nothing special to him.

Yet it was still something of a surprise that she had left him with no sort of message. Yet he had to concede that he had not been too vigilant about keeping in touch with her while he was away for three weeks either. Perhaps she was just seeking to punish him in the way that women managed instinctively to do so well.

So he had settled down to writing his book. He was feeling an urgency to shake this one down and move on rapidly to his next project. Besides he felt he might be pushed into various commitments for DICE in the coming weeks. So head down and get on with it.

Later that evening Stevie's best friend had called to say she had also been looking for her for some days, had not received any message to suggest that she was going away. She wondered, particularly with all the violence on the streets just recently, whether she should be calling the hospitals or the police. Tom suggested gently that perhaps this was just a wee bit hasty. While she accepted his counsel, she jokingly asked Tom if they'd had a row and he had done away with her on one of his trips to far-flung places. Once he had reassured her and finished the call, he sat down and started to take the disappearance just a little more seriously.

After a good night's sleep had chased away the last of his jet-lag he set off early and fully refreshed for that day's follow-up meeting of DICE. While they waited for the others to arrive he mentioned his concerns to Sir Joseph. The old man of course knew Stevie from the trip last year to the Congo and so he was being knee-jerk placatory though none too interested. That was until Tom mentioned that she had apparently joined some organisation called BiCogNaIT. Now he had all Sir Joseph's attention; the old man immediately ordered his team to look into her disappearance.

The meeting proceeded and reviewed some further snippets of data that had been gleaned on these Gene Genie people. Sir Joseph judged that he now needed to broaden the discussion to include the ape-man incidents, gNOS and BiCogNaIT.

Tom was startled at the mention of gNOS and their tattooed operatives and explained about the treatment meted out on him in South America at this security team's hands. Brain's camera phone picture of the tattoo on the security guard at the London break-in was shown to Tom, he confirmed his South American captors had borne the very same symbol on their foreheads.

He explained to the Professor how, while he had been angered by his treatment, he had still found time to feel sorely disappointed that the symbol was not something Sumerian or Phoenician to be used as material for his book. The facts that particularly rankled were that they had taken his rubbings of the stelae, DINAR was being less than forthcoming with new ones. When he got out of this meeting he really needed to chase them up.

As the chair of the meeting Tom decided he should try for some sort of control of the wide-ranging discussions. He spoke aloud as he scribbled on a whiteboard.

'My god, this just gets more convoluted. Let me try to summarise what we know. First of all you had these gNOS guards running all around London interfering with a Met Police operation. They were apparently pursuing a humanzee that had reputedly been developed by BiCogNaIT to become Robocop and the Terminator all wrapped up in one hairy bundle.'

The Professor smiled, 'It all sounds more like Hollywood, than Cricklewood!

Tom continued. 'This breakthrough transgenic achievement was managed by this brilliant BiCogNaIT woman geneticist you mentioned, Marsha Davenport. She is also the person who employed my Stevie, who then promptly disappeared. Then we have this fast-growing retail operation Gene Genie that is springing up everywhere, also dealing in innovative genetic activities.'

Sir Joseph commented, 'Surely these three organisations must be connected in some manner?'

Tom nodded. 'Let's not overlook the two further names that I have thrown into the ring, Mission and Tyndale. I am pretty much convinced that Mission was into genetics too. They were certainly collecting DNA. But I can't begin to imagine quite how they might fit in with these others? It can't be just a coincidence that this same gNOS operation turned up in South America at that Tyndale campsite, right out in the middle of Lake Titicaca. They're clearly acting as the security arm for BiCogNaIT and for Tyndale, so are they just a shared contractor or are they in fact somehow connected?'

Sir Joseph shook his head. 'I'm sorry but this old man feels it is just too incredulous a coincidence that they should happen to emerge at the same time. All my instincts are that these must be linked in some manner.'

Tom agreed but commented, 'Yet all we have on Gene Genie is that its progress is still proceeding at a breath-taking pace. As I understand it your team has failed as yet to uncover the source of its central funding?'

Brain added, 'We do know that there is a distinct Gene Genie connection with this BiCogNaIT. When we were there it was doing a lot of lab work for the retail group.'

Tom queried, 'Again that could just be a simple supplier and service purchaser relationship.'

Sir Joseph continued. 'What rankles most is that this gNOS team is running all around the world in a far too cavalier manner for my taste. It has the distinct tang of that other American habit, of extraordinary rendition. I've never been a fan of loose cannons.'

Tom wanted to move the debate forward. 'There have been no further sightings of the ape-man and to all intents and purposes the BiCogNaIT operation might be viewed as a bright young organisation that is pushing at the biological, genetic and pharmaceutical boundaries. I don't believe Stevie would have had anything to do with them if they weren't well respected. None of the rest of their work looks anything like as controversial as the transgenic humanzees.'

Sir Joseph was insistent. 'The most compelling issue for me is that the more my team has tried to find out about these organisations, the less we know. This is what is tweaking my instinct that there just has to be something amiss. Please appreciate that my organisation is one of the top intelligence agencies in the world. We are intimately interconnected very closely with most of the others. And yet all our combined efforts have got us nowhere on this. That just would not happen unless there is something seriously out of kilter.'

As he said this he was thinking that the largest intelligence agency active in the world is the Roman Catholic Church. It had always been the biggest intelligence gatherer in the world, its experience stretching back for two thousand years.

He particularly admired its capabilities in keeping their secrets. Would that he could say the same of his own organisation down the years! He dismissed them as not being relevant to this matter, but he could not have been more wrong.

As the meeting was coming to a close for lack of any real progress, a member of Sir Joseph's team interrupted to advise him that they had managed to trace Stevie. She had apparently flown direct to Tunis on a British Airways evening flight a few days before. Her booking had been part of a group booking of thirteen seats, all booked and paid for by Dr Marsha Davenport of BiCogNaIT who herself was one of the group.

The tickets were all return tickets, evidently the Tunisian authorities always insist on this, but apparently all their return flights had been left open. Sir Joseph expressed his confidence that his office would be able to establish her local hotel in Tunis, certainly before the end of the day. At least in this matter his team could make some progress!

It was quickly decided that Brain should accompany Tom to Tunis to find out just what BiCogNaIT was doing there. Sir Joseph arranged for his team to rush around organising tickets, but it was the Professor who came up with the cover story.

It was he who drew the connection with Tom's latest book. 'Tom, I trust that you appreciate just what sits right at the heart of Tunis?'

When Tom looked vacant he added, 'Tut tut. Research just isn't quite what it was in my day. I've long suspected that today it's all a matter of presentation and no substance. Carthage, my dear young friend, Carthage. You should know that this is where many of your Phoenicians moved and transformed themselves into Carthaginians!'

'Of course, I realised that it rang some distant bells when Tunis was mentioned but I was concentrating more on Stevie and just why she might have headed for there. My immediate thoughts were white slaving! I made no connection with my research!'

'You and Brain could claim to be following up on the research for your book.'

'And, that's not just a cover story. I always wanted to go and look at Carthage and try to see where it might fit within my current archaeo-astronomy project!'

# Chapter 27 - *Tamegroute, Morocco*

The annual *Moussem* festival had gone off very well. The population of the small community had been impressively swollen by many pilgrims, there to celebrate the life and deeds of Sidi Mohammed ibn Nasir and his son Ahmad; for it was they who had founded the order of Sufi known as *Nasiriyya.*

Ahmad had brought back such a range of literary riches from his six Hajj pilgrimages and it was these that had laid the foundation for Tamegroute's famous library.

As it was every year, the community spirit had been lifted as the people contemplated these great men and their works, words and deeds that had reached right around the whole Islamic world. This festival was an annual opportunity to inspire those currently studying at the school and to extend the reputation of this otherwise rather sequestered place.

The first sign of any problem was a truck crashing right at the centre of the village. A mangy group of chimpanzees had marauded for almost an hour before each had been cornered and caged. Several had just been summarily shot when they proved too awkward to capture. It had been a brief interlude, quickly forgotten.

The very next day a Tunisian visitor to the village visited the local doctor to complain about his high temperature and the debilitating pains he was experiencing in his stomach and joints. He presented with an overwhelming feeling of listlessness, of sapping fatigue and weakness. The relatively senior local doctor treated him with little success. He was particularly frustrated that only three or four days earlier a very capable UNHCR team had been based right there in the village taking blood tests as part of some anti-AIDS protocol; surely they would have been able to assist this visitor much more thoroughly than he could with his paltry supplies. But the local officials had hastened them on their way so these non-Muslims would not be around to interfere with the festival.

The doctor closely monitored his patient, recording that his eyes were extremely bloodshot and a little later noting that he began to cough and vomit. The patient declined rapidly. First he began showing traces of blood in his vomit, then he worsened with extreme diarrhoea with clear traces of occult blood. He was rapidly dehydrating despite their pumping him with fluids. The alarm bells were now too deafening to ignore.

The doctor had earned plenty of experience with malaria and dismissed this as the cause. He also established early on that it was not a form of virulent influenza. But upon referring, in some despair, to his old and dusty medical books he narrowed it down to just two equally awful alternatives. He had to conclude that typhoid or Ebola haemorrhagic fever were the most likely diagnoses that would fit with all these symptoms. He instructed his staff to try to notify the UNHCR team and get them back to the village to assist.

When four more patients presented with similar symptoms he really began to panic. He was therefore immensely relieved when the UNHCR team speedily arrived back at the village. He was quite surprised that they had been able to drop what they were doing and respond so quickly but immense relief overcame any curiosity that this might have caused.

He felt relieved as the 'UN' team established a strict quarantine regime; only those dressed in full protective gear were allowed to approach the patients and then only to start further IV drips and a new course of medication. He was particularly delighted that they brought all they needed with them so they were not going to be a drain on his supplies; they were the answer to all his prayers. In consulting with the doctor the team encouraged his belief that this was Ebola fever. But any joy in the confirmation of his diagnosis was dissolved by their prediction that the likelihood of death was expected to be somewhere between 50% and 90%.

The local manpower and resources rapidly became overwhelmed as further cases were reported across the next few days. The civic leaders were delighted that this 'UN' team was prepared to take the lead. They themselves were of course increasingly keen to stay well away from those who had become infected.

When even more 'UN' people arrived they found they could very gratefully detach themselves almost entirely from any handling and treatment of patients; particularly good news now that some were beginning to die.

The village held a series of interminable and heated meetings that led to a complete stand-off between the small local medical team and the rather larger group of local government officials. The medicos wanted to report this outbreak but the officials wanted to avoid a mountain of paperwork, particularly as many of those afflicted were not even Moroccans. The officials were largely appointed, funded and controlled by the local businessmen and they were clear that they didn't want the news to damage the village's already tenuous livelihood.

The officials finally won the war of words and adopted the approach that it was better to assess the overall outcome of this outbreak before acting precipitately. Besides they could see no sense in rushing out news before they really knew what was happening.

Anyway, the UN was there already and clearly in charge. They could take any flak that might result from the village's delay in reporting.

Dom Berkeley's team, led by Buck, took full advantage of this confusion while the outbreak spread steadily and surely throughout the populace. The death count rose remorselessly. It was not within the earlier estimate; instead it was looking as if it might reach closer to 100%.

Buck had impressed upon the locals that they could not let anyone leave the village and risk spreading the deadly infection. He was delighted when a local businessman offered to post roadblocks. It was clear that the businesses this individual managed were securely founded in crime and extortion. The roadblocks would be manned and sustained so long as the UN team provided him with generous funding.

Buck was amused that for quite a small investment he had his perimeter established without having to involve his own team in any way. The fact that this was being done by local thugs only served to conceal their presence while they managed this community.

Their Coptic Crew, as Buck had nicknamed them, had been charged with gaining control of the library. They had moved to achieve this as soon as the first problems had been experienced; once the epidemic was in full spate they were able to take it over without resistance.

Within a few days they had worked their way through the archives and crated up what Samuel Shepherd had required to be shipped back to him in Arizona.

The Mission team had been protected from the infection. Of course, as it was they who had introduced it, it had been a simple matter to take all necessary precautions. Buck's only problem was keeping the story straight between his close team who knew precisely what was happening and the others as they arrived to take over the community. These others had to remain convinced there was an epidemic and that they were helping to stem it.

They made sure that many of the senior locals became infected and were struck down early. For Buck the good news was that any desire these officials had to report or manage the outbreak naturally subsided commensurately with their contraction of the illness and their death.

Those in the vicinity of the village naturally heard rumours of the outbreak, and of the death toll. Most sensibly found reasons therefore to be elsewhere. The very few who tried to reach relatives in the village were turned back by the roadblocks where they heard increasingly terrifying descriptions of what was happening inside the quarantine area.

If the villagers had been less self-engrossed they might have commented on the ever- increasing flow of vehicles and people that were arriving each day. They would perhaps have found time to be impressed by the UN's forward planning and logistical prowess. Among the vast array of supplies they received were a number of small diggers that were used to dig the required mass graves.

It was all happening so quickly, not something Africans often experienced.

They might also have wondered why the excavations were always at night and why they were operating beneath large tarpaulin structures.

Of course Buck's team was ensuring that nothing could be noted from any prying over-flying satellites. Each morning they ensured that all caterpillar tracks had been carefully erased.

Within just five days Mission had established complete control of Tamegroute.

# Chapter 28 – *Carthage, Tunisia*

The ruins of Carthage stretched out before them as they strolled quietly through the area. It had only fallen quiet now that the helicopter, after taking an inordinate time about landing, had taken off, hovered over the nearby heliport for an age and then finally clattered off across the bay.

'Explain to me again why you actually wanted to come here to see this bunch of old rubble?' Brain was completely bemused by what could possibly be interesting there.

Tom replied, 'As I told you, I've been commissioned to write a book on the subject of archaeo-astronomy. I can't begin to tell you how readily I get drawn in by this sort of subject. I call it one of the 'weird' sciences. I love all the quirky and contra-indicated stuff that comes out from a discussion of these topics with their proponents.'

'I would have expected you, as a scientist, would be more likely than me to dismiss any bizarre or offbeat thinking.'

'Well, as an absolute minimum I usually find the detailed analysis of such unusual notions helps me to harden down on my thinking. Pretty often it triggers off new thought, a new angle, a new direction. I find it's best not to question this sort of thing. I can't begin to tell you the strange directions you can end up pursuing, or the destinations you can reach.'

Brain smiled. He had originally thought that Tom was a bit of a prima donna, very arrogant about the power of his own intellect. But they had now shared a number of experiences that had fostered a strong mutual respect; though that didn't stop them sniping at each other's profession.

'And perhaps even more importantly there's the little matter of generating some useful articles or papers that can keep you out there in the public eye!'

Tom didn't rise to the bait. He was only half-heartedly involved in the conversation. He was, perhaps a little belatedly, thinking in detail about where his relationship with Stevie might be headed. It had become fairly serious, but not yet reached the point of any real formality or even the suggestion of their moving in together. But whenever he was in the UK seldom did more than a few days go by without them spending time together. Maybe now he had to accept that the relationship was much more significant than he had been prepared to admit. Why else was he prepared to drop everything and rush to Tunis to try to find her?

Brain had been a good companion for the journey. He was not someone who was in your face all the time. He was quite happy to sit in silence. In fact Brain's quietness had been because he couldn't stop thinking through quite why he was there. He was trying to make some sort of sense of what these companies were up to. The various organisations had turned up without warning into his area of interest, or rather Sir Joseph's, and that amounted to precisely the same thing. The old man was expecting Brain to come back from this trip with some real insight into what was going on. It was a big ask, just where should he start?

They were beside the Tunis Gulf at the site of the Roman Baths of Emperor Antoninus Pius. The baths had been constructed around 150 to 160 CE and the significance from Tom's perspective was that they were built a few centuries after Rome's victory in the third Punic War. This was the war that had marked the effective destruction of the Carthaginians and therefore of their forerunners the Phoenicians.

Once Tom had completed his look around the baths, they walked on, both engrossed in their own thoughts for a while until they reached the hill named *Byrsa,* the name derived from the Greek word for a bull's hide.

Tom stopped and looked around, 'You know, I realised that I have a perfect image in my mind of Princess Elissa, or Queen Dido. She was the founder of all this, of Carthage. She had to be formidable this Elissa; she'd fled all the way from Tyre, ending up here in north Africa some time before 800 BC. Just imagine a single woman making her way in those times. It was so much a man's world back then!'

Brain was content to let Tom prattle on. Besides he found it was quite interesting stuff that he usually trotted out.

'She skilfully hoodwinked the locals who she found living here already by asking if she might buy a piece of land from them. She said all that she needed was something the size of a single bull hide. When they agreed to her terms she arranged to have the selected hide cut so finely that she could encompass this entire sizeable hill.' He waved his arms around to make the point. 'I was thinking that Elissa must have been just like our own Ellise Jacobs. She would have had the balls to have come up with something like that too!'

Ellise was the athletic, forceful and forthright member of the American organisation, the Office of Oceanic and Atmospheric Research. She had been there with them up in the Arctic, when they had managed to thwart the Brotherhood's plans.

'Come on admit it. You were well in to her, weren't you?'

Tom reddened. 'We've not really spoken since you came barrelling in and saved our skins up there.'

'Yes, but you can admit it to me here and now. Just between us. You would have, wouldn't you, if Stevie hadn't been on the scene?'

'Who knows?' Tom had uncomfortable memories that jarred with his recent thinking about the strength of his relationship with Stevie. He decided it was safer to change the subject.

He smiled as he said, 'Moving smoothly back to this remarkable Princess, or Queen. She founded Carthage here and that was generations before Rome itself was created by Romulus and Remus. From here the Carthaginians went on to control much of the western Mediterranean. You've heard of Helen of Troy and how her face was said to have launched a thousand ships, well Queen Elissa inspired the Carthaginians to build a fleet that was every bit the equal of any of a major 19th century European colonising powers. They used it to become the long-lasting trading superpower of its age. Its basic civilisation was securely underpinned by the development of strong agricultural methods.'

'So what was it that halted them?'

'The Romans decided they wanted to expand. To achieve their goals they had first to wage three costly Punic Wars upon Carthage. These lasted for more than a century before Rome was able to seize what Carthage had built.' He turned to look around the area from the vantage point of the hill.

'After winning that final war, the Romans' fury was awesome. First they burned Carthage's huge fleet. That was pretty darned wasteful of them. Then they burned the city itself. Vindictively they felt that even this was not enough so they are said to have sowed salt into its lands to punish them even further. Not only was that a horrible thing to do, you also have to appreciate that salt was such a very valuable commodity back in Roman times, so it was a sizeable statement. Legionnaires were often paid in salt; it's where the word 'sal-ary' comes from! But then the Carthaginians terrified the Romans so very much; their mothers would taunt their kids that if they misbehaved Hannibal would come and get them.'

Brain commented, 'I'm always amazed by how much we have deep-rooted inside us that comes down to us directly from the Romans. Do you remember that Monty Python 'Life of Brian' sketch when they kept asking "what have the Romans done for us?" Well many a true word… At military college they explained to us that today's concept of 'third time lucky' comes directly to us from the legionnaires. The first two rows of their tortoise formations were pretty vulnerable, so it was considered much better to be placed back in the third row, to be in the third was lucky. But I always thought Hannibal was a Roman?'

'No, he was very much out of Carthage. He was a considerable military man; I think you would have liked him. Of course you know about him arriving from Spain and crossing the Alps with war elephants; everyone knows that snippet. But he successfully occupied parts of Italy for around a decade. He had some other pretty remarkable successes too. Who knows how the world, or at least Europe, would have looked if the Romans had not eventually beaten him.'

Brain commented. 'While I was at Shrivenham we were told that Hannibal was one of the great strategists, apparently both Bonaparte and Wellington were great fans of his. But I really did think he was a Roman. Hang on, there was a quote of his that I had to learn for an exam. What was it? It was a bit like where there's a will there's a way. Something about if there is no way forward then we'll just have to make one.'

'He certainly left a lasting impression. It took another two thousand years before the modern mayors of Rome and Carthage were prepared to finally meet up. It was as recently as 1985 that they formally declared peace between the two cities!'

Stevie and Avril were part of a group that was just then climbing another part of the Byrsa hill.

After their first meeting at the Congress Centre the two young women had gone out for a drink and had readily built up an instant rapport. Avril had found herself explaining to Stevie all about her paternity issue; somehow it felt easy to confide in this woman who was around her age and had similar interests. Stevie proved such a good listener and, as she was not involved with any of Avril's relatives, she was able to talk over the various ways forward without any bias or self-interest.

Perhaps simply to balance off their relationship Stevie found that she, fresh from Marsha's meeting, had wanted to talk through her childhood vision of Perpetua.

Over the next week the two of them had found themselves caught up in the whirlwind of meetings that Marsha kept organising for them. Marsha apologised for the frequency of these meetings, all being so telescoped. She was planning to be in the UK for such a short time, she wanted to make sure that they could seize every opportunity. But she need not have worried because the two women were hooked; they passionately looked forward to all these meetings. Both had come to realise just how empty their lives must have been before this. They now appreciated that prior to meeting Marsha they had become increasingly defined by their jobs. They had thrown themselves into their work rather than into building a circle of friends; they had foregone any sort of social life. Yes Stevie had Tom, but he was so seldom around.

Stevie and Avril were being mentored within a group of twelve women ranging in age from 25 to their late 30s. Marsha had jokingly named them her 'Anglo Apostles' and she definitely put such an effort into her time with them. Stevie wondered whether she had lost any real interest in developing the new BiCogNaIT facility at Culham, though her workaholism ensured that this work still progressed.

The mentor group had rapidly melded into a strong inter-dependent team, and when Marsha offered them the opportunity to meet face-to-face with the founder of the Perpetua Order they had all jumped at the chance. Most would have readily paid to go themselves.

As they climbed the hill Avril appreciated the added significance of this Tunis trip for Stevie. It was a journey towards the very location of Saint Perpetua's martyrdom. She knew it was more than twenty years since Stevie had her experience with the school's statue of the saint, but Stevie had explained to Avril that it still felt to her like yesterday.

Avril had not heard of more than the apparent 'vision'. She knew nothing of what had followed and thus she could not fully appreciate the memories that were now being raked over, fresh and raw in Stevie's mind. If she was completely honest with herself Avril thought it must have been just a youthful dream, a fancy. Hadn't Stevie mentioned that it happened soon after her mother's death? But she would never have thought to voice this conclusion to her new best friend. So she was surprised by Stevie's current demeanour.

'You leapt at the chance to come to Tunisia and visit the old stomping ground of your Perpetua. Why are you so quiet now that we are actually here?'

Stevie had indeed welcomed this as her opportunity to reach out to the saint. It was a chance to try to understand, finally, more of her childhood epiphany. This was something that she had buried very deeply and for far too many years. Now there it was all back, right at the front of her mind, with all her emotions in turmoil.

She now accepted that everything since that evening had never felt quite so real, nothing had ever approached the same significance. The appalling abuse by the priest had intruded on something wonderful, this had disconnected her from the original vision. Its impact had become contained within the hard shell that she had created to block out his foul attentions. On the journey to Tunis she had recovered that original feeling with all its intensity.

Now she was in Carthage, right where Perpetua and Felicity had met their awful ends. Surely she should be feeling something. There ought to be some sort of sign now that she was there?

'I just hoped that once I got here I might be feeling something, anything. But all I can sense is every one of those eighteen hundred years that have passed since her martyrdom. Somehow that huge passage of time is proving too intrusive. It's clouding any possible perceptions I might have expected. It's blocking out any possible communication with her. I guess really I'm cross with myself. How could I have fooled myself into thinking that I could connect back with that life and death from so very long ago?'

Stevie had read of the original Phoenician city and the bull-hide story. She had learnt too of the subsequent Roman city of Carthage founded almost a century later upon the razed original. She assumed that the salt sown on the land had all been subsumed by then to permit the Romans to rebuild and repopulate the city.

Roman Carthage too had become successful; it had grown to become second only to Rome. Stevie imagined it must have had a deep-rooted frontier character, a free and enterprising spirit. It was not so surprising that early Christianity would have flowered in this desalinated soil. That was of course up until the point that the then Roman emperor had decided that conversion to Christianity or Judaism should become a crime punishable by death.

Perpetua and Felicity, two young women, both new mothers, had been thrown into the arena simply for not being prepared to forsake their Christianity. In the arena they were attacked and gored by a wild bull. Stevie wondered just what it was about bulls and this place.

# Chapter 29 – *Carthage, Tunisia*

Stevie and Avril were walking up the Byrsa Hill buried deep within a large group. They were climbing towards a site where Marsha had described a necropolis that had been revealed a few years earlier. Stevie had become particularly excited when she learned that a church had been uncovered that had been dedicated to 'her' St Perpetua.

After a sapping climb in the heat and humidity the guides indicated they had arrived at their goal, but as they received no further directions, they assumed they were waiting for someone to arrive.

Approaching from the other side of the hill, Tom and Brain could see a large group beginning to assemble ahead of them at the top. They wondered what the attraction might be. As they got closer Tom watched a striking figure sweep across the track to join the group. Something about him clearly exuded some authority over the sizeable audience.

Tom realised that he had noticed this individual earlier. It was the man who had arrived in the noisy helicopter down by the baths. Something about the proportion of his head to his body and the big shock of grey hair stamped him out, this was still visible protruding from beneath his headgear.

Samuel Shepherd brushed a hand slowly through his mane of silver hair and used silence and an exaggerated, almost theatrical pose to bring quiet down upon his audience, consisting of those invited and any onlookers. If you could put aside the fact that Tunisia did not have a very large Berber population, then he looked absolutely magnificent dressed in a traditional yet somehow flamboyant Berber outfit, more tourist than Tunis.

Tom was unaware of exactly what costume it was, he recognised it as Arabic, but it really did look incongruous on this evidently non-Arabic individual.

Tom thought the man looked more a caricature than in character, and commented so to Brain, 'He must have bought one of those costumes the Spanish use in their Moors and Christians fiestas held all along the costas.'

'Brothers and sisters,' Shepherd was calling them to order. He did so firmly though without shouting. His band of followers drew a little closer to be sure they could hear him. But as they shuffled closer he raised his voice ensuring he would be heard both by his group and those on the periphery of his congregation, attracted to join the group.

'We are here to recall an age of clarity of Christian belief, a time well before the mandarins of the Roman Catholic Church were allowed to meddle. We are going to travel back to one of the earliest turning points in Christianity, turning points that have regularly plagued the Word. We go back to a time before the bureaucrats of the Church had tinkered with the scriptures, which be assured they have done consistently down the many generations since Jesus Christ.'

Brain commented on the man's accent, almost to himself, 'North Texas, perhaps New Mexico.'

'Here we are standing on ground that was originally inhabited by one of the very early peoples of mankind, the Berbers.' He theatrically waved his hands down and around his costume.

'They spread early humanity from our origins in east Africa, migrated all along the fertile southern shores of the Mediterranean. The Berbers were competent farmers, not the wandering nomads we are led to consider them today. They controlled North Africa and southern Iberia, bringing order and prosperity to those powerful sites of our early history. At one time the Berbers even ran the 22$^{nd}$ dynasty along the coast in mighty Egypt. And make no mistake; it is their genes that constitute 75% of those who live here today. We shouldn't be confused by their Arabisation, their conversion to Islam. Their DNA still proudly bears a marker, M81 - the mark of the Berbers.'

Tom was confused and commented to Brain, 'These Bible Belt evangelists don't usually espouse science. My previous experience of such preachers is that they usually choose to ignore it as a rather unfortunate contradiction to their boundless belief. As in, if you have faith then why would you possibly need the certainties of science?'

Brain was on a different tack. 'Gene Genie, BiCogNaIT, gNOS and now some Bible-basher talking about genes! There has to be a connection in there somewhere?'

'Quintus Septimius Florens Tertullianus, whose name today we usually shorten to Tertullian, was just such a Berber. He lived a good long life from 160 to 220 CE. After his conversion from paganism in his late 30s, he wrote over forty works, this was some of the earliest Christian literature. It was he that effectively set the Roman Church agenda. He first coined the term the Trinity. It was he who defined what a soul is, he who attacked many of the heresies of the time. So what drove these people, who had espoused and cherished early Christianity? What drove them towards Islam?'

He counted his points out on his fingers, 'It was bureaucracy, red tape and, last but not least, an early saint! The Berber Christians had a pure faith and clearly wanted to maintain it this way. It's true that when the Romans started to persecute the early Church during the 3$^{rd}$ and 4$^{th}$ centuries, many weakened. They defected and renounced their faith, weak apostates, turncoats, cowards. They were all keen enough to return later when the persecution relented. But the other Berbers knew them clearly for what they were, unworthy!'

Shepherd spat out this last word with vehemence, and continued. 'The Berber Christians demanded they pay penance. They made them remain outside the church for some years where they had to seek the prayers and blessings of those who had remained sincere. If they worked long and hard at this, then perhaps some time later they might be admitted to kneel just inside the church during the services. They would have to work even longer and harder to earn the right to eventually stand within the congregation. And they decided that it would take a supreme effort on these returners' behalf ever to be invited to take the sacrament.

'I have instructed many of you gathered here, on the great prophesies of Daniel and Revelations. I warned you that the first seal of the Revelations has been broken. The first horse of the Apocalypse is loose. This is the white horse that represents the false prophets who seek to confuse and lead us from the Path.'

Tom looked around the group. One section was clearly made up of young Americans, smiling with the orthodontic symmetry only that country seemed to want and to achieve. Dressed so neatly and conservatively, he would have assumed they were Mormons. It was only as he scanned their faces that he spotted Stevie within their number.

'The Catholic bureaucrats, were so easily misled by the false prophets, happy to let these apostates simply to walk right back into the Church, even permitting some to re-assume their roles as priests. They were ready to allow them not just to take the sacrament but also to give it! Simply by apologising! Hadn't these ingrates received their forgiveness and been welcomed into Christianity when they had been christened? So when they had forsaken their faith in the face of oppression, hadn't they forsaken that forgiveness too? By readmitting these weak people it could only lead to a weakening of the Church, a weakening of the Faith.'

Tom watched some of the 'congregation' throw up their hands to the sky as if in despair of these lost and confused individuals whom Shepherd was describing. He tried to work his way across to where Stevie was standing, she was very clearly involved with this group.

'This was how bureaucracy took its toll here. In the 5th century a committee was held across the sea from here in Arles, France' he pointed out across the Mediterranean. 'This committee of bureaucrats decided that these pure North-African Christians were wrong and declared them a schism. Within a century they were being called heretic. Perhaps the Church simply feared how they might get enough priests if each had to be shown to have been constant and steadfast in his belief. But is this a good criterion upon which to build Christianity? At the same time these faithful early Christians were called heretic, just for wanting to secure the true Word.'

A few 'hallelujahs' were shouted from among the group. Tom and Brain were finding it difficult to get through the tightly-packed crowd to where Stevie was standing, they paused to see if an opportunity to speak to her would present itself.

'Then there was the saint I mentioned, and let's not forget how someone becomes a saint in this ever weakening Church. Their names are put forward and yet another committee meets to consider the claim for canonisation.' He looked across the heads of his followers. 'I have no idea who made the joke first, but the local beast of burden here in Africa, the camel, is said to be a horse created by a committee. Foul-tempered, obstinate as a mule and impossible to deliver anything like a comfortable ride. Just pause and think of any committees that you have joined and how they operated. How it is the least competent and most outspoken who rise to become senior officers of any committee. Ponder what it means to be a good committee man or woman!

'Now let's pause and think of those centuries of meddling, petty arguments, expedient solutions, politicking. It's this that made the Church today a weakling, enfeebled by its own inner machinations, without the moral strength to lead the world. It's unable to confront its opponents from a position of rectitude, no longer credible as the recipient and guardian of right-thinking.'

His voice had risen with the heat in his comments and his emphasis led to an explosion of spittle over the heads of his acolytes. They appeared not to notice. He gathered himself and once more spoke steadily and quietly.

'Let me be clear that there is no doubting the brilliance of this saint, Augustine of Hippo. He too was a Berber, born in nearby Algeria, brought up a Christian. He was educated at a famous school that boasted grammarians, novelists and a whole host of martyrs.'

He paused at this word then looked over the heads of his followers, 'Let's not forget that martyrdom too was a key part of early Berber Christianity! You too need to prepare for this possibility. Particularly as now I am able to advise you that the second seal of the Revelation has been broken, the second horse has been set loose. This is the red horse that many call 'War'. Once again we need to look beyond our modern use of this word. War has been omnipresent since the beginning of time. The red horse is not war per se, it represents the absence of peace. You will see global disquiet, peaceful neighbour suddenly arguing against neighbour. Mark my words; there will be a time of general unrest that stretches all around the world.'

Tom felt a chill on hearing these words, that sort of unrest was already evident in the major cities. It was also the way in which the words were delivered and received, the man's followers all had beatific smiles on their faces clearly accepting the potential of martyrdom. For the first time Tom reappraised the man, he whispered to Brain, 'This preacher might actually be dangerous.'

He observed a camera crew following this man's every word and action, presumably to be broadcast on to his followers elsewhere in the world. Tom knew that these evangelists were no slouches in their use of modern communications technology.

'We were talking of Augustine. He was taught about Latin and Greek scholars and of their thinking while living in that school which was established within a town that was part Christian, part pagan. But he was trained in the early Manichaean form of Christianity. This branch of the Faith was at the time very widespread. Its books had been translated into Greek, Latin, Coptic, Persian, Parthian and even Chinese. His Manichaean belief, his training and his strong intellect were rewarded. He was sent here to Carthage to further his education. Later still, his Manichaean friends funded his move to Italy to become a professor in both Milan and Rome.

'So how did he repay these valuable friends and patrons? Many, many times over! Manichaeism was later defined by the Roman Emperor as a heresy because it had linked the God of Christianity to the gods of Zoroastrianism and of other earlier faiths. The Emperor therefore imposed the penalty of death for anyone found to be following this heresy. It is then perhaps understandable that Augustine made sure he was seen to switch and adopt the core of Roman Christianity. Yet in his writings he still managed to insert his Manichaean beliefs - right at the very heart of Christianity. His thinking and writings very perceptibly changed the concepts and beliefs about the fight of good versus evil, the concept of original sin, the concept of hell, the need for priests to avoid sexual activity... Quietly, stealthily from within, he changed the Church more towards the ideas he had learnt while directly pursuing his Manichaean faith.'

He had listed the items slowly, pausing to allow each member of his throng to take time and call to mind these issues, or at least their own appreciation of them.

'So here we are at the site of this early Christian crossroads where many early beliefs fought for pre-eminence. They fought to keep out other earlier religions. They fought to keep the message delivered by Jesus Christ pure and untarnished. Did this particular saint and the outcome of his meddling ensure the early Church would follow the true path? Or was the Church led down a by-road by this intelligent, well-meaning but none-the-less misguided soul? Who is to say that perhaps, by his manoeuvrings, it was he who ensured they would never recover the original path again?'

Tom was following the discussion and considered the question. He said to Brain, 'I bet he believes that he's the one who can say!'

'I say, let's seek out an even earlier time. Let's travel back further in time and consider what happened right here, for this was a very busy centre for the early Church. We'll go back beyond the synod in 419 CE that declared Pelagius a heretic, back beyond the Conference in 411 that declared Donatism as yet another heretical schism. Think on the fact that history, just like the modern Church is not a record of who was right, just of who won!

'We'll go back even further; on past the Council of Carthage held at the end of the 4th century which defined the books that would be permitted to be included in the Bible. Who knows what ended up being excised, what fell off their table to be considered mere apocrypha?

'No we will pass on back beyond the many synods that were held right here in the 3rd and 4th centuries – meetings used to edit, manipulate and shuffle around the concepts in order to declare the approved structures and beliefs. Just who was it that gave them the monopoly on these matters?

'No, we return to a time before these dilemmas and dalliances with the Truth. We go back to a time before these early crossroads had been reached and the choices made, before these many fateful decisions made by compelling thinkers and by thoughtless committees. Let's return to a time when the Church was fresh, when it was the heart that guided, not the rhetoric.'

Tom commented, 'Pot? Black? He was a fine one to bad-mouth rhetoric.'

He was still trying to work through the throng getting ever closer to where Stevie was standing when abruptly the throng surged. The preacher had walked across to a mound of rocks and the crowd rushed to follow in his footsteps, the movement like a swirling flock of birds. Unfortunately this rearrangement carried Stevie deeper into the group and further away from Tom wiping out all of his progress.

Shepherd paused for a long moment, 'Beside us here are the remains of a church that celebrated the purity of a young mother, Perpetua. Her family pleaded with her to recant her Christian faith, to deny what her heart and soul told her was true.'

Tom was still trying to reach Stevie, but suddenly stopped, pole-axed by the use of the name Perpetua; so that was why Stevie was here! He recalled vividly the various conversations when he and Stevie talked about the saint and of Stevie's childhood experience. She had also confessed, in haunting detail, about the years of abuse that had followed her visitation. So why was she here, choosing to put herself through all this again by coming and listening to this awful man?

Shepherd was still holding forth. 'Let's not forget her young female servant, who induced her own child so it would arrive early, emerging into this early Christian world in her eighth month. She did this so she could be sure to join with her mistress, both to become martyrs to their beliefs; both to send us all a clear message!'

Stevie was rapt, 'Yes,' she shouted internally. 'This man actually understands. Finally Perpetua has reached out to me within this group, through this man.'

'It was Perpetua and Felicity who sent out a clarion call of clarity that still echoes down the centuries. Their message was that there is a pure faith, one worth standing up for and declaring, a set of beliefs worth dying for. This was not some lifeless thing thrashed out around a committee table by self-serving officials. It was an idea that back then was new, clean, pure! Now I call upon all of you present to recover that idea. We must recapture it and take it out there into this wicked world.'

He paused, theatrically turning his back on them. 'Just out across these waters is Gibraltar or Gibr-al-Tariq, for literally it means the rock of Tariq. This Tariq who gave it his name was Jabal Tariq, a Berber general. Five hundred years after the martyrdom of these young mothers, he landed a force upon Gibraltar from where he sought to take control of southern Spain in the name of his Muslim faith. So committed was he to his cause that he burned his ships and declared, "There is nowhere to run away! The sea is behind you, and the enemy is in front of you: There is nothing for you, by God, except only sincerity and patience."

'We're here so many centuries later and our goal is to reverse his mission. Metaphorically I have brought you here and together we have burnt your boats. You are my disciples. You each have a group that you must lead out into this continent. The sea is over there. Put it at your backs and face south. Take our message out to every corner of this vast continent. Show them the error of their ways, the wrong paths they have been taking. Proudly proclaim the message of Perpetua!

'For it's all in her, and our, name. Perpetua, has the Latin roots, *perpes* – continuous and uninterrupted; *petere* - directed towards. We do know our way. We will be resolute. We are on our way to salvation. Nothing can make us turn from the Word. Don't let anything stand in your way. Your direction is clear - ever southward until we have brought the Light to this Dark Continent!'

# Chapter 30 – *Mumbai, India*

## STAR India Special Report

"Trouble in Kashmir does not often hit the headlines these days, because trouble there is all too common, but perhaps the cause of this latest rioting and these recent deaths is rather more 'hair-raising' than normal.

This is Pete Galloway, reporting for Star India, from Srinagar in Kashmir, a beautiful yet very troubled part of our world. It sits in this glorious valley, and one would be forgiven for imagining that it might be secure here, contained, as it is, neatly between the Himalayas and the Pir Panjal Range.

It is has always proven something of a nexus, literally and figuratively - a crossroads that has often been caught in a crossfire. China lies to its north and west across the Himalayas, and currently holds several disputed areas within Kashmir. Over the Karakoram Range to the north-east is troubled Afghanistan, whose people once controlled the whole of Kashmir. To the west and south lie the two states that believe they should own Kashmir today, these are of course Pakistan and India.

This region was organised into a single state of Jammu and Kashmir while under the management of the British Empire, but this denied its basic realities, its significant regional differences. The area to the east, Ladakh, was always essentially Tibetan and Buddhist in its approach. The more populated central valley had been invaded by the Mughals and later the Afghans; they imposed a Sunni Muslim rule that is still largely its make-up today, though it also contains a strong Hindu minority. To the south of the region Jammu was invaded and annexed in the early 19th century by the Sikhs; today it contains a much more confused mix of Hindus, Muslims and Sikhs.

When the British granted independence to those around this region in 1947, new boundaries were created under its 'Partition' arrangement. It was judged that because three-quarters and more of Kashmir's population was Muslim, that the Maharaja would automatically and immediately opt to join with Pakistan, rather than India. But his initial hesitancy to come to any clear decision led to strife, which first Mountbatten as the outgoing Governor-General and then the UN tried to manage. Since then regular periods of unrest, strife and two formally-declared wars in 1965 and 1999 have left this region's sovereignty even further confused. Today India holds perhaps a half of the area, Pakistan a third and the rest is annexed within China.

The city of Srinagar sits upon the banks of an Indus tributary, the Vyath as it is known locally in Kashmiri. The area here abounds with lakes, perhaps laying foundation to the legend that Kashmir was originally one large lake that was drained by a Hindu sage.

This reporter last visited the city when the city fathers came under huge criticism for a policy of poisoning its stray dogs. With the number of feral dogs being well over 100,000 in a city of only 900,000 human inhabitants perhaps they might just have had a point? It was the rather brusque approach back then that had caused the furore.

Now there has been this latest incident that has brought me back here. The city attracted hundreds of thousands of Muslims to its Eïd celebration, which took place without any trouble. Central to the city's attraction is its Hazratbal Shrine, a beautiful white marble mosque beside the Dal Lake. It is this mosque that houses the Moi-e-Muqqadas relic, said to be a small tuft of the hair of the prophet Mohammed.

This relic is claimed to have been brought to India from the holy city of Medina by a descendant of the prophet. To keep it safe from the invading Mughals it was later sold on to a wealthy Kashmiri. However it was seized by the Mughals and the Kashmiri was imprisoned; later to die in jail. The relic then eventually found its way circuitously back into Kashmir. It was held here by the descendants of one family and only released for display on a small number of occasions each year.

After these Eïd celebrations were over these keepers, called the Nishaandehs, were on the point of receiving the relic back into their safe-keeping. A military style heist was mounted and the raiders actually managed to seize the relic during the fracas. Despite being unarmed, many of the worshippers nearby rushed at the raiders only to be cut down by automatic fire. The final count was horrific, thirty-two dead and more than fifty wounded.

The raiders initially seemed to have been stalled and constrained within a circle of their own vehicles, but in fact they proved to have been waiting for a helicopter to whisk them away, this was duly achieved.

Initially it was believed that the self-sacrifice of the worshippers in overwhelming the circle of vehicles and recapturing the relic had achieved its purpose, the raiders left without taking their prize; or did they?

The glass case containing the hair was broken in the raid and the Nishaandehs now believe some strands of the prophet's hair may have been lost or stolen. They cannot be sure as no empirical measurement of the hair has ever been permitted to be undertaken. However they insist that their familiarity with the relic does mean that their impression that it is depleted should be taken extremely seriously.

Given the fanatical desire to acquire such religious relics, did these masked raiders get what they came for after all? Local law enforcers have thoroughly examined the abandoned vehicles without finding any clues; they are still trying to identify the helicopter that was involved. The raiders were clad entirely in black and wore masks; no race or nationality could be discerned from the observations of the survivors. The authorities are checking all routes out of the region, but it appears the thieves made good their escape.

Perhaps this is an open and shut case of "hair today, gone tomorrow"? This was Pete Galloway for Star News, Srinagar, Kashmir.

# Chapter 31 – *Tunis, Tunisia*

Tom couldn't wait any longer and decided the time had come to push his way roughly towards Stevie as the congregation was beginning to break up. It became obvious that the extremely large overall group was made up of several predefined sub-sections, and these were now gathering together and beginning to move off promptly.

From perhaps a dozen metres away and over the heads of the milling crowd Tom called her name. She heard him and turned. A look of surprise flashed across her face to be replaced immediately with a lovely smile. But his shout had also alerted Marsha Davenport who was standing right beside her. She immediately tapped Stevie on the shoulder to get her attention and engaged her in earnest conversation.

Tom had relaxed his thrust through the crowd. Now he had made Stevie aware that he was here he was content to let the situation unfold. He felt confident that she would want to speak with him once the flurry of movement had died down a little.

Marsha turned from Stevie and motioned to some young men who came to her side. She pointed at Tom and three of them started across the crowd towards him. Several others took close order on Stevie who with her group was hustled away off down the hill. As she left Stevie looked back over her shoulder at Tom with a slight look of alarm but she did not stop or attempt to come back towards him.

Tom forced his way through the throng even less politely, speedily closing the gap with the three guys who were coming just as urgently towards him. He saw no particular threat from these smiley Mormon-esque young men. When he reached them the three young men closed up to stop his forward progress. When he tried to push one of them out of the way another took a grip of his arm and swung him around.

Tom protested, 'Look that's my girlfriend over there. I just want to talk with her. I have no argument with you.'

'She doesn't want to see you.'

'You have no basis for saying that. Let go of my arm.'

Brain, who had been watching this unfold with the aid of a little distance, saw that each of the three men had a tattoo on his forehead - just like the gNOS security guards. He still had no idea what the tattoo might mean to suggest, but there were similarly marked individuals right in among this Perpetua group. The connection with BiCogNaIT and gene research was clear. Earlier this Perpetua preacher had also been talking about genes. And there was this Gene Genie operation. What could it all mean? How and why were they linked? He felt the pressure, knowing Sir Joseph would expect him to establish what it was that they were up to.

He circled behind the three guards and stepped in between them unnoticed. A forearm across the windpipe of one, a swift turn and a returning elbow across the nose of the second proved pretty effective. Now he could turn to deal with the one who was manhandling Tom.

Though he had the benefit of surprise with the first two, the original struggle with Tom had drawn attention from their colleagues who were now rapidly making their way to the point of the argument. Brain sized up the third man, all the time aware that a loose line of other guards was forming. Perhaps eight to ten of them were now making a loose muster line to cut Tom and Brain off from Stevie. One or two of them looked quite useful, and he stopped to take stock.

The man holding Tom released him and pushed him into Brain, then stepped backwards to join the muster line. He said, 'Just get the message. She doesn't want to see you.'

Tom had already lost sight of Stevie, and put up no resistance as Brain ushered him away. There was clearly no way through.

Marsha, who was being shepherded away with the rest of the group, manoeuvred herself alongside Stevie and asked, 'Who was that?'

'Tom Carter, my…. I guess you'd say he's my significant other. But he was in South America? How did he come to be here?'

'Did you leave him a message to say where you were going?'

'No, nothing. Perhaps it was research for his book that brought him? I know he was looking into the Phoenicians, Carthaginians, but he never mentioned any plans to come here. A pretty huge coincidence though.'

'You understand why I couldn't let you speak with him. Not now, not when we are so close.'

Stevie was hanging back from the rest of her group. She turned and looked back up the hill. 'No, not really. He wouldn't have changed anything. I could have taken a few moments to explain where I was going and why.'

'Precisely. It's a very delicate moment. We don't need anyone interfering at this stage. There will be plenty of time for you to bring him up to date when we're all safely installed in the village.'

Stevie was still quite evidently unsure.

Marsha leaned in towards her. 'Perpetua chose you. Perpetua needs you.'

Stevie came to a halt and intoned, 'Perpetua chose me. Perpetua needs me.' She stopped looking back, and turned to face Marsha, concentrating on what she was saying to her in a quiet, simple and direct manner. When she had finished speaking they both continued down the hill, Marsha striding on ahead.

Avril slowed and fell back into step beside Stevie. She asked, 'What was all that about?'

Stevie looked at her blankly, 'What?'

'Who was that man back there, the one who called out to you?'

'Oh, nobody significant.'

Brain had led him at a rapid pace away from the scene and seemed to know what he was about, so Tom rushed to keep up, 'Where are we going?'

'Back to their hotel. I didn't see any sign of their luggage on the hill, did you? So they have to go back to their hotel at some stage. With a bit of luck we can catch up with them there.'

Tom had not been thinking straight. He couldn't understand what had just happened back there. Stevie would never walk away from him like that. Would she? Then she had come there without letting him know. She had left no message, now he had just watched her calmly walk away from him. Just what was the goal of that woman who had brought her here? Who was the evangelist who ran this Perpetua mob? And why were they using the name of the very saint who had had such an impact upon Stevie in her childhood?

'You think I might get a chance to talk to Stevie?'

'Look, while you may be here for Stevie, we also need to know just what these various organisations are up to. The whole situation keeps on getting weirder. The old man, Sir Joseph, certainly has a good nose for when something is out of kilter. You must have noticed that those guards who confronted you were from the same team involved with that ape-man business. So we now have another connection between these organisations, but what it is I couldn't even begin to guess!'

'I do need to speak with her though.'

'Relax. Both of our objectives would indicate we need to talk with Stevie. So let's go find her.'

Brain's rapid pace had achieved his objective and they arrived back at the hotel before the others. They had already been there earlier in the day and enquiries had revealed it was block-booked for a convention "Early Christians in North Africa". They had not been able to get access to the organisers or any material on the event; they were advised it was a closed meeting and not for public access.

They did learn however that the delegates were all out of the venue for the day on a social programme. As no sessions were planned within the conference centre, Brain had indulged Tom by allowing him to view some of the Carthaginian ruins, just to add a little colour to their cover story. Lo and behold, in doing so they had caught up with the group anyway.

They slipped into a quiet room off to one side of the reception area that would provide a good view of any arrivals and departures. Stevie's group arrived back a few minutes later, supervised by a group of around half a dozen guards who made a cursory inspection of the lobby and watched as the women collected their keys and went to their rooms.

Marsha called out loudly enough for Brain to hear. 'Please be prompt our coach leaves for the airport in eight minutes. We will have plenty of facilities at the other end so don't be too fussy with your packing.'

Brain watched as the lift that Stevie had taken rose to the eighth floor and then came back to the lobby; clearly her group was all accommodated on the same floor. Helpful!

The guards watched until the last members entered the lift and then promptly left the lobby. Either they were going to patrol outside or they had to go to another hotel and pack for themselves.

Brain waited until the lobby was bustling with other Perpetua groups who must have taken a rather more leisurely pace back to the hotel. While it was at its busiest and most chaotic he hustled Tom over to the hotel's stairwell and led the way up to the eighth floor at a speed that left Tom almost retching as they paused at the fire door giving access to the rooms.

Brain left Tom to catch his breath as he made a quick recce of the floor. A few minutes later he was back and led Tom along the corridor and to a small side room. The room was extremely warm, clearly no aircon was being wasted on the public areas, and the noise coming from the ice makers and vending machines it housed was unpleasant. Its merits were its location directly opposite the lifts, a small glass panel provided a good view across the corridor enabling them to monitor any comings and goings.

Sure enough, in a few minutes Stevie appeared with another young woman and pressed the button to descend.

Tom rushed out of the room, 'Stevie. It's me!'

She turned and made no effort to avoid his hug, but was not particularly demonstrative in return.

He kissed her cheek and asked, 'What are you doing here? Why didn't you leave me a message to say you were coming? Why did you let those people keep us apart on the hill?'

Stevie said nothing but Avril asked him, 'Look, just who are you?'

'Hasn't Stevie explained? I'm Tom!'

'Yes, I can see you're a guy, but what have you done to make Stevie like this? She was fine before you shouted at her back there on the hill.'

'I don't understand what's going on. Just who are you?'

'I'm Stevie's friend, Avril.'

'She's never mentioned an Avril.'

'Well snap-jinks! She's never mentioned a Tom to me either!'

Stevie looked confused. 'Perpetua needs me.'

Tom placed his hands on her shoulders. 'Look at me, Stevie. What have they done to you? Four weeks ago Perpetua was just a horrible incident in your past, something you had enormous difficulty telling me about. Telling me was one of our turning points; it marked a new level of commitment between us.

Don't you remember how we celebrated after we had both confessed our innermost secrets, my brother, your vision and its aftermath?'

Stevie's eyes conveyed nothing at all to him. No recognition, no sign that she was hearing what he was saying.

He allowed Avril to brush off his arms.

She said. 'Look, it's clear she doesn't want to talk about it. I don't know who you are, but I accept you do know Stevie. If you really care for her then let her pursue this. We're both going to a retreat in Morocco, something we want more than anything else in our lives at the moment. We've planned it for weeks and we're almost there.'

Tom couldn't believe the lack of expression in Stevie's eyes. Usually they were flashing all over the place. When her mind was active it always showed in her lively eyes. Even at peace they were a huge part of her appeal, bright and sensuous they showed her extreme intellect. Now she was like a husk. What could have changed her in just a few weeks? Or, was it something he'd done that had prompted this reaction?

The lift arrived and Avril helped Stevie to take her case into the cabin. Tom was stunned by Stevie's stupor. He just stood and watched them.

Brain called as the doors were closing, 'Where in Morocco?'

Avril didn't have time to consider whether she should answer. She replied without thinking, 'Tamegroute.'

# Chapter 32 - *London, UK*

The Foreign Secretary called the meeting to order. She took her seat quickly to avoid any nonsense of the men making a point of waiting for her to sit first. But she also rushed so that she could observe as coffee cups were discarded and those assembled slowly took their seats around the large table.

She was amused to see the pecking order automatically establish itself. She had deliberately not set up a seating plan and watched as this diverse group warily eyed each other as they selected what they judged to be their appropriate location at the table. If she had in fact chosen to set a plan then there would only have been two notable differences from the way things ended up. She watched this, not sure if the person who had overreached his status had done this wittingly, or if the other had deliberately demoted himself in some act of modesty - or more likely artfulness.

She started the meeting by getting straight to the point. 'So, my colleague across at the Home Office has asked that we consider who is behind this current wave of hate crimes? Does anyone have any thoughts, or better still, any real information?'

The collection of individuals around the table stayed silent. She noted one or two deliberately trying to avoid her eye in case they were picked out for comment.

'OK, I see. No-one has anything to say.' She smiled around the room giving everyone the opportunity to disagree. Seeing no takers she turned to the Professor. 'Professor Groves, can you perhaps update us all on the sequence of events?'

'Certainly.' The Professor shuffled his notes. 'The first isolated incidents started a month or so ago. They were so thinly spread, so varied and, frankly, so unusual in their nature, that they did not show up on the normal crime reports or statistics as being significant. We have therefore had to backtrack through the records to identify the earliest events. From this backtracking our belief now is that the very first of the sequence was an anti-Semitic attack in Bath.'

Flicking through the notes issued for the meeting, Sir Joseph interrupted, 'I believe you mean this attack on a Jewish businessman.'

'I take your point. Semites include all the supposed descendants of Noah's son, Seth. Strictly the term covers all Jews, Arabs, Assyrians, Phoenicians and Babylonians.'

Sir Joseph mumbled, but loudly enough for most to hear. 'I've not noticed too many Phoenicians or Babylonians walking down Milsom Street of late.'

The Foreign Secretary smiled at the exchange. 'Well, I guess the Rastafarians would have seen off any Babylonians that were foolish enough to turn up. Please, let's not get sidetracked. Professor.'

'So chronologically we have this then as our first instance. BANES, Bath and North East Somerset, is not somewhere you would expect this sort of trouble. The emergency planning for the area focuses upon its several civil and military airfields, and the maintenance of the strategic links of the M4 and the busy rail service that pass through it.

'In the 2001 census the authority had a population of just under 170,000. Fewer than 5,000, that's less than 3%, were from the BOME groups - black and other minority ethnics. I could find no stats on the Jewish population per se. But what I think this stat shows is that Bath is no hot bed of ethnic diversity. The only record of a synagogue that I could find, suggests it was flooded back in 1894 and became derelict by 1911. So I can only guess that their numbers in Bath must be rather limited.'

Sir Joseph commented. 'Very interesting as all this is, I do trust that we do not need to go into this much detail on each of the incidents.'

The Professor raised his arms and then let them drop at his side. 'Of course not, but this was the very first, so we need to see what started it and whether it might connect with the others in some manner. That's why I thought the background important.'

The Foreign Secretary was still enjoying this. She banged her fist on the table and with a broad smile she said, 'Objection overruled. Please continue Professor.'

He nodded his appreciation to her. 'So nothing about the locality would suggest a catalyst for this attack. The victim was not a particularly devout Jew and was not in any denomination that meant his attire would stamp him out on the street as being Jewish. This was no music-hall moneylender, there was no funny hat or hair-do, he was not even particularly well off. He is a middle manager, a retail district manager with a London-based operation.

'His attacker was a near neighbour who lived four doors away on a quiet, what I guess you would call middle-class, housing estate. He was not a known racist, no shaven-haired hoodie. To all intents and purposes he was a responsible community member with a wife and two young children. The two men had no particular connection other than the proximity of their homes. Their wives and children were certainly aware of each other from their children's school and probably through local shopping and entertainment. No history of dispute between them had been recorded; others in the neighbourhood thought them all to be mild-mannered, hard-working individuals.'

'So what happened?'

'It was a frenzied attack without any seeming provocation. The victim arrived back from work at his normal time and as he got out of his car he was attacked with a golf club. The attacker was shouting racial abuse as he repeatedly slammed the golf club at his defenceless victim. Fortunately the victim managed to get the car door between them to deflect a number of the blows. The attacker then moved on to systematically smash the car's windows and lights; apparently he was pretty determined and didn't miss a single panel. Muttering increasingly foul racial slurs, he walked back to his own home and once there carried on as if nothing had happened. It was all over in a few minutes. The victim received a number of nasty blows; all photographed and recorded later at the hospital. Most seriously he had two broken ribs and six broken fingers from warding off the attack. He was lucky.'

Sir Joseph muttered. 'If that's lucky, I'd hate to know what would have happened if he had been truly unfortunate?'

The Foreign Secretary wanted to move on. 'What did the investigation of the attack come up with?'

'The attacker has no memory of mounting the attack. He certainly cannot justify his actions. He can think of no reason why he did what he did. He's full of remorse, and completely confused.'

'Drugs? A tumour?'

'No, nothing could be found to justify this. Nothing at all.'

'So what came next?'

'It would appear that the next event was further down the M4, across the Severn Crossing in Newport. Seductively nearby, but actually it's in a whole other country of course. This one was even more bizarre. A quiet 62 year old man, English, but who had lived in South Wales for almost forty years, had brought up his children in Wales. He suddenly launched an attack on a Welsh female neighbour. This too appeared to be racially motivated. He came across as being vehemently anti-Wales and the Welsh, yet all his adult life had been wittingly spent among the targets for this abuse.'

The Foreign Secretary asked, 'What was the nature of this attack? Sexually motivated?'

'No. It was an extremely brutal and systematic beating. Unfortunately the poor woman was unable to find a refuge. Though she is very unwell, she would not press charges. This too would have fallen outside our consideration without the backtracking.'

She pushed him on. 'Cycle forward a little and catch us up with the more highly publicised events that followed on from these.'

'These first two attacks and one or two others were exceptional in that they did not spark any reaction or retribution. Later ones took place in areas where the racial tension was already highly strung, and at the point of snapping. With these the local police generally only became involved when a full scale riot was already in place.

'With two communities at each other's throats they were highly likely to be recorded as incidents of civil unrest and those would not appear within our stats either. Of course very few of those involved were prepared to talk about what instigated them in the first place, or to talk at all. However good police work and intelligence traced several of the incidents back to an originating event that was not too dissimilar to our first two. They were each carried out by an unlikely initial protagonist who attacked a single victim; no sort of previous history, no apparent provocation to the act. The troubled locale and its inherent problems were triggered by the initial event and a major incident blossomed from there.'

Sir Joseph commented. 'I guess it was like France a few years back when localities competed to see who could burn the most cars.'

'No, that's the strange thing. All these inciting incidents are clearly individual one-on-one crimes against the person. It's just in the ensuing chaos that some collateral damage has taken place in terms of vehicles or properties being attacked or damaged.'

The Foreign Secretary flicked through a file before her. 'Yes. In looking at your analysis there are not many of these inciting incidents where a weapon was used - the golf club, a few knives, but no guns.'

'The attacks were all very personal, almost primeval in their ferocity. Few of the perpetrators are prior criminals. I would guess therefore they did not own and probably had no obvious means of obtaining a weapon. Nothing was premeditated. They suddenly attacked, the victims were doubly unfortunate if some weapon happened to be close at hand. Of course the subsequent reprisals were more likely to involve those more familiar with weapons and their use.'

She queried, 'But though the antagonists appear to have been racially motivated there is no significant racial dimension within the attackers or the attacked?'

'That's just one more strange aspect of this outbreak. The stats don't show any particular race within the ranks of the victim or the protagonist. And the incidents are too widespread to be propagated by an air or water-borne chemical or any form of nerve agent. Just one of the many theories proposed and discarded.

'The attackers involved have no connection - personally, geographically, commercially, politically or racially in terms of them or their victims. We have even had all their work and home PCs analysed to see if they visited the same websites or chat rooms. But there is absolutely no correlation.'

'Professor, thank you so much for your detailed overview. It very successfully highlights why my honourable colleague asked us to investigate. It's clear that there is much that we just don't know and as yet cannot understand. Can anyone sprinkle any insight, any bright ideas?'

She was amused to see so many usually commanding, not to say egotistical, individuals trying hard to make themselves look invisible.

'So, Sir Joseph, I'm afraid it's over to you. We need your team to go over these reports and look for any sort of connection, any catalyst for these attacks. Currently we have twenty-six dead, hundreds injured and the courts are backed up with the cases. We are desperately in need of your usual insightfulness to get us somewhere with this.'

He mumbled, 'To get the press off your back, more likely.'

She caught the comment and smiled at him. 'Yes, that too. What else do you think you are for? Last time I looked it was the Intelligence Service, and I choose to put the accent on the word service. A speedy service with a smile would be good.'

# Chapter 33 - *Marrakech, Morocco*

The smiles on the faces of the Royal Air Maroc crew were all well and good, but Tom and Brain could not shake the concern that they had arrived in Morocco a whole day after the Perpetua team had reached there. Playing catch up they had eventually found a very cheap deal that had taken them from the Carthage-Tunis airport directly to Marrakech.

At the airport it took an inordinate amount of time trying to arrange for the hire of a 4x4. When that proved impossible they had to settle on a sturdy looking van for the drive to Tamegroute. The rental agency map of the area they had been supplied with proved pretty vague; but the purchased service station maps were no more helpful. The drive ahead was evidently going to be an arduous one and, despite Tom's frustration, Brain made sure they paused and took time to stock up with water and supplies in Marrakech.

Brain made a series of phone calls and arranged a rendezvous with someone called Pierre. He explained Pierre had been an officer in the French Foreign Legion. They met with him in a dubious and scruffy café where Tom felt they stuck out like sore thumbs among the other patrons; it was the sort of place he would never have considered entering alone. Pierre sat with an unlit cigar hanging from his lips. It was clear that, whatever he might once have been, he was now securely installed within the local rackets and the criminal fraternity in Morocco.

Brain surprised Tom when he surreptitiously flashed Pierre a roll of US dollars to demonstrate he could pay for the weapons and ammunition he had been negotiating to buy. He showed the money but insisted that they needed to see the weapons first. A surly assistant appeared from the rear of the café and Brain drove them all across to a nearby building in a dark quarter of the town. After a thorough inspection of the weapons, Brain handed over much of the roll of cash.

Once he had secured the deal and the money, the Frenchman became much more talkative and helpful; clearly this had been an unexpected windfall for him. He provided them with a good map and some detailed advice on the best route to take. Following his advice they left Marrakech and drove up through the Atlas Mountains towards the city of Ouarzazate.

Tom's hastily purchased guidebook described this destination city as the gateway to the Sahara. Tom was controlling his frustration by reading out titbits aloud from the book while they trundled along. Apparently the city had been a small crossing point for traders to pass from the south to the northern coastal areas. It was forced to expand when selected as a military garrison town during the French colonial period.

The city's most famous son, T'hami El Glaoui, had clearly led a very colourful life. To Tom this was all beginning to sound a wee bit as if their destination was somewhere close to the edge of the known universe - until he read that it was home to the Atlas Studios. These studios and Ouarzazate had provided the setting for a number of movies including Lawrence of Arabia, Cleopatra and, somewhat more recently, Gladiator.

They had booked ahead and secured rooms at the Vallée Drâa hotel in Zagora; this was the nearest sizeable place to Tamegroute itself. As they had no idea what they would be walking into they decided to make an approach cautiously based from there, rather than barrel straight in. Brain had not used their own names for the booking; from one of his many 'poacher's pockets' he had instead produced a credit card issued to one of his cover identities. Tom was no longer surprised by anything that this enterprising man might do and so went along with the flow. Anything that got him back to Stevie; he desperately needed to solve the mystery of her journey and particularly her change in attitude.

Tom read from his book that Zagora and made a note to have his picture taken in front of the famous Timbuktu road sign before he tucked the book away and drifted off to sleep while Brain battled the way on to the hotel; at last in a blessed silence.

The road block was manned by children; Tom calculated that if the ages of all three 'soldiers' were added together it would probably barely reach forty. But Brain quickly warned Tom not to underestimate them; they and their HK45s clearly meant business.

Brain admitted to being confused by their weapons of choice, for these were American weapons. He would have thought it far more likely for them to have been equipped with the world's more readily-available and omnipresent Kalashnikovs. More confusing too, these American weapons of theirs were in pristine condition. He would have expected these boy soldiers to be carrying cast-offs that had seen generations of use and abuse. Where had they come from? Did it have something to do with the American organisations they had pursued here?

They were trying to drive to Tamegroute from Zagora and this was the second route that they had used; the first had yielded the same outcome. The boys at the roadblock made clear they were not interested in conversation, or perhaps their English was too poor. Certainly they were not prepared to give any explanation for not allowing them to pass. But then their weapons did all their talking for them.

They knew the village of Tamegroute was quite small. Tom's guidebook listed a few mosques and mentioned a famous library containing old illuminated Qur'ans and even a 500-year old translation of Pythagoras into Arabic.

Apparently Tamegroute did have a thriving cooperative specialising in making green and brown pottery; but it boasted no hotel, and nothing by way of eating out or evening entertainment.

So what precisely was Stevie doing there? Where could she be staying? Why would some evangelical Christian movement be in such a godforsaken place? He smiled on realising his thoughts were rather appropriate. As that evangelist had said in Tunis, God had been forsaken here for Allah.

On reaching Zagora they could already appreciate that they were on the edge of the desert. The Draa Valley spread ahead of them to a wall of mountains set right out at the distant horizon. From the map they knew it must be the Anti-Atlas range which cocooned the valley in a scoop stretching around for more than 270 degrees.

The one notable breach in this wall of mountains was located straight ahead, pointing south east directly out into the Sahara. If they tried to get around the roadblocks by passing around the range to come back through that distant route it might take all the 52 days advertised back on that Timbuktu poster. They surmised that they would probably meet a similar road blockade on that approach too.

They established that there were only two roads along the floor of the valley heading in the right direction and they had now tried both of them without success. To their left was a large amount of sand drawn up into impressive dunes with no sign of any traffic having ever crossed them; certainly their old van would not make any progress across that terrain. Brain concluded their only hope was to wait for night and trust they could sneak around the boys through the palms and other greenery.

He reckoned they had a few hours to kill before sundown and decided they should go back to the hotel and prepare properly for the 'incursion', as he insisted on calling it. Tom used the opportunity to ask around in the hotel, to see if he could find out anything about the roadblock. He eventually found a porter who explained there had been an outbreak of some disease reported over there. The porter went on to say that there were constant problems with people coming up from the south. Usually it was AIDS that they brought with them, but it was rumoured that this time it had been something more serious.

Tom was now really concerned for Stevie. What the hell was she doing putting herself at risk like this? Surely this was not some misguided missionary zeal in which she had become involved? He just hoped she had taken precautions against whatever this disease might be.

They also established, in talking to the porter, that the boys' roadblocks were in fact sited about a hundred metres up the road from a somewhat more official UNHCR version. He explained that apparently a local gangster, or warlord, had negotiated with the UN for some lucrative payments and equipment in return for his men maintaining the roadblocks. The gangster was vigilant as part of his posturing to show who was really in charge around there.

They could discover nothing more; even Brain's calls to the UK and enquiries being made from that end could establish nothing about the reported outbreak of disease.

Brain insisted they both take a nap and that Tom should change into dark clothing. Later, when they were in the hotel car park ready to leave he blackened up their faces, the rear of their necks and their hands. He instructed Tom to empty his pockets and remove his watch and placed the items under the passenger floor carpet of the van.

They drove back towards Tamegroute and pulled over to the side of the road beneath an overhanging tree. They were still some fifteen hundred metres from the roadblock, they waited for their moment.

Tom remembered an early role-playing computer game his parents gave him to use on a vintage Sinclair ZX81. After he had fiddled with the cassette recorder's volume for what felt like hours he finally managed to load the programme and the software started to work. The early computer's memory was so tiny that there were constant interruptions as it loaded each subsequent phase of the routine. During these many pauses the screen always displayed the text 'Time Passed'. This was precisely what they were doing now, parked up under the large tree, allowing time to pass until night fell.

When it did it was with no discernible dusk or sunset; the sun quickly dropped below the mountains and it was dark. The contrast in temperatures, either side of this nightfall, made Tom feel chilly.

They made their move. He kept in mind those hard-looking little lads holding weapons. They may have looked far too big for them, yet the combination was still deadly. What if there were others patrolling the areas either side of the roadblocks? But he knew Brain was well-trained for precisely these sorts of situations. He would follow his lead very closely, very accurately and extremely quietly.

Why and how did he keep getting himself into these situations? There he was, an oceanographer operating so many miles from the sea, being put at risk yet again by that wily old spymaster. At least this time he could reassure himself that he was there for Stevie.

Brain's pace was slow and painstaking until he judged they had inched beyond both the boys' and also the UN roadblocks. After this he strode out more purposefully and less carefully. About ten minutes into this faster section of the journey they came to a long high fence. It looked new and it was dominantly blocking the route.

Brain though was completely unperturbed and followed it around southward, away from the roads, all the time looking for a weak point where they might penetrate it. Then unexpectedly the barrier petered out. The fence was obviously still under construction; the builders must have started with the section spanning the two roads, but a few hundred metres brought them to the end of the constructed wall.

Tom whispered, 'Suppose they have do have some terrible contagion within the village. Are we being smart by breaking in like this?'

'Look, the disease I'm interested in is the sudden flurry of related organisations that are clearly up to something. They're like some new plague; coming here, dragging along your girlfriend. It's a rash that Sir Joseph insists we scratch until something drops off and tells us what this is all about. Anyway you're the scientist, digging into things all the time. Surely you want to know what they're up to here.'

Pressing on they crossed a field grown tall with something or other. It was odd to see this crop, whatever it might be, prospering right beside this desert landscape. Previously the local vegetation had all been pretty sparse; the soil was clearly very rocky where it wasn't just pure sand. But this field was startlingly vibrant, verdant and just too organised in comparison to its surroundings; definitely it was out of the ordinary here.

As they emerged from the crops at the edge of the field, Brain motioned to Tom to drop to the floor and stay still while he edged forward on hands and knees to a small berm; it was perhaps some sort of irrigation mound; he wanted to see what might be up ahead. After a few moments he motioned Tom to join him and passed him a pair of night vision binoculars. Tom accustomed himself to the strange green world they displayed as he adjusted them to his eyes.

'My God! The buildings look exactly the same, not at all like anything I've seen here locally. Look, they have exactly the same set of buildings arranged around a few large central communal buildings. It feels like it's some sort of UFO that took off and followed me to land all the way over here.'

'What are you talking about?'

'It looks to be precisely the same set-up as that Tyndale place I saw just a few weeks ago. That one was located on the Isla del Sol right in the middle of Lake Titicaca – up at high altitude in Bolivia!'

# Chapter 34 - *Chiang Mai, Thailand*

Will Patterson cursed Dom Berkeley as he took each of the 309 steps up the Naga stairs to the monument. It wasn't just the heat and the humidity, Will was reasonably fit and could take that in his stride. It was the wild goose chase that he was convinced this particular task represented.

Dom was obviously insecure in his role as leader, he used every opportunity to try to put Will down. Will could not understand it. Dom was the boss-man and Will and the others truly respected that fact. They each did their jobs and this should have made Dom feel more secure, but somehow it never did. Their individual successes seemed more to wound him, rather than build him up. Since the debacle in Hebron Dom was also less keen to deal with the field activity himself. Will would love to have found out precisely what had happened over there. He suspected that Dom had screwed up somehow.

Doi Suthep rose almost 1,700 metres above the nearby city and it had taken an hour from the hotel to follow the road through heavy traffic just to reach the foot of these stairs. He could have paid the additional 20 baht to ride the funicular but he needed to assess the major route personally, both in and out of the site. Halfway up he realised that he could have ridden the funicular up and then completed his survey on the way down but now it was too late - quick in and out was the objective.

Because he had not managed the whole process himself he had a nagging feeling of doubt about the exercise; after all Dom had organised it. Will thought that Dom appeared to be increasingly accident-prone; being followed into the South American retreat had been just one of the more recent issues. Perhaps he was losing it? Maybe it was time for Will to step up?

This target was in a pretty remote location with only one route out. What if Dom had not thought it through properly, or worse, what if he had deliberately set him up?

One of Will's concerns was the proximity of a major Thai royal residence where the ruling family escaped the heat, noise and pollution of the current capital. But he had asked around and established that no royal was currently in residence. Security in the area would therefore hopefully be light, any response likely to be slow and pretty cursory.

This extremely ornate temple on the mountain top was one of the most important to the Thais, forming the focus for huge pilgrimages. But today at this high point of the rainy season, the humidity feeling close to 100%, the temperature certainly at a sapping 36 degrees C, the visitor numbers were understandably light.

Surely this was going to be a complete waste of time? The legend that brought him here told of a monk named Sumanathera who in the 14th century had a dream that led him to Pang Cha to look for a relic, rather too fortuitously for Will's taste, he had duly found it. He claimed that this was the shoulder bone of the Lord Buddha. Will's first question was, if it was such a significant item, why was it just left hanging around there for him to find? Pretty implausible stuff!

Then this monk claimed that it had magical powers, it could glow or vanish and it could transport itself. He took it to a King who had been delighted, celebrating its discovery with a ceremony and offerings, but it was found to exhibit none of its claimed special powers. After this the King, quite understandably, told the monk what he might do with his relic. Will fully appreciated the King's reaction. If it had been his call then he would have said that the monk could keep it too.

Will shrugged himself out of his boots; because entering the holy place required this. He regretted that he would have to lose them. They were well worn in and he was not looking forward to breaking in the next pair over the coming weeks. Why hadn't he bought a cheap and disposable pair of trainers and worn them up here? Local markets could have provided him with anything he might want in the way of dodgy 'branded' footwear. That was the problem with this heist, lack of proper planning.

It was all rushed after Dom had stupidly mentioned his niece's trip here and related the story of the relic to Shepherd. Now there Will was with a cockamamie plan that was all a little too reliant upon surprise.

He trusted that he would be the one who sprang the surprise and not be on the receiving end of one himself. Dom had not been at all impressed when Will had reminded him of the six Ps in their last telephone call.

'Proper planning prevents piss poor performance,' Will had said.

Dom had replied angrily, 'If you can't handle a bunch of meek monks armed only with robes and sandals then you're no part of my team! Just do it!'

Will blamed it all on another king who had not been able to leave well enough alone. This King had heard of the monk's relic and asked him to bring it north. When this second King acquired it, it apparently did show some magical powers and better still it apparently cloned itself. One part remained exactly as it was and the second was created slightly smaller. Yeah, right!

The larger piece was placed in a *chedi* or pagoda, at Wat Suan Dok, while the smaller piece went walkabout. The second relic was placed upon a white elephant. Will was exasperated that no-one was able to explain why they had chosen to do that! The elephant had tromped off through the jungle, tramped up this mountain, trumped three times and then promptly tripped off its mortal coil. The king decided that this must be 'a sign', he ordered that this temple be built here.

Will reflected, 'Surely, no-one can actually believe that this really is a piece of the holy man's body? The monk was clearly one big chancer.' Yet, whatever the truth of it all, here he was dispatched across the world to steal it.

Will climbed, in his bare feet, up the further twelve steps into the inner courtyard. It was dazzling in the sunlight, an unreal place of gilt pagodas, umbrellas, shrines and statues all glistening in this most holy part of the temple. The styles were a bizarre mixture of Thai and Indian designs, the result just a little too bright for Will. Bling bling Buddhism!

As he walked around he recognised a Ganesh, then a replica of the Emerald Buddha. So much was crammed into this quite small area that it was an assault on the eye. He thought it sad that much of this gilt-work was 1990s reproduction, little of it actually clad in the original noble metals. His guidebook indicated that any gold used in these parts had been carried off by the Burmese many years back. Still he guessed if this gilt had been real then he would not have been the only one up there planning a heist.

Will knew the government in Thailand was an extremely ephemeral entity. It was around eighty years since Thailand had wrested control from the old Siam in a coup d'état. Siam had always been a strong absolute monarchy. Notably it had been one of the few south-east Asian states that had proved powerful and diplomatically skilled enough to avoid being colonised by avaricious European nations.

Yet in less than a century the nation, now called Thailand, had recorded more than a score of dissolutions and prime ministerial resignations, and become victim to a dozen coups d'état and people's uprisings. Will felt that there must be something fundamentally wrong with this nation; a country that on the face of it was full of apparently gentle, pleasant and very smiley people and yet it was so politically erratic.

Another contradiction against this topsy-turvy political backdrop was that King Bhumibol Adulyadej had been on the throne for over sixty years clocking up the longest reign in the world. Will assumed that his palaces and throne must have been far removed from the deep-rooted corruption that enveloped his subjects and particularly his politicians and armed forces.

There he was, standing before the main copper-covered *chedi* where the relic was said to be stored. It was a monk of dubious motivations who had discovered and cloned it originally, Will thought it only fitting that another monk was about to steal it from the Wat, or temple.

Will was aware that the monkhood in Thailand was as flawed as every other part of its society. It was their custom that at some stage every boy should spend time serving as a monk, in a sort of religious national service. Evidently still others took up the saffron robes merely to escape justice. This resulted in the monkhood becoming a repository of all types of dodgy individuals, few of them saw it as part of the job description to forsake any temptations.

Dom had made arrangements with just such a monk and Will was waiting to be approached by the crooked cleric. He had seen enough of them moving about on this square inner sanctum, had watched them all carefully, but was completely taken aback when the monk who approached him looked no more than ten years old.

The lad came straight up to him. Having recovered from the shock, Will ducked his head and bent at the knees as he had been advised. The boy blessed him and passed him a small piece of paper. Written on it in English were the words 'Follow me'. Will assumed that the real contact was using this boy to keep his own identity secret.

The boy-monk walked him steadily around the main pagoda and along a cloistered area that off to one side bore a complex series of paintings setting out the stages of some sacred tale; Will assumed it was like some Buddhist 'Stations of the Cross'. He was led across to a broad terrace which at its far side had a balustrade providing a panoramic view of the nearby city.

The boy went to a desk at one side of the terrace and reached beneath it to recover a small parcel. Will furtively looked around but nobody was showing any interest at all. He looked at the half a dozen tourists who were taking so much trouble to get their panoramic shots. Will smiled, knowing that most of these shots were destined to remain on their digital camera memory chips, few would make it as far as a PC, probably none of the views would ever get printed in any format.

The boy handed him the parcel and Will was overwhelmed by a sense of detachment from the circumstances. Part of the feeling was his wondering how he could be sure the parcel contained the relic; but he had to accept that it had already been removed from the pagoda, and that this was it. The lad had already disappeared to who knows where. He hesitated but then thought to hell with it. Even if it was the relic who knew whether it ever had any connection to the Buddha anyway?

He recognised his other emotion was one of disappointment. He had come up here steeled for a chase, some degree of hue and cry; but the whole procedure had turned out to be calm and matter of fact. For some reason no-one there was aware that their most holy of relics, from the most holy of shrines, had gone missing. Assuming that the parcel truly did hold the relic and it had any sort of veracity!

It was so uneventful that he could have taken the funicular back or even taken his time down the steps. His planned exit now felt far too melodramatic, but again he shrugged and decided to go with the flow.

He opened his backpack, took out a long coil of thick rope and crossed to a series of bells that he had seen several of the tourists taking turns in sounding. The scaffold that held them was reported to be strong enough for what he planned; he certainly hoped that this was the case.

Right next to a sign telling visitors not to push the bell, he attached his rope to the scaffold with a good knot that he tensioned by putting all his weight into a tug. This was to check that the scaffold showed no signs of give against his pull; he was confident of the knot. He took the other end of the rope and tossed it over the side of the balustrade, quickly rappelling down it to the road far beneath. The few visitors who even noticed him thought that it was some ritual or entertainment and stayed well clear. Only one had time to take a fuzzy picture that was destined to be erased once he got back on the tour bus.

At the base of the rope he ran barefoot across to the road. You couldn't get away from monks here, one had caused the road to be built in the 1930s. He had challenged every local village to each build ten metres of the track. They had responded and built the whole thing in six months.

Will's colleague from Mission was waiting with a hire car, he ran to the vehicle and climbed in. They travelled on down the monk's road, past a large statue of him sat at the bottom of the hill, then rapidly became lost in the Chiang Mai traffic.

Will was relieved it had all gone off so easily, but retained every one of his doubts about the value of this little sideshow. The two Americans' only difficulty was remembering to drive on the left, like the Limeys. Will's fears of Dom having set him up receded as they became buried in the traffic passing around the city's moat and on towards the airport.

# Chapter 35 - *Double-T R, Morocco*

Stevie and the other Anglo Apostles appeared to be stamped out for special favour once they had reached the Tyndale Tamegroute Retreat. That mouthful of a name had rapidly been shortened by those living and working there to become the 'Double-T R'. These favours for the Apostles were evidently bestowed because of their close connection with Marsha, who they came to realise held a very exalted position within this organisation.

They had already learnt much from Marsha of the organisation, and about the seven levels of priesthood, the Perfects that existed within the Perpetua Order. Now they came to appreciate that Marsha herself was a Seven, also termed an Apostle. This was a status that had been conferred on fewer than forty individuals globally. They had also been made aware of a planned maximum of only seventy for this level. Marsha explained this as a clear piece of motivation and indicated that she fully expected each of them to aspire to that status. Her use of the term Anglo Apostles was no joke; it was a goal!

As yet they had not even been admitted into the Perfect status; they were mere acolytes. But they had been told that they were being prepared to leap directly in at the third level. It had never been explained precisely why they were to merit such rapid advancement.

In the first few days they saw that at all formal retreat meetings Marsha sat proudly at the left hand of Samuel Shepherd, the Leader. In these meetings he regularly sought her counsel, constantly involving her in discussions and asking for her input on issues of significance.

To his right, Daniel Lehri was also omnipresent. He was introduced to them as a Canon. This confused Stevie as she had thought she knew by now that the Perpetua hierarchy was made up of the Patriarch, then the Apostles or 7s, Bishops were 6, Deans 5, Prelates 4, and then on down to 3, 2 and 1, the Pastors, Deacons and Perfects.

Marsha explained that a Canon was also a Six. Apparently this term was used only for those who would run the retreats. This Daniel would undertake for Double-T R once it was completed and whenever Shepherd and the other 7s were off elsewhere.

Daniel was a quiet, almost brooding presence and this was not helped by the sinister looking tattoo on his forehead. To Stevie it resembled some sort of hieroglyph and yet it was formed from almost LED like numerals. She found herself trying to decipher it. It looked a little like a squared off £ symbol sitting on top of an E, or was it a reversed 3? Below this, was it an upside down T or a sideways H? She gave up trying to work it out.

Daniel caught her inspection and glared back until she noticed and looked swiftly away. He was clearly a very moody sort of person. She surmised that he was probably impatient for the leader and Marsha to leave and allow him to get on with his job.

On arrival Stevie was delighted to find the twelve Brits had all been assigned to share a dormitory. They were developing a really strong team ethic and spirit that she would have hated to have lost. She could not remember when she had last had such a close coterie of friends; this was something she realised she had always yearned for without ever having been aware of that need within her.

Externally their dormitory looked like something from an old Second World War movie but inside it was well appointed with air-con and all modern conveniences. So modern that, unbeknownst to them, every room had all-round video surveillance, day and night. In fact anything that might be said anywhere in the retreat was being monitored and recorded at the central buildings. The 'Big Brother' television series would have wept for the quality of the monitoring systems; high definition video with silent electronic optics rather than noisy motors driving the tilts and zooms; voice activated audio systems with software to seek out certain keywords that would alert an operator and generate a report.

They soon found that they were all expected to participate in the many combined worship, exercise and meditation sessions which were announced constantly via their networked televisions and computer screens. These were more frequent and certainly much more physically demanding than the Muslim five-times-per-day *Salats*; theirs of course did not involve facing Mecca; instead they had to gather communally in front of the nearest big screen. The timings did not have any logic or regular programme so they had to be ready at any moment to break off from what they were doing to attend the session.

The sessions themselves however did follow a reassuringly consistent format. They always opened with one of the Order's signature multi-image presentations. During these Stevie often looked around and noted that these seemed to calm, almost sedate, most of the others, including Avril. But she herself experienced no such pleasing affect. She wondered if there was something wrong with her that she did not respond like the others.

Following the initial presentation, usually an introduction was made by Samuel, Marsha or Daniel. This short session talked of progress in the construction of the retreat, or presented news from the outside world; though the news shown was of uniformly dire and depressing material. Stevie assumed this was a pretty naked attempt to underline how much better off they all were inside the retreat; she thought this was just a little too trite and obvious but, judging from their conversations, the others lapped it up.

After this short interlude there might then be a fairly strenuous warm-up and series of exercise routines, followed by a cooling-down and a meditation session. Several of those around her found the exercise quite testing, but Stevie, who was fit and supple, looked forward to them.

Generally next came some sort of 'teaching' session from one of the three leaders. They talked of the Truth, the Word, the coming Judgment and of their Salvation; all four words were regularly stressed and Stevie visualised them as very clearly capitalised!

The session was always rounded off with another fast-moving video and audio presentation. Stevie was surprised there was to be an endless supply of these; initially she had thought they would be like television companies' 'ident' segments which would become very rapidly repetitive and annoying. No such thing there; a new one followed each session.

The mass of the general population was working on the construction of the camp and its fence or toiling in the fields. Organised in two shifts, they toiled in the early morning and late evening, presumably to avoid the extreme of the heat at the middle of the day. The Anglo Apostles were thankfully allocated more sedentary tasks and while the rest of the retreat's personnel wore loose Arab clothing they were permitted to stay in western dress. None of them realised this meant they therefore stood out from the others and were thus more easily monitored.

Stevie was advised that she would be working at the main laboratory. On her second day at Double-T R, she finally got to see it. She would be working under the supervision of Hannah, a Sixth, to whom she was introduced by Marsha.

Hannah came across as being aloof and this was not at all what Stevie expected from someone with the lofty status of a Sixth. She had no real basis for this impression apart from having expected her to have been more outgoing, more engaging, more gregarious, and frankly a lot more interesting than she was.

On the first day Marsha and Hannah walked her around the large laboratory where perhaps fifty or more technicians were actively engaged in something or other. Or was it, as Stevie suspected, that they were all being so industrious because Marsha was there? Stevie saw it was a much bigger operation than she had expected out here at the edge of a desert.

Marsha had explained, 'Your work here will be to a large extent what I interviewed you for at Culham. The anti-ageing research is still a major part of our task. We also plan to be pretty active, if not to specialise, in stem cell work at this facility. You will be working alongside a team involved in biogenetics and bio-fuels. Effort will initially be concentrating specifically on providing a benefit for our own community here; Samuel has set us the goal of complete self-sufficiency. But, as Hannah will explain later, in this main laboratory she is also supervising a wide range of research into ethical dysgenics.'

'Sorry?'

Hannah looked pointedly at Marsha to see if she was going to comment. Marsha waved a hand dismissively at her to do so. Hannah exhaled loudly.

Stevie thought that if Hannah was a Sixth then her current behaviour was no particular advertisement for progressing to that level.

Hannah, seemingly reluctantly explained. 'Dysgenics, as a term, was probably first used during the First World War. It described the fact that the fittest young men were being sent to the trenches to die and that this was going to lead to a massive degradation of the gene pool. The old and infirm left behind would be all that was left to carry on the human bloodline. In the 1960s Shockley, one of the inventors of the transistor, also used the term when he complained that the future of mankind was threatened because those with low IQs were having many more children than those with high IQs; thus also leading to a distinct degradation of the gene pool.'

Stevie looked confused. 'Isn't that eugenics?'

Marsha leapt in when she heard the word. 'Certainly not! Look, let's get some terminology shaken down. Eugenics became discredited in Nazi Germany, somewhat unjustly because the Holocaust was not really about eugenics; it was instead the deadly elimination of what was perceived as an inferior yet competitive race. There was no attempt at improving the gene stock, more the elimination of an undesirable strain. The Germans practised eugenics too, but not as much as the Swedes. Even the US and Canada had been much more active than the Germans...'

Hannah interrupted her, 'At the Nuremberg Trials the Nazi defence of their work in eugenics was actually that they had been inspired by the earlier American research.'

Marsha glared at her, and then stepped on ahead on their inspection tour. 'You should know that eugenics was extremely well supported by your Winston Churchill, by George Bernard Shaw, by Alexander Graham Bell. All great people, each of them appreciated that the future needed us to look closely at just how we might improve humankind.

'And now it's becoming urgent. In the last twenty years the world population has increased by over a third. Staggeringly, it's now racing up towards seven billion. When I was a child, and I'm by no means ancient, it was only four billion! The resources to cope are simply not there. And how many of these extra billions do you think are likely to make any contribution like say an Einstein, or a Pasteur, or Descartes, or Leonardo?'

Stevie disagreed. 'Surely that's exactly what we have to hope - that every generation will throw up its share of great people who can lead us forward?'

Marsha snapped at this. 'Hope is not nearly enough. How can great people be heard above the clamour and demands made by this huge over-population? A huge population that's in a steep decline, based upon any measure of intelligence or physical capability that you might like to apply. We allow too many teenage births; the mothers are only half-formed themselves. Now we have selfish women wanting to have children into their late 50s and 60s; when they just won't have the energy for bringing up the child properly, seeing it through. Then there are those of all ages who are so ignorant, throughout pregnancy they smoke and drink no matter what harm they are told that this does to the child.

'Even where nature has already concluded a woman should not become a mother, what do we do? We give IVF treatment, so that they can beat the rap. It doesn't matter what mental problems, disease or disability a woman has, her right to be a mother is currently allowed to take absolute precedence over any objections.'

Stevie was not going to be put off by Marsha's somewhat unusual display of temper. 'So you're suggesting that we should just neuter those who have limited intelligence or undesirable physical attributes?'

Marsha snapped out of her diatribe, realising that she was showing far too much emotion for this subject; but trying to overcome petty prejudices was a constant battle of hers. She calmed down as she explained. 'But it's always been that way. It's always been in our nature to seek out gene diversity, by travelling between communities. Our sense of beauty means that the better physical specimens look for and acquire the more attractive, more capable partners. For hundreds of years we have either stopped or hindered the mentally incompetent and the disabled from procreating; China still does. Many countries still require a blood test before a marriage. In Cyprus they use prenatal screening to reduce thalassaemia on the island. It used to occur in about 1 in 150 births, it has now been almost eradicated altogether.'

Hannah added. 'In my mother's Jewish community, because of our tendency towards inbreeding, we have used the *Dor Yeshorim* programme together with careful matchmaking to fight off a series of diseases that were particularly prevalent within our numbers; Tay-Sachs, Bloom's syndrome, Gaucher, Niemann-Pick, just to mention a few.'

Marsha continued. 'Now at last, with such major advances in gene research we have the scientific knowledge and the tools to tackle conditions like Huntington's and haemophilia. Are you suggesting we shouldn't do this because of an obvious abuse and a historic misunderstanding from the last century?'

Hannah exploded at this comment. 'The Holocaust was an historic misunderstanding! I really don't believe you said that.' She stomped off to her desk in another part of the laboratory.

Stevie was uncomfortable with this subject but felt a need to calm things down and move on. 'Marsha, you know that I believe in and fully support genetic research. I guess it's just that I have some catching up to do, some re-education by looking at this...' Stevie looked after Hannah, '...perhaps a little more dispassionately. So what did you say? It's ethical dysgenics, not eugenics?'

'You have to appreciate that we're not just playing with words. You have to look back and appreciate history in order to go forward. The Holocaust generated decades of emotion that clouded the appreciation of this subject. In fact many more people died in Russia defending their homelands than died in the Holocaust, but we never hear about that. Any sympathy for them was lost behind the hate engendered by the formation of the USSR and its Iron Curtain. Eugenics literally means good or well-born, and surely we would all prefer that for everyone, I guess?'

Stevie was still concerned. 'Of course, but there is a moral dimension too. We don't want this to lead to designer babies - people able to choose the sex, the looks and the capabilities of their children. I'm not sure I believe any of that as being a power for good.'

'We're still a long way from making that possible. We're currently only at the level of steering propensities, making it more or less likely for a characteristic to be present or activated.'

'So what exactly are we doing here?'

'We are providing experimental work based around the findings we have established by comparing the huge database that our IT team has been gathering. They have assembled an amazing number of individual genetic records, from both the living and those dead. In comparing these, and the history of the individuals' lives and achievements, we are pinpointing areas of interest that we can investigate here. Hannah will show you what is necessary later.'

Stevie asked. 'I meant to ask about that. When I used my PC earlier today I had to request web material to be collected, collated and supplied via the server, rather than being able to directly connect out to the Internet? And my email doesn't work externally either?'

Marsha led her off to another part of the laboratory as she replied, 'It's just teething problems here at Double-T R. Give us some time and you'll have everything you need. Let me show you the final leg of the work here.'

They entered a sectioned off part of the laboratory which turned out to be an animal testing and holding facility. On one side a whole series of cages housed mice, rats and other small animals. The opposite side was like a farmyard with a fenced off area containing pigs. The long rear wall had caged primates, and a big set of double doors leading beyond.

Marsha marched along the cages. 'We have a whole series of investigations going on here.' She stopped by one cage and pointed at a rat with what looked like a human ear on its back. 'This for example is quite a simple exercise in growing cartilage that we have copied from others. Human cartilage cells are implanted on a mesh, which is implanted in the rat and cartilage grows to fill the mesh. Then of course a cosmetic surgeon can use it.'

'Does it bother the rat at all?'

Marsha commented. 'No, there are no ill effects. We tend to use the Wistar and Sprague-Dawley strains of rat here. That one is a Wistar; you can see it has a slightly wider head and a shorter tail than the Sprague-Dawley. A female by the size of it, they're usually about a hundred grammes lighter than the male. You see that we use no metal in the cage as this can damage them, and we take care with the bedding so there is no ammonia build-up. It's a complete myth that we hurt them. They are our partners in research; any sign of distress and we would resolve it.'

Stevie was left in little doubt that the solution might be pretty final for the rat. 'What's through those double doors?'

'We'll save that for later.' She turned to look Stevie directly in the eyes. 'Perpetua chose you. Perpetua needs you.'

Stevie relaxed visibly. 'Perpetua chose me. Perpetua needs me.'

Marsha calmly instructed her for a few minutes, and then said, 'For now just settle in and read up on the current projects. You and Hannah must become friends.' Marsha pointed across to Hannah at her desk and used the opportunity to exit the laboratory.


Stevie found Hannah deeply engrossed in something on her screen, giving the distinct impression she did not want to be bothered. But Stevie felt somehow compelled to make friends with her so dismissed her natural reticence and asked, 'How long have you worked with Marsha?'

'I never have. That bloody woman thought I was getting too close to Samuel and so has just had me posted to this retreat.'

'That must have been great. You actually worked with Samuel?'

'Yes, I did. Very closely.' She said this with some feeling. 'I had become part of his inner bishopric, travelling with him and assisting him with his ministry. You cannot appreciate the demands on his time; they are just so incredible.' She became wistful. 'He has so much to do, all over the world. He's such a great man!'

'You sound as if you are English, are you?

'Yes from Guildford in Surrey originally. I was travelling on my gap year when I came across Perpetua and joined up.'

'I thought you said you were Jewish?'

'Half Jewish, from my mother. She was never really committed to Judaism. Dad, an Irishman, was not too religious either. You know, the usual Paddy, no real religious convictions but he would still fight you for them. Back there I just used my Jewishness to wind her up. I think deep down Marsha is like a big stick of rock; open her up and it wouldn't be Brighton written there, it would be Bigotry.'

Stevie was extremely confused. She felt desperate to become friendly with Hannah and yet this was the first sign of any friction or temperament that she had encountered within the Perpetua team; until now everything had been warm and welcoming.

# Chapter 36 - *Double-T R, Morocco*

Stevie and Avril met up after their long working day and were not ready yet to collapse into their beds. They went for a stroll before what they assumed would be the last big-screen session of the evening.

Stevie asked Avril about her visits to the village of Tamegroute. 'It was just how I imagine the Marie Celeste must have looked. Completely empty. It was as if all the villagers had run away a few seconds before I arrived. That was the very worst thing, seeing all their belongings laid out in their homes, as if they were expected back at any minute.'

Stevie asked, 'So everyone in the village was killed by this Ebola thing?'

'As good as. Those who survived are very poorly, still in strict quarantine. We don't hold out much hope for them.'

'How awful it must be for you, working inside the field hospital, watching all that suffering with very little hope of saving them.'

'Nursing care is my training. Life and death are something we learn to confront every day, it would be nice if life was actually an option here. But working in the NHS the most distressing thing I ever dealt with before today was when I was doing a locum at an STD clinic. That was just self-inflicted suffering and embarrassment. These poor people here are something else, their coughs sound so painful and all we can do is to help keep them comfortable. Not that we ourselves are at all comfortable constrained within those hazmat suits, in this heat! I'm not having a bad hair day by the way; it's a bad dose of helmet hair. Joking aside you can't really give any comfort or reassurance when you're tucked away inside a suit.'

'Will these last few survive?'

'It's not looking too hopeful. They think it's been brought up from the Congo.'

Stevie looked surprised. 'Gosh, I was in the Congo only last year, with Tom.'

'He looked nice. He certainly seemed quite taken with you back in Tunis?'

'Yes, I need to follow this thing through here first. It's much more important for now.'

Avril looked curious, 'But what do you hope you can achieve?'

'I have absolutely no idea. I just know I have to be here.'

Avril grabbed her hand. 'I do know what you mean. I feel like I belong right here too. Despite what I was just saying I really am completely at home here. You guys are my family now!'

Stevie gave her a hug then told her a little of the conversations with Marsha and Hannah and how she had been a tad disturbed to see the first signs of any friction, and frankly some downright cussedness on the part of Hannah.

'Well, we're still human and haven't reached Paradise yet.'

Stevie laughed. 'You're right of course. I just hoped it might be different here.'

'Well it's certainly that. While you are locked away in your laboratory I have to travel over to the village. The Ones, the Perfects, who work in the fields are a pretty earthy lot, oversexed if you ask me. I don't think that I've managed a trip in either direction without seeing someone at it. They're just like rabbits among the vegetables.'

'Really? We have the animals in the laboratory that we encourage to breed so that we are self-sufficient in our test subjects but there's been no hanky-panky. Or none that I've spotted.'

Avril explained. 'I asked around while across at the village. Regular sex is pretty much encouraged here and yet they discourage any formal relationships.'

She looked across at a group of fit young men working in the field and giggled, 'Perhaps you're wrong and we are already in Paradise?'

# Chapter 37 - *Double-T R, Morocco*

Tom had been left by himself at the berm for perhaps ten minutes. Brain had left him with the binoculars so he was straining at everything he saw moving inside the camp. But it was all too indistinct; the green vision would have made it difficult to recognise his own mother.

The silence was suddenly broken as an electronic tone sounded and he watched as people began moving off at pace in all directions. Had Brain set off an alarm? Where was he?

He watched and it became evident that it had not been an alarm. It was obviously a prayer time as they all gathered on mats in front of a large screen; but it was too far away for him to see or hear anything from out there. Should he move forward? Brain had been clear that he should wait right there and he did appear to know what he was doing.

He strained to try to see Stevie but almost everyone was in Arab garb so she could have been any or none of them. Eight to ten minutes later and the prayer session was over, most of the individuals moved back indoors.

He had not expected to spot Brain, thought him too expert at his tradecraft for that. But then the night-vision binoculars clearly picked out his body heat as he exited the camp and started to make his way back towards Tom.

Everything appeared to be going off without a hitch until a Jeep emerged from somewhere and seemed to zero in on Brain's position. Four men jumped out and started to fan out in a line to quarter the area. Their choice of direction could not have been made by chance and they looked sure to uncover Brain. They carried large torches and a beam from one momentarily flicked across his binoculars creating a large flare in the sights and in his vision.

He watched helplessly as the torches made their way directly to where Brain had been; but he realised that he wasn't entirely helpless.

Running along the top of the berm as fast as he could, he repeatedly shouted out, 'Over here numpties!' The torches flashed towards him and the four changed direction. They were only about four hundred metres away.

He dropped down the berm and turned into the crops deliberately running against the grain for what felt like a hundred metres at least, meandering and braking down the tall plants. Then abruptly he turned and ran back for what he hoped was about a third of the distance. He then set off down a row, being careful not to disturb the plants; twenty or so paces along this row he stopped. He picked his way carefully between unbroken rows and gently let the plant slip back into the way it had been. He did this again and at ground level reached through to smooth away his footprints. He repeated this for five or six rows, feeling sure they would be upon him at any moment.

Finally he used the moon's position to pick a route directly away from the camp, this time with a little less worry about leaving footprints behind him; now he needed to add distance for he was not sure if the torchlight had revealed his ploy. Hopefully it would be some minutes before they worked out where he had gone?

The terrifying fact was that he heard and saw nothing as he crossed the field. Before he reached the far side he paused to listen. Perhaps they had not bothered to follow him? Perhaps they were circling the crops right now and would be waiting for him to emerge at the other side? He felt huge pressure to move on and get some distance between him and them. But something made him pause just a little longer.

He must have subconsciously picked up some distant noise which gradually became more distinct. Someone was approaching. Whoever it was sounded as if he was just a couple of rows over. He couldn't see a torch. How was someone following him through the thick crops without a light?

He put the night-vision binoculars to his eyes and saw the heat source of his hunter maybe ten or so paces away. Did he have some form of night vision too? He had a clear view of his pursuer's head and shoulders, thankfully he looked quite small but he could make out no sign of binoculars or a night vision device. In fact his hunter was raising his head as if to sniff the air.

The tracker must have detected something and advanced directly towards Tom. As his pursuer pushed through the crops Tom knew it was vital to act decisively. He swung the heavy binoculars overhead using all the momentum that the neck strap could provide and crashed it down onto the head of this pursuer. The hunter crumpled noiselessly and showed no sign of getting back up. There had been such satisfying contact, to Tom the thunk sounded so loud he feared it must attract any other pursuers. He wasted no time in pressing on across the field.

The young humanzee lay unexamined and dead behind Tom, his small skull crushed by the binoculars.

When he reached the edge of the crops Tom cautiously lay on the ground and looked all around from floor level; he saw nothing, no footsteps or heavy breathing.

He rose and sprinted as fast as he could to the nearest trees, not daring to look around or hesitate. If anyone had a video of this he would be humiliated for years to come. He ran lifting his feet high and placing them down squarely, terrified that he would catch a root or a small rut and go crashing to the floor. He must have resembled some dressage horse, though he would have argued more like a rugby winger stepping out of a tackle.

He made it, and now there was all manner of heavy breathing, namely his own. He feared it drowned out any sound that might be made by a pursuer. The one he had coshed in the crops had him worried. Had he really been following by smell alone? . He forced himself to slow his breathing down so he could listen carefully as he scanned the field and the edge of the crops with his binoculars. Nothing.

He made his way back out and around the fence line, giving it a very wide berth. He pressed on back towards the two roadblocks. Thank God for the moon, it was all that gave him any idea of where he was headed. But first he needed to find one of the two roads. He pressed on until he saw the track illuminated like a ribbon by the moonlight.

He was a bag of nerves as he picked his way slowly around past the roadblocks, or at least where he assumed them to be. He dropped to the floor and held his breath as someone appeared ahead, then he exhaled loudly when it proved to be Brain.

Brain asked, 'Where the hell have you been? What took you so long?'

'There's gratitude for you. They would have found you if I'd not diverted them.'

'There would have been four fewer of them to worry about if they had!'

'I've no doubt you would have given a good account of yourself, but it was four on one.'

'Yes, you're right. I guess thanks are in order. Now we need to get out of here before they come looking. There're only two routes, so it won't take them long to work out where we are.'

As they walked back to their vehicle Brain explained, 'The place was clearly a religious community of some sort. From what I could see self-sufficiency and all that sort of tosh is their main aim. You can relax. I don't think that Stevie is in any particular danger from these Holy Joes. It all looked pretty pastoral and polite.

'The good news is we've now joined up all the dots. While they were having their Bible-bashing meeting I was able to take a look around and see that there's a very modern laboratory there.'

'Presumably that's where Stevie will be working?'

'Probably. There was still quite a lot crated up and I saw logos for gNOS, BiCogNaIT and Gene Genie - and now we can add in this Perpetua. They all appear to have some involvement here. I grabbed any documents that I could find – though there wasn't too much of interest.'

'Don't forget we now have to add in two further organisations, Mission and Tyndale.'

'You're right they must be connected in too. Certainly Tyndale is. Much of the documentation I collected has its logo at the top. But I got one hell of a shock when I looked in one of the windows and saw one of those bloody bonobos!'

'A what?'

'It's a long story. And I'd only have to kill you afterwards!'

Relief flooded through Tom when they reached the point where he could see their rented van parked up ahead. It was one very inelegant, dull box-like shape but to him right now it looked like home, parents, and a steaming big slice of sticky toffee pudding all wrapped up in one.

As he reached out for the van door he felt a sharp blow to his neck. He had no idea where it came from, but he couldn't stop himself from falling to the ground. He instinctively put his hand up to his neck and even in the moonlight there was no mistaking that it was covered in blood, his blood.

Everything now seemed to be happening in slow motion. Brain bent over Tom, who tried to speak but could only manage a gurgle.

Brain assessed the wound and looked serious. The ringing in Tom's ears made it difficult to understand what he said.

'I'll level with you. It's a very bad wound. Keep your hand pressing hard here. Look, if I try to get you out of here you'll probably die. Your best bet is to let them take you back to their labs.'

Then Brain was gone, leaving Tom trying to process what he had been told. He attempted to move but he felt so completely, mind-numbedly weary. With what felt like an out-of-body sensation he watched his pursuers arrive and bend to assess his condition. It felt like a lot of time passed, he felt himself slip away from it all.

# BOOK THREE

**Gustave Le Bon**, a French social psychologist, 1895

*'Crowds are never thirsty for truth. They demand illusions…'*

**Jean de la Fontaine**

*'The power of crowds is only to destroy.'*

**Sigmund Freud**

*'A crowd is trusting and easily influenced; it is non-critical… …Whoever wants to influence it*
*doesn´t need to present logical arguments. It is only necessary to paint the most alluring images, to*
*exaggerate and to repeat the same concept several times.'*

**Arthur Schopenhauer**

*'All truth passes through three stages. First, it is ridiculed. Second, it is violently opposed. Third, it is accepted as being self-evident.'*

# Chapter 38 - *Double-T R, Morocco*

Stevie had settled into something of a routine in the laboratory and at Marsha's suggestion was slowly, yet surely, working at developing the beginnings of a reasonable relationship with Hannah.

Yet despite finding some degree of pleasure in her work she found that she was also very confused. After all, she had only agreed to come to North Africa to pursue her interest in Saint Perpetua, but then the organisation, named for the saint, had hurriedly moved her on to Morocco, well away from the site of the saint's martyrdom in Carthage. She had been moved on before she felt she had a proper opportunity to explore where the saint had lived or to experience the location of her martyrdom; Stevie felt she had allowed no chance to let the saint find her, reach out and speak with her. This was what was causing her confusion. She had never been asked about, or agreed to, this side trip.

Still, grudgingly she had to admit that she was enjoying the work that she had been assigned. She felt she was able to make a difference. She was therefore not yet of a mind to do anything about her state of confusion; besides each time it rose to the surface of her consciousness it rapidly became overwhelmed and suppressed by something else from deep within her.

In fact it was these equal and opposite waves of confusion and distraction that were what was really disturbing her. Both sensations appeared to be outside her volition. Just what was happening, she had always prided herself on an extreme self-control?

Marsha had initially been omnipresent at the retreat but had of late become a less frequent visitor to the laboratory. Stevie had to admit to being a tad relieved about this as the more she was learning about Marsha the more complex she appeared to be. Certainly she was a brilliant scientist, but some of her beliefs and principles were proving to be more than a little offbeat to Stevie. Her fear was that the constant exposure to these thoughts might eventually start to change her own. She could feel it happening already. But why was this able to take place, she had always been very independent of thought?

She realised that this was at the root of her concerns. Her previous certainties were being slowly yet surely undermined and eroded there. She was unaware that she was dealing with the programming that the retreat employed rather better than most of the others there. This was in part because Marsha was handling her programming somewhat differently from the others.

Today Stevie was reviewing the results of a long series of animal tests based on using stem cells for gene targeting and repair. If she was perfectly honest she was delighted she was not being asked to be involved in the handling of the animals themselves; she would have hated the possibility that she might be doing them harm. Somehow the pages and screens of data were safe, impersonal, or perhaps she thought that it should be 'im-animal'. She was pleased with this invented term as 'inanimate' certainly didn't get close to covering the thought properly.

The last meeting with Marsha had been one of those occasions when the older woman had exhibited both sides of her character - her insight and, what Stevie had begun to fear might be, her insanity.

Marsha seemed to always be keen to develop Stevie's understanding of the work, and on that occasion she decided to start with a provocative statement.

'There is no such thing as evolution. It's really just changes in our DNA that are created by inaccuracies of cell replication.' Marsha delivered the thought and waited for Stevie's reaction.

Marsha saw that it was clear from Stevie's body language and from her characteristic rapid eye movements that Stevie didn't like the premise at all.

Stevie responded, 'Aren't you looking through the wrong end of the telescope? Surely the host creature's relative success or failure is reflected by the surviving DNA that remains to take the strain forward.'

Marsha was delighted by the comment, though concealed the fact. 'That only works if you assume DNA to have always been there. You need to be aware that there are two distinct forms of cell, eukaryotes and prokaryotes. Eukaryotic cells include protists...' Seeing Stevie's lack of recognition of the term she paused to explain, '... protist is the name given to varieties of algae and protozoa. Eukaryotes are also present in the more complex organisms, from fungus through plants and animals, including us of course.'

'That's pretty comprehensive, so what was the other type that you mentioned?'

'Prokaryotes. It's really a term that covers the cells in two other types of life form, bacteria and archaea. Prokaryotes are much smaller than eukaryotes, in part because they don't have a nucleus. Back to eukaryotes, the word comes from the Greek meaning 'good nut', the origin presumably referring to the fact that it does have a nucleus. But where it gets really interesting for us is when a eukaryotic cell also contains a mitochondrion.'

'Why? Because the mitochondrion contains DNA?'

'Precisely. Why does it and how does it? That's the interesting thing. Let me explain. The mitochondrion is a vital organelle within the cell. I believe you already appreciate that it's essentially the cell's chemical energy plant? It is essential to drive our metabolism. The mitochondrion also controls signalling - the way in which cells communicate with each other, so each individual cell knows of its role within the scheme of things in its organism. It's this signalling that enables it to maintain its integrity, its immunity and to trigger repairs for example. The mitochondrion also has a vital role in cell differentiation which is the way a less specialised cell, like a stem cell, can be altered to fulfil a specific purpose. Plus, as you've been considering, it has a role in ageing and cell death. All of that packed into one little organelle.'

'Organelle?'

'It's just the diminutive form of organ. Just as the major organs are the vital constituent parts of our bodies, a series of a dozen or more different organelles are the vital components of our cells. The mitochondrion is interesting from a DNA perspective. Most of the DNA is in a cell's nucleus, but as you know there is a quite separate genome within the mitochondrion. And the DNA within this genome most resembles that other branch of life, prokaryotes.'

'You said that there were two types of these?'

Marsha smiled, 'That's why it's so good to have you here. You miss absolutely nothing. Yes, there are two, bacteria and archaea; some argue that they shouldn't be lumped together at all. Bacteria and archaea share a major feature though - neither usually contains any organelles. It's amazing that archaea were only classified and recognised as a separate classification as recently as the late 1970s, and yet they add up to around a fifth of the total biomass on earth! It was initially thought that they could only live in extreme environments, like hot springs, salt lakes, polar areas and deep in the sea.'

Stevie had a flash of Tom and his stories of such places. 'Tom told me about when he used a submersible at extreme depths in the Pacific. He said it was amazing to see so much life teeming around what he called a black-smoker, a release from a deep geological rift. He said that the very specialist life forms down there are called thermophiles.'

Marsha grimaced at the use of Tom's name though she wanted to press on with this session. 'Many believe that those very thermophiles are where all life on earth started. Archaea are like that; in their various forms they are able to take nutrition from all manner of sources. Some survive just on sunlight, others from a variety of organic and inorganic compounds. For example they're found in huge quantities amongst plankton and they're present in swamps emitting methane. Some use carbon dioxide from the atmosphere to obtain carbon as their fuel. Still others live in the gut of animals, including us, and feed upon acids.'

'They produce methane?'

'Straight to the point again! As you are aware methane is a major greenhouse gas, representing a fifth of the world's total emissions. Methane has increased by 250 per cent across the last 250 years, from 700 parts per billion to 1,750 ppb. Yet carbon dioxide, despite all the current fuss, has only grown by a third in the same timeframe, rising from 275 to 365 ppb. Methane is also known to have twenty-five times the effect on our temperatures compared with that produced by $CO^2$.'

'So are you saying that controlling these archaea could reduce the greenhouse effect?'

'Wouldn't that be wonderful if it could? But unfortunately methane enters the atmosphere and then breaks down into $CO^2$ and water, and of course plants, animals and we humans need both. Methane is also the constituent of the natural gas that we are currently pretty dependent upon too. It's not just down there below ground for us to pipe to homes and industry. There is a lot of it at the bottom of the sea. It's given off by volcanoes, by hot mud-fields, from dying vegetable matter. It's emitted by swamps and solid-waste landfill sites. And our domesticated cattle break wind at both ends to create around 16% of all the methane out there!'

'If archaea exist that live on a variety of compounds, might there be the chance to find one that would consume rather than emit the greenhouse gases?'

'I have certainly been looking for just that, collecting archaea samples from all over the world. It's not that easy as most are only detectable from their nucleic acids. They are therefore difficult to find and preserve long enough for us to be able to use in the laboratory. We need to be able to make a detailed examination and learn how to manipulate them. We have managed to isolate quite a few though, but we're not in fact seeking to stop global warming with these.'

Stevie thought that this was the brilliant Marsha. Here she was at her very best, able to make complex issues seem straightforward, able to enthral with her evident enthusiasm for her subject. She realised this was quite reminiscent of Tom and his same way with words. She always felt mellow as Marsha covered this sort of material. But then the other Marsha appeared.

'Let's get back to the mitochondrion and how it got its DNA. As I said its genome looks somewhat bacterial in origin. It's therefore a mutation, either an invasion from a bacterium or perhaps it was placed there by design?'

'Surely it must have been evolution?'

Marsha snapped, 'Didn't I start this discussion by saying there is no longer any such thing as evolution? The genes act far too slowly. In fact they try to constrain us and play no part in our development. We have to override them by going forward jerkily by trial and error, essentially by accident. We are no longer governed by this process; if we ever were?'

'Sorry but I don't understand?'

'We were designed.'

'If you mean designed by a creator of course then I fully agree.'

'No, designed by others. I've been working more closely with DNA than anyone has managed before. I have ready and exclusive access to the most significant database of individuals' DNAs. Not just those alive but a huge number taken from our history and prehistory. I have an overview that was never possible before, and as a result I can clearly see the design that is implicit there.'

'Everything about us is remarkable. I agree that we cannot be here by accident.'

'No, now you're not listening to me! There are clear genetic markers, right there within the DNA that were quite evidently put there by a designer. They were there to direct our development of course, but also so that when the time was right, someone could finally interpret them, so that we might realise our purpose. I am beginning to learn what it is that we are intended to become.'

'I don't understand?'

'I'm wasting my time. You aren't listening. Don't you see? I know, I know!'

Stevie had been more than a little disturbed by Marsha's outburst. That was why, today, she was trying to lose herself within her work and not ponder this bizarre declaration any further.

She was not going to be allowed that option, because Marsha came and sought her out. She appeared completely unaware of the effect she had created at their last meeting. In fact she acted as if it had not happened, as if she had nothing for which to apologise. She invited Stevie to stroll around the retreat, mentioning that she believed she thought and spoke best while on the move.

'Today, I thought we should consider those stem cells that you are working with at the moment. Stem cells are completely unspecialized cells. They don't just have the ability to renew themselves but they can also differentiate, emulate and create any other cells to fulfil a range of different functions. It's the loss of our stem cells or at least their reproductive ability that is the most evident cause of ageing.'

Stevie had decided not to comment on their previous meeting and was content to engage in this latest discussion. 'So how and why are they lost?

Marsha nodded to someone who they passed; she was treated like a top celebrity at the retreat. People stopped what they were doing and gawped at her. 'It's the cells themselves that weaken and die with time, and they take us with them!'

'So how are we planning to beat what I would have said was a pretty natural outcome?'

'Today, here, we have arranged a ready access to an endless line of stem cells that we can apply to maintain and repair our bodies.'

'I thought there was some restriction in the use of them?'

'There was a great deal of emotion about the use of embryonic human stem cells, which of course required the use of a human foetus; though you can also acquire stem cells from the umbilical cord that would normally just be discarded at birth.'

They had reached the compound wall, which Stevie noted was getting closer to completion. Deep down she was not at all sure that she was happy about being walled up inside a compound. Marsha turned them back towards the laboratory.

Stevie asked, 'Is that the only source of human stem cells, - a foetus or its waste products?'

'There is another type that can be garnered from a child's milk teeth and then there are also some adult stem cells. There has also been some recent success in converting skin cells.'

Stevie pondered aloud, 'Do all of them, no matter where they are found, behave in precisely the same manner?'

'Well spotted! Adult stem cells have been used for years in bone marrow transplants to treat leukaemia and other bone or blood cancers. These adult stem cells are relatively limited in terms of their 'reach'; they can only create cells that are quite close in function to themselves. It's the embryonic ones that are much better for our purposes because they have no such limitation and can virtually transform and create any sort of cell or tissue.'

'To obtain these we would need to set up some system to harvest umbilical cords?'

'That was the case.' She did her thing of stopping and looking deep into Stevie's eyes; evidently she was trying to reach a decision. Whatever she saw must have reassured her.

Marsha made no secret of the fact that she had high hopes for Stevie, though she was none too specific about what this meant. One effect of this was that Stevie was only lightly controlled. Marsha wanted the young woman to come to the fore of her team without being too altered or manipulated. She had learnt that too much programming tended to limit an individual's creativity and wanted all of Stevie's to be unrestrained; her DNA profile had shown her as very special.

'We have found another way.' She suddenly walked with much more purpose directly back to the laboratory.

'You can appreciate that with unlimited access to stem cells our work can accelerate in so many directions. Many years back I realised that this crunch point would be reached and so I focused on how best to resolve access to a ready supply line.'

They reached the laboratory and Marsha led the way back through the work area to the animal compound. One of the surly guards, of which the retreat had a plentiful supply, unlocked a door that Stevie had yet to penetrate. They both stepped into a compression chamber and the door wheezed closed behind them. Marsha moved forward to a retinal scanner that unlocked the inner door, which she swung wide open.

Inside it looked to Stevie like a Hollywood movie's representation of a cell block. Before her was a large central area with chairs drawn up around a television. More tables and chairs clearly were used for eating or playing cards and board games. On the wall was a dartboard and there was also a table tennis table.

Around this central area, stretching along both sides and double-tiered, was a series of 'cells'. This assumption was further confirmed by their metallic construction, the heavy locks and tiny porthole windows.

What stopped Stevie in her tracks were the 'inmates'. This impression was formed as they were all dressed in the same overalls which reinforced the feeling of this being a jailhouse; there must have been more than a hundred of them.

They looked like small humans but the musky smell clearly said otherwise. A small group walked across to greet Marsha and signed furiously to her. Marsha held a signed conversation with a large female that was clearly, by her body language, the head honcho.

A young male stood within the group assessing Stevie in a way that could only have been described as lustful; his lips were almost dribbling with interest and he kept running a thick tongue across them. He was clearly unhappy with Marsha's response to the female's questions, but at the same time was carefully respectful of her.

Marsha turned and explained, 'This is one of our humanzee colonies. They are a cross between bonobos, that's a variety of chimpanzee, and humans. I developed the strain and have refined it over many years.'

'Are these what sparked off all the fuss in London?'

'Yes, it was one of ours. A silly girl became too close to them and let one escape.'

Stevie fully understood the 'silly girl's' attitude when several 'children' made their way over to her. They reached out to hold her hand, looked up into her eyes with such trust and joy that her heart just melted. She knelt and played with the children as Marsha continued her dispassionate description.

'To all intents and purposes they are human, but we haven't as yet managed to develop their voice boxes. We are only able to get rudimentary noises from them. Though their much expanded brainpower does mean that they can sign very capably, very expressively too. Their thought processes prove to be not so very different from our own.'

Stevie rose and with a 'child' holding each of her hands she walked along the length of the room. She came close to an open 'cell' and made it clear to the adult female inside that she'd like permission to take a look around. The female signed something that Stevie could not understand but also clearly waved her inside.

The 'cell' was furnished like a small apartment. Perhaps it was a little thin on furniture but the walls made up for this with their heavy decoration, displaying an array of artwork and crafts.

Marsha explained, 'They are very creative, if rather *naif*. We have worked hard not to force our culture and imagery upon them so they can follow their own course. For example the videos we show are mostly factual natural history programmes, which they seem to really appreciate. As you can see they do not try to draw photographically. They don't try to capture a perfect representation of what it is they see; they have a far more conceptual approach.'

Stevie said, 'From what I've seen so far, I think their artwork would be readily accepted by any human gallery.' She made a point of thanking the female and showing her appreciation of the room before she left. As they walked further along the 'cellblock' she said, 'This is fantastic. What you have achieved here is remarkable.'

Marsha explained, 'Man and chimpanzee are just a little under 99% the same so far as DNA coding is concerned. In fact we diverged from them only five million years ago. We have one chromosome fewer than apes; it appears that two of theirs have fused into one within our structure. The work done on the genome shows that there was not a sudden and complete split between the two species. We may have mated with each other across a very long period then stopped at some point in our two developments. There are some 14,000 gene sequences that have diverged much more than the others, it's those that I focused upon.'

Stevie realised that she was clearly being challenged to a game of darts, something in which she had never shown any particular skill. A very young male was an extremely accurate player and Stevie was stunned when he chalked up their scores, handling the subtractions speedily and without error.

'Interestingly one of the areas where we are different is in our immune system, the genes that govern cell death. At some stage we mutated these so that our genes do last longer. The Lord gives and he also takes away, and we are more prone to cancer cell growth; and that's at the very heart of the anti-ageing problem.'

The game over, Marsha promptly led them back to the secure exit. Stevie realised as they were leaving that Marsha had done absolutely nothing with the humanzees. She had shown no particular interest in them, other than to respond to the female's signing.

As they came out into the laboratory it finally dawned on Stevie and it felt like a blow to the head. 'Gosh! I must be so slow. So what I assume you are telling me is that these humanzees are your ready stem cell line?'

'Yes. You may have noticed the lasciviousness they exhibit. It seems to be hard-wired into them to be very sexually active so they are quite a lusty production line.'

'Please tell me that you take only the umbilicals?'

Marsha turned to her and intoned, 'Perpetua chose you. Perpetua needs you.'

Stevie replied, 'Perpetua chose me. Perpetua needs me.'

# Chapter 39 - *London, UK*

The chubby TV anchor turned to his female sports presenter. 'Now we welcome Libby to the studio, with all the day's sports news.'

He was of an age that still felt that a female should not be presenting football news. It was not just that they couldn't understand the offside law, it was simply unnatural. Today they even had women commentating on football matches. That could never work for him. It was just plain wrong. His wife would even sit at home during an international and half-way through ask what team was in which colour!

'Libby, I understand that most of today's back pages have gone with the off-the-pitch antics rather than the play itself?'

Of course women had always presented the news, and the less able but pretty and ambitious ones had used weather reporting as a route to fame and fiancés; now they were taking over sport. Fortunately most of the public in the station's focus group interviews and research still preferred a male anchor, someone with 'bottom', with gravitas. The sports presenter would have readily agreed that he had a lot of bottom, but she would not have granted him too much gravitas.

She started to speak and he interrupted her yet again.

'It's all too common at the moment, and not just in sport.'

She gave him a sideways look and paused to check that he was finished. Verbose old sleaze-bag.

'Yes, Connor, it was all so unexpected. Who would have thought that Danny Bright might be a racist? He'd just finished the first half for United and six of the starting line-up had been black players. He'd never shown any problems playing with them before. In fact a team spokesman has pointed out that when they were on the road he always roomed with Cyril Koriche, the Cameroon international. United had worked well as a team; in that first half they were only narrowly denied a goal by the woodwork.

'It was as they got back to the changing room that he is reported to have viciously attacked several of them while shouting dreadful things. It took the rest of the team and several of the training staff to restrain him. He didn't come out for the second half and his team mates were so shaken up that they ended up losing the match. Any hopes of the championship this year have probably receded with this unexpected defeat.

'In Australia, England has just lost the second test by seven wickets...'

Her few minutes of sport concluded, her autocue scrolled to the hand-back line. As usual it was a line that would set her up for the anchor to have a cheap shot back, for him to look good at her expense. So she ignored it. 'That's all for now, more sport in thirty minutes.' She beamed at him, sitting beside her.

He had been ready for his prepared punch-line and as she studied his face the briefest of flickers showed when he realised that she had denied him his daily dig. But experience and professionalism concealed it from his viewers.

'We're joined now by our crime consultant, ex-head of the Flying Squad, Brian Petersham. Brian, just what is going on out there? Vast tracts of Britain have become no-go areas at night, crimes of violence are at an all-time high and it's no longer just about sink estates or turf battles between rival drug suppliers. Apparently law-abiding and reasonable people are suddenly expressing hate, and not just racial hatred. Some of it is just pure and simple hate, allegedly.'

Brian commented, 'This time it's not about a re-jigging of the official statistics either! I don't think that even this government could work out a way to hide a threefold increase in crimes of violence. In the last National Crime Statistics it was boasted that overall crime was down by several percentage points, though albeit there were still 11 million crimes reported annually! They claimed only plastic card crime, vandalism, robbery and drug offences had shown a rise. Figures showed that violence against the person had dropped a percentage point or so.'

Connor stopped his flow, 'What about this recent wave?'

'Let's leave aside sexual violence for this purpose. There are over two million crimes of violence each year, so for us to understand what's happening more thoroughly the police need to grade the incidents they handle. Just as they say on 'Crime Watch' there has been little cause for panic for most of us, until now. You see a little over fifty per cent of all violent incidents reported do not in fact lead to any significant injury being sustained. An individual's risk of being subject to a violent incident in the UK has been only around 3%, though it's a little more for men than women. Nationally last year there were just 17,000 incidents recorded as 'most serious' violence against the person.'

Connor commented, 'I have here the report commissioned for today's Telegraph and it shows there have been approaching 11,000 'most serious' violent incidents where injury has definitely been sustained in just the last ten weeks. My arithmetic has never been that good, but even I can see that would mean more than 50,000 across a year if the incidence of incidents remains where it is.'

Brian nodded, 'That's where my stat of a threefold increase comes from. The fear is that across those ten weeks it has been on a rising trend and not consistent. A colleague plotted a graph for me to show if the trend holds then I daren't tell you where we get to by the end of the year!'

Connor turned to camera, 'So what is being done to get this violence under control? We have the Home Secretary talking to us in twenty minutes time. Do text or email us your questions so that we can raise them during the interview.

'And do take part in our survey by pressing your red button. Today we are asking "Should the Government be putting the bobby back on the beat to combat this wave of violence?" And let's see, currently 79% of you have voted "Yes".'

# Chapter 40 - *Double-T R, Morocco*

The retreat's heavy daily programme of regular group meditation and exercise, overlaid by an ever increasing series of one-on-ones with Marsha, combined with her heavy workload in the laboratory left Stevie with little time to dwell upon Saint Perpetua. She found by the end of the day that she usually just about had the energy to get back to the dormitory before crashing out. She was exhausted both physically and mentally.

Tonight Avril had come back to the dormitory in tears. One of her favourite patients had finally succumbed. It happened just when they were beginning to feel, given so much time had passed, that the young lad must have pulled through the worse phase and be coming out the other side.

In fact between tears she reported that there had been a total of five deaths that day. This meant that the field hospital based in the centre of the original village of Tamegroute was now to be closed. There were no remaining patients from the dreadful outbreak. The village had been utterly wiped out along with all those who had the misfortune to have been attending the festival.

Avril tried to cheer herself up by pointing out that she would no longer have to live in the sweaty bio-hazard suits and that would certainly be a blessing. 'Perhaps I might start to put a bit of weight back on!'

Stevie, in consoling Avril, made a suggestion. 'Look why don't you let me ask Marsha to arrange that you work with me at the laboratory? At least that way we should be able to spend much more time together.'

Avril explained, 'Nice idea, but you're too late. I've already been advised that I've been selected to become part of the Canon's office, one of Daniel Lehri's team.'

'That doesn't sound so good. I always find he's a bit of a cold fish.'

Avril nodded, 'I do know what you mean. I guess it's that he's not very *sympatico*. Marsha may be behind this. It seems to me that she wants to get one of the Anglo Apostles posted into all the various key locations. I think she plans for us to become her eyes and ears here. Daniel certainly wasn't initially terribly welcoming. He acted as if I'd been foisted onto him.'

'I wouldn't want to get on the wrong side of him. He's got what they used to say about that politician, "There's something of the dark" about him.'

Avril continued. 'I had a long meeting with him early today, and there really is something about him that does put you off. I sorted out one thing. You know how we were confused that he's called a Canon and not one of the usual seven grades of perfect? Well he explained that one. It's because he works for the Tyndale organisation and not directly for Perpetua.

'Tyndale is the team that actually sets up and manages the retreats. Apparently each of them has to be designed and created to have everything that you would expect of a thriving small city. It's one hell of a task. You do have to admire him and his team for their skills and commitment.'

'How many of these places are there then? And just how many people are planned to be housed here?'

'Daniel explained there will be a dozen of them, and each will end up housing 12,000.'

'That's a lot of people, and I don't understand why they would want to start this right next to a "plague" site?'

'Nor me. 12,000 I think is about the size of my old home town, Cobham in Surrey.'

Stevie laughed at this, 'In your new role you have to promise me that you'll make sure we'll have fewer Chelsea footballers and absolutely none of their WAGs!'

'He tried to motivate me by saying that if I do a good job here then I could be part of the commissioning team at some other retreat.'

'You can't leave me here, alone.'

'There's little chance of that, at least not for a year or more. Daniel explained the size of the task. They've had to build big diesel power plants augmented by solar panels, all set well away from the retreat. Then there are huge water pumps to supply our needs from aquifers that fortunately lie deep beneath us here. Who would have guessed that there's water beneath this desert? Then there's all the sewage, waste removal and recycling. It all has to be created and managed from scratch out here.'

'I don't understand how you would fit in with all that?'

'He's explained that Marsha proposed me. I'm to work directly on his staff, to liaise and manage the team that's in the process of establishing a full hospital here, not just a clinic. It's to be a fully functioning general hospital.'

'Nurse to hospital administrator?'

'Precisely. After my time here, it is a bit of stretch. Believe me, following my latest experience that will come as one big relief. I don't think I could bear to ever lose another patient.'

'Poor you. It must be so awful. I can't even bring myself to become involved directly with the animal testing for fear of damaging them. I can't begin to imagine caring for someone for weeks only to lose them.'

Avril clearly didn't want to go back to that topic. 'There's a huge amount of work to be done to set up the hospital, though I was surprised to see that a lot of the equipment is already up and working. There's a huge cryonics department planned. You would probably know more about that area than I do?'

'Cryonics? You don't mean cryosurgery?'

'No, the plans and documents clearly say 'cryonics'. I thought I'd wait and ask you?'

'I believe the term cryonics refers to freezing humans and animals that have an irreparable disease in the hope that one day they can find a cure, then defrost you and remedy the problem. I went to a meeting about it while at Culham. From what I remember, most of those who attended were against the idea, mainly because the safe resuscitation of a frozen human hasn't been shown to be readily replicated. Some denied that it had ever really satisfactorily been achieved. There was something about tissue damage being the major problem.'

Avril was unimpressed, 'Even if it was fully guaranteed, I don't understand why anyone would want to go through that?'

'They would need to be pretty desperate, but I guess the assumption is that their identity could be preserved until a cure is found and then they'd be reignited.'

Avril was unconvinced, 'Surely religion teaches us that our identity is in our 'soul'. What happens to that if it is frozen? Would it survive a long period of such a dormant existence? What if it left your husk never to return?'

'Precisely. But from what I heard people are not even bothering now to keep their whole body. It's just their heads that they freeze. Imagine waking up without a body and in another time in the future where you know nobody?'

Avril shivered at the thought, took a deep breath and decided to change the subject. 'You know you were talking of animals earlier, there's even going to be a large farm here. I mean a stock farm with animals and not just the current crops, oh, and even a full zoo.'

This gave Stevie a sudden flashback that broke through Marsha's conditioning. Once broken she regained all her critical faculties.

She now recalled what it was that she had learnt about the humanzees, how they were being used, or rather to her mind, how they were being abused. Those lovely gentle creatures with so many human qualities locked away in a cellblock, expected just to procreate, and then merely to provide the stem cells used in the laboratory.

She also remembered that Marsha had not done anything to confirm or deny that they reserved their harvesting just to the umbilicals. Marsha couldn't possibly be taking their foetuses and babies, could she?

She realised that the whole process in Morocco could not possibly be ethical; she concluded perhaps that was precisely why the retreat was located out in the wilderness and not somewhere like Culham where the regulatory system would be sure to have stopped it in its tracks?

Now they were meddling with cryonics. So many questions. Just what was it that they were really up to? She decided that she must try to find out.

Then just as suddenly as she had experienced this conditioning breakthrough, it was gone. It was as though all the fresh thoughts had been written up on a chalkboard and someone had walked up and rubbed them off, or rolled them around to the other side.

Her negative memories and thoughts were replaced by a flush of excitement about her work, about living there, about her friendships. Marsha's conditioning had just kicked back in.

# Chapter 41 – *Colorado, USA*

In difficult conditions Ellery Scott, or Elzo to his mates, had so far handled everything that they had thrown at him. He had been a little concerned when they took DNA samples for he assumed that his might be found somewhere on the government databases. But presumably he had passed on that matter too, as he was now scheduled to meet up with Trajan Milos, the Operations Director of gNOS.

Scott was, of course, Mark Elliott using one of his CIA-created 'legends'. When they checked on Elzo Scott they would find he had no family, had dropped out of High School, had drifted around the country never staying anywhere long, not able to hold down the jobs he had taken. They would learn that he had recently shown more staying power as a security guard at a government establishment, where he had been promoted but without chance of further advancement. He just hoped these guys couldn't hack into the government DNA database and uncover his identity. On his next face-to-face report he would feed this thought back to his minder.

Mark was currently seconded from the CIA to DHS, the Department of Homeland Security. The Homeland folk had inherited so much work and, to be frank, created so much work for themselves since 9/11, that junior CIA men like him were regularly rotated through their teams to help out.

The US was currently experiencing the same increase in hate crimes on its soil as the rest of the world, though perhaps it had just taken them a little longer to notice; in the US these had never been a particularly rare occurrence, even before the new wave had begun to strike. The US and UK intelligence services pooled information on this sort of thing quite routinely but neither had any particular leads as yet.

Quite separately the US side was also intrigued by the sudden rash of Gene Genie shops, particularly as they hailed originally from their side of the pond. gNOS and BiCogNaIT were also from the US of A, but local intelligence had found only circumstantial connections between these organisations.

As part of one investigation instigated into these organisations, Mark had been challenged with trying to penetrate the gNOS structure. Both intelligence services had the gut feeling that these various organisations were part of a global conspiracy of some sort. It certainly seemed that gNOS was somehow central in that it ran 'interference' and security for the various other operations in this unholy, or perhaps given Perpetua, holy alliance.

A disenchanted ex-employee had been extremely informative and useful to the investigation. He had advised how best to come to the attention of gNOS without becoming too obvious.

Mark was instructed to drift into a private compound that was housing an ever-larger collection of apparently disparate groups. He and his colleagues had established there were many different groups here. Some were pursuing new-age dreams, there were those with a fundamentally religious objective, and then there were the doomsday-cum-survivalist types. And finally there were those who just railed and howled against the establishment in all its forms, complaining about both actual and perceived policies.

Once inside Mark had been instructed to schmooze the Aryan Nation offshoot within the camp. They were perhaps the nastiest of the lot. Back in 2005 their main group had sought an Al Qaeda alliance! He had been advised that gNOS tended to watch the intake of this group closely and then get to any likely candidates for itself before the full Aryan Nation initiation, when, for example, various hate tattoos were obligatory. Mark hoped the informant was right. He did not think his CIA future would be enhanced with 'HATE' tattooed across his knuckles.

Even though it had been created after passing through the chrysalis of the Church of Jesus Christ Christian, the Aryan Nation had the unmistakable DNA of the Ku Klux Klan running through its beliefs. This 'delightful' church taught that all non-whites were 'mud people' with no soul, no chance of salvation; and Jews were devils, one of their evil attributes being an ability to control the media. Its followers had refined and relished their own hate crimes long before this current wave had frothed around the world.

The various groups had been drawn to this compound pretty much to fester and to feed upon each other's fears and obsessions. Much of their paranoia had been channelled into achieving a readiness state for they believed it was only a matter of time before the establishment would come down the road to confront them as they had at Waco. The fitness regime was therefore something right at the heart of their beliefs, something of paramount significance to them.

The FBI had agents under deep cover to report on what was being said and done, to look out for anyone on their and the world's watch lists. Mark had been briefed by the local FBI office when it was explained that most individuals had been identified and their often extensive records pulled. These had revealed the expected strings of juvenile and motoring offences. Only a few were really bad 'mothers'; and these were all within the Aryan Nation group!

The informant had explained that a strong performance on the compound's military obstacle course was a vital precursor to getting noticed. Mark had therefore visited an army base where he was given a full week's intensive training on the likely elements. He had surprised himself by how much better this enforced repetition had made him; he made a mental note to do more physical activity in the future. Clearly he could be pretty capable if he only cared enough to take the time to pursue a regime.

On arrival at the compound he had been chased through the course by two individuals who had obviously done this for a living at some stage. As the tempo increased and they too showed signs of getting hot, they stripped off their sweatshirts to reveal '*Semper Fi*' tattoos confirming his original assumption; they had both been marines.

He always knew why he had never wanted to join the military and this current activity only served to confirm his prejudice. He had clambered up a tall climbing wall at the first attempt; before his recent training he knew he would not have made it. But after the climb he rappelled down the other side into a muddy ditch; minutes of hard graft to move forward just about three metres. Pointless!

He'd had much the same thoughts when he'd first seen the Great Wall of China with its ludicrous climbs and drops. If the Chinese had located it just a few kilometres south, as he would have done, then it could have been more simply built across a plain. Just what was it about the military mind? Did they just not apply the mush behind their foreheads at all? Senseless!

What kept him going was this sort of railing against military mindlessness. His training and this fuelled determination allowed him to make it to the finish in good time and still in good order. The two minders were clearly surprised but they were not about to admit it; instead they led him directly on to an assault course. They acted as if this was a normal part of the process. It was not, but they were determined to find a weakness in this different discipline. Fruitless!

This part Mark could have done without any pre-training. It consisted mostly of clambering under netting and over obstacles while live shots were being fired around him. The course was intended to see if the individual would flinch or freeze when weapons were in use. It was not as physically demanding and he completed it without any concerns. In the past he had been subject to shots fired directly at him in anger and not been overly bothered. This part was a cakewalk.

Clearly he had passed this first of the induction processes with flying colours. As a direct result he was introduced to an inner sanctum when his homework on the hotchpotch of small-minded hatreds paid off in an 'interview'.

The next step was a series of psych tests, the most notable being when he was placed in a freezer unit and after ten minutes asked to answer questions and solve a range of math problems. Subsequently he had to stand to attention as a guard while two instructors shouted and cursed at him, calling into question his lineage, his sexual proclivities and his manhood; virtually spitting in his face as they ranted.

So this was his reward for a week of discomfort - finally a meeting with the big man himself, Trajan Milos. In reviewing his file earlier, Mark thought it was a perfect case study of how to create someone with a deep and unfettered capacity to hate.

Back during WWII, Nazi Germany and Fascist Italy had combined to set up and support Croatia as an independent state; of course this new nation had been determined to curry favour from its two sponsors. On the banks of the Sava, a tributary of the Danube, they had built five concentration camps in a complex called Jasenovac. These camps had contributed to the 'Final Solution', killing many internal opponents as well as any Jews and gypsies.

Trajan's family had been from the region of Kozara, a naturally beautiful mountainous area; today it is located within what is modern Bosnia & Herzegovina. His grandfather and father, the latter just a boy at the time, had joined up with the partisans during that war and they had both become engaged in the Battle of Kozara. A force of three thousand partisans augmented by tens of thousands of lightly armed and trained local volunteers had held off an assault led by 15,000 German troops ably supported by 22,000 Bosnian troops. The partisans had punched well above their weight and inflicted losses of four-times their own.

His grandfather had been wounded in one of the pitch battles and was carried off to join up with several hundred others who had been wounded. They were gathered at Široka Luka, but their position there had been overrun and all were ruthlessly slaughtered.

After their eventual defeat many of the Serbs, including most of Trajan's family, had been simply herded off to the camps at Jasenovac. Today's Jasenovac Memorial Area lists around 70,000 victims of the camps, but this is claimed by some to be only a fifth of the actual total that had been exterminated. All were victims of ethnic cleansing and this was fifty years before the term became infamous in the region.

His father aged eleven was already by then a veteran of many engagements, had joined up with the Fifth Krajina Brigade and survived to see Tito become leader of the Socialist Federal Republic of Yugoslavia.

Years later, Trajan himself saw action as a young man in the Bosnian Serb Army. He was a junior officer within an artillery group and so was not indicted, as many of that army had been, for the war crimes and for the genocide they had wrought. He instead managed to find his way to and into the United States at the end of the 1990s. He had gone on to co-found gNOS in the early oughties.

On their first meeting Mark could see Trajan's bitter history on his battered face but his attention was drawn to the tattoo on his forehead. It was the same as that photographed on gNOS operatives in the UK. He wondered if he dared to ask what it meant, what it was for?

# Chapter 42 - *Blackpool, England*

It was party conference season, again! They seemed to come around ever faster in the Foreign Secretary's less-than-humble opinion. She found the main sessions were no longer at all meaningful for her. They had become so stage-managed, a mish-mash for the media - no controversy, no schisms, just a series of well-crafted photo opportunities and word bites in time to catch the evening news. The choreographed standing ovations were becoming ridiculous affairs where the crowd had to persist and outdo previous occasions with their plaudits.

These days she felt that from her perspective the real outcome of the conference was much more about what happened in the side and fringe meetings. These were where ministers needed to be seen and to be heard to sustain and advance their careers. Picking which to attend was the critical issue. She found most of her effort needed to be applied to a careful selection of which of these side meetings she must be sure to attend and which she must avoid like the plague. She had been caught up in one of these interminable meetings and so had arrived just a few minutes late to this briefing session.

Sir Joseph had decided to keep his powder dry until she arrived, and was preparing to modestly accept her highest accolades for his exceptionally good work. Before he could begin to give her his news, she showed that she was determined to grill him on quite another matter.

'So what have we learnt of Tom Carter? Is he alive?'

Sir Joseph was also distraught over the plight of this capable young man, and felt responsible for his loss, but automatically went on the defensive. 'My field operative had little choice but to leave him to their care. If he had moved him, where could he have gone? He assessed, correctly I believe, that if he had tried to carry him away from there, then he would surely have died. Carter had much more of a chance with them. They had facilities located nearby that could save him.'

'Only if they were of a mind to do so. Weren't they the ones who shot him in the first place?'

'There does appear to be a religious-based organisation assembled there. We can only hope that they would be forgiving and caring; if only to find out what we know.'

The Foreign Secretary was not going to let him get off so lightly. 'So is there any sign of them having taken him and treated him? Or did they just let him die there at the side of the road'

'I am afraid that we have no news at all, Foreign Secretary. The remote compound is not easy to penetrate with 'hum-int' on the ground. Look at what happened to Mr Carter. From the air our satellite imagery shows us a steadily growing community, but we cannot see into their buildings other than to look for infrared signatures, and they do seem to be shielding several of their facilities.

All we can really see is people working diligently in the fields. Sorry but we have no information on his whereabouts.'

She liked to see this arrogant old man squirming, particularly as he was not very good at it. She thought he therefore needed a little more practice. 'So just what have you been able to find out about this community?'

'Before the unfortunate incident on the side of the road…'

She snapped back, 'Unfortunate? You deliberately sent this high profile member of the British public to wander into harm's way; and it was not for the first time!'

'He is a Navy reservist, and not just a simple member of the public.'

'Those are weasel words!'

The Professor sought to resolve the deteriorating atmosphere. 'Foreign Secretary, I can confirm that Tom went there of his own accord. He was pursuing young Stevie Tasker with whom he is romantically involved. We could not have stopped him going there, even if we had tried.'

Sir Joseph beamed his gratitude. 'Precisely. He would have gone with no support, we sent him along with a top field man. They had achieved what they were there for and it was truly unfortunate…' he stressed the word, '…that someone managed to snipe poor Carter just at the last.'

The Foreign Secretary was not placated. 'So what did we learn that was of sufficient value to justify this debacle?'

The Professor chose to answer this. 'The community there is called the Tyndale Retreat and Tom had seen another of these in Bolivia when he visited recently. Apparently they looked just the same set-up despite being thousands of miles apart, on two different continents and in entirely different climates. We are of course researching this Tyndale organisation.'

'Why Tyndale?'

'We can't be sure but the most significant Tyndale was William Tyndale. A 15th-16th century scholar who ignored the Old English and Middle English translations of the Bible and went back to the Hebrew, Greek and Latin texts to produce a much-printed better version. Print was of course then very much in its infancy. Much of his efforts ended up being used later in the Authorised or 'King James Version'. He was not honoured or lauded for his work; instead he was burnt at the stake for being a little too Lutheran for his time.'

Sir Joseph commented, 'Bad enough to be burnt at the stake for your work, but to have it done to you in Belgium! I always felt sorry for that American pop singer from the 60s, Gene Pitney when he died in a hotel room in Cardiff and not "24 hours from Tulsa".'

The Foreign Secretary was taken aback by this comment; Sir Joseph knowing something of popular music was nothing short of a complete surprise. But she wasn't going to be outdone by the old fart. 'Though quite appropriate given one of his other hits was "Town Without Pity".'

The Professor smiled at the interplay. 'Tyndale was apparently defrocked, strangled and then burnt. This is interesting in that only Anabaptists at the time were supposed to be burnt, not Lutherans. What may be relevant is that one of the followers of this Perpetua Order who fell out and left it is accusing its leaders of holding some Anabaptist tendencies.'

The Foreign Secretary had had enough of the religious history lesson. 'So these retreats are named after a minor historical figure with religious credentials. What precisely are they doing in them?'

Sir Joseph, now feeling he had relaxed the mood with the Gene Pitney comment, chose to answer this one. 'We have uncovered at least six of these around the world. They have been developed recently and quite secretly. Further they usually seem to be founded upon others' misfortunes. In each case we have noted that there have been prior or coincident incidents in the area that have seen a heavy death toll of local inhabitants. Then these retreats spring up like a weed directly within the vacated territory. It is far too much to be a coincidence for all six of them to share this common feature.'

The Foreign Secretary pushed the heavy folder away. 'Rather than I read this tome, tell me what you mean?'

Sir Joseph explained. 'This one in Tamegroute for example. The local village was wiped out by an outbreak of a virulent disease and while everyone else was giving it a wide berth these Tyndale people moved in, apparently with absolutely no fear of catching the devastating illness. Any innocent organisation would surely be a little more circumspect. You can't help but make a connection between this and Dr Marsha Davenport. It sounds to me more than likely that she has developed pathogens or other biological weapons that are used to clear the way for the retreat.'

'You have other examples?'

Sir Joseph continued, 'The Uros who live on and around Lake Titicaca had some sort of flesh-eating disease at about the time that the Bolivian Retreat appeared on the Isla del Sol. Also in South America, there is another retreat close to the city of São Gabriel da Cachoeira. It's built on the lower slopes that rise up to become Brazil's highest peak, Pico da Neblina, right up against the Venezuelan border. Here a tribe of Nheengatu speakers were wiped out by some unidentified disease that then conveniently made way for these Tyndale people.'

The Professor commented, 'At the moment they seem to be using these biological materials against local and isolated small communities. Our big fear has to be what happens if they should later choose to do it against a large city!'

Sir Joseph added. 'Another concern, when you see what they are up to, is whether these are being developed into a series of Jonestowns. You may recall it was also South America, in Tomana, where Jim Jones gathered almost a thousand followers of his Peoples' Temple and had them all commit suicide. And worse, these Tyndale Retreats look to be planned to be a lot bigger than that!'

'Why in these particular places?'

Sir Joseph answered, 'We have to take the word of a lapsed 'Perpetuan' for the criterion for the locations. Perhaps you'll excuse an apparent Americanism if we call them 'Perps' for short? Well anyway, he advises that they don't appear to have suicide on their minds, instead one of their major fixations is extending their lives. This is also apparently something of a speciality for Dr Davenport too. As part of this Perp's interrogation by the US authorities, it appears the choice of location may have been motivated by a US National Institute of Ageing research project that investigated the most long-lived communities around the world.'

The Professor picked up the story. 'The USNIA report has shortlisted and analysed four particularly long-lived communities. The first was the Nicoyan Peninsula of Costa Rica, where men reach a century four times more frequently than those in the USA; and that's achieved of course within a radically inferior healthcare service. The second was in Sardinia, where several mountain villages also have a high rate of men reaching a century, contracting fewer major diseases and enjoying much longer, healthier lives. Then Okinawa in Japan was also an oasis of long life. Perhaps the strangest of the four was Loma Linda in the San Bernardino valley of California, where there was a long-lived largely vegetarian Mormon community. Strange, because the community sits over water that was polluted by poorly dumped rocket fuel and also 'enjoys' some of the worst air quality as it is located downwind from heavily-polluted Los Angeles.'

He slid a thick copy of the report across the table to the Foreign Secretary. 'The report's conclusions were that these communities share several factors: a reasonably high altitude; inhabitants who eat less meat and more fruit, vegetables and nuts; inhabitants who remain very physically active. Personally I'm delighted to see that the drinking of red wine was also a regular feature too.'

The Foreign Secretary slid back the report without examining it. She was getting restless, already beginning to think about, mentally preparing for, her next meeting. 'So they find these locations that fit the profile and just kill the sitting tenants? What sort of people can do that without qualms? And after they have done that, just who is it who lives in the retreats?'

Sir Joseph took up the briefing. 'This is where it gets intriguing. The main community consists of members of this Perpetua Order. We know also that the security is run by this gNOS crowd, those who were running around chasing down the humanzee that was loose on London. By the way my man did spot a number of humanzees at the Morocco retreat.

'Carter had mentioned to my operative yet another organisation, called Mission; of course we are now striving to learn more about that. My instinct on what we have currently is that Mission is the team that infects the target communities. It sounds like one of the nastiest parts of this operation. Then, this Davenport woman has her research organisation BiCogNaIT that must be tied up in it all somehow. She is certainly well connected into the Perpetua Order. God knows why it all has to be quite so complicated?'

'What's with this BiCogNaIT name? That doesn't sound particularly religious to me.'

The Professor replied. 'It's a popular trend that science is exploiting, though Davenport seems to have seen it rather earlier than most. It's the convergence that many scientists are noting and investigating in the previously separate fields of biotechnology, cognitive sciences, nanotechnology and information technology. One report, funded by the US National Science Foundation back in 2002, said... Well let me read the beginning of their executive summary.'

"In the early decades of the 21st century, concentrated efforts can unify science based on the unity of nature, thereby advancing the combination of nanotechnology, biotechnology, information technology, and new technologies based in cognitive science. With proper attention to ethical issues and societal needs, converging technologies could achieve a tremendous improvement in human abilities, societal outcomes, the nation's productivity, and the quality of life."

The Professor passed over another bulky report and pointed out a diagram near the front. 'Perhaps the title to their first illustration says it best, *"Converging Technologies for Improving Human Performance."*

Sir Joseph added. 'But I fear that in Davenport's case she interprets this to mean merely improving performance within defined roles, as in factory drones, or agricultural labourers or more worrisomely as warriors.'

The Foreign Secretary was confused. 'Is she doing anything demonstrably wrong?'

Sir Joseph shook his head. 'If anything she has a clean bill of health from their Department of Defense. She has clearly contributed to a number of their pet projects, pun intended. And she's quite a big employer too.'

The Professor added, 'She stole Bill Gates' quote when asked why she took on all the top graduates in those four scientific areas, saying "I employ them so that no-one else can!"'

'You can confirm that she is tangled up with this Perpetua Order too?'

The Professor smiled, 'Yes she is and that means that God is perhaps the linking theme. Tyndale the Bible translator, Perpetua the religious cult, gNOS must surely have some connection with Gnostic - even the word Mission has religious undertones. This plethora of names and organisations is all so very confusing. Perhaps they're all taking too literally the saying that "God moves in a mysterious way His wonders to perform".'

The Foreign Secretary commented, 'Well it's working; we can't fathom out what they are up to. Perhaps you're looking from the wrong side. Don't they say that "the devil is in the detail"?'

Sir Joseph pressed on for he finally judged that his moment had arrived. 'We have had one major breakthrough Foreign Secretary. As a result you will be owed a great deal by your colleague at the Home Office. As part of this investigation we had also included the Gene Genie retailer as they seemed to be linked to BiCogNaIT and gNOS, and suddenly became so active in the same time frame. It now looks to us as if Gene Genie has been the catalyst for the wave of hate crimes.'

He now had all the Foreign Secretary's attention as he continued. 'One of my team plotted the hate incidents, their timings, and compared these with the Gene Genie store opening programme and, eureka, she found a direct correlation.'

What he would never admit was that one of his overworked team had simply picked up an overloaded lever arch-file and it had done what they so often do, deposited all the documents right across the floor. As this floor was particularly slippery the pages had not fallen in any convenient blocks. The clerk, not being familiar with the material, had some difficulty in re-inserting the document. She had painstakingly to resolve precisely which document went into which section of the binder.

When she had worked through all the material she ended up with two maps left over because annoyingly no legend had been applied that could help to identify either, just a figure number. She was busily trying to establish which went into which section when she realised that they were strikingly similar and pointed this fact out to the case officer.

'With your permission Foreign Secretary I am arranging a series of simultaneous raids to close down this irksome shopkeeper.'

# Chapter 43 - *Double-T R, Morocco*

All those within the Double-T R were unexpectedly gathered together just as sunset was beckoning. They assembled and sat on the floor in a scalloped piece of cleared land that offered itself up as a natural amphitheatre. They instinctively joined up with their own working groups and were amiably chatting as night fell. Those who normally worked the fields were particularly ebullient, delighted with this unexpected evening off.

A warm party atmosphere developed as large bottles of various drinks were passed around those assembled and many were sharing cigarettes too. Stevie took a sip of one of the bottles and passed it on, but the smell of the cigarettes indicated that they were not filled with simple tobacco, so she elected not to take a drag on one of these.

Suddenly a light picked out Samuel on a small rise. Resplendent again in his Berber outfit, he was sitting astride a donkey climbing to the top of the rise. It could so easily have been a risible sight but somehow he managed to pull it off. He dismounted and raised his arms to an amazing cheer. The video cameras were capturing this and sending it to all the other Tyndale retreats by satellite link.

He then drew his hands together as if in prayer. 'We are gathered here today in simple service to Christ. Here we are not polluted with the trappings of the modern world, there is just a natural fellowship forged through work and worship. Make no mistake, what we are recreating here is the Kingdom of Heaven where it rightfully belongs - right here upon earth.'

Stevie heard a few around the audience shout out 'hallelujah'.

'Today is July the 22$^{nd}$ which is a special day for us. It is the feast day of a very, very special woman - Mary of Magdalene.'

This time rather more of the audience called out 'Hail Mary'.

'Despite the early Church leaders having attempted to edge Mary out of the Bible, thrusting her away from the centre of the holy story and trying to discredit her as the fallen woman of scripture, Mary Magdalene has managed to retain a strong presence. She still reaches down to us across the two millennia that have passed since those significant events.'

Stevie found herself relating Shepherd's words to some of the teaching that Marsha had given her and the Anglo Apostles. The American had explained the way that women had been marginalised right down through the years, how generations of men had controlled and enslaved them. Stevie had never been particularly feminist but just lately she had begun to find Marsha's accounts extremely thought-provoking.

Marsha had suggested it all started with the 1$^{st}$ Council of Nicaea, back in 325 CE. This meeting, held in modern-day Turkey, was the first truly ecumenical meeting assembling around 300 of the Church's then 1,800 bishops from around all its early communities.

Only twelve years earlier persecution of the Christians had been halted by a series of decisions culminating in the Edict of Milan. This Council was the first opportunity seized by the early Church to set itself upon the right course. Most Christians are made aware of the fruits of this Council when they learn the Nicene Creed, one of the more positive outcomes of the meeting. Much of the month-long meeting was dedicated to dealing with the many perceived blasphemies and heresies that had emerged in this early Christendom. At this Council they attempted to come to some agreement upon a single approach for the future.

An inordinate amount of the Council's time was dedicated to separating the date of Easter from that of the date of the Jewish Passover; trying to ensure that the two would never coincide. It was the Council that came up with the idea of Easter Sunday being celebrated on the first Sunday, after the first full moon, that follows the vernal equinox. Stevie had always wondered why Easter could move around so much from year to year, it seemed to her almost extravagant in its range of dates. She wondered if Tom would cite this matter as a major example of archaeo-astronomy in his book?

Shepherd pressed on. 'Mary is still considered a saint by most modern branches of Christianity. Appallingly she is revered based upon a confusion that was deliberately introduced in the third century, when she became wrongly identified as the repentant fallen woman. Mary Magdalene is therefore canonised quite incorrectly as a symbol of penitence, and not known for her true status - for her own works.'

Stevie was trying to follow the sermon but was aware that quite a few around her were obviously forming up into couples, openly snuggling and cuddling up to each other. Some were actually lying out in a full clinch. She nudged Avril and pointed this out.

'Yet even according to that much-edited and propagandist modern Bible, and particularly in the apocrypha that have been discovered and published more recently, she clearly had a very prominent role back then. We know it was she and the Virgin Mary who went on that third morning to find the Saviour's tomb empty. It was she who felt the need to uplift and motivate the disciples after His death. It was she who was called the 'Apostle to the Apostles'. She it was who had the other disciples jealously asking why Christ kissed her so frequently, asking why he spoke through a mere woman rather than them. Their fears that He somehow favoured her over them. And yet kissing was such a major feature of the early Church. Members of the congregation were encouraged to exchange kisses and not a modern 'mwah' or air-kiss; these were directly upon the lips.'

Stevie was startled when he appeared to be smiling out directly upon those who were now removing clothes and clearly preparing to have sex, right out in full view of everyone. She and Avril exchanged amused yet embarrassed looks.

Stevie tried to ignore them, instead thinking back to what she had been taught about the Council of Nicaea. It was this Council that suggested that as Christ had only chosen to call male apostles then there should be no female clerics. In the Jewish faith there had always been female prophets, even a female 'Judge'. Other religions had goddesses aplenty – Isis, Athena, Artemis, Freyja, Diana, Aphrodite, Venus... The Orthodox Church still reveres Sophia. The main thrust of Christianity had been directed by this Council to revere just a Father, a Son and a Holy Ghost.

'How many of our female Perfects assembled here, and being reached through our global broadcast, can empathise with this issue? As women within their previous careers, pressing hard up against that 'glass ceiling'; able to see through to the other side, but discrimination keeping them firmly constrained beneath it. How many have tried to smash through the ceiling only to be used, abused or discredited as strumpets or defamed as lesbians for daring to try to break into a masculine province?'

Samuel paused and looked around providing the camera operators with a close-up opportunity of his broad smile. The drinks were now flowing more steadily and even Stevie found herself taking a deep draught on the wacky baccy.

'It's understandable therefore that modern fiction and non-fiction, seeing this historic unfairness dealt out against the Magdalene, should have routinely tried to reinstate her. Many in recent years have sought to show her significance was because she was in fact the wife of Christ, some even claiming it was their wedding where He turned the water into wine; that it was for this reason he talked with her privately, kissed her frequently. This is yet another attempt to contain her, constrain her, to give her the subordinate role of wife. Why can't they just accept her and acknowledge that she was a leading apostle? What is wrong with him kissing her, loving her? Why must that make her his wife? In the Perpetua New Order we shall never be embarrassed by love. It's a natural thing, something to be encouraged.'

Stevie had been told by Marsha that the original apostles had travelled with women known as sisters. They had been invaluable as they were able to spread the word into places where male apostles could not reach. Clement of Alexandria had called them 'fellow ministers'. The early Church had also recognised and encouraged deaconesses. Yet this Council had ended all of that! Stevie, in her annoyance at this fact, took another deep draught on a joint.

'After His death, Mary travelled to Ephesus and helped build one of the seven founding churches. Her skills in Greek assisted in spreading the Word outside the confines of Judaism. It is her gospel and her writings upon which we at Perpetua base our creed. Hers is the Truth that we cherish as the first-hand account of the life and passion of Christ.'

Marsha had promised her Apostles that they would be shown the full gospel according to Mary Magdalene, that the Perpetua Order had a more thorough copy than had ever been published elsewhere. This secret gospel she promised would be used to remedy all the lies.

'No other figure in history can have had such a terrible campaign of deliberate misinformation. It was Pope Gregory I in 591 who barefacedly said *"She whom Luke calls the sinful woman, whom John calls Mary of Bethany, we believe to be the Mary from whom seven devils were ejected according to Mark."* In doing so he managed successfully to confuse three Biblical individuals and most specifically managed to discredit the Magdalene. But even he, six hundred years after the events, only dared to call her a *peccatrix* or sinful woman; he was not prepared to use the word *meretrix* for prostitute. It was left to later generations to add this additional charge; yet another example of the Church abusing its editorial powers!'

Stevie was beginning to get angry. Hadn't women always been at the forefront of Christianity? It wasn't just her Perpetua and Felicity. Other women who were martyred for the early Christian church included Cecilia, Agnes, Lucy, Blandina, even Saint Peter's wife. And Saint Antonia of Nicaea had been martyred at the very place where the Council was held, just nineteen years before it!

It would not have occurred to Stevie that she had never heard of these names prior to meeting Marsha, that she had never previously entertained a feminist thought. Without her being alerted, Marsha's subtle programming was having an impact. She had never previously felt moved to militancy about anything, before now. As she finished smoking the spliff, she found her anger was dissipating and she was feeling a little more mellow.

Fewer were calling out now because so many had found rather more creative uses for their tongues. Stevie was no prude but one part of her felt that this was all beginning to get rather too shameless; couples close to her were engaged in fellatio and several enjoying full-on sex. It was as if they were all drunk, yet they'd had so little of the drink. Whatever, it now looked as though this evening was irrevocably turning into a full orgy.

While taken aback by these brazen actions, she had to admit that she was at the same time being turned on by what was happening around her. Her sensible streak still thought that surely this was being disrespectful to Samuel's presentation, of which she had to admit that she too had begun to lose track. She struggled to focus back to what he was saying.

Samuel paused, and then said with stress, 'No, this is much more. It is a deliberate attempt to rewrite reality. Don't underestimate the power of evil. Evil has been there, right at the heart of Christianity throughout its development and history. We wear a crucifix proudly, yet conveniently forget that Christ was nailed to that cross, to have the life drained from Him painfully and in the most barbaric way. He was no terrorist, had not threatened the authorities and yet they took Him, scourged Him and cruelly murdered Him. His message had been a passive one. He taught of love, respect, caring. In this awful act of theirs, He revealed to us, so clearly, all of the evil that abounds out there in our world.'

The love-making paused at this serious tone, so Samuel threw his hands in the air, 'My Perfects, he also demonstrated how, with faith, we can and shall overcome!'

This brought about another wave of hallelujahs and the couplings started again with greater gusto. Stevie was becoming increasingly desensitised by the activity around her. She realised that she was becoming concerned, wondering why she and the other Anglo Apostles were being so signally ignored by the others. She felt herself losing some of her recent confidence; perhaps the others thought there was something fundamentally wrong with them. She didn't appreciate that it was merely their different clothing and their connection to Marsha that had stamped them out as 'other', stopped them being approached, involved.

Samuel extended his hands to two young women who were obviously waiting for this moment. 'My Perfects, let us build the Kingdom of Heaven right here.' He led the two girls off towards his quarters as Hannah glared after them; for that had been her role before she was posted here by Marsha.

Stevie having been aroused, had felt that this was all working up to something, but now she feared it would all end up as one huge anticlimax. She had entertained such expectations earlier, when there had been real meaning for her in the sermon. A feeling in the air had been developed that was almost electric, and now Samuel had left and she could feel it all dissipating; for her at least.

She looked around to Hannah and recognised that she too was sharing the same feeling of somehow being let down, forgotten. This Hannah resolved by reaching across to Stevie and gently kissing her on the lips. Before Stevie's sensible core had time to think, they had both lustily turned this into a full-blooded kiss. First their tongues explored each other's mouths lightly then increasingly aggressively, their hands began to caress and then explore each other's bodies.

They soon found that their clothing was a nuisance, a hindrance, so they shrugged it off and joined the others gyrating on the floor.

# Chapter 44 - *Kent, England*

Will Patterson spun down into the train seat. He was using this down time to contemplate his current situation. He had been promoted to a Level Six through his successful work with Mission, but he knew that if he had not ended up working there he would probably have happily described himself as an agnostic. He had recognised that to advance in Mission it was best to maintain an apparent fervour, show commitment to the beliefs and tasks set out by Shepherd. Yet his instinct was never to be considered by anyone as any form of sheep!

Here he was off chasing relics, again. Though at least this was the big one! He even had help along with him this time, Buck was along for the ride. They had also recruited some local Perpetua adherents as there would be some heavy shifting work.

Will's phone sounded and he saw that it was Dom, calling him for the umpteenth time to check on some pernickety detail or other. As he pressed to accept the call their train entered the tunnel under the English Channel; satisfyingly he saw that the signal disappeared from his screen.

'Oh, what a crying shame,' he thought, sarcastically.

At least in Europe Will felt relaxed that he understood the mentality of his likely adversaries. The Thais he had met in Chiang Mai were confusing, on the one hand mild, yet somehow rebellious too. Then there was the huge sex business and all the drug trafficking; he supposed he would never get around to figuring them out.

The mystery of the Thais was pretty straightforward compared to the myths and legends surrounding their target for this trip. Much debated by the early Christian Church, this enigmatic woman was clearly of major significance to Shepherd.

Will found this female influence confusing, what he saw and knew of Shepherd made him appear a member of the 'old school'. He was aware the preacher partook of the pretty young converts regularly, so he had assumed a strong streak of misogyny or outright chauvinism in the man. Just when you thought you had defined him he showed awe and respect for women.

The Order was named for a woman, Perpetua. Regularly sermons delivered by the old man featured other women too. Marsha featured very powerfully in the Order's hierarchy. When he had the time he thought he should look at this matter rather more carefully.

Today's woman of interest was the big one, Mary Magdalene. He had transited through the UK long enough to learn that the Brits added to her mystery by deliberately mispronouncing her name, they seemed to say it as Mawd-lin, despite the spelling! Go figure!

## Chapter 45 - *Double-T R, Morocco*

Tom stirred and scratched the top of his head, then noticed that the American fellow from Carthage was sat next to his bed. He was still dressed in his ludicrous Arab get-up.

Where was he? Was he dreaming? He tried to lift his head but he was still far too drowsy, too weak, and slumped back onto his pillow.

'Ah Mr Carter, I am so pleased to see that you are recovering well. I'm delighted to welcome such an esteemed guest to our Tamegroute Tyndale Retreat. You are our very first VIP visitor. My name is Samuel Shepherd and I am glad we could be of assistance to you with our meagre facilities here.'

Tom tried to speak but found the words wouldn't come out; he made a sort of grumbling sound.

'No, don't try to talk yet. You have too much connected to you and there is currently all sorts of stuff actually still in your throat. You should be recovered enough for much of it to be removed tomorrow and then you will be able to talk freely. You see, we needed to repair the damage to your neck. The bullet went straight through the upper part of your trachea, your windpipe. You're very fortunate that you were right here because we were able to do something for you.'

Tom was still a tad confused about what was happening, where he was, but he was fully aware that it was this man's team that had shot him. Without that attack he wouldn't have needed their help.

'I am told that elsewhere they usually look to use an aortic graft for this sort of thing. Be thankful that it wasn't your oesophagus, your food pipe. The usual treatment for that is to take a colon graft.' He chuckled, 'Then your detractors could really accuse you of talking through your *derrière*. Our team has repaired your windpipe but you currently have a silicone stent ensuring that it keeps its integrity. This will need to stay with you for a few months. The rest will be removed later today or tomorrow.'

In his head Tom was replaying what had happened. He remembered that Brain had left him for dead by the side of the road. Bastard!

'I hope you don't mind but I have been sitting here reading the manuscript and notes for your new book. We found it in your abandoned van. It's absolutely fascinating! And what do you know, it just happens that I think I am in a unique position to help you with some of the background to the very thing that you have been trying to discover - a unification of the various early beliefs.'

Tom sighed internally, though no sound actually emerged. Why was it that everyone thought they could do your job, improve upon your work? Everyone's a critic because they once read a book!

Shepherd would probably want to relate everything to the Bible and his own beliefs; worse there was no getting away from him. He was literally a captive audience for this preacher who obviously loved the sound of his own voice.

In a flash of self-discovery he wondered if this was how others felt when he himself cornered them and pontificated. If so then he promised himself to be more thoughtful in the future. Well he could try.

'I feel your doubt, but honestly I think I can help join up some of your loose ends. First and foremost I really feel that you urgently need to investigate the Caduceus. You know, the medical logo with two snakes coiled around a staff. You will find it makes extremely interesting reading. It's used all over the place. Military doctors have it on their badges - it's most commonly used today in a medical context. Yet in fact that's all largely based on something of a confusion. The mistaken belief that it is the symbol Hippocrates used, when in fact what he used was the Rod of Asclepios.'

Shepherd paced around the room as he developed his argument, 'It's unclear whether Asclepios was considered to be mortal or a god. He was the son of Apollo and of course stories abound of gods coupling with mortals. When the Romans had a plague in 293 BCE it was Asclepios that they approached for assistance. He came in the guise of a snake..

'His imagery and symbol, the Rod of Asclepios, has just the one snake coiled around a staff. You really do need to look into the whole subject of serpents. In the Orthodox Churches Sophia's transmission of wisdom to us mortals was embodied as a snake. It's a symbol used by the Gnostics too. And, it was of course a serpent in the Garden of Eden that brought knowledge to Adam and Eve.'

Tom thought, 'There you go! I knew we would end up with the Bible at some point.'

'If you could speak you would be saying that the serpent was evil, that it tempted Eve away from her god. You, as a scientist, must accept it could not be correct for Adam and Eve simply to stay put inside that perfect Garden, having everything laid on and provided for them, without any effort to be applied on their part. Living blissfully ignorant of the real world and how it functions, that's not a life as we know it. It's certainly no sort of a scientific life.'

Tom wanted to fall back to sleep, but he also wanted to know and understand what this man was about; the man who had somehow lured Stevie away from him. Where was he going with all this?

'Then you may be thinking the story of Adam and Eve is just a fable, or is the correct term perhaps an allegory? I vote for allegory, for this fable was something that can be interpreted to reveal a hidden meaning. We at Perpetua think it is based upon an oral traditional story passed down many generations and by many races before it ever became encapsulated within the Bible.

'Gnostics believe this physical world of ours was created by the Demiurge, a serpent with a lion's head. It's not just Christianity that talks of serpents; the Australian Aborigines have their 'rainbow serpent'. And, of course as you know, yet another allegory talks of a similar slippery creature, though perhaps a slightly more aquatic one, Oannes. Oannes was the bringer of early knowledge to the Sumerians, for them to found their civilisation. Unrelated early civilisations, serpents bringing knowledge, perhaps this is your missing link? Who then were these serpents?'

Tom audibly gasped at this. Was Shepherd just playing with him or did he in fact have some insights that could help him round off his book? This was his very last thought as he lost his fight to retain consciousness and slipped back into a deep sleep.

# Chapter 46 – *Colorado, USA*

Mark was woken very early and led by Trajan and others out through the compound and into the dense woods until they reached a clearing. He had noted that several of the gNOS personnel dropped back and posted themselves at various distances to stop any of the others from the compound who might have decided to follow them; this would take care of the FBI deep cover men, so he had to accept that he was out there on his own.

He had no idea what was expected of him so the adrenalin was coursing through him. Had they blown his cover and was this to be the end? Was this IT? The IT that every undercover agent feared and yet expected must happen one day, despite all their training and subterfuge.

They reached the clearing and the others formed a respectful circle around him and Trajan. So if this was it, it would be the top man who would despatch him. Trajan looked pretty useful and Mark realised he had never really had to use his combat training in earnest, ever! It had all been theoretic exercises and training; now it looked like he was in for a practical!

Trajan broke the moment by smiling. 'So Elzo, I'm told you recorded good times and good reactions in all our various tests, but in my life I have seen many athletes turn and run when it came down to personal combat. Come on, try and take me.'

Trajan was used to people staring at his tattoo, and understood that most could not bring themselves to verbalise their curiosity about it. In fact he saw it as something of a test in itself. The way in which an individual responded to it, whether they asked, how long they took to ask, the way in which they asked; these gave him the measure of the person.

Mark went for broke. 'That's an interesting tattoo. Japanese?'

Trajan smiled. This Elzo had passed his initial test at least. He had asked about it straight out, he had already tried to categorise it and 'Japanese' was a more informed guess than the more common Chinese.

'It depicts the characters JHWH.' He paused to await a reaction.

Mark asked, 'Are you Jewish then?' But as he did he stepped forward and went for Trajan, kicking out a foot towards his opponent's knee.

Trajan was warming to this young man. Clearly he was seeking an advantage with words he thought might offend and put him off guard. He had sidestepped the blow easily. But there was also a deeper appreciation in the young man's use of his knowledge, his very economy with words. He clearly realised JHWH was the Hebrew for God, Jahweh or Jehovah, minus the vowels as was their custom. But he had wasted no words, did not want appreciation for his knowledge, he had just got straight to the point.

'No it isn't signifying my race, but my religion. Are you religious?' Trajan stepped forward but then dropped to a crouch and snaked out his leg to sweep away Mark's. The younger man was quick and able to leap over the limb. On landing he regained his balance instantly and launched a kick at Trajan's stooped head.

'Well, I was brought up in a strict Baptist community, so I do know my Bible. I had it beaten into me from a very young age. As a grown man I've never really dedicated much time to thinking what it is that I believe for myself.'

Trajan had expected the counter and neatly dodged the kick. He grabbed Mark's leg and thrust him off balance. 'Well in fact I'm Gnostic.'

Mark was delighted that his belief about gNOS and Gnostic was correct but kept any evidence of joy at this revelation from his face. He regained his balance and stood back at a safe distance, assessing his opponent afresh. He realised that Trajan certainly knew what he was about. 'I know what agnostic means, but don't really understand what it means without the 'a'?'

The two men circled each other, no hurry on either side, each looking for the next opportunity. 'That's because the Roman Church decided we were heretics and have vigorously tried to destroy us, since the first century. Gnostic simply means knowledge or enlightenment. That's what we seek in our religion, knowledge; and particularly knowledge of our inner self. That's where we believe we can find comfort, enlightenment and only through these things will we be granted our salvation. We awaken our *pneuma*, that vital spirit that lies within us. Our aim is to release our creativity and through this develop our soul.'

Mark started to think, 'What? Develop your soul by becoming a security guard?'

He had no time for further thought as, in a manner of unwitting poetry; Trajan had used the word 'creativity' as his trigger to attack. He feinted in one direction and, as the younger man moved backwards trying to escape contact, he had time to pick his spot and deliver a heavy blow to Mark's left shoulder.

Darn it, that hurt! The whole of his left arm felt numb. He realised the intent as it would now be difficult for him to direct it, and hard to deliver any accuracy or force with it. He couldn't afford to lose the function of his right arm the same way so adopted a stance that kept it furthest away from the Eastern European.

Mark replied, 'That sounds pretty straightforward. I don't see why that would in any manner be considered a heresy?' The man appeared keen to tell him what he'd come to find out, so provided he could stay alert, conscious, then this could end up being quite a quick investigation. That would certainly suit his purpose.

Trajan was circling, keeping Mark on the move, alert to any attack. He recognised Mark's quickness of mind in keeping his right side away from their likely point of contact.

'We Agnostics know that the world was created by the Demiurge, not by God. We appreciate that there are in fact two side-by-side worlds - the physical and the spiritual. Our heresy is this knowledge and then it's down to guilt by association. In pursuing our Truth we find we believe in many of the apparent villains of the Bible. We hold to a different opinion of Judas Iscariot for example. He was not the betrayer that many mistranslations have claimed. It is not as Pope Benedict XVI says that Judas freely chose to betray Jesus as "…an open rejection of God's love…", but instead we understand that he was specifically following Christ's instructions. Even the accepted canonical Gospels record that Jesus, during the Last Supper, had said to Judas, "What you have to do, do quickly." He knew what Judas was doing, because he had planned it!'

Trajan momentarily looked to one of his men who had coughed. Mark was lightning quick this time. He stepped in, spun right, crouched left, turned and kicked up from the ground, managing to land a heavy forearm blow to Trajan's chest. It rocked the man backwards but Mark correctly gauged that he was overplaying his lack of balance, he had done this so that Mark might be tempted to follow through, when the gNOS head was in fact all too ready for him.

Mark sensibly held back, in part because he wanted to hear more. Apparently in this combat situation he was permitted to ask questions openly that he would otherwise have had to edge up to in any normal circumstance.

'OK, so I understand you're saying you support the little guy…' he gestured to himself ironically, '…caught up and destroyed by the greater plan?' He indicated the man's supporters gathered around them.

Trajan looked at the man he knew as Elzo a little more carefully. Was he mocking his words? This was a reaction he had encountered many times and he had a heightened sensitivity to any hint of ridicule. His inspection revealed no confirmation either way but his hackles had been raised by the comment and he launched a furious attack of his own, landing a fist to Mark's kidney as he tried to dodge away. The pain was excruciating. Trajan evidently knew where to inflict the most agony, and in a fight he also had the presence of mind to deliver the telling blow with an economy of effort.

'Elzo, you look like you could be an asset to gNOS. But you will need to understand something of us and our beliefs before we can give you anything serious to do for us.'

Mark had to take a few moments to recover from the kidney punch and resorted to circling furiously. 'What can I tell you? I have to admit that I was never particularly inspired by my parents' religious beliefs, but I've always been very open and willing to learn.'

Trajan smiled at the reassurance. 'Down the years the Church has pursued us vengefully for our beliefs. At every turn and every generation they have sought to wipe us out; but our knowledge persists. Essentially we believe the world was created by the Demiurge, deliberately to confuse and confound us, to keep us from learning what we really are, what we can become.'

Mark was still sore but could see that Trajan was ready to take things further. He just needed to nudge him onwards. 'Why don't I know about you already?'

'Because the Roman Church has always controlled the press! Look how they discredited Judas as the betrayer of Christ, how they sidelined Mary Magdalene as a whore; Mary was a Gnostic too! You have to come to appreciate just how truly evil the world is, how there are forces at work to conceal the truth, to screen the knowledge.'

Mark launched another attack only to find Trajan had predicted it and wheeled away. 'So where do you get your knowledge?'

'We have access to a whole series of original texts, but then there are many other publications that have come to light recently that do not form any part of the Canon of the Bible. Originally they condemned us as Sethites for our belief in the sanctity of Seth. We believe for instance that Seth was the *Logos* and that Jesus was merely the Seth reborn. You may not know that just as Jesus was created rather than born, so too was Seth. As the Apocalypse of Adam explains, he was created by three men "whose likeness I was unable to recognise"; created to replace Abel after Cain had murdered his brother.'

This time Trajan caught him napping. He was guilty of listening to the words and not watching the man carefully enough. Blows rained down on him in rapid succession, but he felt that his assailant was pulling them, not delivering the full ferocity of which he was capable. The only way to make him stop was to go to ground, a dangerous option if he was determined to follow through. Mark was relieved to learn that Trajan did not follow him down to finish it.

'I can see that this would be pretty controversial!' He got up and made to dust himself off, but threw a handful of dirt straight at Trajan's face. The Slav put a forearm up to shield his eyes and this gave Mark his moment. He performed a neat judo throw and deposited his opponent on the floor. He did not want the man to come at him seriously, did not want him to lose face in front of his men, so followed Trajan's earlier lead and simply stepped back from his momentarily prone form.

Trajan smiled his acknowledgement of the move and rose to his feet. 'They attacked us as Ophites because we revere the serpent that first brought us Knowledge. Down the centuries they have tried to define us as Docetists, Valentians, Marcionists, Montanists and Manichaeans, as if somehow in managing to define us they could better expunge us. As Cathars they successfully mounted a full crusade against us in the 13th and 14th centuries; they believed that they had wiped us out.'

'Now Cathars I've heard of! But I'm even more confused as to what it is you believe.'

'Valentinus in the 2nd century said it best; he should have been Bishop of Rome but was passed over. His writings identify that there are three types of people on this earth of ours - the spiritual, the psychical and the material. Material people are caught up in the world that the Demiurge created and so are doomed. The psychics can attain some form of salvation, but it is only the spiritual who can receive the gnosis and achieve a return to the Pleroma.'

'Is that something like achieving Nirvana?'

'Precisely.' Trajan came in direct, fast and hard and bulldozed Mark backwards. This time he followed through and joined him on the floor. The older man started a blow to Mark's throat that would clearly have disabled if not despatched him, but he didn't follow through. Instead he mussed up his hair. He got up and walked back across the clearing, deliberately offering his back to Mark. Mark chose not to take up the opportunity and instead climbed to his feet and dusted himself off; with no ulterior motive this time.

'Can you become spiritual or is it something you are born with?'

'From our various tests I can advise you that you have all the attributes to become a spiritual person.' Clearly this test too was over as Trajan stretched his arms wide and continued. 'Well done. You handle yourself well. I see that you use your mind not just your muscles!'

Mark put out his hand to shake on it. 'Will I have to get one of the tattoos?'

As Trajan took his hand Mark spun his man and aimed his own blow to the face but stopped short. 'You told me what it says, but what does it actually mean?'

Trajan clapped his final effort and slapped him on the shoulder. 'You say you know your Bible. There are profound messages buried deep within it, particularly in Revelations. We can help you to interpret it with time, but right out there in the open it says in chapter 14:

"And I looked, and lo, a Lamb was stood on the Mount Sion, and with Him an hundred and forty and four thousand, having His Father's name written in their foreheads... ...And they sang as it were a new song before the throne... ...and no man could learn that song but the one hundred and forty and four thousand who had been redeemed from the earth."'

Mark was surprised that an otherwise intelligent person would interpret this to mean that he needed a tattoo on his forehead!

'When the seventh seal is opened and the fifth angel has sounded a trumpet, out of the pit will come locusts, "And it was commanded them that they should not hurt the grass of the earth, neither any green thing, neither any tree; but only those men which have not the seal of God in their foreheads..."

'So, at the end just 144,000 will be saved, and we intend to be safely among them!'

# Chapter 47 - *Double-T R, Morocco*

The many cameras around the natural amphitheatre had saved a graphic record of the evening. As they worked their way through the video footage Samuel commented, 'Marsha, your stuff last night was just too fast-acting. It became clear that I was beginning to get in the way. I had so much more that I needed to say in this presentation but I realised I had to leave it there.'

Marsha was having her hair groomed. 'It's OK. We just need to do a little studio work now, a bit of cutting here and there to finish off the package. We let the other retreats believe that it was a satellite problem. Dieter, are we ready to go?'

They were in a classic two-chair studio interview, a stark and featureless infinity wall behind them, the background would be added in later.

'So I believe we're going to come in after I'd just said *"...the evil that abounded in the world?"'*

Dieter called out, 'Yes, that's it. We're running.'

Samuel started. 'Even at the very beginning the unworthy, the lazy and the evil have always been present. Just imagine if you can, Christ's teachings could have been lost to us forever because of a petty squabble between His followers.'

Dieter saw that Marsha with all her skills was not good in front of camera. Her facial expressions were just a little too forced as she asked, 'And who were those who could not just follow his teachings?'

'Christ's own relatives wanted Christianity to stay firmly fixed within its roots, remain solely within Judaism; they saw his ministry as only being of relevance to other Jews. Fortunately it was a second group that history ended up following, led by Saul, St Paul. He it was who took His message outside Judaism and made it truly international, to espouse the Gentiles too; and he it was who carried St Peter along with him.'

Now Marsha was smiling just a little too beatifically, 'Your teachings have shown us that this historic Church regularly tinkered with the truth? Oh sorry. Please cut there and I'll try again.'

She composed herself, breathed deeply and said. 'Your teachings have shown us that this historic Church regularly tinkered with the Word?

'That's absolutely true. First there was the Word and then there was the Church. Back there at the very beginning there was another party, another direction, one that the early Church decided to hide from us. These were the teachings of Mary Magdalene, "the Apostle to the Apostles".'

Marsha prompted, 'Her teachings were ignored?'

Samuel was in super close-up. 'In her gospel she forecasts what in fact happened when she cautioned the disciples with what Christ had told her, "*Do not lay down any rules beyond what I appointed you.*". He and she both knew that the great danger would be those who came behind them changing the rules to suit their own times and their own tastes, to alter the Word as they saw fit.'

Marsha was enjoying this; she felt that they worked well as a team. She was totally unaware that Dieter was leaving her out of shot for much of this. He had concluded that her expressions would interfere with the message.

She asked, 'But Mary, this amazing woman who was there constantly at his side, who witnessed the crucifixion and the resurrection, was vilified by the early Church, her message discarded and excluded from the Bible.'

'It was not just the early Church. It's so sad but we are all victims of the beautiful and glorious paintings and icons that have been sponsored by the rich merchants down the years. These are such powerful images that they become the accepted fact for many of us. Those pictures have editorialised and marginalised Mary Magdalene. They show her with long and uncovered hair. It is often red hair, and frequently she is dressed in red too. Each such picture compounds the original lie; she is routinely depicted as the whore that Pope Gregory had sought to suggest by his proclamation.'

Marsha nodded to the camera. 'Down the centuries it's always been easy for a man who fears a woman, to brand her as loose, unworthy, or alternatively a witch. So we have to ask ourselves just what precisely was it that Gregory feared? Why was this woman such a threat?'

Samuel, again dressed in his Berber costume, rose from his chair as he continued. 'In the Eastern Orthodox Church there is a different belief. They believe that Mary Magdalene led such a blameless life that the Devil feared she might have become the one to deliver Christ into the world. The Devil therefore sent seven demons to torment her; those same demons that Christ later cast out in the Gospels. But we know that the Gospels confuse two biblical Marys.'

Marsha realised that the camera was at last on her, so looked resignedly deep into it, 'The hard fact was that a woman could not legally bear witness in those days. This is why it was so significant that Christ chose her and sent her to the disciples to tell them that He was risen again. She said "*Do not weep and do not grieve nor be irresolute, for His grace will be entirely with you and will protect you.*" She it was who helped the disciples to rediscover their backbones. All the editors down through the years, most of them male, have not managed to remove this apparent anomaly.'

Samuel was pacing with the camera following his every move. 'In her gospel Mary tells us so much. Just before one fragment of her gospel becomes lost she reports that "*The Saviour answered and said, He does not see through the soul nor through the spirit, but the mind that is between the two that is what sees the vision ...*". So it is the mind that we concentrate upon in the Perpetua Order. The spirit is what drives you, the soul is your eternal being, but here, living in this Kingdom of Heaven on earth, it is your mind that must direct you.'

'Samuel, you mentioned that it was to Ephesus that Mary Magdalene travelled with Mary, the mother of Christ. That's a location of which we hear so very little from today's Church.'

He walked back and sat down. 'Ephesus is in fact a very significant place. The Revelation was written in Ephesus; it was of course addressed to the seven early churches, the first named being that at Ephesus. Paul certainly wrote a number of his epistles from there; one was addressed to the people of Ephesus themselves. It was also where John, the author of The Revelations, lived and later died. Even in the second century the church at Ephesus still had significance with Bishop Ignatius of Antioch famously writing to its congregation.'

Samuel had given a signal to Dieter; the camera zoomed in on to his face which was brilliantly illuminated. 'So together let's rediscover Mary Magdalene who was largely edited out by the Church. Then let's rediscover Ephesus - clearly a significant location, largely overlooked and forgotten today. I can reveal to you now that it is directly from Ephesus and directly from the teachings of Mary Magdalene that the Perpetua Order has received its special knowledge.'

Dieter called out, 'Thank you, that's perfect. No need for another run.'

The studio team cleared away and left the two sitting back in their chairs. Dieter remained in the control room working on the edit. His loyalties lay with Samuel, for it was Shepherd who had recruited and advanced him.

He was not drawn to Marsha as so many others of the Order; she was too much of a control freak for Dieter. He could see something deep in her eyes that he did not find at all comfortable. If anyone had asked he could not have explained why, but he decided to leave an audio recorder rolling that would pick up the conversation in the studio.

Samuel was not in a good mood. 'You do need to be much more careful in the future, Marsha. We were going out live to all our followers with that outside broadcast. OK, so Dieter made it look as if there had been a satellite failure, and we later suggested that our enemies had interfered with the broadcast. So I guess nothing was lost, except time, but we know that is in short supply. We need to understand why Carter and his colleague were here? And just who was it who got away from us?'

Marsha smiled, 'He's just a love-sick puppy chasing after his lost girlfriend. It's yet another case of a man's little brain ruling his big one.'

Samuel jumped up and began pacing. 'Is it really that simple? You lost that bloody monkey in London and this Tom is a Brit with a military background. Now it's the Brits who lead on this enforced closure of our Gene Genie shops. Carter turned up in Tunis and now here. How did he know where we were? Are they on to us?'

Marsha was using her little girl voice, trying to placate him. 'We always knew that they'd link the hate crimes to the shops. No-one in the franchise has any idea of what they were doing, they were all too happy with their income to question anything. We expanded our database enormously through the use of these shops. Don't forget that this way we had others do the work and they took on the costs for us too. We've already erased the routines in the franchisee PCs that sent the DNA records on to us, and we've disposed of the routines where we controlled the local selections.'

Samuel was not so easily pacified. 'Are you absolutely positive that no-one there can lead this back to us?'

'As part of the franchise agreement they had to buy their PCs and all their supplies from us. They happily took our word for the fact that the specialist second swabs they used were just an antiseptic. Someone may eventually discover it was these second tests, requested only after we had analysed their initial DNA results, that enabled us to selectively use the mind-changing material.

'There are those out there who might be able to "reverse engineer" what we did, but they probably wouldn't be able to see the hormonal imbalances we introduced, for they will appear as natural. They will probably be able to discern the chemicals we used to interfere with the R-complex; that ancient, very advanced, part of our brain that we mammals share with reptiles. The place where we triggered their emotions to accentuate their fears and this generated their hatred. But by then it will be far too late for them to do anything about it.'

Samuel was still not ready to relax. 'We have just eight of the retreats up and running, so Mission is a little behind target while the Perpetua recruitment is right on track.'

Marsha walked over to him and stroked the back of his neck. 'The Gene Genies did their job for us. The various franchisees and senior franchise managers on seeing lucrative livelihoods disappear will cause such a fuss with their local and national politicians. This will cloud any investigations for weeks and months. Don't forget all those they tested will still have had their MPW gene tweaked irreparably and will continue the attacks; that too will give the authorities enough to keep them occupied.'

Samuel snapped back, 'You scientists, always hiding behind formulae and acronyms. MPW?'

'Male Pattern Whiteness, or if you prefer it the "hate gene".'

'So why doesn't it have a code like VMAT2, the "God Gene", the one we test for before admitting someone into Perpetua?'

'Dean Hamer is a behavioural geneticist working within the system. He therefore applied proper designations to his findings for the "God Gene"; he believes in scientific nomenclature. Conversely MPW was the term applied by a US team when they investigated white unemployed supremacists in the States, they were a little more interested in the media than in the scientific community.'

'Why is it categorised as male?' He took up a challenging stance. 'Women can be pretty hateful too; like you taking Hannah away from me and posting her to this retreat!'

Dieter was alone, deep inside the control room, just finishing off his work on the broadcast. He had not been particularly interested in what was being said between the two but this caught his attention. Back in Arizona he had made it clear to Hannah that he was interested in her, but his interest had remained unrequited because this old man had selected her as his very own. He was still smitten, had never really forgiven Shepherd for this. He checked that the audio recording was still capturing the studio conversation, covered the device with a clipboard and decided it best to leave the room in case they realised he had been privy to their private conversation.

Samuel was now beginning to relax, yet still asked. 'Perhaps it's time for us to go secure and move into LTR?'

Marsha took both of her hands in his. 'We have far too much left to do before we can go there.' She looked deep into his eyes and said, 'You are the Leader. The world needs your leadership.'

He intoned, 'I am the Leader. The world needs my leadership.'

She whispered some directions to him, but the microphones still captured her words. Samuel listened intently then stopped his pacing and sat down.

Clearly now completely relaxed, his patriarchal style was back. 'Can you please run the video of the Perfects for me?'

Marsha went to the control room. Not noticing the audio recorder running beneath the clipboard, she pressed the button to set up and run the video. She stayed there allowing him to feed his ego from the recording.

Samuel called out, 'Pause it there please.'

She went back into the studio to see what it was that had caught his attention.

'Marsha, you tell me that this young beauty locked in an embrace is none other than Tom Carter's girlfriend. I can now see why someone would follow her to the ends of the earth.'

Marsha smiled, 'You remember I told you all about Stevie from Culham. She's the one, I have selected her for us. I've not used the general conditioning on her that we apply within the retreats. I knew you'd want her to remain bright, independent and wilful.'

She was thinking, 'I have almost completed the placement of my team right at the very heart of Perpetua. That accomplished I can control it from a distance, without needing to hang around in these awful retreats.'

'I see. I think therefore I am in need of a meeting with her, very soon.'

# Chapter 48 - *Double-T R, Morocco*

Tom finally woke again. He was surprised to find Shepherd was still at his bedside. He was no longer wearing his faux-Arab outfit, which helped somewhat to confirm Tom's waking impression that he had been sleeping for quite some time.

He deliberately came around slowly, taking the time to notice rather less equipment around him. When he swallowed he realised that much of the clutter in his throat had been removed too.

'How long...?' He had a coughing fit as he tried to continue his question.

'Don't force it. You will be sore for a while yet. To answer your unspoken question, you have been asleep for the best part of a day since we last spoke. Our doctors have kept you sedated to aid your recovery. But they've told me that I can offer you liquids.' He passed a plastic beaker and assisted him to take a sip.

Tom thought it bizarre that the man, Shepherd was it, had not challenged him as to why he was there? No comment about how he was shot, or more significantly why he had been shot. Well, he certainly wasn't going to volunteer anything. He instinctively felt that he should not mention Stevie, even though every part of him wanted to ask Shepherd to let her know that he was here in the retreat. He was already beginning to feel better, but thought he should conceal any signs of recovery until he was ready to get out of there.

Shepherd showed no curiosity whatsoever in this matter and patiently waited to continue his monologue, still calmly seeking to shape Tom's next book.

'Now where were we? I believe I was developing the story of the caduceus for you, and had mentioned the story of Eve and the serpent. Before we pass on from that story, let me just mention that there are many who believe the staff in the Rod of Asclepios and the one in the caduceus come directly from the wood of the Tree of Knowledge in the Garden of Eden.

'I also explained that that the story of Adam and Eve is a re-hash of a much earlier telling. You may in your research have come across one of the earliest human works of literature "The Epic of Gilgamesh"?' He didn't wait for an immediate response but pressed straight on, 'There are two versions that usually get quoted, one of these is Sumerian. One of the earliest uses of the caduceus symbol is in fact Sumerian, to depict the fertility god, Ningizzida. Ah, I thought that might get your attention. The Sumerian version was produced 2,000 years before Christ and the other, which was a later Akkadian version, was produced perhaps 700 to 800 years later. Do you know of it?'

Tom gulped as he said, 'Know the name.' and signed for Shepherd to continue, suggesting his voice was still too painful.

'Gilgamesh was shown as a ruler on the Sumerian king list at about 2,600 BCE; so these versions we have, would have been passed down by word of mouth and only written down much later. I feel sure this is not too dissimilar to the process that delivered us the Bible Gospels. The later version of the epic opens with "He who saw the deep..." and is taken to mean he was the one granted special knowledge.

'These very early Sumerian and Akkadian records are very intriguing. They talk of an earlier time when life was perfect; perfect as described in the Garden of Eden! They talk of the creation of mankind by some other being or god. They talk of knowledge being passed to humankind by some strange being, the serpent Oannes; their Gilgamesh, our Eve! It was the Sumerians who first mentioned the anger of a god and a great flood; their Ziusudra, our Noah! So is the Bible just a plagiarism? Or is it that, as I believe, both record an archive of a much earlier belief passed down for centuries by word-of-mouth?'

Tom was intrigued by the thinking, perhaps this preacher had something he could use after all.

'I guess they are not so very far apart geographically, the two peoples.' Tom then spluttered to cover his sudden long sentence, but he need not have worried for Shepherd was pressing on regardless.

'The creation story in the Bible has Adam being formed out of "the dust of the ground", and then while he slept "he took one of his ribs, and closed up the flesh..." Shepherd flicked through Tom's papers.

'In your notes here you comment on those early people in South America, in Tiwanaku, believing that their god made humans from clay too.' He scanned for the name.

'Ah, here it is, Viracocha. I was intrigued enough to look him up. He was an Inca god too, acclaimed as the bringer of knowledge and civilisation. There is also an aquatic reference in that he rose out of Lake Titicaca and eventually disappeared into the sea; apparently his name literally means "sea-foam".'

Tom was trying to dedicate part of his mind to assessing where he was, how he might escape. He had to confess that what Shepherd was relating was not without interest, so he relaxed and listened to this man, while trying to assess his weaknesses. Liking the sound of his own voice was the first of course, but Tom accepted that he was just as often guilty of this too.

'The Sumerians had a god who made man out of clay too. They go into rather more detail. The clay figures are combined with the flesh and blood of a god, then more gods spit onto the clay. The process involved a gestation period and a womb broke open to deliver the first human. This taking of ribs, the mixing up of flesh and blood, is interesting when you consider that these early people would have had no knowledge of surgical procedures. Within the limits of their knowledge and their language, these sound like pretty good attempts of someone without any such knowledge trying to describe a modern medical scene. Gilgamesh himself is described as two-thirds god and one-third human, what we might call a genetic hybrid today.'

Tom insisted and grunted out, 'These are all fables, legends.'

'Are you sure? Then let's look again at that early symbol, the caduceus. It appears on some Mesopotamian cylinder seals as early as 4,000 BCE. The Greeks depicted their messenger of the gods, Hermes as holding the symbol. Many suggest that he was based upon a much earlier Mesopotamian deity. The Romans applied the same symbol to their god Mercury, he too carries the caduceus.'

He pulled out a picture of the icon.

'Now just take a good close look at it. Imagine for a moment, just what else it could be seeking to represent? It can only be the double helix, present deep within our DNA? And this clear symbol has been handed down to us from time immemorial, from a time when our human antecedents could not possibly have known anything of its significance!'

# Chapter 49 - *Saint-Maximin-la-Sainte-Baume, France*

They had arrived in Saint-Maximin-la-Sainte-Baume late in the evening. The local team had rented a small gîte just outside the town and they had piled in and crashed out.

An intermediary had paid over cash to complete the transaction. It was ideal for their needs, adjacent to a country house which they had confirmed was currently empty. Across its three floors there were three bedrooms, two doubles and a twin, though the Americans were none too keen on the notion of a shared bathroom. Then it conveniently had a large shed and a carport where they were able to accumulate and assemble all their equipment.

Each of them wore gloves and took care to place every scrap of rubbish into waste bags that they would take with them. Fine grills were placed over the bath plug to capture any hair or other body debris and this would be disposed of similarly. Aggressive cleaning fluids would complete the clean-up as they left; they would do everything to ensure that there would be no trace of their presence.

Will was impressed; it looked as if Dom had organised this one properly, finally! Or perhaps he had just lucked out in his choice of local operatives. They rested up for the morning, then in the afternoon the two Americans took a leisurely stroll through the town and around the church behaving as typical tourists, taking a plethora of photos that could be studied back at the gîte.

It was a pretty sleepy place, but then Will was amazed how many times he had travelled through a French town seeing no-one - all the shutters drawn, not even a sleepy cat or dog to indicate it was anything other than a ghost town. All that was needed was a local variety of tumbleweed to make it fully authentic.

This town had a commanding presence; apparently it was the largest Gothic building in the whole of the south of France, certainly it looked impressive. It perched broodily above the town, almost pink in the afternoon sunshine. Will had always been uncomfortable with huge buildings that looked as if they were designed to threaten the local community rather than attract them. He thought they said loudly and clearly, 'Bow down before me you mere mortal!'

All that construction cost in terms of human toil and resources, and in this particular case over a full three centuries, to end up with something that was threatening. If he must follow a religion, then this certainly could not be his choice.

Will had allocated Buck the dubious pleasure of checking that none of the relics were being held in either of the nearby shrines. This had entailed Buck schlepping all the way up to the cave-church high on a hill close to the town where, according to legend, the Magdalene spent thirty years at the end of her life. She was certainly meant to be long-lived for her era.

He was amused by Buck's displeasure when he also advised him he would need to make the even steeper climb up to the cliff-top chapel where the locals believed angels had carried Mary each evening for her final devotions; Buck's comments were certainly not for the ears of angels.

Will himself was standing inside the basilica looking up at the ornate walnut pulpit while reading his guidebook notes about it, describing how it held seven detailed carved scenes depicting the Magdalene's life. But his studied anonymity as a tourist was blown to pieces when his phone resounded around the otherwise still church. He really needed to change the tone from the recognisable CTU chiming used in the TV series '24'.

He took a second to see that it was Dom calling before he pressed the reject button, but he accepted that he needed to leave the building and return the call because Dom would persevere.

'Yes?' He kept his voice deliberately neutral when Dom responded.

'Why didn't you take my call?'

'I was inside the Church recceing for tonight. Why did you call?'

'To check all was in hand, of course.'

He couldn't help himself in saying, 'Well I'm afraid it's not, but only because I've been interrupted in the middle of my inspection.'

'No need for sarcasm. If you kept me advised on progress then I wouldn't need to keep calling you. You are just one part of a well-oiled series of missions over which someone has to retain a clear oversight. Do I need to wet nurse you all?'

Will thought, 'Well, you do have the man boobs for the job!' But he said, 'Let me do my job.'

He closed the call, switched off his phone and angrily went back inside to seek out the route down to the crypt. Dom was getting beyond a joke. In Will's view this constant calling was further evidence that the man was losing it. Then perhaps this might just lead to an opportunity for personal advancement?

Sure enough he found the stairway and light switch and passed down through a heavy door into the crypt. There was no sign that either door could be locked or might be secured later in the evening.

Inside the crypt he studied the 4th century monumental work that held the four ornate marble sarcophagi, each with a carved biblical scene; and there too was the shrine said to contain Mary Magdalene's remains. Of the brass head he could find nothing. Perhaps it was in the main body of the church? He looked around but could see no sign of it.

Buck came back to the gîte grumbling about his onerous climb, but his words fell on deaf ears as Will still remembered climbing more than three hundred steps in Chiang Mai; though he had to admit the downward journey had been much easier. Buck confirmed there was no suggestion of a reliquary in either of the shrines, so they could relax until that night when they would enter the basilica.

They went about this with brutal efficiency. One of the local team was positioned outside each door to deflect any interest their noise might attract. Tom had concluded there was no simple way of reaching and opening the lids of the sarcophagi. Buck and he took it in turns to use a large sledgehammer directly on the marble sides of the sarcophagi. They were not very resilient having been designed merely as decoration rather than any form of secure structure.

Neither gave a thought to the works of art that they were destroying, or the resting places they were defiling. The noise of their work was deafening within the crypt but the heavy doors meant that little sound escaped to attract any curiosity.

Buck paused and asked, 'Do you believe these things hold anything of real value, real saints?'

Will laughed, 'Who knows? Isn't religion all about faith? If these things truly are precious then it doesn't seem to me that the Church is aware of it; absolutely no sign of any security here or at the other shrines I've been to.'

'What are we doing with them? Building shrines of our own?'

'They are all going to Dr Davenport rather than Perpetua, so I've no idea. Reminds me of the text on an old army T-shirt that I would like to tweak and reprint to say, "I joined Mission to travel and expand my mind, to visit exotic places, meet interesting people - and rob graves."'

They both chuckled as they used battery-powered hand tools to punch holes in the inner containers and then reached into each to take some of the remains. In three cases they came up with parts of a hand, and in one a sternum with a segment of a ribcage. They checked with a UV light to see that the bones had some residual material on their surface and carefully bagged each piece separately.

They next turned their attention to the Magdalene shrine which they attacked with gusto, eager to finish up there. It was completely empty. They looked around the crypt for any other likely location but found none. Will gave Buck a challenging look to see if he would have any argument, and reached back into one of the female saints' sarcophagi to extract another sample. That way they would still return with five relics for Dom. Buck's look confirmed he too was happy to let Dom resolve the issue back at base.

Within an hour the sacrilege in the sacristy was complete and they were on their way home.

# Chapter 50 - *Double-T R, Morocco*

Stevie woke with the mother of all hangovers. A deep pulse pounding in her head suggested something in there wanted to escape the pressured confines of her skull. Her ears rebelled against a constant white noise source, like a combination of fingernails being filed, and then those same nails being scratched across a chalkboard.

She was cold, so cold. Worse something heavy was pinning down her arm which had become completely numb. The taste in her mouth gave the impression she had eaten a strong curry and not used toothpaste for days. As she opened her eyes she started to cough, a dry hacking cough as if she was a long-term heavy smoker.

She put aside her discomforts when she realised that she was lying out in the open air; and worse she was completely naked!

When she investigated further, the weight on her arm proved to be Hannah, also lying there brazenly asleep and unclothed. She managed to work her arm free without waking her but this just added to the catalogue of woes as her arm came painfully back to life.

So it was real! She had thought it was some weird dream she had been having. She had been shocked, even deep within her assumed dream, that she could have shown interest in another woman. That was why she had been content to treat it as some sort of nightmare; she had absolutely no doubts about her true leanings. She had never detected an iota of interest in that particular direction before.

She had to get away! If she did then somehow it would become less real and perhaps she could begin to forget the night's events which were now all too vividly flooding back to her. She started the slow process of thrusting these memories to the back of her mind. She was unaware of it, but she was filing the whole incident close to where her childhood abuse had been stored for so many years.

She gathered some clothes, any clothes that she could find. This just couldn't be happening to her. Sleeping out in the open, naked, gay sex, with all these others around her, what had she been thinking? She couldn't really have done with Hannah what was now replaying in her mind, could she? She felt sick and started to retch.

She picked her way carefully through the field. It was like she imagined a battlefield might look, with all these bodies just lying around. No, what it looked like was that old master painting the 'Rape of the Sabine Women'. This hadn't been rape; it had all been consensual. No the scene she was surveying was not that. It was more like an illustrated work she had seen years ago the horrific imagination in Dante's 'Inferno'.

Somehow she managed to get back to the hut, thankful to find it empty. How could she face Hannah when next in the laboratory?

Over the next hour or so several of the other 'Anglos' struggled back in one by one, all looking much the worse for wear and all strangely insular. Thankfully each remained silent on the night's events, but not so Avril. She came back, looking equally bedraggled, but sporting a broad smile on her face; and clearly she wanted to talk about all in graphic detail.

'What a night!'

Stevie could not ignore her, so feigned enthusiasm, 'Yes, Samuel's presentation was very interesting wasn't it?'

'No, not that, after! It was absolutely incredible. I think I made love to at least three guys last night. I was absolutely and completely insatiable. I've no idea what came over me but I just couldn't get enough. I felt so liberated, so empowered, so horny!'

'Listen to yourself, that's just not at all like you talking!'

'I know, I know. I've never felt like that before. I know it's shameful, but it was also pretty spectacular too! I felt completely wanton! Last night I was certainly wanton it!' She subsided into giggles at her own joke.

Stevie couldn't help but smile, 'You're so shameless. Just look at that smile on your face!'

Stevie was thinking she wished she could somehow find that wantonness, but she knew it had been squeezed out of her in her childhood. However she was quite clear that her desire for wantonness did not include having sex with another woman!

'But do you know who they were?'

'Absolutely no idea, and that's what was so very good about it - no trying to remember their names, no awkward breakfast in the morning, no feeling guilty leaving an apartment at the dead of night, no waiting for them to call you back.

'Oh God I almost forgot, one of them did tell me something. He recognised him from his TV appearances apparently. He said that Tom, your Tom, he's here. He's in a private room at our hospital.'

Stevie waited while Avril cleaned up and changed, determined to go straight to the hospital to find Tom. As they were almost ready to leave, Marsha arrived completely unannounced at their dorm. It was the first time she had ever entered their hut. She looked around them all expressionlessly; quite a few of the Apostles took this as a critical observation of their overnight antics and their cheeks flared in embarrassment.

Marsha had of course seen the video evidence of each and every one of their exploits the previous night. If anything the only emotion she felt was a degree of envy for these younger women who were so voracious. She considered this to be yet another incentive to hurry along her work in not just halting ageing but also reversing its effects. Perhaps when this was all over she could recapture some of their sexual enthusiasm and athleticism.

Realising the effect that she was having, she spoke to resolve the matter. 'I do trust that you all enjoyed your very special night?'

Everyone relaxed visibly as Marsha explained she needed Stevie to come with her. Now it was Stevie who flushed. Was it her unnatural encounter that had caused offence?

Stevie wanted to ask about Tom but decided it might bother Marsha. She had made it very clear in Tunis that Stevie should have left him behind her. Marsha believed that Stevie had somehow contacted Tom to bring him to Tunis; and she clearly viewed this as some sort of lack of commitment on Stevie's part. So Stevie decided to keep her knowledge of Tom's presence to herself - for now.

Marsha was unaware of the earlier conversation between Avril and Stevie, and unaware that Stevie already intended to seek out Tom. Dieter, following the revelations at the studio, was currently intercepting and deleting certain conversations.

It was evident that Marsha was not in the mood for conversation as she led Stevie at pace across to the main building. She paused at the door.

'I've brought you here to meet Samuel face-to-face.' Then pressing on rapidly through a maze of corridors, they arrived at a door with a young man standing guard outside.

Stevie's neck instantly reddened at the thought. This was her first private meeting with the Patriarch. All her instincts told her she was to be condemned for her lesbian act, perhaps exiled from the Perpetua Order? Or maybe it was more personal. Apparently he had once held a special interest in Hannah. Was he repulsed by the person who had led her in another direction?

She stepped carefully into the room, not knowing what to expect. He found it was furnished like a luxuriously plush apartment. Low and moody lighting revealed four low settees set around a large central coffee table. A large desk beside oak-shelved rows of books filled one wall, a sophisticated AV system commanded another corner. It looked and felt masculine in its approach, yet it was clearly a comfortable room both to work and to relax in.

Samuel Shepherd was sitting behind the desk, his spread papers bathed in light from a large brass desk lamp. Stevie sensed something missing on the desk, and realised it was that there was no expected PC taking up working surface.

Samuel stood and walked across to Marsha. He took her in a bear hug then kissed her heartily on the lips.

'So tell me who is it that you have brought to meet me?' He turned his attention to Stevie; and it was all his attention. His keen eyes travelled all over Stevie's body. She could not know he had seen every part of her on the video, every action. In fact he could not shake the image he had of her coupling with Hannah; and was wondering if he could dare propose a threesome.

He tore his thoughts back to the present. He could always watch that video again after their meeting; but he could imagine Stevie and Hannah re-enacting the scene for him in private. With supreme effort he managed to wrest his mind back from the thought and his attention came to rest on her eyes.

Marsha could read the man and was excited that he was so turned on by Stevie. Her plan was working. The girl looked flustered and so she came to her rescue.

'This is Stevie Tasker. I told you all about her from way back at our first meeting at Culham; and my early impression has not dimmed with time.'

'Of course, your single most important individual within the Anglo Apostles, your divine dozen.' Stevie looked across at Marsha, embarrassed and a tad concerned by his 'most important' tag. Before she knew it she was grabbed into the same bear hug and he kissed her just as heartily on the lips. 'You are very welcome here. Are you settling in OK?'

Stevie was extremely uncomfortable at the kiss directly on her lips. There had also been the hint of a tongue against her mouth. But she shook off her concern; he was the Patriarch after all. She modestly replied, 'Yes, thank you. We in Marsha's Anglos are a pretty remarkable team.'

'Good, good. Marsha, does Stevie know quite how special they are yet?'

Stevie felt an electric shock at the use of the word 'special'; that was how that disgusting old priest had referred to her while he abused her. He had kept on stressing that she was 'his special one', that they had a 'very special relationship', that it was so 'special' that others could not be told, because they could not begin to understand it. That kiss and now the use of the word 'special' in this context overwhelmed any conditioning. She was now very much on guard.

'No, Samuel, I've left it for you to explain.'

He motioned them to the sofas and walked around the room shaking away the last pictures of that video and collecting his thoughts.

'As you know Perpetua is creating a new order in this tired and wicked world. Ours is a community based upon pure ability and capacity. For far too long we have allowed the human strain to atrophy, to weaken. Sadly today the highest birth rates are recorded by those with the lowest IQs. We allow the disabled and feeble-minded to procreate. We allow those with hereditary diseases, HIV and other terrible afflictions to have children. We use science to give pregnancies to those who can't achieve this naturally.'

Stevie looked across at Marsha. 'Marsha and I have had this conversation before. I have to admit that I feel uncomfortable with eugenics because I cannot establish who is fit to be the judge or jury of what is desirable? For instance, might we have lost Einstein because eugenics would have aborted him for his dyslexia?'

Marsha answered this brusquely. 'It can all be judged by the genes themselves. We now have such a huge database which shows us clearly where the problems lie and the 'jury' can set the boundaries wide enough to allow enough uncertainty to still exist and permit the slow-developing genius through the net.'

Stevie persisted, 'Shouldn't it be for our leaders, thinkers and politicians to debate and define what is acceptable?'

Marsha snapped, 'What? You would want a Richard Nixon, or Ronald Reagan, or George W Bush to be the final arbiters of right and wrong? I wouldn't have trusted them to park my car! They're the very ones who've gotten us to where we are today!'

Samuel waved a calming hand. 'We are talking here of our community, admitting only those who can enhance and advance the Order. You and your colleagues were selected because you have innate special skills that perhaps you have not yet been able to fully realise.'

Stevie flinched again. She really would prefer it if he stopped using that word 'special'; for her it triggered all the wrong emotions.

He continued, 'We have a confession to make. When you joined us you each had your full genome analysed in absolute detail. We compared yours with our huge database and we found that the Anglos have amazing, wonderful, delightful skills. Our new Order has been established to cherish and nurture these skills. You are aware of the Perfect orders?'

Stevie nodded as Marsha explained, 'Yes, I have advised her of the structure, of our seven levels.'

'Fine, fine. As I hope you know, seven is that heavenly number for perfection. The Book of Revelations was directed to the seven early churches, it prophesied of the seven seals and so on. For the same reason we have seven orders of Perfects, reflecting not just the development of the individual but also their inherent, innate skills.

'Some ardent well-intentioned long-term members will be capable only of ever achieving level Three, but you my dear should aspire at least to becoming a Six. And with the right training, that we are pledged to give you, we fully expect to greet you into Seven status at an early stage.'

Stevie was still unsettled by the conversation. When she considered what she knew of other Sixes, like Hannah, she was none too convinced that much happiness had ensued by gaining that status.

Samuel caught her look. 'You don't look too sure this is what you want?'

'No, it's not that at all. Of course I'm delighted that my fellow Apostles and I can look forward to a long and fruitful membership. It's another matter which I have explained to Marsha.'

'Yes, Samuel. I told you of Stevie's vision of Perpetua.'

Samuel walked over and knelt before her, taking both her hands lightly in his. 'If it were not an awful sin then I would be so very envious of you. You actually saw Saint Perpetua?'

'Yes, I was very young, but she appeared to me when I needed guidance.'

'You must not dismiss it as some error imagined by your youth. In fact when you are young you are better able to appreciate the realities as you have not been programmed by the world around you, not programmed to think and see what everyone else sees. As a child you see what you see, without interpretation, without any motivation. It is what it is. How wonderful for you. For me this just underlines your special status. Why were you looking so worried?'

She thought, 'Do stop using that word!' But she said. 'I felt I might be able to recapture something of Perpetua while I was in Tunis. But I was whisked away before I had really settled there. I had hardly any time to reach out to her, or for her to reach out to me. It does feel a lot like unfinished business as a result.'

'I see, I see. You really mustn't feel as if you are imprisoned here. Why do you need to be anywhere in particular in order to open up your heart and mind to Perpetua? She originally came to you in England, I understand. Marsha can show you how to open yourself up to whatever it is you seek. Marsha, you can find time for some one-on-one meditation classes, can't you?'

She nodded. Samuel rose and drew Stevie up with him. 'I am so delighted to meet you Stevie. Marsha, you were right. She truly has a remarkable soul.'

He drew Stevie back into a bear hug but this time one of his hands slid down to the small of her back and he pressed their lower bodies together. It was only for a split second, as if he was testing her to see if she would respond. She found it extremely unwelcome, unsavoury. She stiffened in his grip.

It was the one thing that Stevie would recall from the meeting. It left a sour note overwhelming the rest of the encounter that could have otherwise been so very interesting.

# Chapter 51 - *Double-T R, Morocco*

Tom had been left dumbstruck at their last meeting by the thought that the caduceus was somehow a depiction of the DNA's double helix. It was something that had never occurred to him before. How could someone in our prehistory have had any such appreciation of this very modern scientific phenomenon? It must be pure happenstance.

The caduceus was just an image that was reminiscent of the double helix and Shepherd had jumped to a conclusion after the fact. Then Tom had never considered himself a great believer in happenstance or coincidence; in his life he always found something systematically at work behind any event of apparent serendipity.

Now that he was no longer sedated, he slowly recovered his powers of speech through talking with the nursing staff. He found them a tight-lipped lot. However one finally apologised explaining that this reticence was because they were all worn down by the epidemic they had been fighting there.

Stevie made her way across to the laboratory with some trepidation. Would Hannah be there? How would she act towards her this morning? But she need not have worried as Hannah came straight to her with a look of concern and led her off to a side room.

'You know that those SOBs drugged us all last night. Sorry but now they've just gone too far. First they remove us all to this wilderness, then they try to mind control us with their regular broadcasts and meditation sessions. They keep us on such flimsy diets that we don't have the energy to object and now they're screwing our minds with their drugs.'

Stevie didn't know what to say about this.

Hannah smiled, 'Stop looking so worried. I'm not gay, not even a little bit that way. There's no way I want anyone to know what we did. Ever! I do hope you feel the same way?'

'Absolutely, I still can't really believe that it happened. It's like some half-remembered nightmare.'

'That's because it wasn't you and it was not of your volition. They drugged us, changed us. I thought I knew all their tricks but it seems that in the retreats, because they know they have us imprisoned, they are prepared to go even further. If we hang around here they'll have us mating with the humanzees next. In fact, just imagine. If they'd let them loose last night in our condition we probably wouldn't have known or cared!'

'What do you mean? Are you planning to leave?'

'We're their drones here. They can do what they want to us and who knows or cares. Was it Sigourney Weaver's film that said "In space no one can hear you scream"? Well I'm not sure anyone would hear us from way out here either!'

Now Shepherd was back in Tom's room again and Tom sensed he had some reason for urgency. Shepherd had much more to tell and seemed to be under some time constraint to do so.

'Look, in writing your archaeo-astronomy book you need to be aware that the caduceus was also used from very early times as an astrological image; it represented the forgotten or at least uncelebrated thirteenth sign of the zodiac. Don't forget it was the Babylonians, the direct successors to your Sumerians, whose astronomers first catalogued the ecliptic path of the sun and divided the heavens into twelve zones.'

Tom was on well researched ground, 'Yes I know it was them. They named the twelve zones and invented what they termed the "circle of animals" or zodiac.'

Shepherd wanted the helm. 'In fact they should have created thirteen zones, as the sun passes through the constellation of Ophiuchus from November 30th to December 17th. This zone lies between the two established signs of Sagittarius and Libra but is completely ignored by our modern zodiac system. I've no idea why that happened but it's probably something to do with triskaidekaphobia, you know, the fear of the number 13.'

Tom couldn't quite believe that he was actually choosing to reference the Bible in front of this preacher man. 'I thought that was supposed to be based on the belief that the traitor Judas was the thirteenth to sit down at the table for the Last Supper?'

'True it has shaped the history of that number. Then the baby Jesus had his epiphany on the 13th day of life, the day upon which he received the Magi, and that was not considered as in any manner unlucky. By the way do you know the date of Christ's birth?'

Tom was finding these sudden changes of tack intriguing though tiring. Perhaps he was not as well recovered as he thought. 'Well I guess I always assumed it was on the 25th December?'

'The supposed authority was Saint Clement of Alexandria who lived at the end of the 2nd century CE. Yet he gives us two possible dates - overnight on the 24th/25th day of *Pachon* or the 25th day of *Pharmuthi*, which would in fact place it securely in the spring. So it ought to be much nearer to our modern Easter rather than when we celebrate it at Christmas.'

Shepherd pressed on with his wealth of information. 'The actual year of His birth is also a matter of great dispute. The various protagonists place it at various times from as early as 8 BCE up to as late as 6 CE. It was only a 4th century invention that moved it across to 25th December. This was done completely artificially to locate it at the beginning of the Jewish festival of light.'

Tom felt he should contribute to the process and interrupted. 'Of course any such working out of dates has to take account of Pope Gregory's major change to the calendar sometime around the late 16<sup>th</sup> century.'

'Precisely. Pope Gregory III's changes meant that eleven days of 1582 CE had to be skipped. He it was who also introduced leap years to get us back in sync with the heavenly norms; that's even more archaeo-astronomy lore for your book. For example Easter had got out of sync with the moon by around four days at that time. Let's get back to our Saviour's birth. The established or more informed wisdom places it towards the latter part of that range of dates that I mentioned earlier, usually concluding that it was on the 6<sup>th</sup> January in the year 4 CE. The Bible suggests that the king at the time was Herod and that's not borne out by other historic sources. To resolve this we have to seek out other evidence.'

Tom had to admit he was becoming engrossed by the man's story. Not just his story, he was surprised that he was actually warming to the man and his enthusiasm. 'Does it really matter when it was; does it need to be that precise?'

'I'm getting to that, but you need to appreciate that the Bible is quite confused over its stance on astrology. In the Old Testament's Deuteronomy, Moses quotes the vengeful Jehovah as permitting no astrology, *"... hath gone and served other gods, and worshipped them, either the sun or the moon, or any of the host of the heaven, which I have not commanded...."* Then the New Testament's Luke has Jesus saying, *"... there shall be signs in the sun and in the moon, and in the stars...."*'

Tom could see no problem with this. 'Aren't the two testaments pretty much at odds with each other in many other respects anyway.'

'There can be no doubting that His birth has a very key astrological significance, the Magi's star. This is mentioned less than thirty verses into the New Testament! The Magi were only much later declared to have been kings. They are thought to have in fact been practitioners of Zoroastrianism, a middle-Eastern religion that pre-dated Christ by some five centuries. They certainly believed in astrology and as such would have been moved to notice and perhaps to follow an unusual event they spotted in the sky.'

Tom was ashamed to realise that he had not looked at the Bible stories for his astrological research, instinctively assuming that it would have no relevance to his book. Yet this was clearly one of the most famous pieces of archaeo-astronomy! Tom wanted to urge the preacher on, 'I've read conflicting stories. Do you believe it was a star or a planet that they saw?'

'In part calling it a star was predicated by a star prophecy in the Old Testament, written some eight hundred years earlier in Numbers 24:17. Numbers is interesting for many other reasons, including to pursue the story of the caduceus, but we can come back to that. Linking Christ's birth to a star was probably very useful to the early Christian cause. It helped to fulfil some of the Old Testament expectations which would help to make His birth much more significant. The Magi's arrival seems on the face of it to have had no particular added-value to what was at the time a purely Jewish event.'

Stevie's meeting with the Patriarch had been the final straw for her. She readily agreed with Hannah that their best course of action would be to leave the retreat, but she insisted that she wanted to be sure that Avril would come too. Hannah thought that the more people who knew about their plans the more likely they were to be stopped, but she accepted that Avril should be invited along.

Once Avril had agreed to join them, Stevie insisted that they had to get Tom out too, in case he was used to lure her back. Hannah was strongly against this idea. She questioned whether they should even investigate whether Tom was actually there, fearing that the longer they delayed their escape the more likely it was they would be discovered. Stevie was adamant.

What none of the three realised was that each conversation about escaping was of course being filmed; everything they said in the retreat was recorded. The security team should have heard and intervened well before now, however Dieter had told them that he was running a special project for the Patriarch and he ensured that he alone in the security centre was able to monitor their discussions. He was hurriedly deleting the records as he went. He also took over the monitoring of Avril's office as the three expanded on their conspiracy.

While Hannah organised packing up some supplies and materials for their escape, Stevie was able to get past the hospital security team by virtue of Avril's presence and her authority. Dieter watched powerlessly as they almost walked straight in on Samuel and Tom deep in discussion in his private room.

However the presence of security men along the corridor alerted Avril that something was out of the ordinary. Dieter monitored her asking one of the nursing staff what was happening, and was told that the Patriarch was currently in with Tom. He watched and continued to delete as they decided it would be better to wait until Shepherd had left.

On his split screen he also monitored Hannah as she was packing. Her bending and stretching as she worked displayed her fit body in all its glory; delighting his eye, yet at the same time churning his stomach. His emotions were torn. It was his unrequited love that was driving him to save her, to watch her back; yet in doing so he was also ensuring that she would leave, guaranteeing his love would never have a chance to flourish.

Tom had been drinking freely from the plastic beaker to keep his still quite raw throat lubricated. 'Surely the Magi are just an invention? Wouldn't the gospel writers, preparing their words much later, as Christianity was successfully spreading throughout the Roman Empire, have wanted to showcase the event as being seen at the time as of more than of local importance?'

Shepherd considered his point. 'Perhaps, but let's follow their star a little. Today's astronomers do suggest the most likely candidate could be a planetary conjunction; planets travelling at different speeds and of course different orbits do briefly appear to be in the same place when viewed from earth. When they are so close, the combination of their brightnesses makes them far more evident than normal in the night sky. Research shows that there were no candidate comets or meteors having any significance around that time. Besides if you follow the Gospel accounts, then this phenomenon could not have been just a single event but had to be a series of them; first something happened to lead the Magi towards Herod and then much later something had to shine over that stable in Bethlehem.'

Tom queried. 'I've always been confused by that one. Just how can a star be considered to point at some place on the earth so specifically?'

Shepherd pressed on with his account; obviously nothing was going to stop his flow and direction. 'The Magi would not have set off from Persia without seeing something pretty remarkable. What we at Perpetua have learnt from other gospels that we have uncovered, ones that have yet to be published, is that they did indeed see a conjunction. It happened near the star Regulus, one of the night sky's brightest stars. It's the star they at the time called *Sharru*. It was one of the four royal stars, the stars that by their relative brightness gave the Zoroastrians a sort of shorthand calendar. *Sharru*, our Regulus, was the "Watcher of the South" and heralded the important summer solstice.

'In mid-August 3 BCE it can be shown that there was a conjunction of Venus and Jupiter in Regulus. Their beliefs would have linked this event and it happening within Leo would suggest to them something to do with Judah, this was its symbology for them. Add to this that Jupiter was their king planet and the star's name, *Sharru*, also meant king. Finally Venus, their star *Ishtar*, was also chief among the Babylonian goddesses related to fertility. So these happenings would have certainly gotten their attention – it was as if the stars were shouting at them "Judah, king, king, birth".'

Behind him Dieter only just caught sight of Daniel Lehri as he entered the control complex and had just enough time to switch his view to a video edit that was on his task list. He just hoped the three women would not move from their current location while he was unable to provide them with back-up support.

Tom was taken along with the tale but asked, 'What about its apparent stopping?'

'In mid-September Jupiter had a further conjunction with Regulus, then it appeared to stop and move backwards. Astronomers call this phenomenon a retrograde motion. It happens at times when the earth is running more quickly here on our inner orbit than the distant viewed objects.

'Jupiter later conjoined with Regulus again in mid-February 2 BCE, and it did the same yet again in early May. We can only imagine the huge amount of interest that this would have generated with these early astronomers. The clincher that would have them setting off to find the great king in Judah, to find the "King of the Jews", was when Jupiter, Venus and Regulus all again came into conjunction in mid-June 2 BCE.'

'Where does the caduceus, or this rod you mentioned, fit in with this?'

'We have evidence that these travellers arrived at and journeyed through the Holy Land to meet up with the then king during the sun's transition of Ophiuchus - that's the thirteenth zodiac sign with its symbol being the caduceus. It's one of the forty-eight constellations recorded by Ptolemy; also known as Serpentarius, the serpent-holder; in fact both its names have serpent origins.

'Since the world obtained the capabilities of the Hubble Telescope this area of our night sky has again become popular as it's here where the now famous Eagle nebula is located. You may have seen the popular newspaper photo and subsequent posters showing that enormous cloudy creator of new stars. You surely must have seen those images of three startlingly colourful columns of cloud that have become popularly known as "The Pillars of Creation"?'

Tom nodded, 'Yes, I know the picture you mean.'

'However, apparently its capability to create stars actually peaked back around a million years ago. We are of course only seeing it as it was when the light left it; we're not seeing it real time as it is today. Interestingly, when we use X-rays, we cannot "see" those pillars any more. Astronomers have therefore concluded that a supernova must have destroyed the pillars, and it is estimated this happened around 6,000 years ago. As they are located some 7,000 light years away from us the columns have yet to disappear from any visual observation that we might make!'

'So how come the X-rays are registering the disappearance. I'm no physicist but surely X-rays can't exceed the speed of light?'

'You're the scientist. I'm only reporting what I understand to be the established view on this. Ask me about my own areas of interest and I can probably give you a more complete answer. When they investigated their theory they found there are apparently more than twenty stars out near the nebula that are clearly ripe to go nova; any therefore could be the culprit. It has been posited that the one that effectively destroyed those clouds went nova some 3,000 years earlier. Its effects would have taken time to cross space to reach out and destroy the clouds back at 6,000 years ago. We will have to wait a further millennium until we can actually get to see this disappearance.'

'You'll need to run that past me again. I'm confused on the number of years you're bandying about?'

'What it means is that the culprit supernova would have happened 9,000 years ago. Factoring in the 7,000 light years that it would have taken to get here, then the explosion would have been visible around 2,000 years ago!'

'So I see. What you're suggesting is that the second nativity event was a supernova and it was seen from within that constellation?'

'Precisely and that's not the only reason this particular constellation is of interest.'

'So why is this constellation, serpent-thingy of such interest to you? You can't seriously be telling me that snake-like ETs came to earth from this distant constellation and that they were still meddling in our affairs in some manner, many thousands of years later, when they inspired the Magi to travel to Bethlehem, can you?'

Dieter switched back to his split screen the instant Daniel left. It was with immense relief that he saw nothing had happened in the time he was off air. Everything was exactly as before.

Then Dieter zoomed in on Hannah as she changed her clothes. Briefly she stood naked in front of a mirror, looking for any flaws he presumed. He breathlessly could see not a single one. He feasted his eyes upon her; this was probably his last chance to glimpse the woman he loved with every fibre of his body.

He thought that she stretched and moved just like a young kitten, completely relaxed and unfettered. He couldn't help himself as he ran a DVD of the scene.

Tom realised Shepherd was displaying an acute neediness in his face and in his comments; for some reason he wanted to befriend Tom. Was this his motivation in sharing all this knowledge and his beliefs?

His instincts were correct; in his heart Samuel desperately wanted the world to appreciate his hard-won insights. He hoped Tom might become the one to achieve that for him. He hoped he might be prepared to join them and use his notoriety to become Perpetua's archivist, its press relations officer. Tom had the scientific reputation and the skills that would make the world sit up and listen to the justification for why Samuel had set upon the course that he and Marsha had defined.

Yet Shepherd was becoming frustrated at Tom's unwillingness to see the value of what he was presenting to him, delivering all this valuable material upon a silver platter. He realised this was because in recent years he had only ever preached to the converted; he was not used to a critical audience, with its own thoughts, its own point of view. This was a very different sort of challenge, but one he was committed to overcome.

'I thought you had thoroughly researched the Sumerians? The early kings were called the *Anunnaki*, literally it means those who came from heaven to earth which shows they clearly believed they were extraterrestrials. They said that these god-kings came from *Nibiru*, the "planet of the crossing", and they also claimed they were extremely long-lived.

'The Sumerians original name for them meant "pure and bright"; it was only much later that this was altered to suggest they were godlike or actual gods.

The many depictions of these gods often took a reptilian form. For example, as you say in your book manuscript, *Ea*, was the god of the waters, you do not seem to have noticed that intertwined snakes were his symbol; from what we have found this usage was the very first recorded application of the caduceus symbol.'

Tom didn't wish to interrupt this flow. He realised that, despite his earlier impressions, his book was indeed being finished off for him with this man's bizarre fiction.

Shepherd was on a roll and kept up the cascade of thoughts. 'If you examine the Sumerian royal cylinder seal that you have referenced in your notes, it quite clearly depicts a genetic experiment. Remember what I said of Gilgamesh. He was described as two-thirds god and one-third human - a hybrid.

'The Bible too talks of this sort of thing. In Genesis 6 verses 2 thru' 4 it says "...That the sons of God saw the daughters of men that they were fair and they took them wives of all which they chose ... ...There were giants in the earth in those days... ...and they bare children to them, the same became mighty men which were of old, men of renown."'

Tom wished he had a laptop or a recorder to capture all this.

'So just who were these gods, the ones with whom the human females mated? We've discovered no records of any other earthly-based advanced civilisations that could have convinced these relative sophisticates of their time that they were gods?'

'Interesting, but I'm not sure that you can make this series of references tie up in quite the way you suggest. My publisher gives me a lot of licence, but that's a series of huge leaps.'

'Exactly. It is a leap of faith! So far in our consideration of the caduceus we have concentrated upon the serpents, the bringers of knowledge arranged in such a provocative DNA double helix that just cannot be accidental. However all our discussions so far have ignored the staff or rod itself. If you examine it quite separately then it also proves very interesting.'

Tom recalled their earlier conversation. 'Didn't you suggest that the staff was originally taken from the Tree of Knowledge in the Garden of Eden?'

'Your notes show you are looking for something to connect all these early civilisations spread across the globe. You will need to think about this staff to understand the full significance of the caduceus.

'Take a look at Moses and Aaron; they both used a staff in mysterious ways. Surely it must have been the same one? At the burning bush Moses doubted how he could be sure to make his people stop and listen. God told him to throw his staff to the floor whereupon it changed into a snake - snake mark you! Aaron changed his staff into a snake too. This sort of staff became a symbol of high authority down the years. Greek heralds used them as the visible symbol of their power too.'

Shepherd was bombarding him with references to try to make his point. 'In the book of Numbers a rebellion was quelled and authority established for the Levite tribe to be the natural priests over other tribes. Each of the twelve tribes was required to bring a staff and it was again Aaron's staff that showed magical powers; when he stuck it into the ground it grew almonds.

'The *Haggadah*, the Jewish text that sets out the rules of the Passover, gives an even longer provenance to this rod or staff. It was put to use by Jacob when he crossed the Jordan long before Moses and Aaron used it. You may know 'Jacob's staff' has been the name given to an astronomical instrument down through the ages, though today it is more usually applied to the device where astronomical instruments are stored aboard a ship.'

Tom was stunned that none of this had come up in his research! These ideas were bewildering, but most of all extremely commercial. He hoped he could recall everything; certainly his publishers were going to love it!

'The *Haggadah* also says it was the same rod that David used to slay Goliath...'

'I thought he used a sling?'

Shepherd ignored this comment. '...and it later it became the sceptre of David's lineage, a symbol of authority for his descendant kings; though it disappeared when the temple was sacked. It also says that when he appeared the Messiah would have this staff to demonstrate his authority.

'As I mentioned before, other sources suggest that Adam was given it when banished from the Garden of Eden, that it was passed down to many of the great characters of the Old Testament and the Qur'an. Abraham, Isaac and Joseph are said by some to have had it before Moses. It is also claimed that it was passed on by him to Joshua. Still others suggest that it was on Noah's Ark and remained safe throughout the flood.

'There is even a suggestion that it was given to Jesus so that he might reveal his authority, but that favourite of fall guys, Judas Iscariot, stole it. Then later, when the Romans found no suitable wood for fabricating the cross-beam of the cross for Jesus, Judas gave them the historic rod for this purpose.'

'You can't possibly believe all that...?' Tom had wanted to add the word 'nonsense' but chose not to antagonise the man.

'I am merely providing you with research material. You see we have access to so many documents that you will not have seen. Many have never been published but instead have been handed down to those who were worthy of the knowledge.'

'That's certainly intriguing.'

Shepherd did not respond to the comment. 'In your notes you make clear that you were looking for some unification of these ancient peoples. I believe that in the caduceus, I have supplied you with your "missing link".'

'Rest assured that when I am recovered it's at the top of my list!'

'You mentioned the Inca god *Varicocha* in your notes? Well he was another who was said to have used a staff; many images show him with snakes in his hair or on his clothing. One such image is the oldest depiction of any god found anywhere in either of the Americas; it dates back to around 2,250 BCE.'

'Interesting. I have to confess that my first reaction is that it's implausible.'

Shepherd was annoyed by the reaction. 'Reviewing some of your published work I would have thought "interesting, but implausible" to be a good description of your approach.'

Tom smiled, 'Touché. I really don't need to come all the way to Africa, get shot and hospitalised to find further critics!'

Shepherd snapped, 'It was all spelt out for you there on those stelae rubbings from Tiwanaku!'

Tom was shocked, 'If your gNOS people hadn't stolen them from me perhaps then I would have reached some conclusion for myself!'

Shepherd realised his error and rather blustered, 'You had already made many of the links yourself. Look at what I have given you to consider - a global unifying symbol, the caduceus; the many references to reptilian or fishlike bringers of knowledge; the knowledge of medicine, genetics and DNA that implausibly seems to have been known back in our pre-history; the transgenic mixing of these bringers of knowledge or gods with early man.'

Tom wanted to keep Shepherd sweet so he could begin to learn more of his plans. 'I'm not ungrateful, for the surgery or for the ideas. I guess I need time to assimilate it all?'

'I have left you some material with your notes. I look forward to hearing your considered thoughts later.'

'I have to confess it's stunning what you have set out in our discussions. Can I see the source documents you mentioned?'

'Ah,' thought Shepherd, 'perhaps I have not been wasting my time.' He said, 'Only high-ranking members of Perpetua can see those. Our tests of your DNA suggest that you could be admitted into the Order, but it would take some commitment before you would earn the right to see those particular documents.' He used this as his exit line.

Tom called out to the man's disappearing back, 'And can I have the rubbings back?'

He then slumped back exhausted by the energy of the man and his broad ranging concepts. His instinct was that this was all probably arrant nonsense, but he hadn't discounted its potential 'wow factor' for his book. He needed access to a laptop, and soon, to get all this down!

Samuel and his guards swept off down the corridor and Dieter followed the girls on camera until they came to Tom's room; the Englishman was apparently asleep.

Tom was exhausted by the steady stream of ideas, and had closed his eyes to assist in trying to work his way through them. As he had no chance of access to a PC, or paper and pen, he found it easier to do this with his eyes closed.

His heart sank when the door re-opened, and he assumed that the preacher was coming back with even more. Instead it was Stevie and her new friend Avril who gushed into the room.

Stevie stood back looking concerned as she noted all the equipment around him. 'What happened to you? And why are you here?'

Tom smiled at her. 'It's much better than it looks. I came looking for you of course. I couldn't recognise you as the person I met in Tunis. I guess I might just as well ask you. What's happened to you? Why are you here?'

They stared at each other unclear where to start. Stevie resolved things by reaching down and kissing him on the cheek. 'What happened to put you in this bed?'

'I was shot by your preacher's men for trying to come to see you.'

Stevie was aghast. 'No, there must be some mistake! They wouldn't have done that.'

Monitoring this, Dieter shook his head. Despite her resolution to leave, this Stevie Tasker was still conditioned to believe in some good in the Order.

Tom grimaced. 'I'm sorry to disagree with you, but here I am living evidence of the fact. Brain and I, you remember him? Well, we came to see what they were doing with you here and we were chased away. As I got back to our vehicle to leave I was shot, through the throat. They brought me here and apparently gave me a new bit of trachea.'

Avril nodded at this. 'Stevie, I did see an order go through to the laboratories for that very thing. I noticed it because it was such an unusual request. I didn't know you could just order up such a thing.'

Stevie was stunned. 'Normally you couldn't, but my bet is that they would have used one of the humanzees for the replacement part! One of those poor creatures will have died to save you!'

Avril asked, 'What on earth's a humanzee?'

Stevie took a deep breath. 'I'll tell you later. Look we're all getting out of here. There's something wrong with this place; I've been feeling it for days. Hannah confirmed this even more this morning.'

Tom asked, 'I can see that in your face. What is it that's disturbing you so powerfully?'

'It's just that each time I've begun to feel the strangeness here, I've then somehow been Marsha-ed. She knows precisely when I'm feeling like that, almost seems to know what I'm thinking. After a one-on-one session with her I'm re-motivated to carry on. That can't be right. I'm my own person, able to make my own decisions. I really don't need to be dominated like this.'

Dieter smiled up in his eyrie. 'Now finally you're beginning to get it, to appreciate quite what's going on here!'

Tom was curious, 'There's something more than just a feeling?'

'It's Shepherd for one. The old goat all but touched me up earlier. Worse I'm getting the distinct impression that Marsha is encouraging me to end up as his concubine or something. I understand that's what Hannah had been before.

'Then there's what's happening in the laboratory - the humanzees and so on. Plus Avril's talk of cryonics facilities being set up here at the hospital. And there's your being shot for just wanting to come to see me.

'And, why is it that we need to be out here in the middle of nowhere? It all feels sort of devious, skulking out at the edges of civilisation. Besides it makes supplies and communications awful. Avril, you told me how tough a task it is for Daniel to set everything up here. If there was honest scientific endeavour then we could have been doing it more easily at Culham!'

Avril completely agreed that something was wrong with this place, but then she really hadn't come down completely from her overnight experiences. It was she who asked the practical question. 'How are you and Hannah planning to get us out of here? Should Tom even be moved?'

Tom volunteered. 'I'm OK, honestly. I can walk out of here if it's necessary.'

Stevie said, 'I strolled along the wall with Marsha and there is still a section that is unfinished. We could walk out through there.'

Avril smiled, 'I think I can do a little bit better than that.'

# Chapter 52 - *Kent, UK*

The meeting was deliberately set at Sir Joseph's country pile because a number of non-DICE members would be present. In fact though it was under the aegis of this body, it was not to be announced or recorded as a DICE meeting; it was planned more as an informal briefing of the five who had escaped from Tamegroute.

Present was Sir Joseph with Brain along as a general factotum. The Professor had brought Simon to be a minute-taker. The Professor was there to brief the Foreign Secretary on this otherwise off-the-record meeting. Admiral Bracewell had come with three aides to represent any military interests. These seven instinctively took one side and the two ends of a large rosewood table in the dining room.

Sitting opposite were Tom flanked by Stevie and Avril to his left, with Hannah and Dieter to his right. The five displayed various degrees of comfort in the presence of these obviously senior government officials. It didn't help that that the admiral had arrived from a formal function and was resplendent in full dress uniform.

Sir Joseph took the lead, well it was his home! 'We were all delighted to learn of your escape, and particularly relieved to find that young Tom here has been treated properly.'

Tom caught Brain's eye. The operative gave him a complicated look that Tom summed up as a combination of an apology for leaving him for dead and evident relief at the outcome.

Brain commented, 'I did think through all the options available and I'm delighted that I was right in my assessment.'

Tom made him wriggle just a little longer. 'If I'd had the strength or a suitable weapon to hand I would have happily shot you in the back when you walked away from me. I've had plenty of time to think it through and you were probably right. Fortunately events have proven you so. Just like history, the outcome is all that ends up being recorded, of having any importance. Besides I suppose it did mean I got Stevie out of there.'

## Double-T R, Morocco

Shepherd was incandescent. He realised that he should just have left the man to die; clearly he had underestimated Carter and certainly his medical team must have overestimated the extent of his injuries. The author must have been humouring him; he could never have given any thought to the invitation to join Perpetua.

Shepherd rallied his senior members from around the globe. He called for a satellite teleconference to include Tyndale's ruling cabinet which consisted of the twelve Canons of the twelve retreats, plus his inner sanctum group made up of himself representing Perpetua, Marsha for BiCogNaIT and Gene Genie, Dom for Mission, and Trajan for gNOS.

Shepherd turned on Daniel Lehri first. 'How can this have happened? Five people brewing a plot under our noses and getting clean away.'

'It was Dieter who made it all possible. As part of your personal coterie he was considered to be akin to Caesar's wife, beyond reproach. Without him messing with our security coverage they could not have done this.'

'I understand how they got out of the retreat. How many times did I say you should have finished the wall way before now? Just how could they have escaped the country too? Or are they lying low somewhere?'

## Kent, UK
In fact Avril had been the one who had got them out of the retreat, at least as far as the wall.

First she used her authority to organise a wheelchair to 'walk' Tom safely to the rear of the hospital. In her work at the retreat she was regularly being ferried back and forth to the hospital in a small jeep. She knew the keys could always be found in the ignition and knew her way around the hospital, so was able to get the three of them to the vehicle without being noticed.

She was the one who had instinctively appreciated that any skulking around would be instantly noticed so she simply and confidently drove them across the centre of the compound. The jeep was a familiar sight and no-one took any notice of its passage. She drove directly to the rear of the laboratory where Stevie fetched Hannah and their supplies for the journey.

From there they made directly for the gap in the wall. It was there that it looked as if it was all about to suddenly unravel. They feared a last minute discovery. As they approached the wall they saw Dieter standing right at the centre of the final gap in the retreat's perimeter. Avril was preparing to drive straight at him, straight over him if it proved necessary, but Hannah urged that she should pull over.

Hannah got out. Of course she knew about Dieter's feelings for her; he wore them across his face and in all his actions when he was anywhere around her. He was like some love-sick puppy, which frankly she did not find very appealing, but she believed she could use this crush to convince him that he should let them go.

She was surprised when he quickly blurted out that he had been monitoring them throughout their planning phase and for her sake had been dumping all the recordings of their conversations and actions as he went. He stressed that without him 'watching their backs' they would not have got here.

He pointed to a small bag at his feet, insisted that he wanted to come with them and stressed that they needed to get on with it as he was no longer at the helm in the security office. He explained that he had deliberately damaged the camera system that covered this section of the 'wall' and this should give them enough time to get away, but only if they moved immediately!

They made it safely to Zagora. Tom had urged caution but was surprised and started to relax when he saw the roadblocks of the UN team and local heavies had now been removed. Once in Zagora, Tom found an international telephone outlet and rapidly put in a call to Sir Joseph. With just a few phone calls the intelligence man was able to get them full consular support in case their lack of passports became an issue, even though one of them was not even British. Perhaps as importantly he called up the necessary muscle to obtain assistance in reaching a military airport to fly promptly back to the UK.

Now all safely back in Kent, it was the Professor who took charge of the meeting to debrief each of them, carefully asking them about the Tamegroute Retreat, its objectives and its occupants.

Tom of course could talk only of his hospital room and the conversations with Shepherd, though he kept much of what was actually said to himself. They could read it in his book like everyone else, though it was not at all likely that he would attribute the thoughts to Shepherd.

Instead he described the content of their discussions as a wide-ranging debate of the man's extreme beliefs. He mentioned his extraterrestrial creation theories, and this was confirmed by both Hannah and Dieter as being a central theme of the Order's special knowledge.

Tom summed up, 'He believes that there's a set of serpent-like ETs that have either created us or at least played with or enhanced our development. I have to admit that some of what he said made as much sense to me as anything I learned from the Bible.'

The Professor quizzed them further and then reached a conclusion. 'To me this all sounds like Raëlism, a religion founded back in the 1970s. Raël had been a French motor-sport driver and journalist and I think he'd been a singer before that, so he was not the most likely of religious innovators. Nonetheless he has inspired around 80,000 followers across ninety countries. This Raël fellow also maintained that extraterrestrials had engineered all life on earth. He suggested that he had met with them and changed his name to Raël when he was appointed as their messenger; his ETs were called "Elohim".'

Hannah was uncomfortable at the disparaging tone, lumping their beliefs in with this French playboy, but she answered the implied question. 'So far as I was aware at Perpetua, no name was used for our genetic makers other than 'the creators'. No one to my knowledge has claimed to have met any of them. And our authority spreads right back to prehistory and not to some latter-day Johnny Hallyday!'

The Professor flicked through his notes. 'The Raëlian beliefs focus quite a lot on cloning and on something they call mind transfers. Did these play any role at Perpetua?'

Stevie offered, 'The laboratory was certainly active in all other aspects of gene research, so I would expect that cloning might certainly have played a role at some stage?'

Her question was directed at Hannah, who replied. 'Our laboratory was not engaged in either but then I believe that each retreat tended to specialise in different areas, just as Marsha chose and decreed.'

The Professor was still scanning. 'They do not believe in any supernatural creation just an extraterrestrial interference; and they don't talk much of souls just this mind transfer business. They encourage healthy eating, no tobacco, no coffee, moderation with alcohol, no recreational drugs. They seem to have had a female priesthood largely drawn from the sex industry.'

Avril interrupted, 'Well then Perpetua is very different, because alcohol and drugs were positively encouraged, sex too!'

Tom glanced to his side at Stevie who reddened and lowered her head under his scrutiny.

Simon, the Professor's assistant, had been quiet through much of the meeting, 'Raëlism was founded by a fraudster, its beliefs clearly faulty. We shouldn't automatically write off the Perpetua Order as of the same persuasion.'

The Professor looked at the young man with disgust, 'Both are of the Christian persuasion and for me every man jack of them should be written off !'

Sir Joseph would always proudly write in 'C of E' on any official questionnaire, though he rarely set foot into a church or even for a moment considered that there might be any higher non-corporeal authority.

He decided they should move on. 'So it seems to me of very little value to try and force the Perpetua Order into some pigeonhole marked Raëlism. Besides it is not some stand-alone religion; it is working hand-in-glove with these other organisations, with the Tyndale Retreats and Mission, with the Gene Genie shops and so on. So what we really need to start to understand is what are its aims, its ambitions, its goals?'

**Double-T R, Morocco**

In discussion of the escape Shepherd had also become circumspect about any matters relating to the long conversations he had held with Tom. He was aware all this must be on tape somewhere but this was not his concern.

He felt embarrassed that he had assumed that he could sway the man by the power of his words and with the many gifts he had bestowed upon him for use in his next novel. He had hoped that he would see the knowledge that the Order held as intriguing, appealing, valuable; to feel that it was worth staying around and becoming part of the movement.

He really had cherished the idea that perhaps Tom might become a lay spokesperson for them, would see the value in acquiring and then broadcasting their messages. No time for that now. It was time to consider what damage had been done and what their next steps ought to be.

He looked at Lehri once more. 'We are sure that it was just the five of them who escaped?'

Daniel assured him, 'We have run a complete people and humanzee audit; we've even checked that they took no lab animals and none of the materiel. What we can't be sure is if they have any files with them. There can be little doubt that Dieter had free access to so much here while he was at the retreat.'

Trajan too sought to pacify. 'We have increased the security detail at Tamegroute to ensure there are no further defections. With the increased labour detail now applied the wall should be finished within ten days. All retreats have now installed a tandem operation on all surveillance systems so we will never allow any individual such access or control again.'

Marsha was not as helpful. 'Dieter and Hannah were Sixes. They were part of your closest team, Samuel. What will they have heard and seen? You need to backtrack and think through what damage they might do with their knowledge.'

'It's not as damaging as you might think. Of course as Sixes they know much of the basis of our faith. I would be very surprised if they do not still hold true to many of our beliefs. They are not aware of how we plan to take things forward. They were only involved in the preparation and review of my broadcasts and presentations. They have not even seen the content of the series of future planned global broadcasts. Of course nor has anyone, because I am still working on them.'

Marsha did not agree. 'We must move fast with our next phases and then any knowledge they do have will become rapidly worthless.'

Shepherd reassured, 'I promise they know nothing of our next steps. I don't believe they would even be able to identify where all the retreats are located.'

He decided he was not going to take all the pressure. 'What of your two Anglo Apostles? What might they know that could prove damaging?'

Daniel was quick to respond. 'Avril knew nothing. She was merely an administrator who had hardly taken up her role with me before she was gone. I did say at the time I didn't want an outsider posted into my team. Fortunately I wasn't yet ready to have her operate too closely!'

Marsha waved a tired arm at them all. 'We will achieve nothing if we bicker about who is at fault and to what degree. What we need are solutions. What are we going to do about this?'

Dom spoke up on this one. 'We are trying to trace their whereabouts. They must have kept going north because there's nothing but wilderness south of the retreat. We have sightings of them in Zagora, but then they seem to have been spirited away. Four of them being Brits we have to assume that they somehow got official help. That Carter guy is certainly ex-military, perhaps he's still connected in some way?'

Trajan commented, 'When he tried to get away from the retreat originally he killed a humanzee; that was why we shot at him. I assume we don't want to draw attention to ourselves by suggesting he's a fugitive?'

'Absolutely not!' Daniel had no interest in firing up activity from the local authorities. They had only just finished managing the curiosity of those who had lost family members in the disease outbreak. He needed to be left alone to get his retreat fully up and running.

Shepherd wanted decisive action too. 'We should release the third seal without delay!'

Marsha glared at him. 'If we do agree to do this now then the pressure must be applied on Dom to complete his harvesting of the relics. Once the third seal is released our movement internationally will become much more difficult. Order and control will descend into anarchy very quickly.'

Trajan once again sought to reassure. 'Security at the retreats will be strong. We were always set up to secure them from incoming threats. It was just that we had not spent quite as much time considering there would be anyone wanting to leave. Once anarchy is rife then few would want to leave the safety of our communities. So I see the third seal as a positive step forward.'

Shepherd appeared to be having an internal personal debate, but expressed this aloud as he recounted. 'Our investigations have established that the earth is only intended for 2.5 billion human inhabitants; that is the largest number completely sustainable within its natural resources.'

Marsha realised that it was only at this eleventh hour that he had finally caught a glimpse of how his goals might be perceived by outsiders. The iconic head of their organisation was about to commit to a plan leading to mass murderer on a scale never witnessed before.

She waited, confident that the facts, or her conditioning, would kick in to reassure him that 'his' course was righteous. While this proceeded she was idly pondering that they would need to think up a new word because genocide was the extinction of just one national, racial, political, or ethnic group. Their plan was a more wholesale approach, an equal opportunity extermination.

He continued to express his thoughts aloud. 'We are already approaching 7 billion and we just cannot countenance, cannot allow it to reach the projected 9 billion by 2050; and that's just a median projection! China already has 400 million too many, India a current surplus of 350 million, the USA is approaching 100 million in overpopulation. Russia has 60 million too many despite its vast land mass. Even little UK, curs-ed UK, sits on its tiny island with an overpopulation of 40 million.'

Marsha grimaced. Once again it was the strong woman behind the throne who would have to give the man a push, provide him with the backbone. 'Samuel, we really do need to do this for the good of mankind. We have to fulfil the prophesy. The third seal, the black horse and Rider of Famine, is essential for our plans.'

Trajan supported her. 'It's only a very few places like Australia and New Zealand, Brazil, Chile and Peru, and Indonesia where they are not yet pushing at the fabric of their countries, still living within the means of their natural resources.'

Shepherd recovered from his reverie. 'Yes, and we will emerge from our retreats later to espouse these people, bring them into the Order.'

Trajan seized upon this pause in proceedings. 'Have you yet had a chance to consider my plan to advance our cause in the States more rapidly?'

## Kent, UK

Sir Joseph was summing up the group session before they broke off into separate groups. It was clear that Hannah and Dieter, being longer-term Perpetua members, were still too heavily programmed by the Order and would need patient and careful handling to uncover useful knowledge. Though they had made the break physically, mentally they were still securely back within the religious group.

'Several of you have confirmed that the Gene Genie operation was an accelerant for them to get a huge DNA database assembled, but you don't know why?'

The Professor commented, 'In the UK we accumulated from various police investigations almost five million DNA records for a criminal database, that's around one in every twelve of us. Then it came under pressure to delete those that were not taken from convicted criminals. Human rights and other legislation meant they were required to give them up, despite the benefits for future criminal investigations. This lot being a private enterprise has no such imperative.'

Sir Joseph commented, 'I repeat, what value would these things have to an organisation like Perpetua?'

Stevie had clearly been thinking about this. 'In the laboratory Marsha mentioned that the Order was compiling genetic data from both the living and the dead. She suggested that we were looking into the personal histories behind the DNA, overlaying the lives and achievements of individuals against their DNA, to pinpoint areas of interest that were worthy of investigation. I was only working in anti-ageing research - telomeres and the like.'

Hannah confirmed Stevie's point. 'Yes, others were working with the DNA database and creating a variety of cross references to the achievements of the individuals. Gene Genie of course captured a large amount of personal history on each applicant while they were at the outlets. Those of interest were called back and asked even more questions. In the labs we were only ever engaged in legitimate genetic research.'

Stevie couldn't accept this. 'That's apart from the work being done on humanzees of course.' Some of those in the meeting looked blank at this, so she explained, 'Marsha had created this community of these almost-human monkeys...'

The Professor mused, 'The collective noun is a troop or a tribe of monkeys.'

'...No! This was a community; created just to harvest their genes, to provide stem cells and other raw materials for our research. It was awful to see how sweet and talented they were, all locked away at the back of the laboratory.'

Tom placed his hand on her arm. 'I shall always be grateful for the gift of a replacement trachea; it was made possible only because of this research.'

Stevie was about to say something about the humanzee that would have died to donate this, but choked it back.

Sir Joseph was still on the same track. 'What do they want with this database?'

Dieter finally spoke up. 'I can't really help, but I did once overhear a conversation that suggested the main purpose is some form of backtracking. I was present at a review meeting with Mission reporting on the task they had been set which was to collect DNA from those said to be holy and from primitive societies for the database.

'I also met up with someone from Marsha's team at BiCogNaIT who was extremely motivated by the Genographic Project, the one sponsored by National Geographic and IBM that is using genes to trace the early migration routes taken by primitive people as they spread out to populate the world. That may just have been one of her own personal interests, but at the time it felt as if this might be significant to her approach.'


## Double-T R, Morocco

The teleconference was coming to a close. Shepherd seemed even more withdrawn as the discussion developed; Marsha was forced into taking up more of the leadership role.

It was she who summed up. 'So we are agreed that Samuel should go to Lalibela and prepare for his transmissions. I need to get across to BiCogNaIT HQ to finalise and release the third seal. Dom is to accelerate his programme of data and relic collection. Trajan has approval for his plans in the States to augment our impact quickly and considerably.

'I must stress that timing is everything. We don't want to get caught up in each other's plans or to hinder each other completing these tasks. So let's take the last few minutes to agree a timeline.'

# Chapter 53 - *Colorado, USA*

Mark Elliott had lost them. One minute they were there about 200 to 300 yards up ahead, now they were gone. The traffic was very light on the meandering highway and his luck had held up to this point, he had been confident they had not yet spotted him tailing them.

He had been lulled into a false sense of security as they were out in the wilds with just a few roads, not many turn-offs. If there was one thing he had established was that these cultists liked being out in the wilderness. There had been no intersections for twenty miles, the traffic was getting really quite sparse, and he decided deliberately to drop back some way from them to become even less obvious. But as he rounded the last bend they had just plain disappeared.

He could see clearly for perhaps half a mile, the car was nowhere on the road, ahead was only a single truck. It was not feasible that they had accelerated sufficiently to reach as far as the next bend. He braked violently and controlled the rear wheel skid to nurse the rental on to the not-so-hard shoulder.

He banged it into reverse and snaked back the way he had come, all the way to the crown of the corner. He calculated this would have been the earliest that they might conceivably have left the road but the highway had a huge embankment on this side and there was little chance they could have turned off to the right. He looked across the carriageway and assessed that there were two possible points for the car to have managed to leave the highway.

The first was a small muddy bank but he could see instantly that the only tracks there were old and crumbling. Without hesitation he gunned the car across all four lanes towards the only other likely place. A car was coming from the other direction but it was hundreds of yards away even well after his manoeuvre was completed, yet still the driver flashed and sounded his horn as he passed perfectly safely behind him. Mark swore under his breath. 'Why did these idiots always feel the need to do that?'

He had been anointed to become part of gNOS but seemed to be overlooked as many others in the organisation appeared to respond to some emergency with most of its team suddenly posted off all over the place. He had played it cool waiting on Trajan to make the first move while he continued to pick up any information he could from those who, excited by their new posting, were ready to chatter.

He had remained in the private compound, populated by an ever-growing collection of apparently disparate groups. He had established that the gNOS recruiting team felt here they could gain a cloak of invisibility, sitting at the heart of other groups that were much more likely to catch the eye of any investigators. Plus of course these other groups' members were readily available for tasks that the gNOS team did not want to do, or be seen to do, themselves.

Mark and his controller were monitoring all the comings and goings within the compound. Many individuals had been identified, their records pulled. Most came back with just a string of juvenile offences that had driven these individuals to the edge of society. But then these two came along, the two he was following today. They had been identified as serious international players. And now he had lost them!

He left the road with a deal of momentum, only to find that the down slope was pretty extreme, dropping into a large run-off that had not been visible until it was far too late to change course. All he could do was pump at the wheel and the brakes in the forlorn hope that this was helping as he careered down the bank. While he was pretty preoccupied he still managed to assess that it had not been used by any sort of vehicle in years. Damn it, where the hell were they?

Fortunately he met with nothing solid during his descent and at the bottom a reasonable farm track ran parallel to the highway. He fishtailed and swung along it in his original direction of travel.

As the hire car clattered along the rough track it was shedding its wheel trims and probably more besides. But he had no time to dwell on the aggravation he would get when he next submitted his expenses. But as he had hoped he soon saw that the track crested just a few hundred metres ahead which was the most likely point to rejoin the highway. As he got closer he cursed his luck - there was a deep yawning ditch between the track and the road. He could waste no more time so he piled on his speed as he raced up to the crest. Bizarrely he realised that at this higher speed the bumpy track seemed to smooth out as he only touched down on its high points. He picked out the spot from which he would leap the gap and went for it.

He was relieved when he soared out over the ditch easily; Evil Knievel, eat your heart out! The leap rapidly ceased to be his problem as he emerged onto the highway to find himself closing at a combined speed of well over 100 mph with an enormous truck. He had time to realise that this driver was not wasting any time with flashers or klaxon; he could see him clearly, sitting up there at what felt like three storeys above him. The driver was putting all his grim determination and concentration into standing on his air brakes.

Mark managed instinctively to twitch the car, unknowingly describing a typical rally driver's pendulum swing. He crossed the truck's lane in what appeared from the truck driver's viewpoint to be two crablike lurches. Mark could not have explained what he had done, but mercifully he was clear.

He started to celebrate a little too early as he exhaled after what had been split seconds but felt like minutes. Too early because the truck's brake management system, fighting the natural tendency to jack-knife, still permitted the trailer to swing across the next lane and a half, just where he was now headed! He swung again using the balance of his receding adrenalin to try to perform some further helpful manoeuvre but he was too late. The tail end of the trailer side-swept him and turned him through a violent, full 360-degree rotation.

He could feel his shoulder muscles being pulled at multiple-G, knew that his neck would be in agony for days. The rotation scrubbed off all his speed and he was left between the two carriageways stunned, as much by the emotion of the last few moments as the impact itself. He sat semi-conscious trying to gather his wits about him.

# Chapter 54 - *Caldey Island, Wales*

Dom woke with a start, instantly fully aware. He realised that he had seldom experienced such complete silence, it was almost unearthly. That appeared to be the norm; it was so silent that his ears seemed to rebel, it was as if they were creating a sound to fill the void all by themselves. He realised in fact he must have been lying half awake, stretching his sense of hearing, reaching out to pick up on any noise at all. And something had stirred him to full consciousness; he always trusted his instincts, his survival senses.

Whatever the time of year he slept with the window wide open, never drew curtains or blinds. He finally risked opening his eyes to try to pick out any detail from within the insipid grey nothingness. Dawn was still a little way off, but that damned lighthouse ensured that this quiet island was never quite dark.

This was a location that he had come to circuitously. The first step along the route had been taken some 2,500 kilometres away, with his attack on Mugnano del Cardinale.

Someone was definitely moving around out there, or now it sounded more like several someones. At this time on the island, well before the ferry had started up, there could be no innocent explanation; at least none he could come up with as he lay there.

He only had to pull on his boots to be ready to investigate. He took his HK45 from under the pillow and quietly exited the room. He always got a jolt from holding a Heckler & Koch handgun. Its slimline grip and its general balance felt so right, even when the noise suppressor was fitted as it was now. Eight tiny muted 'expressions' were loaded and ready to level any heated conversations, to silence any resistance to his opinions and goals.

This weapon had always served Dom well, it was his weapon of choice. Somehow when one was in his hand he felt more important, more impressive, just a little immortal. He knew that Samuel Shepherd would never appreciate the simple truths of combat. He would never relish the heightened sense of operating under extreme risk, never enjoy the sense of sheer fulfilment in pitting your own hard-earned and honed abilities against others and emerge triumphant.

Each time he proved others were mere mortals, the experience added something to his own powers, grew his belief in his own immortality. This was where Dom sought and found his own personal enlightenment. He trusted in his salvation every time he went up against another; not enough for him the pastoral pleasures that Samuel preached.

Marsha had recognised all this in him, encouraged him, enabled and permitted him to seek out these luscious moments when he could become all instinct, become one with the weapon. She was the one who outlined how

Samuel's vision would require Dom to play out this role for them; she was the one who enabled and empowered him to fulfil his very special needs.

**Mugnano del Cardinale, Italy**

Dom had experienced one of those 'highs' while at Mugnano del Cardinale; a small place tucked well back behind Mount Vesuvius, around 40 kilometres inland from Naples.

Since the acceleration in Mission's activities, ordered at the recent teleconference, it was a case of all hands to the wheel and it was judged necessary for Dom himself to take on this particular task.

It had been all too easy an extraction; within the basilica Dom had found what he had been seeking for Samuel - and Marsha. There it was, brazenly on open display behind a simple thin pane of glass set into a very highly portable shrine; it wasn't even safety glass! It was built this way for convenience, so the locals could hoist it up onto their shoulders and parade it around on fiesta days, so the crowds thronging the streets could clearly see the relic.

This simple arched cabinet contained a papier mâché figure of Saint Philomena, the effigy holding out a hand that contained Dom's objective - a small vial of the saint's blood.

Philomena's body and vial had been discovered early in the 19th century in some very old catacombs beneath the streets of Rome. Her remains were discovered in one of the very oldest of these, dating back to the 2nd century CE; the catacomb had also contained some early Christian art frescoes. Romans had always tended to cremate their dead but the coming of Christianity and its belief in resurrection had led to the use of these underground cemeteries.

Her story was shrouded in mystery. Philomena was reputed to have been a martyred Greek princess; taken while still a virgin, aged just 13. The painting on her tomb tiles suggest a date late in the 2nd century CE. A palm drawn on these tiles confirm that she was Christian and it was the presence of the vial that initially gave credence to her martyrdom; though more recent luminaries pour doubt upon this latter interpretation.

Her body was found with three tiles closing her tomb and enigmatically displaying the words '*Lumena Paxte Cumfi*'; this expression had no real sense or meaning. But by moving the first tile to the last position this could be interpreted as '*Paxte Cum Filumena*', or 'Peace be with you Philomena'. Some suggest that the wrong arrangement was the result of the re-use of pre-existing tiles from an older burial. As a consequence they prefer to give Philomena a much later date of death – say early 4th century CE.

Once these remains had been uncovered, various individuals began to make claims of visions of her martyrdom. Some also tried to fashion her tale from the pictures found within the catacomb. But virtually nothing is truly known of her life, and nothing in ancient records describes her, or her martyrdom.

It was only after the relic had been moved to Mugnano del Cardinale that her presence was said to have begun having miraculous effects. As a result she became the only saint canonised purely for her posthumous intercessions instead of the more usual recognition of an exemplary life. Pope Pius IX was just one of many 19th century popes who lauded her powers and, with no clear basis, he declared her the 'Patroness of Mary's children'.

Dom had planned to take just a sample from the vial and replace it but he rapidly lost patience when he failed after several attempts to open the simple display cabinet. Instead he chose to smash the glass and take the whole vial. It was the sound of the breaking glass that attracted a minor cleric to investigate what was happening.

While Dom might not have shared all Samuel's beliefs he had one vital rule - three types of individual he would not kill. No police, no children - no priests! When the black-robed figure launched himself he hit out at the cleric using just enough force to shut him up; one blow had sent him to the floor. Examining him lying there lifelessly, Dom could now see that the cleric was very young, with no meat on him. He had gone down far too readily.

He stooped to check that he had not killed what apparently was only a lad. The flowing black robe had confused him; it had given the mere child an apparent bulk. He was much relieved to feel a strong pulse in the boy's neck. On doing so he heard a noise from the body of the church. Still stooped he turned quickly and a bright flash made him drop to the ground.

It wasn't a muzzle flash as he'd assumed; it was a camera. He was up as soon as he realised his error, only to hear someone hurriedly leaving the church. The flare in his eyesight caused by the flash prevented him from discerning any detail of the disappearing photographer.

He looked around outside without any success and decided to get to his car and make his way back to the city at pace. It was only forty kilometres but as he neared Naples the traffic was absolutely dire; his progress became snail-like.

When he did get some forward momentum he could not believe the antics of the Neapolitan pedestrians who would just step out in front of any vehicle, no matter what its speed, and amble their way across the road, for some reason they expected you to stop for them. And this with no sign of any formal crossing point, no common sense in their timing or decisions. It was so infuriating he felt he should clip the heels of one of them to teach him that this was not acceptable behaviour. He guessed he really did not need the hassle right then.

Other than having to watch every pedestrian with extreme care, he felt pretty secure here lost within the traffic, anonymous. He had made good his escape and all that remained was to get to the airport in time for his flight.

He was wrong; he had stirred a monster. His violation of the church, his theft of the relic, his attack of the cleric, all had served to rouse the Catholic Church in all its majesty. Its tendrils were of course particularly deep-rooted throughout Italy.

The picture taken of him had been forwarded by the Church to a group of devout if rather lawless individuals. They were a Cammora family, the Neapolitan version of the Mafia. Its members would extort, cheat, steal, beat and kill throughout the week but would be reliably upon their knees to receive the sacrament every Sunday without fail. They were waiting and looking for him now.

To Dom the roads in Naples were like a labyrinth, but to these others, born, bred and shaped by and on these streets, it was self-evident where he would most likely have to pass. They had a description of his vehicle, his photo and the details of his sacrilege; he had stolen a relic that was beyond precious; he had even beaten a poor *diacono* close to death.

Dom's first sign of any trouble was an Aprilla scooter coming up fast behind him but then, completely uncharacteristically in the slow moving and chaotic traffic, making no effort to pass. The rider had no helmet, talked regularly into a mobile, and more significantly was at great pains not to be seen looking in Dom's direction at any point in this process.

A kilometre or so later the locals were ready to make their move; but Dom was prepared for them. He watched a small car arrive from a side road ahead and then come to a halt forcing other cars to go around it with much arm brandishing and blaring of horns. As Dom approached the halted vehicle the Aprilla rider started to draw alongside him.

Dom didn't even bother to scrub off his low speed. He kicked his door wide open, catching the scooter and sending it into an oncoming car. He launched himself across the front seats and exited through the passenger door just as his car back-ended the vehicle in front; at around twenty kilometres per hour there was no huge impact and he was able to keep his balance and momentum.

This was the sort of moment he had been born for; he silently thanked Marsha for finding him and making it possible. He rolled onto his shoulder between two cars to reach the opposite sidewalk and was up and beside the parked car before they had even reacted to the apparent accident. He shot both individuals in the car causing the obstruction, and was off down a side street while most people were still watching the scooter rider get up from the ground.

# Chapter 55 - *Denver, USA*

Paul Fleischer scooted back to his desk after getting some coffee. 'Don't worry. We have a top CIA operative trailing these two.' Paul was the regional second-in-command and was talking to Robert Krakauer, the local head of DHS, the Department of Homeland Security.

Krakauer demanded, 'Are we to take this as a serious threat?' This was not the simple question it seemed. By this stage in his role Krakauer was often engaged in categorising crises using a sort of shorthand that his organisation had developed. If they reacted to every issue brought to their desks with equal attention, then they would achieve nothing.

More importantly Krakauer thought that without this approach he would have aged a further ten years beyond his biological age. His period in office had already made him look ten years older than he was, and he could ill afford to double up on this opening chasm.

It was this simple grading of a threat that determined how much attention he and others would be permitted to give to it. Should it alter his schedule of meetings and if so, then precisely who should be gathered to discuss it with him, what resources should he apply?

'Serious threat' was quite a significant category, but it was some three grades below the highest threat level that might have been applied. The very top level was termed 'super critical' in the approved file note that had been circulated on the subject of crisis management. Super critical had never really been defined absolutely. It was just assumed that it would be self-evident when and if it occurred. For example any situation with the threat of a biological or nuclear threat to the homeland would clearly merit this highest designation. For now, this meeting was unemotionally being set on course for handling this matter as a reasonably common, yet 'serious', threat.

'It's a pretty strange mixture of groups,' Fleischer, was flicking through his latest field reports. 'About the only thing that you might say they have in common is that they are all white and all extremist. There are several groups that are simply founded upon hate – whether it be directed against the government or corporate-military interests, and then of course against the blacks, the Hispanics, the Jews. You name it and there is a group in there that really hates them. And they hated well before this current wave of hate crimes. Then there are several religious cults in there. These have such a confusing mixture of patriotic and religious beliefs that I can't fathom where one starts and the other finishes.'

Krakauer was also thumbing through reports balanced on his lap. 'It's these two individuals who stand out. The first, Finbar Healey, I see we've gotten some new intel from the Brits on him. Northern Irish, ex-PIRA, Provisional IRA - clearly he was none too happy with the fact that we Americans negotiated the peace over there in Ireland, or that it's holding up pretty well at the moment. So apparently he's become an experienced gun for hire.'

Fleischer added a little ruefully, 'I thought the Irish normally see us as having deep pockets, of value for them with their fundraising and materiel. They're usually very careful not to offend us in case those proceeds begin to dry up. The number of Irish Americans, or those who claim some sort of Irish ancestry, outnumbers the population of Ireland by a huge multiple; and after a few drinks in the Irish bars they're all keen to give money back to the old country. We judge that these thugs do usually appreciate on which side of the pond their bread is buttered.'

Krakauer nodded, 'Yes, but that assumes this Healey is still committed to the Irish cause, or cares about its fund-raising. From what Sir Joseph Maudlin has supplied to us it's clear he's gone rogue, just a gangster really. He'd beaten, knee-capped and murdered his way all the way to the top on the streets of Belfast; only to find when he got there that the game and its rules had changed. Must have been something of a bummer for him.'

Krakauer, always the time manager, pressed, 'And, what about the other one?'

More flicking through papers before Fleischer replied, 'Oh, he's a real charmer. A Serb called Milos Konjović. Back in the day he was very much involved with that mass-murderer Arkan and his group. The group worked in the background to assist with the Milošević thrust to create Central Serbia, though they managed to remain an autonomous group that became very much a law unto itself. Later he worked closely as an off-the-books enforcer for the secret police, their BIA, without ever formally being acknowledged as part of it. Then he went underground and has been involved right across Europe in anything that would pay him well enough.'

Krakauer was shocked, 'How come we at DHS allowed a mother like this to get into the country?'

'Sir Joseph indicates that it was only since a new man took over recently at the BIA that they started to clean up their payroll. Among others this character then came to light. Various initiatives like their 'Operation Sabre' have investigated criminal groups that developed alongside the service and as such had become 'authorised', or as a minimum overlooked. These groups had carried on precisely as if they had official sanction; until their 'new broom' arrived. It was when we sent over this guy's photographs, taken inside the compound that Sir Joseph's team was able to positively identify him from this latest BIA data. They requested further background to be sent over from Belgrade. He was absolutely nowhere in our files before now.'

'Are you making sure we have all the intel from Belgrade into our systems now?' His assistant nodded and Krakauer continued, 'So why didn't we pick him up as soon as he was identified?'

Fleischer responded, 'He was located out there deep inside the compound. It's so full of whackos, that if we'd gone in it would've been, well, a Waco-situation all over again!''

Krakauer paused, started to say something, but decided to move on, 'Gentlemen, let's get back to this letter. Are we sure it came from this group?'

Fleischer picked up his copy, 'We are fairly confident. If we cut through all the bile and the other racist claptrap, they are demanding such fundamental changes to our federal structure that even they can't be expecting any sort of useful response from us. Yet they threaten some sort of major demonstration. They say this will highlight "our basic inability, despite all our technology and military power, to withstand the simple and pure power of Nature". Has anyone any idea at all what they are talking about?'

Krakauer was studying his copy, 'They talk of an enforced return to a more pure style of living, a return to being simple hunter-gatherers. This suggests they think it will be something cataclysmic. They're just a group of dissolutes and backwoodsmen armed with a few automatic weapons and rifles. It makes absolutely no sense to me.'

Fleischer flicked through his file, 'That may have been true until a recent break-in at a nearby army base. If it was them, which we must assume, then they may have recently acquired some pretty large ordnance.'

## I-25, Colorado, USA

Mark couldn't turn his neck to see what had become of the truck that hit him, but concluded in that very instant what must have happened to the car he was trailing. He remembered seeing that other truck trundling along up well ahead of both him and the car he was following.

These guys had clearly seen too many movies! They must have somehow driven up a ramp into the truck. He recalled several films where the ploy had been used, but he had thought it far too artificial an idea - too much the movie cliché and not something to consider in his line of work. Then where would these guys get their ideas from if not from movies?

Still somewhat dazed, he considered whether this meant that they had spotted him or they had just pre-planned this extreme caution from the outset. Clearly the truck could not have just been whistled up once they realised they were being trailed; it must have been planned well in advance. Planned and probably well-rehearsed too. Thus he concluded that, perhaps, he had not been spotted.

He tried to start the engine only to find it was still running, his effort greeted by a loud clanging noise for his mistake. The tinnitus buzzing in his ears had evidently masked the quiet tickover. Again his mind flashed forward to presenting his next expenses claim, he was going to have to be at his creative best. Recounting his rather humiliating series of false assumptions would not be nearly enough. His only way out of this was to secure a positive outcome from the exercise, whatever that might take.

Painfully and carefully he looked back along the highway. Seeing nothing coming he gunned it and was reassured that the rental was still pretty much intact. He had no time to waste on inspecting the bodywork and had to hope that the damage did not make him too noticeable.

After a sustained high speed burst for some eight or ten minutes he easily overhauled the truck on the road and then eased back to watch its progress.

Eventually he realised that one of the many ringing tones in his ear was in fact just that - a ringtone. The display on the handset showed it was his local liaison, probably checking up on his progress, or lack of it.

'Hi Chuck, bad news I'm afraid. I had a little local difficulty.'

The cellphone was having one of its crystal clear moments, 'Why, what's happened?'

'Long story. Thought I'd lost them and in trying to backtrack I had a prang, as my Brit friends would say. I'm OK, a bit of whiplash and a bang to the head. The auto's a bit messed up.'

'So where are they?'

'They pulled a ludicrous stunt. Did you ever see 'The Italian Job'?'

'I saw the original Michael Caine version.'

'Yeah? Well you'll remember the way they ran the three minis up a ramp into the back of a truck.'

'If you think they went to all that trouble then you really must have banged your head'

'No seriously. Other than being beamed up to an alien mother ship that's the only possible answer as to what happened. Anyway I'm trailing the truck.'

'Are you sure they're in it?'

'Of course not. Eliminate all the plausible options and the implausible becomes the only logical conclusion.'

'I just love your fuzzy logic.'

Mark laughed, 'Well I have hurt my head!'

# Chapter 56 - *Caldey Island, Wales*

Dom Berkeley headed for the door. He was on an island in the middle of nowhere and he had decided that someone was coming for him. He thought, 'Me, paranoid? You bet'ya!'

After the incident in Naples he decided not to try for the airport. Instead he had stolen a car and driven his way north out of Italy. He had no choice but to call and tell Will what had happened.

He assumed he could deal with Will later, find some way to counter the loss of face, keep him in line. He'd got the vial, hadn't he? When Will, without question or comment, capably arranged for the handover of the relic and provided him with support to get out of mainland Europe he finally began to believe that perhaps his status was being respected.

Will then proposed that he lay low in one of the locations they had considered for a Tyndale Retreat. Once he reached Caldey Island and saw the name on the guest house into which he had been booked, Philomena, he realised that this was pure sarcasm on Will's part. Or was it more than that? Was Will now planning to take him out?

Caldey Island was a kilometre off the coast of Tenby, a small Welsh resort. The island had been inhabited since the Stone Age, with monks being regular inhabitants since the 6th century. Successions of Celtic monks, Benedictines and presently Cistercian Trappists had called the place home. Their presence had been interrupted only twice, briefly by the 16th century dissolution of the monasteries and a great deal earlier by the Vikings. It was those Vikings who had given the island its name, Keld-Eye, meaning cold island, and at 4 am Dom thought it was certainly living up to its billing.

It wasn't a rebellion by his own team that he now faced. The Vatican had matched his photo with one they had been sent by the Israelis following the Hebron incident. Once the Papal Camorra contacts had failed to recapture their man inside Italy they involved Interpol and this organisation had issued a pan-European bulletin; although this too had achieved no rapid success.

Will had anonymously tipped off a Sky News journalist to link the relic theft not just to the incident at Hebron but to other reports coming from Kashmir and Chiang Mai. The journalist had run a piece showing the photo of the attacker in the church, stooping furtively over the deacon. The item conjectured the lengths to which some collectors would stoop in order to have the dubious pleasure of owning items that once stolen could never ever be displayed or used publicly.

By chance Tom had caught this news item, immediately recognised Dom Berkeley and called it in to Sir Joseph. Now given a name to work with, Sir Joseph's team was able to uncover his entry into the UK when he had used his own documents. It was not long before they found his credit card purchase of an Intercity rail ticket to Swansea. Two Special Branch followers had been waiting for him on the platform at Swansea station.

Dom quietly made his way downstairs to the back door of the guest house and slid the bolts to get outside. As he stepped across the threshold several large floodlights flicked on and he froze in their glare.

'This is the police. We are armed. We will shoot if you do not put down your gun and lie on the floor with your arms and legs spread wide.'

Dom was in turmoil. Had he been sold out? Should he try to shoot his way out?

'Do it now. Or rest assured, we will shoot!'

He felt confident that Marsha would get him out of this, and he put down his gun and complied.

# Chapter 57 – *Wyoming, USA*

The past few hours had been a constant cat and mouse game as Mark dropped back from the truck as far as he dared and then accelerated to close the gap whenever it left his field of vision. As the roads became less significant and the traffic dropped away he took a high risk of being discovered.

He could not understand where they were headed. His map showed they had crossed the Bighorn Basin and were now passing through the Absaroka Range in what he assumed to be a relatively insignificant part of the Rocky Mountains. If they kept going they would reach Idaho and all he knew about that state was that it grew wonderful potatoes. The only place he had ever heard of was the capital, Boise, and all he knew about it was its name, but that was three hundred miles distant. Where the hell were they going?

He took another look at the map. He had not known their destination and he had not paid the extra for the rental to have satnav. The only map he had was a completely inadequate gas station purchase. The whole of Wyoming was summed up in a six-by-four inch area and only the very major physical features got a mention.

They had passed by Cody. Wasn't that Buffalo Bill's name? Currently to his right he assumed he could see Dead Indian Peak. What was it people like Bill Cody used to say? The only good Indian was a dead one. But given today's PC attitudes he was surprised no one had yet gotten around to renaming it something like Good Native-American Peak. Sure enough, almost everything he passed now had Buffalo Bill's name on it.

At least he was out of that awful camp. It had been so claustrophobic in there. He had also feared that having to participate in the constant litany of hate might end up doing him some lasting damage.

His blessed release had come after he had been used as one of a posse of gNOS guards who had secured the perimeter while Trajan was in deep conversation with the two hopefully travelling up ahead of him. Trajan had provided them with some documents and they had pored over them for an hour or two. A hurried discussion with his controller ensued, and instructions passed down from above had ordered Mark to leave the camp and follow these two dangerous men to see precisely what they were about.

Not an easy call. It meant that Mark had to throw away all the work he had done to get alongside this gNOS team. Chuck had reported that other intelligence information from the camp advised that the gNOS team had completely cleared out shortly after Mark had left. They were being trailed but it looked like they had permanently struck from their involvement with that location.

From his gas station map he thought they were heading towards Yellowstone Lake, however suddenly and without any signal, the truck pulled over into a rest area that appeared out of nowhere.

They pulled onto a hard-standing encircled by a thickly wooded area. He made a quick decision that if his 'Italian Job' assumption was correct he should drive on beyond the truck and around the next curve he pulled off into the woods several hundred yards ahead of them.

As he got out of the car he was forcefully reminded of his accident. The pain in his neck was absolute agony and the sudden movement as he stood up made him reel. He had to sit back down and gather his resources. He took several deep breaths and stood again, his determination overcoming the wooziness that threatened to overwhelm him.

Having worked his way through the trees back to the truck he could see the driver was turned dealing with something in the rear cab. He pressed on in the woods moving towards the rear of the truck where he could hear some activity over the noise of the cooling engine.

As he got there he heard the harsh Belfast accent, 'Give us a hand Milo. This bloody thing weighs a fecking ton.'

He was right. There were the two of them setting about assembling something taken from the rear of the truck. He watched as the parts were connected and slowly recognised what looked to his tutored eye to be some form of mortar or rocket launcher - and it was quite a large one.

What on earth could there be of interest? In Wyoming of all places? Perhaps there were some military bases around, perhaps nuclear silos; they were located all over the States and the more secret ones appeared to favour the wide-open spaces. But here? He had passed the town of Cody some time back with its promotional posters for Buffalo Bill's Historical Centre. This was after all the 'Cowboy State' where people came to buy memorabilia and soak up history.

He would guess they were pointing the launcher towards somewhere in Yellowstone National Park but beyond that he had no idea. Perhaps the bears had offended them because they were brown?

Whatever it was, they were soon going to be ready to complete their task, and his mission was obvious - he had to foil them, whatever the hell it was they were about. He had absolutely no idea what their purpose might be. It was a pretty big launcher. What should he do? He could currently see both men he had been trailing, but there was the driver and possibly even a co-driver. He had no idea where the co-driver might be or just who he and the driver might be. Innocent drivers or part of the conspiracy?

He tried to release his handgun from his shoulder holster quietly, cursing his decision to add the Velcro tab. He called the noise that Velcro made as it came apart 'scritching', and he couldn't afford for that distinctive sound to be heard. As each barb of the Velcro released it sounded to him like a firecracker, but thankfully no-one else noticed.

So did he tackle the two he could see and hope he could deal with the others when they emerged? He was weighing up his options, his damaged neck now completely forgotten. As he was formulating his admittedly flimsy approach, the decision-making was taken completely out of his hands.

His mobile started to ring! Dammit! Chuck's timing was always terrible. It was set on a standard ringtone that progressively amplified after each set of two rings. His sensitised hearing from controlling the Velcro scritch meant he had absolutely no difficulty hearing the very first instant of the first tone this time.

His reaction was immediate. Years of training matched by an innate agility allowed a pretty remarkable sleight of hand. Most would have fumbled given the gun already clasped in his right hand and the handset in his right jacket pocket. He flicked the gun to his left hand and thrust his right into his jacket pocket, all in one smooth movement. The local gunslingers of old would have been impressed by his speed. Not pausing to admire his dexterity he threw the handset as high and as far as he could through the trees, as far away from him as possible.

Fortunately it missed the many trunks and branches. He briefly wondered why he could never achieve that on the golf course; any sign of a tree and it turned into a golf ball magnet for him. They say a tree is only 10% wood but he always managed to hit that 10-to-1 outsider every time.

There were a few light noises of its passage through the leaves, which might have been made by a bird or small animal, and it landed perhaps thirty metres away. The whole manoeuvre was so swift that the sound of the phone only began to grow louder as it hit the deck. The early lighter tones and the Doppler effect of the moving phone conspired to conceal its original position and its hasty passage through the trees.

The two at the truck reacted swiftly and both entered the copse just a few feet from him and ran directly towards the, by now, piercing sound of the handset.

Mark seized his opportunity, not stopping to worry about the truck driver or drivers. He had heard only two voices so far. He took the dozen strides to the launcher and expertly assessed its function. He quickly removed a small yet vital component from the firing mechanism and threw it behind the truck to the far side of the road before moving back swiftly into the copse. Thank God for all his baseball practices as a kid; two pitches and both had been right on the money!

The whole process had taken seconds and he heard the tone as one of them reached the handset and pressed send. It sounded like it was the Irishman who grunted a nondescript greeting presumably to try to establish some appreciation of whose phone it was, or at least who was calling.

Mark heard what sounded like the handset being discarded before they moved faster than he had expected and crashed back through the copse towards him. The strip of vegetation between them and his position was quite narrow. It was therefore simplicity itself for the two of them to scour the wooded area almost shoulder to shoulder as they narrowed the distance.

Mark moved away as quietly as he could but they were gaining on him and there was no need for stealth on their part. No choice. He threw caution to the wind and started to run. They reacted immediately to his first snapped branch and started to bullock their way towards him at pace. He dropped to his knees, adopted a two-handed stance and waited. The first to break cover was the Irishman and he took some ironic joy in calmly shooting him through the kneecap. He had intended the same approach for the Serb but, given a few seconds warning, Milos had started to drop to the ground and the shot hit him square through the top of the head.

The Irishman was on the floor trying to stop the blood gushing from his shattered knee. If he had a weapon he had little interest in using it, he was interested only in the pain and stemming the flow of blood. Mark frisked him and removed a flick knife. He had no trouble in attaching a plastic disposable restraint around his wrists, which against protocol he handcuffed from the front so the man could still apply pressure to his wound.

Mark went back to the truck to see who else was aboard. The driver was a huge-gutted redneck who could hardly climb out of the cab when invited to do so at gunpoint. There was no co-driver.

Mark frisked him which was no mean feat given the number of folds of flesh into which he could have concealed a weapon. He expected that the guy might feign no knowledge of his cargo but he proved only too keen to talk.

'You got lucky this time. We've only gotta get lucky once.' Mark was beginning to really hate this saying that came up far too often in articles and films. Now every two-bit hood seemed to use it. Almost as bad as that awful sporting cliché of 'I gave it 110%'.

'What have you got against Yogi Bear anyway? There's nothing out there to shoot at but wilderness, tree-huggers and bears'

'Just where you're wrong. There's a big geezer out there that we don't like, spouting off all the time and we're gonna plug him dead.' He laughed out loud and the folds of his body went into spasm.

Mark carefully considered what he was saying, 'Ah, you mean G, E, Y, S, E, R. Presumably you mean Old Faithful himself? You'd literally be playing with fire. As I understand it the thing's sitting right on top of a bloody volcano. Pretty stupid idea if you ask me - and you'd be right in the path of it.'

'No, we're upwind of it here.'

'Upwind! I don't think a volcano is any respecter of wind direction. There'll be molten rock, lava, ash and all sorts, spread over miles. It would define its own wind direction!'

'That's our point. The eruption will wipe out several of his precious states so the President would have to give in to our demands. He would have had no choice.'

# Chapter 58 - *London, UK*

Tom was amazed, 'They must have been absolutely crazy to even contemplate it. Yellowstone is located over one of the dozen or so real hotspots that we have left on the earth today. The park sits astride a huge magma chamber. There have been three major eruptions in the last two million years, and we are talking really major here. Each of the three explosions was two thousand times larger than Mount St Helens achieved back in 1980.'

Sir Joseph commented with a significant hint of admiration. 'That's clearly what was planned. Who ever thought it up was smart. How else could you use one small rocket and manage to deliver such a whack, punching so far above their weight.'

The Professor chose to ignore this misplaced respect, 'In fact we are already well overdue for another natural eruption, right there, given that the three Tom mentioned took place at 2.1 million years ago, 1.3 m years ago and 640,000 years ago respectively. Even a poor mathematician would be hard-pressed to miss that apparent series!'

Tom picked his words carefully in front of the Foreign Secretary, 'The intervals of this sort of thing are never really that regular or predictable; they just look that way in this particular case. It's true that Yellowstone is a bomb waiting to go off at some time, and it will be geologically soon. We can readily find evidence of the last time that it blew. The amount of debris that was thrown up created a layer of volcanic ash that is deposited all the way across the whole North American continent. Then you have to account for all the damage that it did while its material was up in the atmosphere. It really screwed up the global climate for a very long period before it settled down.'

The Professor talked from his notes. 'Local researchers have shown that the mantle and the geothermal activity in Yellowstone are regularly affected by earthquakes, even those that take place thousands of miles away from it. So it's a place that's already very dynamic and ongoing. Any additional turmoil created there was going to be hugely risky. Gases are held under huge pressure within that magma chamber. Heaven forfend if these had been released by their missile. In an instant that would have allowed the magma to expand. It would have rapidly become exponential and the result would be a gas explosion scattering the crust before it.'

Tom added, 'Without wishing to be overly dramatic, there is one scientist who has specialised in this particular location and he suggests that anything like that would also displace millions of cubic feet of water right there in Yellowstone Lake. So it was likely to create a huge hydrothermal explosion too.'

Sir Joseph moved the discussion focus, 'The annoying thing is that there is absolutely nothing from this that we can pin on these gNOS people. Cleverly they used mercenaries for this attempt. If they had succeeded and sent that missile into the right spot then, from what you are saying, they would have changed the United States into lava beds and driven them back to the agricultural society that they crave?'

Tom answered him. 'Probably a lot worse than that. Forget the greenhouse effect. The dust and debris from this would have created a cold period right around the northern hemisphere, perhaps creating a new ice age. We might even have had yet another major extinction of the species; perhaps mankind might just have been one of those species lost this time.'

The Foreign Secretary got right to the nub of the matter. 'Who could possibly have gained from such an outcome?'

Sir Joseph was the first to consider it. 'Can I assume that those who happen to live in the southern hemisphere would be relatively untouched by this?'

'Yes, that would be the case - at least initially.'

'Therefore one beneficiary would have been these Tyndale Retreats. I am ashamed to admit that I have only just realised the significance that all those locations we know are down towards the southern hemisphere or in it!'

# Chapter 59 – *Köln, Germany*

Tom woke in a strange room with no sense of where he was. At first he feared he was back in the retreat's hospital, but he soon realised that this bed was clearly much more comfortable. He walked across the room to open the curtains and look out on Cologne. He was greeted by the dramatic view of the Rhine and the distinctive twin towers of the cathedral, the Kölner Dom, across on the far side.

This hotel had been recommended for its proximity to the congress that they were there to attend. He was delighted that Stevie was safely back with him and better still she had chosen to travel with him to this conference. She had been insistent that he ought to be resting and not tilting at windmills, again. If he was determined that he was coming then she was going to be at his side.

For himself, he felt fine. His throat would become dry and his voice roughen as each day progressed, but there was no time to spare. These people were up to something and they were not going to wait around for him to mend fully.

However she was not yet entirely back with him. She had insisted on separate rooms at the hotel, apologising that she had things to deal with before they could make a return to normality.

She explained to him that the attraction in going to North Africa had been to learn more of Perpetua, the saint not the Order; and in this she had completely failed. This was part of it, her sense of unfulfilled hopes, but he realised there was more. He was happy to wait until she was ready to tell him, but for now he was content to learn all over again of the many things he loved about her.

After a relaxed late breakfast they decided to walk to the venue. They took joy in the hustle and bustle around them, the sheer innocence of it all. Directly in front of the hotel was an al fresco area where they would be playing jazz later in the evening. Right beside the hotel was a railway bridge being used for rock climbing training and practice; perhaps a dozen or more young people were scuttling up and down its walls.

They walked beside the Rhine passing a steady flow of people, none of whom gave Tom and Stevie a second's thought. The calm feeling here reminded Tom of their walk the previous year alongside the Congo in Kinshasa. It gave the same relaxed impression, the calm after a heavy storm. But then it had proven to be just a brief respite. He hoped that this was not to be the case this time.

They looked across to Köln Beach, an area beside the river where sand had been piled and a relaxed bar was in full swing. They decided they would pay it a visit later, after the conference session they wanted to attend at the Köln Messe or Exhibition Centre.

They had to run the gauntlet of the exhibition to get past and into the conference room. The exhibitors were not just content to wait for you to walk into their space. Instead most of them heralded their products, processes, systems and solutions with display signage and screens. Some also projected images onto the floors and directly onto the passers-by. Many thrust brochures, disks and even memory sticks into visitors' hands.

Stevie was a magpie accepting all their material, even stepping onto stands to get brochures that were not directly proffered. Tom smiled. He thought her mind was just like that large plastic bag, full of diverse information threatening to spill out at any moment. While he needed to immerse himself into a subject to gain value from it, her mind functioned like a sieve taking in the multitude of data and then processing it and finding new connections between otherwise unrelated subjects.

Once in the conference room they worked their way to the rear of the raked auditorium. The conference stream that had brought them there had the uninviting title 'Extropy – exploring the timeline for the trans-humanist evolutionary journey'. The description went on at length referencing Max More and his Extropy Institute, clearly trying to make sure that their use of the term for their sessions would give them no copyright or plagiarism problems.

Tom had researched this term 'extropy' and felt he had been dropped deep into a pile of self-help books, the sort that weighed down airport book shops to be picked up unthinkingly by travellers never to be read. But as he looked through its philosophy it did strike a number of chords.

While the basic tenets sounded peaceful enough, the extropy exponents he found on the Net were calling for new freedoms within a new social order; that was straightforward enough. They called for the removal of what they termed the limitations on progress; limits they claimed were fixed by our current culture and politics.

He thought many of their ideas sounded worthwhile, but his fear for this sort of movement was that the proponents got impatient and tried to bring about these freedoms by aggressive action. Just like anti-vivisection, he was instinctively for it, but then there was that UK group that had taken things too far with bombs, break-ins, threats, even attacking graves. Suppose some extropy group emerged that was not prepared to wait either, one that was prepared to fire a missile into a magma chamber to achieve its goals.

However Tom did inherently appreciate and admire the way that extropy mixed up and merged a host of philosophies and technologies. It was what he termed a weird science; he just loved those!.

One of the goals for extropy was the extension of life to the point of immortality. Strangely most of the disciples of the creed were somewhat passive, happy currently to concentrate upon self-development and maintaining a positive mental attitude. They were prepared to simply wait for the technological advances that they expected would come along to achieve their objectives, rather than actively pursue them.

Another declared principle of the Extropy Institute had chilled him. This was what they called 'Perpetual Progress'. He was shocked to realise that he had not made the connection before, Perpetua to Perpetual. He supposed it was because of Stevie's childhood vision that when he had learnt of the Order he had immediately seen the sainted martyr and not the implied goal in that word. Now he accepted that Perpetua with its DNA databases and genetic research must be looking to achieve immortality.

Dr Marsha Davenport, with an implausibly long string of initials following her name, was advertised as one of an august panel of speakers who would discuss life extension at this conference. Despite what Tom, Stevie and DICE knew or suspected about her, she was being feted as a great scientist, a worthy member of this panel of pundits.

There she was sitting at the centre of the top table. The chairperson used his status to give an unadvertised opening address, seeking to display that he was an authority in the subject area; though he was no scientist himself, merely an editor of a minor scientific magazine from the Netherlands.

Tom was delighted to find that this session, in deference to the panel which largely consisting of non-Germans, was to be delivered throughout in English. It was therefore all the local attendees who had to obtain and wear the simultaneous translation headsets.

The chairperson wound up his opening comments. 'I am confident that many of the people living today can look forward to long, three-figure, lifespans and perhaps given these extended lives they will still be around when we have cracked immortality.'

One of the people at the front of the audience had obviously been 'seeded' to place a question so there would not be the usual pregnant pause when a Q&A session was announced.

The delegate was German and in English his words sounded flat and unemotional. 'Will the panel comment on how they see us dealing with an increased population? Let's apply the current birth and death rates in the West and assume for the moment that the developing world is brought up to our standards...'

Tom whispered to Stevie, 'A bold assumption that assumes our standards are worthy of being replicated!'

Stevie replied, 'Or that we are capable of achieving anything in the developing world.'

The questioner continued. '... and base our forecasts on the current rates shown by the World Health Organisation, then from the year 2000 to 2050 we would have 3.7 billion deaths and 6.6 billion births. That's an increase in world population of 2.9 billion. It will be tough for us to house, feed, water and empower these additional people. Let's not begin to imagine immortality yet, but if your life extension should reduce the death rate by half then we would have to manage yet another 1.9 billion in the world. My question therefore is whether life extension is at all a desirable goal?'

Marsha stayed silent on this one as the other panelists competed to talk about possible benefits. They suggested that with extended lives there would be more time to develop suitable alternative raw materials and power sources. How great thinkers and scientists would use their longer lives to develop these and other riches.

The Q&A proceeded with so many wanting to ask questions that the seeding of the topics had been quite unnecessary. Most of the questioners were in reality more interested in identifying themselves and their organisations or associations and then using their 'question' to expound theories of their own. Regularly the chair had to chivvy them to formulate a question or give up the floor.

Marsha had just finished answering a reasonably technical question when Stevie leapt to her feet. Not waiting to be recognised by the chairperson or being prepared to seek out a microphone she shouted. 'I have a question for Dr Marsha Davenport.'

Marsha looked up, recognised Stevie and turned to someone beside the stage and made some remark. Tom considered pulling Stevie down but it was too late. No-one wanted to interrupt her, and the conference personnel passed along a hand mike.

'Does the panel think that it is acceptable to breed a community of transgenic humanzees so that ready access to their stem cells can advance life extension research?'

Marsha looked openly surprised that the question was so simple. She had expected some verbal attack not this pointless question.

She chose to mock Stevie. 'What is that light I see? Is it perhaps the villagers lighting torches to attack Victor Frankenstein's laboratory?'

Many of the audience laughed at this, turning to see the heckler who had been handled so neatly.

Marsha added, 'Worthwhile scientific advances will always be fought by traditionalists!'

Tom saw that the person Marsha had spoken with had gathered several colleagues and they were slowly working their way back to where he and Stevie were seated.

Stevie was not about to be browbeaten like this. 'All my adult life has been spent in honest scientific endeavour, but there has always been a moral dimension to any such work! It's like drug-taking in sport. Athletes have the expected goal to go faster or further, higher or longer, but we have agreed that it is morally unacceptable that this is achieved with drug assistance. The means does not justify the ends.'

Opinion swung a little as a few of the audience clapped this sentiment.

Marsha saw her security detail was still quite a few paces from Stevie.

'Stevie, you have to understand that we have to become all that we can become. It's a fundamental part of our condition; it's hard-wired into our DNA. If we are to expand out through the universe then we need super-long lifespans. We need to change our very fabric to take the hardship of the long journeys. We need to change our capacities so we can populate the different environments we will encounter. We were never intended simply to crouch on this one planet until the sun goes out. We need to grow wings!'

Six stewards had now zeroed in on their position from all around the room and made a grab for Stevie. One snatched away the microphone before she could make any reply. Tom resisted but one of them pinned his arms while another pulled him out to the aisle, firmly and forcibly but not so that it would provoke the rest of the delegates. As they marched him from the hall he noticed that one of the stewards, the one Marsha had alerted, bore the gNOS tattoo on his forehead.

Behind them Stevie shouted as they manoeuvred her towards the exit, 'We built our so-called civilisation on the pillaging of the earth's natural resources, with absolutely no regard for the other life forms with which we share this ecosystem. Are we in any way worthy to populate other planets, other systems? If we are to extend life, then shouldn't we use it to develop more awareness, more consideration? Breeding and imprisoning a new species is criminal, and killing it to extend our own lives is just unforgivable!'

The doors closed on them as the chairperson was bringing the session back to order. He said, 'Let's not let some tree-huggers deflect us from our important subject.'


Stevie and Tom were led to a small room with a board table and chairs. There were no windows, just the one door. The stewards said nothing, as they forced them into the room and locked the door. Two of them stood outside, backs to the door, yet visible through a small window of wired glass.

Tom asked, 'Did you see that at least one of them was gNOS?'

'Yes, I noticed the tattoo. Sorry, but they were all so complacent, so self-absorbed. I just couldn't allow that woman to be, well, lauded or applauded I guess.'

'You made your points well. I just wish we'd realised that we were walking back into the lion's den.'

'They can't just abduct us, can they?'

'Well, they have no right to lock us in here, but that didn't stop them.'

Tom was looking around but all he could see was a smoke detector built into the ceiling. Neither of them smoked so neither carried matches or a lighter. He studied it more closely and it looked a rather sophisticated device. He concluded that in this public conference area it contained a gas detector too.

He rummaged around in Stevie's bag to find hairspray and a perfume atomiser. He climbed onto the table and just hoped that the combination of the two items sprayed directly into the sensor might provoke a response. He jumped down from the table as an electronic alarm sounded. The two stewards turned and peered back into the room.

They were obviously confused. A sounding alarm required that they escort all visitors and delegates to the nearest hall exit, but their supervisor had stipulated they should keep these two in the room. They were not gNOS, they worked for the Messe on a regular though freelance basis - but the alarm was so strident that it won the battle for their minds. They opened the door and escorted the two to the nearest external exits.

Outside the hall was an area that formed a virtual canyon between the large exhibition buildings. A growing and milling crowd of participants from the exhibition and conference had spilled out into this area, many taking the opportunity to light up a cigarette now that they were out in the open. The stewards clearly had defined duties in such a situation and saw no value in holding on to this pair of hecklers, so they went about their preordained tasks.

Tom led Stevie around the outside of the hall. They had emerged at the loading bay side rather than the public entrance. Tom wanted them away from there as soon as possible. He realised that Stevie's carefully collected set of brochures had been left behind in the conference room. They had come all this way with only ten minutes of a Q&A to show for it! Though Stevie's winding up of Marsha had been useful. He thought she had sounded particularly 'loony tunes' when she was talking of colonising other planets.

It was the fact that everyone else was hanging around expecting to be let back in to the halls that allowed Trajan to spot them. Their purposeful movement along the side of the hall stood out, particularly as they moved from group to group around the various exits. He would have to have been blind not to have noticed them.

He gathered and marshalled his gNOS team and set off on a course through the large crowd in order to cut them off from reaching the exit. Tom was watching for any pursuit and the fact that the gNOS team was so evidently walking away from the hall made them obvious to him too.

He chivvied Stevie to run towards the railway station and they made good progress until he had to stop to catch his breath. It was the first time he had done any real exercise since his operation, the rapid passage of air through his throat had created a reaction. He stopped and stooped as his body was wracked with a series of coughs.

They were closing the gap. He did not have time to be unwell, he started to jog while trying to control his breathing. Stevie was fraught, she wanted him to stop, yet knew they must press on.

Tom managed a shambling jogging rhythm that was not particularly painful to his chest. They were going to make it to the station! He had hoped there would be a taxi rank, but nothing useful materialised. Would there be a queue at the ticket desk? Would there be a train? He was constantly looking back over his shoulder and it was Stevie who had to point out the two men stood at the entrance to the station. They had the distinctive look of gNOS personnel!

Tom had no idea what to do so just pressed on. His only logic that there were two of them at the station and a much larger group was coming from behind. He stopped Stevie twenty paces short of the entrance and looked around for any sign of a vehicle that they might flag down but they were alone on this street.

Their followers also slowed their pace. Now confident of success they closed the gap steadily. Their leader went for his radio, and then looked over his shoulder as a vehicle pulled out of the exhibition parking area and headed their way.

Tom took deep draughts of air as he considered their options but was coming up with no course of action. The large Mercedes saloon moved towards them and stopped alongside. Marsha stepped out.

'I am so disappointed in you Stevie. I picked you out for the highest office within the Order. I allowed you to avoid much of the programming we normally apply at the retreats. I wanted your bright mind unfettered and was offering you personal enlightenment.'

'Pity you didn't allow the humanzees the same freedoms. Didn't you see their paintings, their crafts? They deserve to be treated humanely; no I mean human-ly!'

Marsha snapped back, 'They are lab specimens, no more than that. I created them. They are an experiment created for a purpose - my purpose.'

'To live forever and fly around the planets? Complete madness!'

Marsha had had enough, 'Perpetua chose you. Perpetua needs you.'

Stevie's demeanour and posture completely changed, 'Perpetua chose me. Perpetua needs me.'

Tom shook her. 'No Stevie, stay with me. Don't let her do this to you!'

Trajan walked up to Tom and pulled him away. Tom swung out at him only to see him sidestep and deliver the same blow to the kidney that Mark Elliott had experienced during his 'interview'. He dropped to his knees from the blow.

Stevie looked straight through him. There was no sign of recognition, no reaction of his plight. Marsha beckoned her to the car and she meekly obeyed. Tom tried to stop her but was pulled back by two of the gNOS men. This could not be happening!

He looked around desperately for inspiration and found it. Brain and another guy materialised from nowhere. He learned later they had been sent by Sir Joseph to watch his back and had obviously been waiting for their moment. They attacked the two gNOS men at the gate and then reached Tom pulling him to his feet before wrestling him towards the railway station.

He tried to shake them off, 'Quick, get Stevie!'

Brain shouted, 'The old man made it quite clear there was to be no leaving you on the side of the road again!'

'But they've got Stevie!'

The gNOS team was formed up beside the car, clearly not interested in pursuing Tom. Trajan calmly climbed into the front passenger seat while Marsha slammed the rear door on herself and Stevie. The car moved off and drove away from the Messe towards the city.

Tom couldn't believe it, they had only just pried her away from these people. What the hell had he been thinking bringing her? Yes, she had insisted. He should have been stronger, more aware of the danger. She was such an innocent, and they had taken her from him – again!

# BOOK FOUR

**George Bernard Shaw**:

*'All great truths begin as blasphemies.'*

*'Progress is impossible without change, and those who cannot change their minds cannot change anything.'*

*'The reasonable man adapts himself to the world: the unreasonable one persists in trying to adapt the world to himself. Therefore all progress depends on the unreasonable man.'*

**Max More**, transhumanist and founder of the Extropy Institute:

*'We have achieved two of the three alchemists' dreams: We have transmuted the elements and learned to fly. Immortality is next.'*

# Chapter 60 - *Celbridge, Ireland*

Its country's committed membership of the EU and an attractive tax regime had managed to propel Dublin to reach, at its zenith, the status of the world's fifth richest city in the league table of purchasing power per head of population.

The much larger, star-studded city of Los Angeles only made it to eighth position. Other cities that one would have expected to have scored well proved in fact to be way down the league table. As an example those cities shown as the 25th - 30th richest were respectively New York, Madrid, Tokyo, London, Dubai and Paris.

Dublin's tax breaks had been so very attractive to many American corporations. Companies such as Amazon, Google, Microsoft, PayPal and Yahoo! all chose to establish their European headquarters within the Greater Dublin area. Ireland also managed to attract a number of hi-tech manufacturers like Apple, Intel and Hewlett-Packard to establish plants around the Emerald Isle.

So it came as no real surprise to find that BiCogNaIT's European HQ was located right there on the outskirts of Dublin's urban sprawl, in Celbridge. This town, Tom learned, was one of the largest in Ireland, though it had just one long commercial street as its heart. Its major appeal was that it had no town council to wrap it up in administrative delays, no plague of development or economic planning initiatives to complicate and confuse.

Celbridge has been a settled community for well over 5,000 years. It sits alongside the River Liffey's north bank. Tom, Brain and the rest of the team were booked in to the Setanta House Hotel, an ivy-clad building conveniently located right at the centre of the town. Brain used one of his alternative identities to book and pay for the room in the belief that BiCogNaIT would probably be well informed locally.

Their precautions were in vain as their trip had been reported to Trajan Milos even before the booking of their low-cost Ryanair flights.

## San Francisco, USA

Mark Elliott was beginning to crave flatness; this city was just a little too bizarre with its plunging drops and precipitous climbs. He had been sitting in his vehicle for almost two hours waiting for the SFPD to assemble its crew. It was like sitting in a big dipper carriage making a final tense steady climb before its sudden gut-twisting white-knuckle swoop downwards. Besides his neck still hurt like crazy from his tango with the truck.

He found his mind was wandering. He recalled several dead bodies he had the misfortune to see and to handle, usually after they had been left to mature for some time. He was aware that, for want of a pumping heart, blood collects at the lowest part of the corpse. In much the same way for the last two hours all his blood had been congregating in his butt. The thought had him shifting in his seat as he ran through some simple deep vein thrombosis exercises that he had picked up once on a flight to somewhere. He felt no beneficial effect, though there was the need to rearrange the underwear that had ridden up even further during the process - and this movement brought his neck back into play!

Why wasn't BiCogNaIT located in a leafy science park out on the outskirts of the city like all the other hi-tech companies? But if Mark had to make a guess, he would assume that this site was probably attractive for its close proximity to Nob Hill, right up there ahead of him. In his rear-view mirror he could see the beginnings of Chinatown.

BiCogNaIT's west coast offices were located just off Powell, in a bland six storey building that showed the BiCogNaIT logo on a small and subtle brass plate beside its main door. A CCTV camera guarded the threshold but it had been established that the back entrance to the building offered them no better approach. An SFPD detachment was already waiting at the rear to ensure nothing would exit that way, when they would eventually turn up at the front door with a warrant.

### Celbridge, Ireland

Brain had explained the complications that they would face in Ireland. Though the country recognised the EU's European Arrest Warrant and Sir Joseph had good contacts with The National Bureau of Criminal Investigation at the Garda Síochána, there remained a degree of friction between the two countries' secret services after so many years of cheek-by-jowl antagonism.

For his part Sir Joseph envied the Irish Secret Service for its extreme form of confidentiality. For example it had not followed the trend of other western services, instead steadfastly refusing to name its director. Any commentators in the Republic correctly surmised that the service's members were drawn from among those of the Garda Special Branch, from the army intelligence unit G2 or from the diplomatic corps of the Department of Foreign Affairs. They could only guess at who they were as absolutely no information had ever been published.

Even its political leaders were unusually poorly informed. Charles Haughey, while Taoiseach, said without seeking to hide the hint of despair, 'The nature of this service is such that, even if I had this information, it would not be in the public interest to give it'. During his own term as leader John Bruton commented, 'The nature of secret service payments is such that to subject them to Dáil scrutiny would defeat the whole object of the expenditure.'

The 'Troubles' in Northern Ireland had been over for more than a decade, but the thirty-years of strife had shaped the minds of several generations. Many in Ireland would quickly point to the Troubles having lasted in fact for four long centuries and not just those recent three decades.

It was the residual mutual suspicion that had Brain planning to unofficially break into BiCogNaIT at 2 am, without planning to advise his local counterparts. It was also convenient in that they could coordinate their investigation with what was to happen in San Francisco. While acknowledging these justifications, Tom thought it was mostly because Brain preferred to hang right out there on the extremity of a limb.

Brain seemed to live for these extreme moments; his whole personality changed when he was out in the field. He had confessed to Tom that regrettably the Service was changing, the opportunities for these sorts of forays disappearing fast; for now he was going to make the most of every opportunity while he still could.

Tom felt Brain was being far too melodramatic for his taste but at last they heard that the Americans had got their act together in San Francisco and the time had finally arrived for them to proceed. They were both about to go in.


**San Francisco, USA**

Mark agreed with the SFPD that they should enter at 6pm, in the hope that at the end of a business day there would be a natural degree of confusion when many would be leaving for home. He planned that this would assist with their surprise entry. However attaining the warrant had led to them being twenty minutes late by the time they rapped on the door and presented the paperwork to the receptionist who buzzed them through the front door.

As she lifted the phone to make a call, two security guards appeared from the rear of the entry hall having been alerted by the CCTV. Mark instantly recognised both the forehead tattoos and the attitude. They summarily grabbed the warrant and examined it as if it was some disgusting piece of pornography.

'We will need to run this by our attorney.'

The SFPD lieutenant was experienced at this sort of entry and ignored them. He walked back to the main door and buzzed in his team who flooded through and spread to all parts of the building ignoring the protests of the guards.

He took back the warrant. 'You are welcome to record my badge number...' he flashed it, '... and talk with whomsoever you like, but in the meantime we will be proceeding with our lawful search of your premises.'

Mark stayed with the lieutenant while he first assessed that the guards were willing to comply, and then left two of his own men to hold them in the lobby. He then set off on a general overview of the facility.

They went down to the basement first, this was the level that led to the rear exit of the offices. The lieutenant opened the door and waved to his unit who signalled that no-one had tried to leave by that route, as yet.

The basement was self-evidently a storage facility containing many packages, stationery and medical supplies. It also housed a large archive section that Mark hoped would not need too close an investigation. If it did then it would be a huge task; probably his! One of the entry team was already poring over the packages, taking photos and making notes to provide a first oversight of the material.

To one side of the area there was a hatchway that had already been opened and investigated. It led to a huge underground diesel oil repository and two large diesel generators. If the tank was proportionate in depth to its two visible dimensions then Tom estimated it contained enough oil to run the generators for several decades.

The first floor, in using this term in his thought process, Mark realised that he had spent too long in the UK as he now instinctively thought of it as the ground floor, held a series of meeting rooms and offices dealing with accounting, HR, purchasing and so on. It also housed the server hardware. An officer was already making sure that the computers remained available to them. He had severed any outside connections and the server files were being output onto a portable hard drive.

The second and third floors housed a series of working laboratories with rows of workstations and equipment that Mark thought were pretty much the same as those he had seen during his London facility break-in, while hunting the humanzee. The thought had him unconsciously rub at his ribs where the tranquiliser dart had left bruises for some time. Technical officers were establishing what was happening at each station, but they indicated that they had found nothing of particular interest as yet.

The fourth floor was an animal testing facility with a smell that also took him right back to London, but there were only rodents present here Mark glimpsed creatures that initially looked pretty normal, but some had sprouted various appendages like some freak show. He was delighted to press on from there. Up on the fifth floor they passed through an entry secured by a retina scanner. Fortunately the SFPD had already found some way to gain access and the door was wedged open with a large desk calendar.

During the preparation for this investigation it had been established that the offices consumed a huge amount of electricity; to support the organisation had signed a special deal in place with Pacific Gas & Electricity. The contract guaranteed their heavy requirements and there were strict obligations for PG&E to maintain an uninterrupted supply. The organisation was clearly a belt-and-braces operation given their installation of the diesel generators, presumably to backstop the utility company arrangement. Clearly they wanted to maintain their regular supply, but what was it for?

It was only on reaching the fifth and six floors that they finally learned why all this power was necessary! On the fifth floor they confronted a huge array of cryonic cabinets, organised floor to ceiling in long rows. Mark estimated that there were over two hundred of them on this floor.

His first thought was that there must have been a huge amount of steel added to the floors to take all this weight, but why wasn't all this down at ground level? Just getting it all up there must have taken huge additional effort. If the San Andreas or Hayward fault should have one of its regular grumbles then it would probably all end up down in the basement anyway!

## Celbridge, Ireland

Tom first met Brain's colleague James on the bank of the Danube. He was a big man, quietly capable and reliable. Because of their reticence in offering names Tom had originally nicknamed him Brawn. When he learned it was actually James, but it was unclear whether this was his first name or his surname.

It came as no surprise that it was James who had recc'ed these Irish premises and he that would lead the entry. With the information he had gleaned they found it easy to surprise and overwhelm the two security guards who, while clearly gNOS, must have been low-level, why else would they be allocated to the normally uneventful overnight shift? Certainly they put up no resistance as they were cuffed by plastic grippers to a large radiator and skilfully gagged.

The team passed on into the building to see what they might find. Tom was still hopeful that they would discover Stevie incarcerated somewhere here or, as a minimum, they would find a strong lead to where she was being held.

As in San Francisco, they too found the early parts of the huge warehouse-like facility had been given over to a large laboratory. Neither Brain nor Tom was particularly interested in this area which they assessed was probably just a cover for the real operations undertaken behind it.

They pressed on until they came to a door secured by a keyboard entry device. Brain nodded to one of his team who set about gaining them access. Tom used the time to scan the nearest lab workstations but there was nothing to show what was being carried out there.

An audible ping indicated that the door was finally open and they all filed through. James led the others with Tom tagging along while Brain hung back in the lab looking for something to wedge the door open. He wanted the escape route to be unrestricted if they should need to leave in haste.

The rest of the team passed along a corridor and carefully pushed through swing doors into a rear room. Showing their training the four secret service men quickly fanned out as they entered, making sure they offered no easy group target. Tom hung back until they declared the area safe, though he assumed the greatest threat might be a confrontation with a humanzee. On the way there Brain had confessed and joked about his assault by the female; now Tom knew it was not just their greater strength that he should fear.

Three huge floodlights suddenly bathed the area in crisp detail. The entry team went to ground and were careful not to look into the lights. Tom could not help himself and got a huge area of his eyesight burnt out for his trouble. He ducked back out of the swing doors waiting until his sight recovered.

Brain was coming down the corridor having secured the first doorway. He hugged one of the walls and went to look through a small inspection window in the swing doors that opened on to the rear area.

A disembodied and amplified voice boomed out 'So what have we got here then?' Disembodied because the team scanned the room to reveal nothing. The area had an upper level that hugged the four walls leaving an open atrium at its centre. There could be any number of people up there above them, but unless they chose to peer over the edge there was no way of Brain's team knowing.

The disembodied voice had an American accent. It continued, 'The Irish Larceny Act of 1916 has an amendment 23B that states "a person is guilty of aggravated burglary if he commits any burglary and at the time has with him any firearm". It goes on to say, "A person guilty of aggravated burglary shall be liable on conviction to imprisonment for life".'

James had found a stairway to the upper level and was carefully picking his way up it.

The speaker paused then added, 'I don't suppose any of you, except perhaps Mr Carter, will have any valid proof of your true identity. That may cause you a few problems. It may be best that Sir Joseph Maudlin denies all knowledge of you rather than risk further upsetting his Irish peers. By that I mean the Irish Secret Service, and not the English gentry! So I guess that extradition may prove not to be an option for you.'

Brain slipped back to the labs to look for anyone that might seek to cut off their retreat and Tom decided to follow him. As Brain moved into the lowly lit area a figure launched itself at him and the two rolled away from Tom's view. Brain curled and used his assailant's own momentum against him. He managed to get on top of the man and landed several solid blows to his head.

'Stop right now!'

A second guard pointed a gun at Brain and moved towards him. Presumably his boss wanted the British team captured and not killed as from his vantage point he certainly had every opportunity to finish off Brain.

'Get off of him. Slowly! Now let's see any weapons!'

Tom bent down to pick up the fire extinguisher that Brain had used to wedge open the door. Just what else were they for? Holding it in both hands he ran the few steps to the guard and crashed it down on his head thinking 'Who needs guns when there's always a handy fire extinguisher lying about? This was becoming something of an unfortunate habit.'

It was obvious by the way he crumpled that Tom's man was not going to get up again any time soon. In the meantime Brain had spun and kicked the first guard in the head as he was beginning to get up. Still groggy from the earlier blows he too slumped back to the floor. Tom's manoeuvre was much less balletic but he did manage to catch the door before it closed.

Brain searched the two guards as he said, 'Look, we've secured the exit. Now we have to go back and get my men out of there. Take this pistol. I've released the safety so it's just point and squeeze. But do keep the gun pointed at the floor as we go along the corridor. We don't need a friendly fire incident!'

They both went quickly back down the corridor.

In the rear room it was clear that their antagonist liked the sound of his own voice. He was still taunting them without showing himself.

'So what do we do with you? Call the Gardai and hand you over? Or perhaps we should just deal with you directly in our own way.'

James had finally made it up the stairs without being noticed. He cautiously looked around to see a group of five individuals, one with the megaphone. They were in a group keeping well back from the balcony, clearly enjoying their moment. He wished he was equipped with a machine pistol or better; with one short blast he could have taken them all out. But they had been sent to look for information and this was not a shoot-to-kill assignment.

One of the basic principles of any military engagement was to interrupt the 'control and command' of the opponent; so he calmly shot the man with the bullhorn through the fleshy part of his thigh and ducked out of sight.

Trajan had been enjoying his moment, he was just saying, 'I want each of you to step out of cover to the centre of the...'

The excruciating pain in his leg felt initially like a cramp as it was so unexpected, but as he reeled from the impact he looked to see the ragged hole in his trousers and he could feel the blood already seeping from the wound. He squeezed the area of damage while beckoning one of his men to give him his uniform tie to use as a tourniquet.

The other gNOS guys had dropped to the floor. They had no idea where the shot had come from but they did know that there were only two stairwells so they moved towards them.

Given the sudden silence the three Brits on the ground level seized their opportunity and made it back through the swing doors where they waited for their colleague. James was halfway back down the stairs as two gNOS guards arrived at the top. Without hesitation, given that Trajan had been hit, they shot him in the back.

James was wearing a Kevlar jacket so the force of the first shot succeeded only in propelling him down the stairs; but one of the follow-up shots caught his right arm and he dropped his handgun. He hit the floor grabbing his injured arm, then tried to crawl away towards the swing doors.

One gNOS guard sprinted down the stairs to kick him onto his back. Brain stood at the doors trying to see what was happening on the upper level before committing himself to a rescue. Tom pushed past him, 'I'm not going to be accused of leaving anyone injured by the side of the road!'

He sprinted for the downed man with his gun thrust before him. As he got closer he sprayed shots and by chance one hit its target and the guard reeled away. The second guard was at the bottom of the stairs and hesitated long enough for Tom to cannon into him and crash him back onto the stairwell. He went down with a huge crack on the edge of the metal slat staircase.

Tom looked towards the one he had shot, calmly considering whether he should finish him off. He was at the same time shocked to his core. Only a year ago the thought of killing someone would have been completely abhorrent. What was happening to him, that he could now assess whether to let this other human being live or die? Fortunately the man was almost literally licking his wound and looked of no further threat.

He helped to lift James. Thank God it was not his leg that had been hit, the big man was able to assist. Tom helped him back towards the doors. Brain took over when they got close while the other Brits sprayed covering fire towards the stairs and up at the gallery.

Trajan's voice on the bullhorn was more strained this time, 'This is not over, Mr Carter. You need to remember my name. It's Trajan Milos, and don't forget we have your girlfriend. Perhaps I will give her to my men as a plaything. Or throw her to the humanzees that she likes so much. Once she's tasted that particular monkey meat she won't want to look at you!'

Tom made to make his way back into the rear room but Brain pulled him away. 'There will be other opportunities where we set the ground rules. Come on, let's go!'

They made their retreat cautiously but there was no attempt at pursuit.

Safely in their car Brain asked, 'You are a crazy man when you get your dander up. But nice work. You seem to have the vital thing that every soldier needs, and that's good luck. Mind you, if either of those guards was of any use then you'd have been a goner.'

James was patched up and seemed relaxed. He was amused at the much smaller man's earlier performance. He slapped Tom on the back and then held up his hand in a 4-finger V, the Vulcan salute. 'May you live long! And your luck last longer! Next time we go into action I'm going to make sure I stand right behind you!'

Brain added more seriously, 'If there's anything worse than one of my team getting himself shot, it's when it's clear that someone tipped them off. They knew we were coming, and they knew you were there Tom. They were lying in wait for us. I thought those two we tied up gave in too easily. They were obviously just a decoy. It's just as well they weren't as good as they thought they were; but there's one thing that's absolutely sure - we appear to have ourselves a mole!'

### San Francisco, USA

Mark urgently needed to call in some support - scientific support that could begin to explain quite what it was they were looking at. The BiCogNaIT staff they were holding appeared to know nothing of the top two floors and certainly were not prepared to answer any questions.

He had already learned of the failure in Dublin, of the possible betrayal, of the injured man. They really had to make the very most of their successful surprise entry here. He and Tom had discussed who would have known of the Dublin break-in and yet not be aware of the one in San Francisco. By factoring in both it was quite a small list for them to pursue from both ends.

By now the BiCogNaIT executives would have become fully aware of the San Francisco facility search, so Mark kept back enough personnel at the labs to make sure there could be no chance of a counter-attack.

They already had IT specialists at site. These had been readily recruited from the nearby SVRCFL, the Silicon Valley Regional Computer Forensics Laboratory located just outside the city in Menlo Park. All phone lines to the facility had been isolated on arrival and they believed they had rapidly disconnected the server from any chance of any outside contact. They were keen to avoid any chance of someone externally accessing and cleaning the files.

On their first review they had advised Mark that there was not much held locally; perhaps the really sensitive stuff was remotely stored. Now they were backtracking to try to identify quite where it might be located. There were two regularly accessed locations, one somewhere in the continental USA, the other routed in such a way that they thought it might be in Europe or more likely the Middle East but they could not yet track it back further than the general region. And they stressed that it could be that evidence had been deliberately left or planted to suggest that these areas were of significance while they were in fact nowhere near the server's location.

Fortunately a kernel of files was still held locally under separate passwords and this was where they were currently focusing their efforts.

It was understandable that San Francisco should be well versed in IT crimes. The local FBI department had specialist units for computer intrusion, for industrial espionage, for crimes relating to the theft of intellectual property or of copyrighted materials and one for any physical crimes relating to the semiconductor industry. The San Francisco Division covered the North and Central coast regions of California engaging around 11,000 agents and 15,000 support personnel.

Mark had been advised that his BiCogNaIT investigation had been defined by the local FBI as a 'white collar' crime, though usually this category meant various forms of fraud, bank fraud, wire and mail fraud or money laundering.

Mark had established therefore that not one of the 26,000 local FBI personnel was at all appropriate for the sort of work that the organisation had been pursuing. As a result there had been frantic calls around the many federal offices to find anyone who should be alerted about their findings.

It had taken hours, most of these on the phone trying to call people away from dinner tables or from their homes, but at last the technical support had arrived in the shape of two research biologists from the SSCRM, Stanford Stem

Cell and Regenerative Medicine team, and a complete SFPD Crime Scene Investigation squad.

The dawn had come and gone and Mark was feeling very hyper as a result of all the coffee he had been drinking, but finally the advisors were gathered in one of the meeting rooms on the first floor ready to deliver a preliminary report.

Luke, one of the two SSCRM personnel, had elected himself as spokesperson. 'Well, it will take a little time to be sure but we believe that there are three things going on up there. The least controversial I guess are the cryo units. These are holding a number of heads of followers of this Perpetua Order. We found a list of their names.'

Mark thought he had misheard him, 'Heads? What do you mean? Just heads?'

Luke smiled at this. 'Yep, it's not new to this mob. There are a number of people who believe cures and increased longevity programmes will be achievable in just one or two decades' time. So they pay to have their bodies, but now it's more often just their heads, preserved at or just before the point of death. Their hope is that they can be revived later, then cured or have their lives extended. Or, as I'll go on to explain, they hope that other solutions may by then have been found.'

The senior SFPD CSI person was a small, pale, mousy-looking woman called Raquelle. Mark thought if ever a name was a mismatch this had to be it.

Raquelle added. 'Just storing the heads is of course a much cheaper option. It uses a much smaller cryo unit for example; more can be crammed into the space available and there is a commensurately lower power requirement and so on. Interestingly from the files we found it was not so much a one-off payment made by these people. They appear to have pledged all their worldly wealth across to this church of theirs.'

Mark was still trying to get his head around this idea, then smiled at his unwitting choice of metaphor. 'So, what, they get revived as a head? Just how useful could that possibly be for them?' Still perplexed at the thought he added, 'I guess at least they wouldn't be able to let their heart rule their head again!'

They were all far too tired, dragged from their homes in the middle of the night, under pressure to come up with information, all pushing too hard for results, so nobody found this remotely amusing.

Luke continued. 'Perhaps the next item we found might answer your query. There is a series of experiments running up there trying to do a brain dump.'

Mark questioned, 'Why is it that I'm not getting the feeling you're using 'brain dump' in the conventional sense of the words?'

Raquelle took up the question. 'No, this is an attempt to record and transfer all the neural path connections - to capture the experiences, memories, opinions, beliefs and personality from an organic brain and transfer it across to an organic computer or to another organic brain.'

'What, they can do that?'

Luke smiled, 'That's what they are attempting to do. We can't yet establish if they are having any success. Just trying it breaks every bioethics code that there ever was, and for my taste there are all too few of those currently. Whatever, based upon the ones that there are, they have certainly driven a Hummer right through them.'

Raquelle continued, pulling out a document. 'They are in direct convention of all sorts of laws and morals. It's not as if they didn't know. I even found this copy of the President's Bioethics Committee report displayed in their bookcase upstairs.'

Seeing Mark's lack of recognition she flicked through it and quoted.

'It says for example, "Biotechnology and the life sciences have astonished the world in recent years, but they have also disoriented people by raising a whole new set of ethical issues. In response, a new branch of moral philosophy has emerged, bioethics, whose task is to grapple with the ethical challenges of cloning, stem cell research, genetic engineering, in vitro fertilization, drug therapy, new techniques for arresting the ageing process, and aspirations to conquer death itself." They seem to have taken these items as a virtual 'to do' list; certainly each of them is a goal for these folk. They are dabbling in all of them.'

Mark asked, 'I can just about follow what you're saying, but has this committee come up with any guidelines or laws that we can charge them with breaking?'

This was clearly something Raquelle felt strongly about.

'Unlikely, because it's really all based upon what you believe. It comes down to your definition of our humanity. Are we just a complex organism that lives and dies and then that's it? Or, do we have a soul? If you believe the latter then the sort of meddling these people are doing is an attack on the very dignity of our humanity and might be threatening our eternal soul.'

Mark topped up his coffee cup rather than comment. He was thinking, 'Well I guess from that, it's quite clear where you stand on the matter.'

Luke obviously disagreed too, but he wasn't prepared to keep his own counsel on the matter.

'The brain is something physical that we can all thoroughly appreciate and calibrate. It's the few pounds of grey mush trapped up here inside our skull. But whenever I try to read anyone on the subject of the mind versus the brain I tend to lose the plot very quickly. With some of the psychobabble I almost lose the will to live. I guess I just have to accept that I don't have the brain power, though I would suggest the lack of time, belief or interest, in establishing quite where the brain and the mind might cross over or where they don't. As for the soul?' He raised his hands in defeat.

Raquelle wasn't going to let that pass, 'It's a question of faith…'

Luke was warming to the fight too, 'Precisely, faith. Let me see now. Doesn't that mean to believe something even in the absence of any proof? Not something we scientists would normally care to acknowledge as an approach.'

Mark was the voice of reason. 'Look, we've all had a long night; nerves are bound to be frayed. Didn't you say that there were three thrusts going on up there? Either I missed it or you didn't mention a third.'

Luke answered him. 'Well, the third is the very spookiest. It's real Frankenstein stuff, I'm afraid. We mentioned earlier that they are trying to download the contents of a human brain. Of course one objective is to do this from one human brain to another, presumably a younger human brain. They are also seeking to download it to an organic computer.

'In this particular case that's organic as in living tissue. They have been multiplexing up a series of lower-order brains that connected together may be sufficient to be a suitable receptacle for a human brain dump. It must be some sort of primate that they have been using.'

Mark slumped back in his chair. 'Of course, that's it. That's what they're using the humanzees for!'

# Chapter 61 – *London, UK*

Back in London Tom was distraught, wondering quite what was happening to Stevie and distressed by the lack of any success from the Irish expedition. He had managed very little sleep and as result had lain in late while pondering where she was and what he should or could be doing better in order to get her back?

He was therefore somewhat relieved when his reverie was interrupted by Sir Joseph. He was calling an emergency meeting to review something new that had been uncovered.

Dieter had been enjoying his period of enforced 'house arrest' with Hannah. While of course he craved his freedom, he realised that it would have one large and severe disadvantage - it would mean Hannah would be on her way too and he would probably never get to see her again. In fact he felt he could never have dreamt up a more perfect scenario. She had to spend time with him, give him lots of attention. It was in some ways a case of them united against the universe. He really felt they were developing a proper relationship for the first time. Who knew where this might lead?

As a result of his ebullient mood, Dieter had become much more forthcoming with his interlocutors from the British Secret Service. He asked for and received the use of a PC and was surprised to find that some of his access to the Order had been left ajar. He explained that he had given himself back doors into the servers from the 'get-go' as he was useless at recalling passwords. He needed these other entry points squirrelled away to ensure he could always get access.

Using one of these back doors Dieter discovered a work-in-progress video that Shepherd was working on, presumably with Dieter's successor - and he was able to download it.

Around the table Tom saw it was all the usual suspects who had been gathered. The Foreign Secretary was as usual bracketed by two officials who would offer no comment or input. Instead they would scribble away minutes for the session. Tom was amazed they did not use recording devices or laptops for this purpose; presumably the FO must still have a typing pool somewhere in its bowels. He imagined rows of old maids with wayward hair sitting in Dickensian rows, and secretly hoping that a Russian spy would seduce them for access to the files. He must concentrate. It was all this talk of moles!

He and Brain had already held a preamble meeting and, based upon access to information about the Irish 'incursion' and not about the San Franciscan event, they had identified those who could have been the mole. It was agreed to watch these few suspects carefully through this meeting and in an effort to narrow down the field.

The meeting's objective was set out succinctly by the Foreign Secretary, 'We are here to glean anything that we can about the intentions of these organisations. From the information I have received about this video I understand that they have reached a new stage in their plans. Certainly if they are now preparing to send out broadcasts to the global media they are becoming much more brazen. Why do they suddenly want to attract the world's attention? Previously they have been reasonably stealthy in their approach and shunned publicity at any cost?'

Sir Joseph took up the preamble, 'I had more than enough when those Al Jazeera people broadcast that twisted Saudi's thoughts while he was skulking away deep in his cave. We really don't need any more holy wars beaming out to us from the Middle East! This is their proposed broadcast, which looks as if it is very close to being the final version. Probably best if I just run it and we all take notes. We can go back to any point to study it more carefully if required.'

He started up the recording.

Shepherd appeared on screen, "I'm ready to go!"

The lighting of the studio suddenly increased so his head and shoulders were brightly lit against a pale white background; the effect made his face look as if it shone. He composed his expression into a required look of avuncular warmth that reluctantly delivered a note of discipline.

'The world changes and it changes today! These are my revelations! My revelations and not those of St John. He addressed his Revelations to seven like-minded early communities around the Middle East, but my gospel is intended for every part of the modern world, whether urban, rural or remote. It's for those of every political shade, for all genders, colours and beliefs. Listen carefully, because the world as you know it changes today!'

The Professor commented, 'Well he certainly got my attention.'

Tom grimaced, 'I can't forget that he's the one who has got Stevie too!'

Simon, the Professor's assistant, seemed to want console him, 'He's so clearly a man of god. You should not be concerned.'

Tom made a face at this but chose not to comment.

Shepherd was now shown walking across a field and Tom realised this was the reason Sir Joseph had gained the Middle Eastern impression. It was not the sort of landscape you would find in an English home county. Sparse and coarse vegetation, loose rocky soil and there was something about the angle of the sunlight, the quality of the light that said Middle East.

Tom nodded at Sir Joseph, 'I do agree that this location has the look of North Africa or the Middle East about it. It's the soil and vegetation that suggest it. Or has he managed to find somewhere in the USA that allows him to take on the look of Jesus in the Holy Land?'

Shepherd paused in his stroll and turned to camera. 'Let me start by providing you with a parable for life - life as it has become today. It's intended to highlight what pointless lives we have chosen for ourselves, to illustrate how worthless we have all become. You should think of it as a mirror turned upon your own existence. Look closely at this. Ponder the message and you will begin to recognise your own shortcomings.'

Sir Joseph agreed. 'You're probably right. If it's to be a parable then he has certainly selected the right setting.'

Shepherd proceeded. 'This parable is about Joe. He's an average sort of guy, the type raised in the heart of a thriving and thrusting city within the western democratic system. As a child he was brought up within, and to be respectful of, his mother's church. At her beckoning he was baptised, attended Sunday school, joined the choir, served at the altar, was confirmed.

'He soon grew out of his childhood beliefs when his friends showed him that his religion was irrelevant out there on the neighbourhood streets. He came to realise that his friends' values reflected modern life much more accurately; and he shed his religion.'

Shepherd had disappeared from the screen. It was now showing a montage of old newsreel footage in black and white with the odd item highlighted in colour to illustrate his script. Sir Joseph looked at one of his team and prompted, 'Try to trace the more unusual items used in this sequence. We might get lucky with a photo library that can advise us who they have licensed them to. I imagine a lot of it is just public domain material.'

Shepherd was back on screen. 'At school he was very physically capable. He could probably have succeeded at any sport he chose, but he lacked any real commitment to pursue one. However a coach spotted him and set out to inspire him to try out for the riches and kudos of professional sport; so he shed his friends and pursued his sport.

'Quickly recognising his mix of capability yet lack of tenacity, the coach supplied him with performance-enhancing drugs to make up for the lack of time he devoted to any practice and training. Drug-enhanced, he did well enough to get drafted, but a regular string of injuries progressively dampened his enthusiasm for the sport.

'In fact he slowly abandoned all his high school beliefs, the very few he had ever bothered to develop. He never really grasped the meaning of sportsmanship; for him it was about stretching the laws, fooling the officials. As for team spirit, why should he take a hit for the team? What was that about? He pooh-poohed the importance of the taking part, it was all about the winning.

'He sought all the shortcuts, any means of ignoring the conventions so he could reach out more speedily to relish the rewards. Over time he believed the very top individuals in his sport lacked any personality. He decided that the clubs and sporting authorities and their selection procedures were all established with a bias against people like him who held strong opinions and retained a life outside their sport. He shed his sport, but only just before it could shed him.'

The images moved from black and white to colour as the next section advanced.

'He met Maria in the neighbourhood. They dated, and found that they needed to get married when she fell pregnant. They set up home, raised two kids. Their kids were denied absolutely nothing by Joe. Perhaps initially it was a case of overcompensating for his own failed youth, but progressively it was as much to cover up his ongoing series of infidelities.

'In truth Joe did set out determined that the children would get the advantages that he did not have. He pushed them to concentrate on their education, only to find they pushed right back at him. At each stage of their lives he made sure they had the latest gadgets and fashions, never understanding that there was much more joy in the expectation than in the very short-term happiness from its realisation.'

Again Shepherd's image was replaced by the montage of images based upon black and white newsreel material.

'Too late he came to understand that he gave things to them far too early, often providing items that were more appropriate for much older children. None of the fads satisfied them for long. Their appetites were always voraciously applied to attaining the next vogue rather than appreciating what was to hand.

'The world had changed since Joe's childhood. There was no street life for his children. They were driven to school each day by Maria. Occasional sleepovers with friends were their only personal contact. The social Internet sites were where they did their hanging out.'

Simon commented, 'Well, we should have no difficulty in recognising these people. The world is certainly rather too full of people just like that.'

'That may be true of the West, but I thought his message was intended to be global?' Tom commented.

Shepherd pressed on with his parable. 'Joe soon grew out of any interest in his family too. He had found little real joy from parenthood and this accelerated once he realised he could readily find sex without commitment or responsibility elsewhere. As he aged he became even more jaundiced by life as he experienced a decline in his success on the singles' scene. Now the partners he met turned out to be far too clingy for his taste. They were too often seeking some form of commitment from him. Today he is seriously contemplating buying himself in a Thai or Filipino bride - for sex and housekeeping. He only wants to consider any commitment upon his own terms.'

Brain quipped, 'This Joe can't be too bad a judge then!'

Simon made a face at this comment, 'The man's a complete degenerate.'

Tom decided something about the Professor's PA was a bit off today. He had previously attended meetings and been like the Foreign Secretary's aides, scribbling notes and making few comments, probably because he recognised his lowly status at this table. Today he was becoming much more voluble.

Another series of images came on the screen as Joe's early work was mentioned. Starting out as black and white images they slowly changed to colour.

'Joe trained in construction and soon formed his own business, subcontracting his labour to larger contractors and only directly seeking smaller jobs. Initially he had to work hard to be accepted by the large contractors, had to learn all their procedures. Once he had safely secured their contracts he concluded that they had no real idea of how to run their own projects. He knew better what it was they needed. He knew how to cut corners and find the work-arounds that would speed up the task. He knew how he could save on materials, much of which he would then use on his own direct jobs.'

Sir Joseph commented. 'He sounds like the sort of builders I meet - Messrs Bodgitt & Leggitt. I do begin to wonder if all this was inspired by 'Joe the Plumber'. You know, the working guy who got dragged in to the Obama/McCain election trail?'

Simon muttered, but only Tom caught the comment, 'I think you will find it turns out to be Joseph the carpenter!'

'In the meantime Maria stays at home alone, where she expands her waistline as she slavishly follows the soaps and reality TV shows while reading gossip magazines. She delves into celebrity Internet sites further to feed her envy and prurient interest in their lifestyles. Her 'neighbourhood' has become this ever-changing, ephemeral global celebrity scene. She no longer finds time, being too fearful to try, to meet the rather too real people that she sees outside her doors.'

The video returned to a close-up of Shepherd.

'Joe, our modern everyman, has now developed a clear belief structure from his life and from many years of propping up the local bars. Each night, he can be relied upon to talk passionately about the failings of national and local politicians. To him they are just a long line of actors and shyster lawyers - self-serving idiots pandering to the latest line up of deep-pocketed lobbyists.

'He doesn't bother to vote anymore, because he knows he can't make any difference. Buy him a drink and he'll wax lyrical on the failings of bankers who took back his house, wouldn't finance his business plans and more recently threatened his meagre savings through their own mismanagement. After some early jingoistic pride expressed at the Iraq 'Shock and Awe' event he now echoes his father's post-Vietnam views about current conflicts, views fed by his choice in newspaper and what he gleans around construction sites and bars.'

Shepherd paused, the camera focused upon his eyes.

'So this is the basis for our modern parable of Joseph our humble carpenter and his wife Mary!'

The Professor smiled at the comment, 'Oh, quelle surprise! That's all just a wee bit too trite and obvious for my taste!'

Simon responded, 'It's just a parable!'

Tom found himself closely studying Simon who had forecast this biblical carpenter reference earlier. Might he be their mole? Could he know where Stevie was being held?

# Chapter 62 - *Selçuk, Turkey*

Marsha started their teleconference with an update on the raids at her two facilities.

'I can't hide the fact that the intrusion at San Francisco caught us unawares. We do believe that we managed to delete any damaging local data, most of it is kept off-site anyway, but of course they will have seen the work that we were doing in the laboratories.'

Shepherd was much more worried about the way in which they were being tested and attacked from all sides. 'Perhaps we need Trajan's team to mount a counteroffensive against these individuals who have been raiding our facilities. Until now we've been content to carry on and secure our programmes, to assume that we'll reach our conclusions before they can cause us any real interference. Perhaps we need to go on the offensive?'

Marsha scoffed, 'Trajan was supposed to be fully prepared for them, lying in wait for them at the Dublin facility, and yet they got away!'

Even on Marsha's PC screen she could see Trajan's eyes harden at the comment. He quickly responded, 'We were only tasked with making sure they got no information. No-one had instructed me to detain or despatch any of them. I believed that I was to remain discreet at this stage.'

Marsha dripped sarcasm, 'Now let me see. Dead British agents in Dublin. Local cause for concern, or more likely one for celebration?'

'They got nothing for their troubles. Each side took one casualty. Sadly as you know I was the one on our side. Perhaps the good doctor might like to manage the task herself next time?'

Samuel was bored with the exchange. 'What happened cannot be changed. Please let's move on. I've almost finished editing the first global broadcast so we can act on that within the week.'

Trajan was not ready to let it drop. 'I can move on the two key individuals as soon as you approve it. This Tom Carter should represent no problem at all. I have a personal reason to deal with Mark Elliott. He was the CIA man who led the SF raid. He tried to penetrate gNOS personally and he will regret the day he walked into our camp.'

Will tried to hide his smile as Marsha responded. He was not sure if anyone else caught the double entendre, given Trajan's leg injury.

Obviously Marsha had, 'Let's not make limp threats! We need to stay with the programme. If Samuel has the video ready to go then we have a series of urgent things that need to be resolved right now and these need to be secured. Plus, we now need to get everyone inside the retreats. Trajan and his team must concentrate upon preparing to keep out anyone who might turn up at our walls. We need no other projects or distractions.'

Samuel was content to move on, 'Marsha, where are we with the material?'

Marsha smiled, 'We have the stocks of the material ready and now, prior to your broadcast, Mission must move on to field testing.'

# Chapter 63 - *Ephesus, Turkey*

Marsha finished the teleconference and was delighted that the next phases could now get properly under way. It had felt that everything had been moving in slow motion. Now she could start to resolve her own part of the planning - her rebirth and quest for immortality.

She was delighted that Stevie was becoming her old self again. She had relaxed her conditioning very gently because she did not want to harm her at this late stage. She had such high aspirations for Stevie, but for now she needed her relaxed, compliant and free of conditioning. She certainly did not need some zombie for the next step. Stevie had to be fully aware and on her mettle through the critical final phases of their strategy. Marsha knew she had to prepare her thoroughly. She could afford no more failures.

Stevie assumed that Marsha's objective was somehow to convince her to become a key lieutenant, a right-hand-woman of sorts. Well Marsha could just dream on. It wasn't going to happen.

It was evident today that Marsha had information to impart because she suggested they walked out in the open. Stevie had come to recognise that this was clearly Marsha's preferred approach for any sort of factual transmission session.

They quickly crossed a road and headed southwards. Marsha explained that the road led from the city of Selçuk just off to their east and ran west to both the airport and the coast. Stevie correctly surmised that to Marsha part of the attraction of this particular location was that it afforded a wide variety of rapid escape routes.

Marsha started their walk by describing where they were. 'This place is very special for me, a location of huge significance to womankind. Originally established way back in the 14th century BCE, by some very fierce and extremely independent females, the Amazons. A dynasty of warrior queens who each led their all-woman army on various successful forays around Asia Minor.'

Stevie was confused, 'I thought that they were just mythical. Weren't they just legendary characters depicted as fighting with centaurs and other fictional beings?'

'No, that's not the case. Recent burial findings suggest that they were very real indeed. A number of women have been found buried with bows and several with their own invention, the battleaxe.'

Stevie shuddered at the thought but said, 'If I opt for burial I guess I would want a few treasured items of jewellery buried with me.'

Marsha snorted at this. 'They were remarkable women from a time before we were all subjugated into liking pretty shiny things. Just imagine the dedication. Did you know they even cut off or burned off their right breasts so that these would not interfere with their use of a bow or a spear? They mated just once a year and only on their own terms, and not one of them was allowed to marry before she had killed a man in battle. No wonder the Greeks and Romans, pretty bloodthirsty in their own right, feared and yet to some extent worshipped them too.'

Stevie thought these were not particularly endearing attributes, but chose not to comment.

By now they had passed across some cultivated fields and were beginning to climb a small hill. Marsha paused, took Stevie by the shoulder and turned her. She pointed off to the east where they could make out the outskirts of Selçuk.

'Just before the entrance to that city over there, another famous woman was commemorated. She inspired the creation of one of the seven wonders of the ancient world, the Temple of Artemis. Artemis was of course Apollo's twin. She was the daughter of Zeus, the issue from his infidelity with Leto. Artemis too has very martial overtones. Her symbol is the silver bow and arrow and she is usually depicted holding a bow and arrow or a spear. She was the goddess of the hunt; her Roman equivalent is Diana. By all accounts she was quite bloodthirsty too, reputedly killing or arranging the deaths of many including Adonis and Orion.'

'Back then all their mythology was extremely aggressive.'

'Don't you see we have been conditioned down the years. We started out just as capable as men. Our DNA didn't preclude us from being the warriors, the hunter-gatherers. We just got subjugated by religions and nations into being the child-rearers, the homemakers. We allowed ourselves to be convinced that we were the weaker sex because of our smaller frame. The right weapons wielded competently do not depend upon size. Then they seduced us with fashion, usually designed specifically to please them. They placated us with kitchen implements, furniture, interior decoration, bling. And we just lay back and took it!'

Stevie didn't like the look in Marsha's eyes and chose to change the subject. 'Will we get a chance to see the temple?'

'There's no point. At around 400 CE a bishop of Constantinople led a mob that destroyed it. The Emperor Constantine had it rebuilt but an earthquake and a fire damaged it again later. Today there's only one pillar left standing, much of the rest has been re-used down the years. The followers of Artemis proved darned tenacious, at least the local followers whose living depended on the sale of statuettes of Artemis. When St Paul first came to preach, these tradesmen rioted against his new Christianity, the same Christianity that discredited its early female leaders.'

They had been climbing steadily and came to an ancient grotto which they were able to look down into from their vantage point.

Marsha smiled, 'There are no women here. This is the 'Cave of the Companions' where the infamous seven sleepers were reputed to have slept away for a century or more. The story has been regaled by both Christians and Muslims. The Christian story is that they were being persecuted for their Christianity by the Roman emperor Decius in 250 CE and they hid from his men in this cave. They were hunted and found to be sleeping inside the cave - typical! The Romans sealed them in, and there they stayed until around 375 CE when a local farmer opened up the cave and was naturally stunned to find they were all still alive. The seven men, some say accompanied by a dog, thought they had been sleeping for just one night.'

'Muslims tell the story too?'

'Yes, they talk of them sleeping for three centuries and naturally their story involves the prophet Mohammed. He was challenged to relate the story of the seven sleepers and had to refer to the Qur'an to do so. Some say he had to rely upon revelations supplied to him by *Jibreel*, their Angel Gabriel. The moral of the tale according to Islamists is that it proves the Qur'an is not simply the words of Mohammed. Given that Mohammed needed to refer to the scripture to answer the query and didn't just know it for himself, it is truly the word of Allah.

'It's the Christian motive for the story that I understand much better. The tale was rather conveniently revived when the whole notion of the Resurrection was being challenged by the early Church.'

Marsha turned away from the grotto and led them back down the hill.

'Behind this hill are many of the remains of the city of Ephesus, at least those that have been excavated to date. Perhaps we might take a look at them another day. Probably the most interesting feature there is the Library of Celsus that used to be home to over 12,000 scrolls. There's both a large and a small amphitheatre and a gladiator graveyard was recently found over there too. The Romans built this place into a great city graced by a whole series of baths and one of the most sophisticated aqueduct systems.'

When they got back to the road a 4x4 with a gNOS driver was waiting for them. He set off without a word as soon as they were both inside. As they drove Marsha finally seemed prepared to reveal her true purpose for the excursion.

'So where should I start? How do I begin to explain to you the significance of what it is that we in the Order know and understand? First you have to remove the over-emotional notions that we have developed for the significance of us and our bodies, and begin to appreciate the fact that in reality our body is just a simple chemical engine. It might help if you can understand something of the remarkable arithmetic involved when it comes to the chemical reactions that create and sustain us.'

Stevie did not want to be imprisoned either physically or mentally. She would try to escape at the first opportunity but for now she had decided that her best approach was to humour Marsha; not too obviously because Marsha was far too smart and too insightful to miss any such attempt.

'You know that every one of our human cells contains forty-six chromosomes or molecules?'

'Yes I do.' Stevie saw an opportunity to follow up on the thought, 'I find it quite sobering that while we like to think of ourselves as some sort of superior, higher-order being, in fact the humble donkey has many more chromosomes, more than sixty I believe. Even the simple goldfish has over a hundred – and the potato has two more chromosomes than us!'

Marsha smiled away her point, 'Yes. As we women know, it really seldom has anything to do with size! You need to appreciate that each of these chromosomes in turn holds an average 400 genes, in the case of chromosome 1 more than 4,000.'

Stevie nodded, 'Yes I learned that from the background reading you supplied while we were back at Culham.' She was thinking that this seemed so long ago, so far away.

'So you will know that this all adds up to we humans having a total of between 20,000 and 25,000 genes. Uou need to appreciate that each of these genes is in turn made up of a series of nucleotides. Our genes can be as short as one thousand nucleotide base-pairs or as many as several hundred thousand of them.'

'That's all those combinations of As, Cs, Gs and Ts?'

'Yes, they're the four chemical bases that form the basic building blocks of our genes, all sequenced within our DNA, or deoxyribonucleic acid. The letters themselves stand for adenine and thymine, guanine and cytosine. Though in RNA, ribonucleic acid, the thymine, or 'T' nucleotide, is substituted by another. It's expressed as 'U' for uracil.'

Stevie was being jostled about as the 4x4 took to poor roads to reach their destination. 'I think it's pretty awesome that you can design and build something as complex as a human being with just these four, or five, building blocks!'

'You have to appreciate that there is an extremely long set of them. Our total DNA contains some three billion base-pairs all built up from those nucleotides. It's not just humans of course, these nucleic acids are present in all living organisms, including bacteria and archaea. They contain all the genetic data for an organism's well-being, development and function.'

Stevie felt she could risk one little jibe, 'I don't understand then why that doesn't make you want to protect all forms of life, given that we all share so much in common?'

Marsha either didn't hear or chose to ignore the comment. 'But for you to start to understand our chemical engine it's best deciphered not by looking down at these base-pair levels, which is about as edifying as looking at streams of computer machine code – all the confusing arrays of 1 and 0 'bits'. They only really start to become interesting when we look at them arranged into what you might consider as the equivalent of a computer 'byte'. In this case it's when they are organised into sets of three consecutive base-pairs. These are called codons or triplets.'

Stevie decided to not pursue her point. 'Yes I read about them too. Aren't they able to be arrayed in permutations of 4 x 4 x 4, so a total of 64 combinations?'

'That's true. It's these triplets and their specific sequence that is interpreted by our cells to create amino acids. These amino acids then translate to create essential proteins. Some of these are the enzymes we need as catalysts to drive our metabolism, others drive cellular activity like our immune responses, and so on.'

'So it's this detail and intricacy, encoded deep down within our DNA, that determines what we are - donkey or goldfish, potato or humanzee?'

Marsha broke off from this discussion as they arrived at their destination. 'I brought you here to a place where three recent popes each made a pilgrimage - Paul VI, John Paul II and Benedict XVI, all came here to visit this very holy place. Muslims too recognise it as a special site. Intriguingly the Qur'an mentions this particular woman more times than she is referenced within the New Testament. For this is where St John fulfilled his promise to Jesus to protect his mother after his crucifixion. The Virgin Mary was brought here to see out her days in safety.'

'I thought she was supposed to have gone with Mary Magdalene and Joseph of Arimathea to south-west France?'

'You've read far too much fiction. Ephesus was one of the seven early churches. She was kept safe here where she could lead a simple, chaste and good life. Another powerful woman who didn't need a man to make her decisions for her, didn't need a man to make her contribution at all.'

They walked around the site of the house, first passing a wall that was festooned with slips of paper upon which pilgrims had written their prayers.

Marsha wanted to get back to her theme for the day. 'Take a look at this wall and its thousands of prayers that pilgrims and other visitors have placed here. Imagine if someone said that just one part of one of these dozen and more major sections was considered to be of any significance and all the rest could simply be ignored - a patently ridiculous thought! But that's precisely what most scientists have said about our DNA.

'They have branded around 95% of its content as 'non-coding' DNA, termed by many others by the pejorative expression 'junk DNA'. They have reached the startling assumption that it has no part to play in defining us! That's 95% of all this information that the established wisdom currently says is just worthless clutter, meaningless stuff. I could never believe that any sensible investigator would be prepared to accept this broad conclusion, but it appears that most of them have done just that!'

Stevie was using the prayer wall to encapsulate the thought. 'It is rather a huge proportion of the whole to be considered of no importance. Is it that they believe that we have grown out of it? That evolution has left this clutter behind as we have moved on and gained higher skills?'

'Yes, that has to be the basis for their faulty reasoning. Even if I thought that was the case then I would still want to delve into it to see if we had some earlier skills that, though they have waned today, might still be of value to us again, either now or in the future. Wouldn't you?'

Stevie joined a queue to get some water. It was signposted as being holy water, having miraculous qualities as it derived from a spring that ran beneath the Virgin's home. 'I feel as if I should make a wish?' She swallowed gratefully, her wish of course was to get away from Marsha, 'And are you saying that no-one is doing research into this junk DNA?'

'Very little has been done, or at least next to nothing has been published on this - which is not quite the same thing.'

Stevie walked on to the house, 'So is that what you've been doing?'

'Now don't rush things. I need to take you there after you know just a little more. First, are you aware of all the research that is going into developing organic computers?'

'Of course I've heard the term but I don't really know anything about what it means.'

They were in a small queue to enter the house of the Virgin and Marsha assessed that there were few around them showing any great knowledge of English. Anyway this subject was too esoteric for most, so she chose to press on.

'Organic computer developers are designing systems based upon a quaternary system, using the nucleotides A, C, G and T as their 'bits', in preference to merely the current binary on or offs Alongside this there is also a great deal of activity looking at creating a means of data storage within living proteins. After all it is proteins that our brains use to strengthen our synapses and create our long-term memories.'

'So they're building these computers out of organic matter?'

They entered the small building which was T-shaped, simply furnished with a bedroom to the right and a kitchen to the left. It was dominated by a raised marble altar set before a wall of simple brickwork. Inside a large niche above the altar was a figure depicting the Virgin. They both knelt briefly and crossed themselves.

As they left the house Marsha commented, 'I thought that you should see this place. It's so calm and tranquil. You can imagine her, mourning the loss of her son, trying to rationalise this with the incredible growth of the religion that he had inspired.'

'I was always taught that the Virgin died and had her Assumption from Jerusalem?'

'Most churches are agreed that she did rise to Heaven, but on the detail they aren't necessarily of the same mind. The Roman Catholic dogma is very vague. For example in 1950 Pope Pius XII declared only that she, "having completed the course of her earthly life, was assumed body and soul into heavenly glory." So he fudged on one of the key issues of difference. He remained silent on whether she died and rose again, or if she was taken off to heaven body and soul before her death. Likewise on the subject of its happening in Ephesus or Jerusalem there is also no consensus.'

They walked back towards their waiting vehicle.

'These organic computing trendsetters, those who think they are blazing new trails, are in point of fact thousands of years too late to be considered at all innovative. It's all been done before! Deep down within that 'junk DNA' there are messages from our creators that have been left there for us.'

Stevie felt she should tread very carefully fearing anything she might say would betray her incredulity at the suggestion.

However Marsha rushed on not noticing any reaction. 'It's these messages that defined our evolution and set its steady pace down the centuries. Once we could read and understand these messages then we could forecast forward from them and see how we need to evolve further. These messages show how we must change our very nature. For one thing they will show us how we can live longer, even become immortal.'

Stevie couldn't help asking, but controlled the delivery of her words very carefully, 'And you are saying that you can read these messages?'

'Not well enough yet. You have to appreciate that our DNA is being altered all the time. With each mating the nucleotides we discussed earlier are not always replicated precisely. The most common of these is a single-nucleotide polymorphism. Using these, the Human Genome Diversity Project was able to trace the early geographic migration of humans as we left Africa and populated the world.

'Then DNA is constantly rewritten both by nature, through radiation and UV for example, and by nurture, through the individual's poor diet, stress and the like. Our DNA's in-built instructions do of course try to remedy most of these changes, to get us back on track, but they can't eliminate all the errors and mutations - and across all human development these amount to a huge number.'

'Then you can't read them?'

Marsha was clearly not prepared to admit this was the case, 'This is why Mission has been collecting as many early human DNA traces that they can find from all over the world and in particular has been seeking out samples from those in our history who were discerned as being special - in particular those who were considered during their lives to be holy.'

Stevie blanched at the use of the word special, but asked, 'Is that something to do with the "God Gene"?'

'No, that's VMAT2, a gene that Hamer suggested predisposes those who have it to develop an inbuilt capacity for religious thought. To express it differently, it predisposes them to have the desire to reach out beyond themselves. It's just one part of the current human condition. From our investigations we concluded that our creators may have put this gene in there deliberately, as a sort of defence and control mechanism. It acts as a social regulator.'

'Hannah told me that this is the gene that you test for before admitting someone into the Perpetua Order?'

Marsha grimaced at the mention of Hannah. 'Precisely. She's right, we make sure all our Perfects have a strong dose of that propensity. It directly affects their emotions and the modes of consciousness of the individual. To function many of our control techniques used in the retreats depend upon the Perfects having this gene.'

Stevie couldn't stop herself, 'Do I have it then?'

'No, you have a reasonably neutral status in regard to VMAT2. You were not selected for that propensity. In fact you were selected more because you don't have it at all strongly.'

'I'm not sure I will ever be comfortable with the idea of your conditioning?'

'We need to do this for most of our members, you have to appreciate that the evils of the world are so adept, so intrusive. All we are doing is helping to clear our followers' minds of any distractions.'

Stevie thought to herself, 'Somehow I would find that easier to believe if there was no fence around the retreats, no locked doors keeping the humanzees constrained, no gNOS guards!'

She asked, 'So if it's not the God Gene that you are looking for in these holy people, what is it?'

# Chapter 64 – *London, UK*

In the uncovered video broadcast, that Perpetua was planning to give a wide distribution, Shepherd was pressing on with his parable. Members of the DICE team were taking their own view on the content of this and making notes as it proceeded.

Shepherd was explaining, 'Every parable needs its message - its moral lesson - and this one is to be no different. After living for some forty years on this earth, say half of the normally allotted lifespan, absolutely nothing lasting has reached out and touched these two individuals. Not a thing has inspired them. Their imagination has never been captured by anything other than fleeting fads. Not Joe's mother's religion, not friendship, not parenthood or honest toil; he never offered any commitment to his sport, certainly not to his many women, nor to any institution whether political, financial or military. Maria has at least developed a belief system; but she believes only in the power of those idols that she worships. She feels more alive through experiencing their affairs, marriages, adoptions, break-ups, addictions and rehabs.

'So just what precisely are they for - this seed of Man? What is the purpose of this proud outcome of so many millennia of our species' strivings, passions, beliefs and development? Sadly the answer is nothing. They have no direction; they serve absolutely no purpose. Their only value is through their spending and consumption which, when amassed with millions just like them, shores up our ailing industrial system - a system that is burning up all our resources and wasting any reserves of energy and a system that reaches out to ruin our home planet through its excesses.'

The Professor commented aloud, 'Well he's absolutely right there. I'll give a big amen to that thought!' Simon muttered something but Tom didn't catch it; just what was the man 'on' today?

The camera was still tight onto Shepherd's face, his eyes bright, his smile beatific and bright. 'We all believe that there was once a golden age for mankind, when our communities worked with and for each other, when your elders', your parents' and your teachers' values provided you with useful guidelines and goals upon which you could reliably base your life.'

The newsreel material was back to cascading images across the screen. 'Even then there was hardship and shortage, not the least of which was a paucity of good health together with a low life expectancy. Make no mistake those times, if they ever truly existed, for all their supposed benefits are irrevocably gone. Just as we turned our backs and walked away from the Garden of Eden, so too have we destroyed our original rural idyll, despoiled the homely villages and towns, turned them all into one big urban sprawl and in doing so have replaced all our personal goals with our dependence on destructive industrial and commercial growth.

'In the West, corporates were early to identify their vital industrial unit as the happy nuclear family. Parents and children would aspire to live in architect-designed little boxes, would work long hours to fill them with the latest advertised material fads, and would be coerced to pursue all the latest fashions. Just where is that ideal consuming unit today?'

Tom commented to the Professor, 'This was your point at that conference, retail as God.'

'Now we have more and more single parent families, there is a growing legion of stepfamilies and many of the rest of us now choose to live alone. There is only one certainty in life, other than death and taxes, and this is that the values you have earned, learned and developed will not in any manner be applicable to your children, because times change! And incidentally these children of the future will increasingly be created by insemination and through the use of in vitro methods. And soon they will become subject to genetic screening and alteration as well.'

On the screen Shepherd was walking again, climbing a slope on a barren landscape with hills in the distance. Sir Joseph briefly paused the image, 'Do mark this point in the video. Perhaps we can work up some profile from the formation of those far hills?'

He started it up again and Shepherd pressed on. 'So what should we do? Many will ask how we can walk away from all that we have built. Surely there is a way that we can recreate that lost golden age. They wallow in nostalgia for a dream that was probably never really there, except in our imaginations.

'We at Perpetua are not prepared to delude ourselves any further. We are committed to bringing about a real change to the world. Just take a good look at our modern existence on Mother Earth. These days we do better appreciate it for what it is, a single integrated system of living organisms that is completely interdependent. Life is precarious, precise, precious.'

Tom commented, 'Well that's for sure!'

'Now take a look at what we did to it. Like wild animals we have fought to establish our petty national territories and empires. Nations have been created just as bestially by 'pissing' competitions along their borders, each drawn and redrawn "red in tooth and claw". Nations have been sustained by arms, by hate, by religion, even by sporting prowess, and all secured by the fears, jingoism and racism fostered by governments and their militaries.

'Yet these borders often constrain and corral those from many different and diverse backgrounds and beliefs; after all they were only arbitrarily defined by history. Today our modern communications rail against these borders and they have proven porous to economic and political migrations. These borders have always been completely useless in terms of halting ideas, but today's technology means notions can fly right around the world without hindrance. Borders offer little resistance to our increasing reliance on electronic financial transactions and to our World Wide Web traffic. In reality they only exist as a concept shored up by passports, airport security, border patrols, anti money-laundering regulations - a whole paraphernalia of controls that seek to sustain the illusion of governmental control.'

Those around the table passed no comments. If asked they would each deny it vehemently, but the man's words and his delivery were holding their attention. He was a strong orator and his words were compelling, but just where was all this heading?

'Just look at the way in which we organise those nations. Is there any single statesman, any political party or system from anywhere in the world that we can point to as a paragon of virtue, as operating for the common good of its constituents? No! Our leaders of every persuasion are by definition self-publicists, often corrupt or out-of-touch, regularly autocratic or weak. They proselytise policies that, while they may be well meaning, usually prove to be ill-judged and routinely are poorly implemented.

'We should be questioning why we even need to elect representatives these days. Via some form of internet poll we already have the technology which would enable us to be directly consulted and asked to define or choose between policies. Electronically we could make the major decisions for ourselves!

'Take a look at our health systems. Pharmaceutical companies have the capability and capacity today to rid the developing world of many of its ills; but they don't, because where's the profit in that? Our own Western health systems have become a bureaucratic quagmire, wallowing in unnecessary expense and paperwork, propped up and inflated by insurance and welfare systems that are being increasingly stretched by our ever-growing, ever-ageing populations.

'So, I can hear you thinking, well what can we do? Well a much more lyrical visionary than I said it all so very elegantly.' He read the words without trying to sing them,

"'Imagine there's no countries, it isn't hard to do,
Nothing to kill or die for, and no religion too,
 Imagine all the people, living life in peace...
 ... Imagine no possessions, I wonder if you can,
No need for greed or hunger, a brotherhood of man,
Imagine all the people, sharing all the world..."
'It was John Lennon who proposed that
"...the world will live as one.".'

# Chapter 65 - *Kénitra, Morocco*

'Field testing' Marsha had said, and here they were, the very fields that he was to pose his questions. Will watched as field after field of grains, fruits and vegetables passed beneath them, stretching off in all directions as far as his eye could see.

The helicopter pilot appeared determined to follow every serpentine turn of the river course below them. As they passed over Sidi el Hassan the river's convolutions became a little more regular, the pendulum motion of the helicopter less frantic.

In the distance he could make out the port of Kénitra that had grown prosperous through handling the produce grown in this fertile area. But they were not heading towards the city; instead they were going further west towards an airfield that was defined on three sides by the Sebour River as it made its last few turns before it flowed out to join the Atlantic.

Will was annoyed that he had been allocated the task of testing this new material. It was all well and good for Shepherd to plot and plan everything from his secret stronghold. He chuckled at the thought; it sounded to him like something straight out of Batman movie. It was not so funny that once again it was the Mission team that was put at risk to fulfil one of the old man's aims and decisions.

Will had been content to kick his heels at Tamegroute while Dom's arrest ran its course. He had little confidence that Dom would withstand any interrogation, period! Certainly once Dom realised he had been 'hung out to dry' and the cavalry was not in fact on its way, then Will believed he would become very communicative, very quickly.

However Will considered the saving grace was that this particular task had not been put on their schedule until after Dom's capture, it was unlikely he would be able to lead anyone to their location. It was much more likely that his information would have any investigators turning up at the retreat.

Will understood that this airfield had seen action during WWII, known then as Craw Field it had provided vital air cover for General Patton as he made his thrust through North Africa. Later it served as a secret American base right up until the 1970s when its covert presence was disclosed by a loose-lipped senator back in DC. Now it was a Moroccan army and navy base located just up the coast from Rabat on the main route towards Tangier.

As they neared the military airfield Will was not at all reassured by the way in which the 'copter pilot was moving in his seat, turning his head through some 270-degrees looking around and up to the heavens, worriedly scouring for signs of any other aircraft. There had been no evidence of the pilot checking in by radio before their approach. Will hoped some vigilant air traffic controller at the military base would have registered their arrival.

He could now make out the office unit where he had hired a small facility and a local technical support team. It was adjacent to the airfield and he relaxed as the pilot brought them down safely to land on a large concrete apron that was perfect for their purpose.

Until the material arrived he decided he should use the small helicopter that they had hired for the job. It became a regular sight in the area, evoking no interest in its many comings and goings.

Will was concerned about the battering that the slowing blades were taking while the helicopter was being chocked on the concrete apron. He thought this was probably the most windswept airfield he had ever come across. From his extensive experience all of them were pretty much prone to that condition, but this one was something else. The winds came unfettered from right across the vast stretch of the Atlantic.

He ducked low as he ran away from the helicopter, fully expecting the blades to reach down in the wind and slice him up. It was he who was to be the grim reaper, he who planned to cut a swathe right through the heart of this valuable land and its plentiful harvest.

# Chapter 66 - *Selçuk, Turkey*

They had been driven back to the Selçuk facility without Marsha offering any sort of informative response to Stevie's question about what she was seeking within the database of collected DNA, and certainly nothing about the DNA from the holy relics.

When they were safely back inside the Turkish BiCogNaIT facility Marsha offered Stevie a coffee. She picked up an internal phone to order it, then continued with her narrative.

'I do need you to organise your thinking on these matters. Any emotion gets in the way of our scientific endeavour, too often a weak experimentalist sees things that he or she really wants to see rather than what actually results from their work.'

Stevie was not to be browbeaten, 'Of course I appreciate that. You know that I've worked in research for many years. I've always been able to separate the empirical evidence from the emotion. Surely it is our emotions that drive us on. They're what make us tenacious to get to the bottom of a concept, create the desire for us to investigate and explore how the world around us operates?'

'I'm not proposing that you abandon your emotions, just that you control them; particularly in regard to your concerns for the humanzees.'

'I just hate to see those sweet little creatures locked up and I've not forgotten that one of them must have died to save Tom's life. Of course I'm delighted for Tom to have made a full recovery, but at such a cost!'

'You just have to learn to see them as our experimental assets. Let's not rake over that whole matter again. There are other far more pressing things that I need to discuss with you.'

Stevie decided that she had better keep her own counsel until she found an opportunity to escape, discretion being the better part of valour.

Marsha seemed content with the lack of response and pressed on. 'You are aware that down the generations some individuals stand out, both in their lives and in their personal examples. People that have brought about significant changes, provide turning points in our evolution. Many of them have been considered as a result to be holy, very special in some manner. We believe therefore that by looking at their DNA we will discover further keys to help us decipher the messages contained within our coding much more readily.'

'And have you?'

Marsha was again elusive, 'It's a slow and painstaking process. Mission has collated material from all over, from Aboriginals to Zulus. That's the reason for the choice of name, Mission. It's so very appropriate because they have been charged to be like those early explorers and missionaries. They go deep into jungles, up to the highest mountains, across to the remotest islands. They travel across frozen wastes and into deserts in order to collect data from remote societies. Not only from the living inhabitants, but also from relics and remains and they particularly seek out any leaders or holy people.'

Stevie commented, 'If they have the agreement of those people then I have no problem with their diligent research, but from what I know of your organisation I imagine they probably wouldn't have bothered to observe the niceties!'

Marsha waved an impatient arm at this. 'Then we had the Gene Genie operation. This was so vital for us. Every day it added tens of thousands of current samples to our database. As a by-product from these we could more rapidly identify and select our Perpetua recruits from the many who used the Gene Genie service. Better still we documented all their contact details, medical histories and gathered a degree of detail on demographics to place alongside the recorded DNA. That way we gained even more insight in our detailed investigation.'

'It all sounds a little too intrusive for my liking. I don't suppose that these people signed up to have you play with their DNA in the ways you plan. I imagine it was like Avril, just a paternity test or the like that they sought from their donation?'

'Then they didn't say that we couldn't do this either!' Stevie thought Marsha's demeanour was becoming more strident, more crazy, particularly when she added, 'We don't just rely on sampling humans. What if there is a message or part of a message that has been left deep within the DNA of a whale, a camel or even of a tree?'

At this Stevie called to mind the 'Twilight Zone' theme tune but made sure this did not show in her face or her words. 'So you say you have a large database. How is the analysis going? Do these messages become clearer in the holy DNA samples that Mission has gleaned?'

'Yes they do, but we still need to work long and hard with the database. You can appreciate that we have to keep backtracking down the generations to try to clean up these messages. Ideally we need computing power that would be something of the order of the IBM Roadrunner at Los Alamos Laboratories, and it would need to be working on our task full-time.'

'That is very fast, but I imagine extremely expensive?'

'It's priced at well over 100 million US dollars. We just couldn't afford that approach. Instead we have had to innovate and we created a covert network of distributed computing. Some of our team are brilliant computer designers. They produced and distributed a very sophisticated computer program; I guess you might call it a virus. They distributed it widely through screensavers, viral email campaigns, and by attracting huge numbers of people to download spectacular videos we posted up on social sites, and so on.

'The computer virus does the local PCs no harm; it just short-term 'borrows' millions of computers worldwide, accessing their processing power when their owners are not using them. By networking this resource we've occasionally managed as much as a gigaflop, that's $10^9$. But the access and the processing rate is just far too variable. The available PCs are blinking in and out of our process constantly and we're still some way from having a stable enough projection. But there has been some very good progress.'

Stevie was recalling how her home broadband hub often flashed when her PC was not in use and she appreciated the elegance of the approach. But why wouldn't a virus checker catch it? They had obviously found a way of circumventing it somehow.

They were disturbed by a knock at the door. Stevie was stunned to see it was Karen, one of her fellow Anglo Apostles, who had brought them coffee. She leapt up to take the tray from her and put it down on a table. Then she turned for the anticipated hug accompanied by the expected loud mwahs as they air-kissed.

Karen just stood there bewildered, no sign of recognition on her face.

'Karen, what's the matter? Don't you recognise me? It's Stevie!'

Karen smiled blankly and made no response to the question. Stevie couldn't believe it. Karen had always been one of the most garrulous of their group, not a particular friend, but they had developed into something of a strong team. What could have happened to her?

Suddenly Stevie turned and challenged Marsha, 'What have you done to her? Overdone her conditioning?'

'She's still recovering from a small procedure.'

'Procedure! By that I assume you mean an operation, or an experiment? So it's not just the humanzees. Now we are all considered merely your experimental assets!'

# Chapter 67 – *London, UK*

Shepherd's video finished by showing some disturbing old news footage accompanied by Lennon's 'Imagine', before switching back to a super close up of the preacher.

'So as you can see, I am not claiming these as my original ideas but I shall be the one who will provide us all with the clear route to turn Lennon's goals into a reality. Today the Perpetua Order is committing mankind to step up and finally realise its true destiny. Only when we have achieved this will we then be able to spread ourselves throughout this glorious universe of ours.'

Tom exclaimed, 'That's precisely what that bloody Davenport woman was rabbiting on about across in Cologne!'

'To do this, first we need to live healthily and live much longer. We believe that eventually we will discover how we can become immortal. We are confident that this can be achieved through our latest genetic engineering breakthroughs and other technologies. Our Order has inherited the knowledge to develop the techniques that will make our bodies stronger, become self-repairing. We have information that will allow us to expand our minds. Only we in Perpetua know how to expand these human capabilities and how to free ourselves from our current plight.

'To do this we will need unrestricted access, unlimited resources and energy. We need to be unfettered by nation-states and their politics. We need no authorities, no false religions to hold us back. All that is about to happen was foretold to us by the one true religion, by Daniel and by St John. Sadly the world has been far too ready down the years to choose to ignore the true Word.'

The Professor was making copious notes, the latest to remind himself that he must read the books of Daniel and Revelations again to try to understand precisely what this madman was talking about. But Shepherd was all too ready to fill this gap in understanding.

'The prophecies described the first horse of the apocalypse as the white one named 'Pestilence'. This first seal was released and has been spreading its plague for many years. You need to appreciate that the pestilence it spreads is not a simple bug or disease. It's the heinous lies that issue from the mouths of so many false prophets, each seeking to hide us from the true nature of the Word.'

At a nod from the Foreign Secretary, Sir Joseph froze the video so that those present could top up their teas and coffees.

Tom joined him and commented, 'Why is it that when these people start referring back to the Bible I find my mind glazing over? Just why do they believe that something written two millennia ago can have any relevance to today? Or tomorrow?'

Simon snapped back, 'That comment says much more about you than it does about them! Besides, I thought you were the scientist delving into archaeo-astronomy, seeking out modern relevance from things that happened from times even earlier than this?'

Tom made a face towards Brain, trying to see if he too was finding the man's change in character as something of importance.

Tom challenged Simon, 'So are you saying that you believe that Revelations is to be taken seriously as a blueprint for our future?'

'When taken alongside other matters, then yes I do.'

Tom countered, 'There are many who believe that every one of these prophecies has in fact already been realised, and all by the end of the 1st century. They say that the Beast was the Roman Empire, that Armageddon was the subjugation of the Christians. For instance if you take the Greek spelling of Nero, *Neron Caesar*, then translate the letters into Hebrew and then quantify it, it totals to the number of the Anti-Christ - 666.'

The Professor guffawed, 'And there was me thinking that 666 was the sum of the ASCI characters that spell out William F Gates!'

Simon exploded. 'That's just so naïve an interpretation. You are supposed to be intelligent men. You have to look at Revelations in the light of what came before it, consider Daniel and Isaiah too. It tells us of the End of Days, the Great Tribulation that is coming. We true believers are to be tested for seven years and we shall emerge all the stronger.' He stood up, 'You fools, you sit here vested with your false authority, with your conceited and wrong views. You actually think that you can stop the Order. This message from the Patriarch is telling us all that the moment is coming.'

Brain grabbed hold of the PA and manhandled him from the room.

Simon called back at them as he was pushed through the door. 'You are already too late to stop us.'

The meeting paused a while, each lost in their own thoughts.

It was Tom who broke the silence as Brain came back into the meeting, 'Well, I guess that's one way of finding our mole!'

Brain looked around, 'That's assuming there was only one. Pity they don't all have that tattoo on the forehead; it would make things a lot easier for us.'

Sir Joseph waited until they had all settled down and the Foreign Secretary had nodded to prompt him to press play on the video remote.

Shepherd was still in close-up and there were some interesting things going on with the lighting of his face to make up for the otherwise static image.

'The second seal is the red horse, the one called 'War', and it has been abroad for the last year or so. But it too is not a literal name, not our usual sense of the word 'war'. Instead this horse has taken away our peace, caused global turmoil by the waves of hatred and civil strife that have resounded right around the world.'

Sir Joseph grumbled, 'We know there's no biblical prophecy at work here. They managed all this themselves through the Gene Genie shops!'

The video was still pressing forward. 'Today, exclusively, I can advise you that the third seal and the third horse will now been released. This is the black horse, 'Famine', and it will be true to its name; it will bring a famine down upon those who are unprepared for it.

'Those in the West should think again on this word famine. This time it will not come to you as a remote concept, something that happens in some far-flung Third World land, something you can watch from the comfort of your recliner and perhaps be moved to send off some small donation or cast-off clothes to mitigate your guilt. This famine will be up close and personal! This horse's rider holds a set of scales. They illustrate that it is your life that is in the balance as this famine will be realised right around every part of the world.

'Prepare yourself, for the time is now. The Great Tribulation is upon us. To survive you will need to free yourselves from the systems and processes of the material world that you have helped to create and sustain.'

The video now took on a style that those in the retreats would have recognised instantly, a cacophony of rapidly changing images. These sought to send subliminal conditioning messages, but few watch home television sets with the intense concentration that the Order could achieve in the retreats, where their converts were reinforced by diet, conditioning and drugs. Despite being aware of this they still used all their techniques even though their impact would prove minimal.

Shepherd's voice-over continued. 'Whatever your faith you need to prepare yourselves for the day of the shrieving. Whether this day for you is the Hindu's *Kali Yuga*, or the Hopi's *Day of Purification*, perhaps the Norseman's *Ragnarök*, or for you it might be the Islamic day of the Last Judgment, *al-Qiyāmah*, or Judaism's end of days, *aharit ha-yamim,* but for we Christians it is the *Great Tribulation* as foretold in Revelations.'

Shepherd reappeared in shot in a close-up. 'If you are truly righteous then you need have no fear. Be sure you use the few weeks that you have left to cast off your material mantle and I shall return with further news once you have had the opportunity to realise the truth of my revelations.'

The video held a still picture of Shepherd with the Lennon song 'Imagine' playing over it.

Sir Joseph had had enough and grumpily switched off the equipment.

He commented, 'This is no biblical revelation, no divine judgment. They generated the wave of hate crimes through Gene Genie shops and clearly they will be the ones trying to spread this famine too. We need to understand how they plan to do that? And need to know this today!'

The Professor replied. 'We have to assume that it will be by another form of genetic attack. That's clearly their skill set, ably provided by Marsha Davenport. It's just that this time it will be aimed at the plant life!'

Tom's mind was racing. 'I suppose that has to be the point of their retreats - places where they have established their own communities, growing their own crops which have presumably been immunised against whatever it is they are planning to release.'

Brain added, 'Their very remoteness assists with the security of their community, with gNOS providing the rest. Where should we begin to look and prepare for their attack?'

Sir Joseph was already looking at how he could formulate an approach. 'We need to start by following their various organisations back to their lairs. By now we have virtually eliminated Gene Genie; those left in that organisation are just patsies - franchisees and employees. So I believe we can ignore that lot.'

The spymaster was listing them on his fingers, 'The gNOS team's role is to protect the other organisations' facilities so we don't need to bother to seek them out. We will automatically come up against them as we approach the others. Mark Elliott has provided us some useful background on them. He tells us that they have left all their normal haunts in the USA, so they must now be in their retreats and tasked by these other organisations.

'As for the Mission team, fortunately we already have their main man, Berkeley. He's under arrest and we are interrogating him for any useful information.'

Brain commented, 'If ever the UK could support extraordinary rendition then this is probably that moment. I know one or two 'specialists' who would get what we need out of him.'

The Foreign Secretary had been quiet throughout the showing of the video, making a few notes of her own and watching these early exchanges, but now she glared at Brain, 'Not even in jest!'

Sir Joseph pressed on without responding to the admonition. 'While we are on the subject of interrogation we should also interview this Hannah again. She helped Tom escape from the Moroccan retreat but she had been working intimately alongside Shepherd until a few weeks ago.'

Tom commented, 'I think that there was very much a 'need to know' principle operating and she was only trusted to minister to the old man's day-to-day needs, not party to much of his thinking. Besides I believe from what Dieter overheard that it is Marsha Davenport who has control of Shepherd. It's time we really turned the screws on the BiCogNaIT people!'

Sir Joseph shook his head at this, 'We've detected in recent weeks that these Perpetua people have withdrawn into their retreats, presumably in preparation for this video's release and its promised famine. We've identified eight, possibly nine, of the Tyndale retreat locations so far. All our intel says that they may already have, or they certainly plan, a total of twelve in total.'

The Professor explained, 'It's all to do with this number of 144,000 that's mentioned several times in Revelations. We understand that they are planning on 12,000 to be in each of their twelve retreats. But that's where I get confused because I thought the number was symbolic, like the 40 days and 40 nights just meaning a long time. And anyway I thought these people were all supposed to be Jews? One important thing about this 144,000 is that they are supposed to have the name of their God on their foreheads so that they can be recognised and redeemed; that's the origin of those gNOS tattoos.'

Sir Joseph nodded, 'So as a matter of some urgency we do need to establish where the others might be. We must mobilise our forces globally while we develop a plan for raiding every one of the locations.'

One of Sir Joseph's team was at the end of the table crashing all this into a laptop as if the old man's every word was holy writ.

The Foreign Secretary broke in on his process. 'Shouldn't we be briefing our allies and their services to assist us, rather than chase all over the place like headless chickens?'

'You saw for yourself that they had penetrated to just two places removed from yourself - your special advisor's PA for goodness sake! How do we know whom we can trust?'

'You've been working with this CIA operative, Elliott?'

Sir Joseph paused. 'Only as and when it suited my purposes. Tom is right. This Davenport woman and her BiCogNaIT crowd are central, and so far we haven't gone after them too aggressively because of their US Department of Defense status. We shied away because we accepted she must be deep-rooted within the system to have become so heavily DoD funded and connected. We feared she would get tipped off if we revealed too much to the cousins.

'BiCogNaIT was clearly behind the chemistry of the hate waves, executed through their Gene Genie shops. The San Francisco raid showed us they are into some other seriously dangerous and weird research too. There can be little doubt that they will be the ones who have developed the approach and techniques for spreading this famine too. We need to identify all their locations inside and outside the retreats. We need to get much deeper into their operations now.'

Tom admired the way in which the spymaster had set out his thinking. He had every confidence that the man would cause maximum impact upon these organisations, but Tom needed to be sure that he was not going to get sidelined by the professionals.

'Look, I want to be involved in any planned attack on BiCogNaIT. I think I can provide you with some background and insight given what Shepherd disclosed to me. I most particularly want to be involved if there is any suggestion that Marsha Davenport is going to be there, for where she is I am confident Stevie will be too.'

Sir Joseph had another thought. 'We need to establish where they filmed that broadcast. Someone needs to go through all the external shots very carefully to try to reference any features, landmarks or vegetation that might be useful. Tom you're a geologist, you may be able to identify something from the terrain. If we can find Shepherd then perhaps we can get him to call it all off.'

The Professor had been quiet throughout all this. 'While you are looking at all that I'm off to read my Bible.' He smiled at the confusion this caused, coming from such a public atheist. 'I want to read the Book of Revelations; I have to confess that I never have. I only know about the Four Horsemen of the Apocalypse, Armageddon and all that from fiction and films. As you all appreciate, from my perspective so too is the Bible a fiction, but it is the prime source that is inspiring this Perpetua movement.'

# Chapter 68 - *Selçuk, Turkey*

Stevie was feeling very mellow, but then that was precisely what Marsha's dosage of flunitrazepam had been planned to achieve - a perfectly quiescent state. "Roofies", as they are often called, are the go-to drug for many treatments; but most commonly known as the basis for the date-rape drug, Rohypnol.

At the dosage administered the drug would not only create a calming effect, but would reduce Stevie's naturally emotional outlook. Subsequently it could also generate a degree of amnesia, but each of these effects was appropriate for what Marsha had in mind. She was delighted that currently Stevie was proving very ebullient and talkative from the drug.

Marsha had judged the time must be right; certainly she wasn't going to achieve any more from her discussions with Stevie. The girl was just so willful, and yet Marsha had to admit that she admired and defended that same trait in herself. She had hoped that she would have had more time to prepare Stevie's mind thoroughly and carefully before starting this vital procedure. But time was running out.

Stevie had proven to be the one who best fitted the bill for what was to happen next. Samuel had given her his seal of approval. He had clearly liked the look, and feel, of her. Marsha thought men are just so stupid. Samuel believed that he hid his interest in other women well, but Marsha always knew when he wanted one; he definitely wanted Stevie.

So this procedure would make everyone happy. Stevie would gain so much from this. She had been born with the mental capacity, now it would be stretched, used more comprehensively and put properly to work. The extra years she would give to Marsha would prove significant too. They would provide more time for her vital work to be completed. Given that additional time she was absolutely confident that she would be able to achieve immortality, for them both. Samuel would then have all he could ever need - Marsha's mind inside Stevie's skin, for all eternity!

As she was wheeled in on a stretcher Stevie's first impression was that the equipment looked just like an old horror movie set, yet she corrected this thought because there had clearly been an upgrade from those movies to include computers. Surprisingly she found she was completely relaxed as Marsha made a whole series of connections directly onto her scalp.

She then made some entries into a computer and looked up and smiled across at Stevie, taking a good long look at her lying there now properly connected to the equipment. Her long slender legs were what every woman would want if they could choose, and Marsha had chosen extremely carefully. Her 'British rose' looks were just to die for, a classic pale complexion, long blond hair, blue eyes. Marsha couldn't wait to look out through those eyes and see that face looking back at her from a mirror.

'We need to run some calibrations before we proceed. You will need to put on this headset and I'll play you something to set the scene.'

Stevie was inquisitive, 'What sort of music?'

'It's not music. They are called beats. The headphones will play two sounds that are on similar but not quite the same frequencies. By modulating these sounds we can then affect the brain as it tries to integrate the two sounds down in the lower part of the brainstem, the superior olivary nucleus. As it attempts the integration your brain creates a third sound, the 'binaural beat'. Using this binaural beat we can then initiate changes in your brainwave activity.'

Stevie giggled, 'That sounds painful. It can't be any worse than a rock concert!'

'On the contrary, the technique has been used for meditation and relaxation; some of its exponents even talk of using it for 'brain balancing', for matching up the differences in your left and right sides. For our purposes it's the way to improve your learning and memory skills, to make you more intuitive and creative.'

'Bring it on then!'

Marsha was amused by Stevie's lack of concern and therefore felt more able to describe the process in detail. 'For today it also gives me the ability to 'jack into' your brain's own internal frequencies. The alpha waves are used when we are awake yet being introspective, it is the beta waves that are used when awake and looking more outward, the delta waves are created during deep sleep, the gamma waves are used for perception, the mu waves are linked with motion and the theta waves with dreaming and intuition.'

Stevie's mind was wandering, 'What happened to epsilon, zeta and eta? I always had fond feelings toward the epsilons in 'Brave New World'. And where did iota, kappa and lambda go?'

'Good question! With EEGs the delta waves are defined as those up to 4 Hz, theta 4 to 7 Hz, alpha from 8 to 13, the alpha range includes the mu. Beta is 13 to 30, and then gamma waves are from around 30 to 100 and more hertz.'

Stevie was completely unaware of what was happening to her and positively gabbled, 'There's absolutely no logic at all to that then. How silly to come up with something to describe our very rational core, our brain, with something that is so completely illogical. What were they thinking of? Clearly too many theta waves were going on that day in the lab.'

'Perhaps. Well it's certainly the thetas that we will be concentrating on. Do you remember that when we were walking across to Ephesus the other day I mentioned that they had found a gladiator cemetery up there?'

'Yes, but I was disappointed we didn't go there. I seem to remember that you were only interested in warriors if they were female.'

'Well it may surprise you to learn that it was the injuries the gladiators sustained that moved Galen, a major physician following in the tracks of Hippocrates, to challenge the previously accepted belief that the heart was the centre of our intelligence. He was a pretty arrogant self-publicist and pretty scathing about most of the established wisdom. Through his observation of injured gladiators and their loss of function, together with his animal vivisection work on the brain and spinal cord, he concluded that the brain was the core of our nervous system and the centre of our intelligence.'

'So why thetas? What do they do that's so interesting?'

'It's because our procedure is heavily focused on the hippocampus.'

'I know that's in our brain, doesn't hippo means horse?'

'Yes, the hippocampus is part of the forebrain, the temporal lobe; and its use of 'hippo' is because it has a structure that looks a bit like a seahorse. Anyway, it's associated with our sense of smell, our olfactory system, but it is absolutely central to memory and emotion. Intriguingly when you examine it carefully, it looks almost as if it was a later 'bolt-on' goody to our brain, something our creators installed to give us new abilities. The cortex narrows right down to one layer there and is more tightly-packed in terms of neurons than any other part of the brain. It definitely looks as if it were an upgrade to me.'

The technicians were performing the same connections to Marsha's scalp and soon all that would remain would be for the software to do its work. Stevie's DNA had been ideal for Marsha's needs. All the tests of her physiology had proven perfect; this was a woman in her prime, now this gorgeous body was going to become Marsha's.

Marsha continued to describe her intentions in the belief that this would keep Stevie calm. 'If you disconnect or damage the hippocampus then you can no longer form any new memories. Much of the theta wave activity happens here and in particular its supra-mamillary nucleus. The hippocampus connects in and out to much of the rest of the brain through the entorhinal complex, and receives its theta rhythm from the medial septum.'

'OK you lost me with all those names. What do they do?'

'Always to the point, that's one of the things that sets you apart from the others. You have to start by distinguishing some subtleties between learning and memory. At its simplest you can start the distinction by saying that to learn Spanish you have to study it, but to speak it you access the memory of what you have learnt. Why I say it's subtle is because of course your accumulation of experiences and memories is often used in the process of inference to develop other learning. So it's not an absolutely clear distinction, but you have to have memory for this learning or inference, and many other processes, to be effective.'

Stevie was trying to follow the description but found her mind kept wandering. 'That's all OK unless your ability to recall these memories becomes wayward! My grandfather had dementia and his access to any sort of memory was very variable.'

'True, but you need to be aware that our memories come in various forms. First there's our sensory memory at the point that we see, hear, smell, taste or touch something. We hold on to that sort of memory usually only for milliseconds. It works just long enough to perceive what it was that we sensed, then unless the brain calls for some action the memory is largely discarded. Then there's our short-term memory which kicks in to record each of our experiences and events as we have them, recording the topography of where we are and so on. It has been shown that this first gets filed directly within the hippocampus. We have the capacity to hold just a little more than a half-dozen such topics simultaneously and each is usually only retained there for less than thirty seconds.'

'That's what most people assume is my capacity, but that's entirely based upon my hair colour.'

'Men are pigs! Of course we all lose those short-term memories unless we choose to file them away into our long-term memory. Once successfully captured there then with regular maintenance a memory can last for our whole lifespan. It's how we store our knowledge of words, physical techniques and places. This sending something to your long-term memory is also processed via the hippocampus but then it is filed elsewhere in the brain.

'Our long-term memory is then usually sub-classified into two sub-types. There is the declarative memory, the term for those things you can call up and describe verbally. Then there are non-declarative memories. These are those that allow us to recall things like how to ride a bike or iron a shirt.'

Stevie was intrigued by the discussion, 'What about those memories that you don't want to recall? And what about the way in which we create false memories convincing ourselves that we did something which we actually only ever imagined, perhaps just read it somewhere, or saw it in a movie? "Is it real or is it Memorex?" my father used to say.'

'Now you're moving into that other hippocampus role, that of our emotions. Most of those are deep-rooted protection mechanisms. For instance if you are startled by a loud noise then your brain pauses everything else that you were doing while it assesses the source and form of any potential threat. Almost immediately it draws on memory to decide whether the right course is to freeze, fight or flee. There is no doubt that we are able to store memories more readily and over a much longer term when emotions are evoked by an experience. Our amygdala comes into play here. Among other things it activates our adrenal system which not only helps with any fleeing or fighting, but also assists the hippocampus in its process of recording a memory.'

Marsha was almost fully prepped yet still wanted to finish the discussion.

'As I said the hippocampus clearly handles short-term memories and is key to the process of them being transferred elsewhere so that they become long-term. What we are therefore wishing to achieve today is not to interfere with your sensory or short-term memory processes. We also want to preserve all your useful declarative and non-declarative long-term memory, while we overlay my own.'

The technicians having completed their preparations now carefully put the headsets on both the subjects and placed a sort of hood over each of their heads.

Stevie's last comment as they attached her hood was, 'Where did you get these? They look like something out of a kitsch 1950s hair salon?'

This was the moment when Stevie would have become concerned and agitated if the Rohypnol was not having its desired effect. It was there to disrupt the chemistry between the medial septum and the hippocampus. Clearly it was working because she was considering the whole discussion and the procedure as some sort of conceptual argument, her defences having been completely suspended by the drug.

This equipment had been tried and tested many times, using countless humanzees as they refined the technique. However the first three attempts with human subjects had left the 'recipient' with greatly impaired function. Marsha prayed that they had ironed out their earlier problems. She really could not afford to waste Stevie. She had no suitable potential replacement. As a result of this fear they would apply the process very slowly.

Marsha knew that few individuals ever manage to overstretch the capacity of their minds, so it could not have been an overload condition that had occurred previously. The unfortunate subjects like Karen could now only perform very routine tasks; their personalities, their emotions and their memories had somehow been completely fried or erased. Just as body mechanisms fought off an invading infection, their trials and errors had shown them that there were similar defensive processes within the mind too.

The human brain is a far from simple organ. In its 1.5 kilos of grey matter it contains almost 100 billion neurons, as many neurons in one brain as there are stars detected out there in our galaxy. On average we have some 70,000 thoughts each day that need to be processed and stored or discarded. The information processing of these thoughts travels around the brain, at its very slowest pace, at over 400 kms per hour - a speed only just achieved, and then only once, by a much modified Formula One car on the Bonneville Salt Flats, so modified that it would certainly have been disqualified from the current Grand Prix by the FIA.

In processing these thoughts a human brain generates more electrical pulses in a day than are generated by all the telephones throughout the world. The brain's neurons connect up via 100 trillion synaptic connections. Each human brain is a truly amazing resource!

So it had taken all Marsha's genius to develop a way of accessing and identifying the salient contents of a brain, a laborious analysis of the chemistry taking place at those many synaptic gaps. What they had not yet resolved was how to capture it as a 'hard copy', though she was confident that her team's work with organic computing would master this soon. All they could do for now was access the memories in one brain and then transfer these to a new host.

Early on it had been hoped that through the humanzee programme they might be able to develop a sort of empty receptacle into which they could make such a transfer. It was soon established that they needed a fully mature and functioning human brain, with solid structures and partitioning already in place, for the process to succeed. Apparently in brains and minds a blank sheet was not a good starting place.

This of course meant that when placing another's memories into an existing mind it was necessary to interfere with the existing connections that had been made between that individual's synapses over a lifetime of nature and nurture, experience and emotion. They had also found that it took a compliant recipient, prepared with the right cocktail of drugs, skilful use of the binaural beat and a gentle and timely process, to 'overwrite' the transferred memories in a careful and progressive way so that the brain was not triggered to shut down or rebel.

The really comforting news for Marsha as she settled down to the process was that the donor subject was always unaffected even when the recipient was damaged. They had now recorded two successes and she was confident that this third time would be lucky too.

# Chapter 69 - *Ceuta, north Africa*

As Tom's helicopter landed in north Africa he was thinking back to that fateful day in Tunis when he had spotted Shepherd arriving on this continent in a similar manner. That landing had been some 1,500 kilometres further to the east along this same coastline. He was reminded of the Berber costume that Shepherd enjoyed wearing so much; this place here had also been of major significance to the Berbers. They had sacked it in 740 CE to displace the Arabs who had themselves invaded earlier to unseat the Byzantines. It was the Berbers who restored the city in the 9th century.

But the city held even more interest for Tom; from the 5th century BCE, it had been the Carthaginian city of Ablya. He just could not understand why it was that this ancient people and their predecessors, the Phoenicians and the earlier Sumerians, were currently stalking him from their long silent graves. Normally he was in full control of his writing projects, but this one was taking on a very disturbing life of its very own.

He looked ahead at Monte Hacho which was believed to be the southern Pillar of Hercules with the Rock of Gibraltar, across the mouth of the Mediterranean, as its northern counterpart. The myths surrounding these pillars were unsurprising for they once marked the limits of the known world and were therefore seen as the departure point to discover new lands. Another legend suggested the fabled city of Atlantis sat out beyond them.

These mythical pillars still feature on the coats of arms of Spain and the city of Cadiz; originally a Phoenician city, *Gades*.

Spread out beneath their helicopter was Ceuta, a rather strange Spanish autonomous city of 75,000 souls which with Melilla formed the southern 'underbelly' of Europe, or perhaps more appropriately its southern bulwark against Africa. Precariously perched at the tip of the continent they were there to stop the modern invading hordes.

The two cities claimed and received significant EU funding to secure their six mile border with Morocco by erecting some very controversial fences. Each consisted of two rows of three metre high wired barricades, interlaced with cameras and fibre-optic sensors. There was a road between them permitting regular and vigilant border patrols.

Tom recalled Shepherd's words about national borders and their artificiality. He had few doubts about the need for this one; the flood of humanity heading into Europe would have taken on a biblical Exodus proportion without this barrier's presence. Spain had policed and regularly stopped around 10,000 a year trying to use Ceuta as a jumping off point. Since the fence construction the number was down to just a few hundred each year; as a result these immigrants were forced instead to use all manner of craft and craftiness to cross the narrow straits in a quest to reach the promised lands of Europe.

The helicopter ride from Málaga had been uneventful but Brain was insistent that they had to prepare for their latest investigation. He explained the information had come from Mark Elliott's team. From material uncovered in San Francisco they believed they had identified the first planned site for a series of releases of this famine material. If they were stopped here then they might just be able to halt the threat.

Brain drilled the team on what they should be looking out for, describing what they might expect once they crossed into Morocco. He gave details of the mercenaries they had recruited to assist them, who had what responsibility and so on.

Brain summed up, 'So that's what we have to achieve.'

Tom felt a sense of pride that at last he was completely accepted as a member of this elite team, no longer just the technical nerd who had to be nurse-maided. From within this warm feeling he smiled and commented, 'I guess we are literally looking for that needle in a haystack, trying to stop any genetic interference with Morocco's wheat harvest.'

Brain grimaced and popped Tom's self-congratulatory balloon, 'OK, you're supposed to be the bright boy of the team. Can you explain to me why they would have chosen Morocco?'

Tom stared back at the imposing Rock of Gibraltar as he answered, 'Bizarrely they turn out to be the twelfth largest producer of wheat in the world. Who would have guessed that?'

Brain nodded, 'I guess the choice was made because they have personnel and resources based down at Tamegroute to prepare and launch such an attack. You suggested that they must have an antidote for their own crops that they're growing at the retreat?'

'Unless they are truly suicidal but they are much more interested in the opposite goal - immortality!'

One of the team asked, 'Then why don't we concentrate instead on trying to find their antidote?'

Brain took back the helm. 'That's of course one part of the job, but our first role is prevention. We need to stop them spreading their grief here. So we all know what we are about?'

### Kénitra, Morocco
He looked around at each of the team, 'If you're waiting for me to give a motivational speech then you've picked the wrong guv'nor, and if you need one then I've got the wrong team! We all know what is required, what's at risk - so let's go do it.'

Will was the sort who always needed to understand the details of a task before he could commit to it. This was probably why deep down he was still not that sold on this religious order. Based on this he had questioned the technicians back at Tamegroute at some length about this material that he was being asked to distribute.

It was not that he needed to understand what had been done by the labs to produce the materiel; he understood even less about how it would set about damaging the crops, or quite how quickly it would have an effect. No, he wasn't worried about these things. His concern was that he feared the material might have some side effects on him or his team as they deployed it. And nothing they had told him had reassured him that these 'lab rats', as he called the BiCogNaIT scientists, really knew either!

One of the team had explained how the material had been fabricated from a series of experiments. What they had constructed was not a single substance; it was much more a lethal cocktail of viruses. They explained in far too much detail how they had taken two existing viruses normally transmitted by aphids among crops and genetically altered them.

That was when Will's eyes started to glaze over as they listed all sorts of acronyms that frankly meant nothing to him and learning of them raised his interest not a jot. They talked of WYLV, wheat yellow leaf virus, and of BYDV, barley yellow dwarf virus. To these they had added two more viruses, with two more acronyms, that they said were normally transmitted by arachnids and mites. Will blanched at this; he hated spiders with a passion and was not keen on insects. When he could be rational about his phobia, which was pretty seldom, he attributed it to the fact that as a child he was made to use of an outside toilet on his uncle's farm, a facility that was festooned with cobwebs sporting fat juicy spiders that had thrived on the plentiful insects the farm attracted.

These other viruses were tediously identified as WSMV, wheat streak mosaic virus, and AMV, agropyron mosaic virus. Will thought it was just wheat for God's sake, a simple crop that you planted and grew out there in a field. How could it have so many complicated problems to merit all those damned letters?

The technicians were not affected by his obvious disinterest in the actual names; they were almost boastful as they described how they had managed to alter these viruses and their RNA strands. They retained their potency but now mirrored fungi. With their resultant material they no longer depended upon the insects alone for now they could equally-well be distributed as airborne spores.

The boffins carried on giving him the nauseating details, recounting how destructive diseases had been combated by the development of new strains of wheat seed, or by arranging plantings later in the year's cycle, and of course through the careful use of fertilisers, better irrigation and so on. As a result the BiCogNaIT strain had needed to be tweaked to circumvent these defences.

Will tried to move away but the experts were on a roll by now, keen to define how the resultant agent attacked plants in a whole new series of ways. It apparently contained a single-strand of RNA of around 10,000 nucleotides in length. Will had no idea what that meant but vague recollections of biology lessons at school were stirred when he was instructed how it would enter the plant and limit its ability to produce chlorophyll, severely stunting its growth.

Another RNA strand added was designed to pass through the plant safely and then attack directly at the growth of the roots. A third strand was destined to invade any seeds so they would become barren and thus any future generation of the crop would be halted too.

It was explained with some awe how a further late addition to the mix was included after Marsha had explained of the Romans' approach in using salt to damage the Carthaginian agriculture. She had finally tweaked the cocktail so a percentage of the fungal spores would pass through the plant without affecting it, only to damage the soil by making it infertile.

So he understood enough to know that the material would attack the plant's growth, decimate its roots, infect its seeds and finally impair the soil that it was sitting in. Will thought it sounded pretty noxious, and asked whether it had been tested on humans.

Typical of scientists, they had not quite answered the question. Instead they described how the composite whole was coated with a protein that would pass directly into the hind gut of an aphid and lie there dormant, not reproducing and not causing its host any harm. When pressed they said, not at all reassuringly, that it would 'probably' do the same in a human.

The point of this was apparently that when the aphid later fed on any leaves its salivary gland would very effectively spread the material. Now that did not sound good at all; the idea that if he ate something he might possibly be spreading this stuff. They explained that they had developed something for his team to take that would 'effectively' kill it. There they went again with vague promises!

Will was relaxing a little at this information, but then a whole new threat was introduced to him; apparently this was their ace-in-the-hole. Quite separately they had bred a sort of super-aphid, to be precise a cross between a phylloxera and a standard aphid.

When Will naturally asked them what on earth a phylloxera might be, they didn't answer straight away; instead they explained that it was a phylloxera that had caused the mid-19th century 'Great French Wine Blight'. The French biologist had pronounced the name of the event in the way that Will might have said 'Remember the Alamo'; with real reverence in the tone. Apparently 40% of France's vineyards and therefore much of its wine industry had been brought to its knees by this humble bug.

They also described how the French wine producers' chauvinism had been dealt a huge blow when it was found that their only salvation was to graft their precious vines with those taken from the Americas; the American vines had developed a resistance to their local natural enemy, the grape phylloxera.

They described how the new BiCogNaIT super-aphid had been designed with several, what Will considered quite disgusting, defence mechanisms. It produced a variety of honeydew to combat and dilute any treatment by fungicide and it also interacted chemically with the plant's tissue to create a gall into which it could hide away from any natural predators.

Through many centuries human civilisations had cultivated naturally occurring cereals to support ever-growing communities. Wheat itself has been domesticated for over 10,000 years; a constant series of interventions had increased yield; hard-won techniques had been created to improve the quality and safeguard the resultant crops. Now for the first time wheat production was going to face not a natural or meteorological threat but a calculated enemy menace designed so meticulously that it just had to succeed.

# Chapter 70 - *Selçuk, Turkey*

Twilight was descending and Stevie found she was recalling details of that day from so many years ago. She had been walking. It was foggy and she did not recognise her surroundings until she was suddenly at a door and entered the school chapel, she was moving forward towards the altar rail. And there it was before her - the statue of Perpetua.

Somehow Marsha was there too. She couldn't actually see her, she sensed her presence; she was watching. How could this be?

Marsha's scoffing voice broke the silence as she dismissed Perpetua's presence, 'It's a simple statue. Look it's a fabricated painted thing, not of a particularly high quality either. Far too much gilt for my liking.'

Stevie dismissed her remarks and smiled, 'Don't you see that's the very point of Roman Catholicism - the guilt!'

She pressed on and knelt at the rail to pray. As she did, it brought to mind the extreme chilliness of the small chapel. It was a time before central heating in institutional buildings. She was not even sure that the small convent would have installed it by today. It was a bone-chilling cold that she realised she had spent her whole adult life avoiding. Back then, so soon after her mother's death, it had felt appropriate. The world had been a cold and unforgiving place.

She felt Marsha's presence growing. There was her voice again, 'You really shouldn't be wasting any time on this old, tired religion. Your knowledge of our Order and of science has taken you much further in terms of your understanding of the world and your place in it. This old religion placed limits on you. The Order and science offer you unlimited horizons.'

Marsha sounded just like the Devil as he sought to tempt Christ in the wilderness, offering him all the kingdoms on earth if only he would bow down and worship Satan. With no sensation of any movement, Stevie found herself back in the retreat at Tamegroute. She was in that rear laboratory area, standing among the humanzees locked away from the world.

'What about the horizons of these sweet creatures? Your science has reduced them to the role of living spare parts, born to serve your purpose. Yet you created them! Where are your parental instincts?'

'Don't waste your emotions on these creatures. Now we are together we have plenty of time to have as many children as we care. You can apply your sentimental nature to their general upbringing while I stretch their intelligence.'

Stevie was shocked, 'You believe that sort of thought constitutes a parental instinct? You need to nurture children, and humanzees; seek out their skills and attributes, not force them down the line you choose while you leave others to nanny them for you.'

Marsha's presence was getting ever stronger. 'Puh-lease! You have to understand that finally the world has moved on. We will no longer permit any child simply to be born. Children were previously an accident of birth, a cocktail mixed up from the incidental DNA available to the parents, mere serendipity. All latent potential was left unfulfilled, frustrated or constrained by a second accident – the accident of their environment, the happenstance of their social status, their political and religious systems. How can it be good nurturing, good parenting, to bring them into a world just to fail?'

Stevie found she was wilting under the strength of Marsha, the dominance of her thoughts. She was thrust right back to her childhood doubts and insecurities, her fears of lacking any importance, of having no worth. This notion carried her straight back to the altar rail, looking up again at Perpetua, looking for a sign, any sign of reassurance that she mattered.

Marsha was right, it was merely a naïve painted plaster figure that stared sightlessly back at her. Looking at it now it was obvious it could achieve absolutely nothing for her. How could she have allowed herself to be so easily fooled? Of course she had been just a child at the time, one of the very children that Marsha had just defined, an accident of birth followed up by a veritable motorway pile-up of an environment.

Stevie felt the force as Marsha pressed in so many places to overlay her own thoughts; but she instinctively understood that Marsha was selecting, seizing on, loci that were already in her brain from subjects they had previously discussed in their one-on-ones.

Now when it was too late she understood why Marsha had spent so much time with her. She had been planting the seeds that she now planned to harvest.

# Chapter 71 - *Kénitra, Morocco*

The information that Mark Elliott had found in San Francisco had come from an unconnected snippet. Among a plethora of internal emails there had been a request from Will for suitably-sized nozzles and a query about cleaning them. Mark had been advised of the Order's planned famine attacks and being a country boy he had naturally assumed 'crop sprayers'.

The email containing the word nozzle prompted him to look for other messages between the two individuals. This brought to light to a later request for details of the weather conditions in Morocco, an exchange about the windy conditions on the Atlantic coastal plain to conclude what would be the optimum heights for discharge from a plane. From this the Okie had got his man, or at least his location.

Brain infiltrated three of his men overnight and they were out there in full camouflage dug in on different sides of the compound. One was hidden in an avenue of trees beside the main route in and out monitoring any road movements. Another was to the east in scrubland beside the river to observe any traffic arriving that way; though that was judged unlikely. James, or 'Brawn' as Tom still liked to think of him, was up to the north beside the main military airfield.

While the other two restricted themselves to the occasional report that all was calm, James was routinely voluble about the deafening noise as aircraft took off and landed.

'I want all this recorded so I can sue HMG for deafness in my old age.'

Brain replied, 'Don't forget, I've met your wife and you may be grateful for some reduction in her decibel levels!'

On the first day they had seen T1, or 'Target 1' who was Will Patterson, come and go on two recce trips in his helicopter, but they did not look ready yet for live crop spraying; apparently these were just joy rides. There were only three other 'missionaries' with him, this being Brain's shorthand term for them. The others present were clearly local hired-help who probably knew nothing of the plan but were being exploited as local grunt for their specific knowledge of the helicopter and crop spraying.

Tom pondered why his life recently revolved around helicopters. Up until a year or so back he had never been near one; now he had clocked up many flying hours and it seemed anyone he was investigating also had one as their mode of transport of choice.

Tom was never that comfortable travelling in that fashion: to him helicopters were far too wayward. Take the one the missionaries were using; the blades looked far too flexible in the wind, not nearly precise enough for Tom's peace of mind.

He had the time to realise he had made a pledge to himself up in the Arctic that he had failed to follow through. Confronted with an urgent need to disable a helicopter he had been disturbed by his complete lack of knowledge about its aeronautic, electrical and fuel systems. At the time he had contented himself with trying to damage the moving bits, but he had made a solemn promise that he would investigate more subtle approaches for any future such occasion; and he had of course forgotten to do so!

This time Brain and his crew were along with him and they had enough ordnance not just to stop it, they could expunge it.

On the second day the scout to the west reported a tanker vehicle approaching the site. It had no markings. It was a local truck with two drivers who looked just that, local drivers. It emerged from the avenue of trees and did not make the first left up into the airport but carried on to the target site. It pulled around to the north and parked up on the concrete apron.

Brain ordered the scouts to narrow their distance and take up agreed sniper positions. James already had the apron in full sight and reported that there was no sign yet of the tanker being connected to the helicopter's rear spraying container.

Brain had billeted the rest of the team on the airfield. Sir Joseph had pushed the British-Moroccan relationship to the extreme to get this agreement and had used a terrorist threat as the cause; well it was essentially true.

Brain had summarily annexed a Jeep that the airport team routinely used for patrolling. They had watched them cross the airfield to the Mission compound as part of regular security checks and their presence would raise no particular concerns with the Mission team.

The Jeep with covered sides and rear concealed five of Brain's unit including Tom. They took a good look at the sky in all directions before crossing the runway, taking a worn path that led directly eastwards so that they would not pass through James line of fire. They followed the path south towards the concrete apron.

The scouts could eyeball 'T1' and two other hostiles, but there was no sign of the fourth as they approached the tableau before them. There appeared to be some squabble about the documentation that the tanker driver was waving animatedly. At least it meant no-one was paying particular attention to the Jeep's approach.

One of Will's team moved forward and struck the driver with the back of his hand. It wasn't a very strong blow. Tom looked out over Brain's shoulder and smiled as he assumed the driver must have been a soccer fan; he fell to the floor as if poleaxed. Any Premier League footballer would have been proud of him.

The co-driver was quick to produce a knife and made a move on Will. It all started to go wrong. Brain's team had been told to try to take these missionaries alive so one of the British scouts brought down the co-driver with a head shot. Then all hell broke loose.

The three missionaries went to ground instantly; each pulling out weapons and crabbing towards nearby cover. They had no idea where the shot had come from but now the previously innocuous Jeep looked a pretty good suspect.

Brain had to turn the vehicle away as a couple of hurried shots were directed their way. Those in the back tumbled out and their movements mirrored those of the missionaries a few instants earlier. The fact of their emergence focused all attention on the Jeep.

The driver of the truck, now fully recovered, took advantage of the melée and made it back to his vehicle which had been idling. He engaged a gear and started to turn back towards the exit.

One of the missionaries ran across to the tanker to stop this. He shouted at the driver to halt and raised his pistol threateningly towards the windscreen. The instruction was that the missionaries were to be taken alive, but of even more importance was that the material in that truck should not be released. A shot rang out and the man with the gun fell to the ground in front of the oncoming truck.

The driver did his best to avoid him but he was crushed by the front wheel and then the rear wheels somehow fouled on the body, trapping it between the double rear wheels and spinning it around sickeningly.

Will shot out both front tyres but the driver was still managing some forward progress despite his rapidly deflating fronts. That was until the rims hit the concrete and jarred the steering wheel from his hands. The front wheels swung around into a full lock and the truck halted.

Will turned now to the attackers and called out towards the Jeep, 'I will assume you understand English! You need to know that I have a grenade and I will blow up the tanker if you don't come out and give yourselves up.'

When nothing happened he shouted again. 'Look, we are all immune to this stuff, but I can assure you that you are so close you will all die!'

Tom shook his head at Brain, 'It's pretty unlikely that it would do us direct harm.'

Brain smiled back, 'Pretty unlikely doesn't sound very scientific. There's not much of an empirical ring to me.'

'OK then. If it's a plant disease it might well be unpleasant but I would say that it can't hurt us seriously.'

Brain was talking on his radio, 'We do need to try and take these missionaries alive if we can. We have to establish where the stuff came from, whether there's more.'

The British team from the Jeep was fanning out; the scouts were still working their way in.

Will was getting impatient and stood up showing the grenade in his hand. He walked towards the helicopter but kept himself in range to lob the grenade at the tanker. 'I don't know who you are but if you have any idea what we are doing then you must be aware that this is very toxic stuff that we have in the tanker.'

The two local drivers had clearly had enough and started to run back to the buildings. Will's companion calmly made sure neither of them made it that far. Two shots sounded; one must have been a clear hit as the man fell and lay inert, but his colleague was obviously only wounded. He lay where he fell, wailing and calling for help in both Arabic and English.

Will reached the helicopter and hauled the pilot out using him as a shield; the gun in his left hand was pointed at the man's head, his right hand was still holding the grenade. The remaining missionary moved from out in the open to join Will at the helicopter and took over responsibility for the pilot.

Brain had taken enough of this nonsense. Nowhere in his plan was there the possibility of these people getting away and he issued James a terse order. The big man rose from his cover, shouldered his RPG and neatly dropped a grenade right beneath the helicopter. The blast almost lifted the helicopter off the ground, its glass cockpit covered in a cobweb of cracks and several small electrical fires started inside.

Tom smiled, 'Why couldn't I have thought of that? Obviously the way to do it!'

The three standing beside the helicopter were thrown forward onto their faces by the blast. Will was the first to get up and tossed his grenade, but a shot rang out and hit him in the forearm. The grenade appeared to be moving in slow motion, eccentrically bobbling forward, it rolled remorselessly towards the tanker. Everyone watched, bracing themselves for the explosion and the potential of its aftermath.

On its final contact with the ground its eccentric shape kicked it off sideways like a rugby ball at the feet of a struggling fullback. It rolled under the tractor unit of the trailer, directly beneath the large diesel engine which took most of the force when it detonated.

The explosion neatly stripped the connection between the tractor and tanker, lifting the cab up and away from its deadly cargo. Tom was petrified as he looked up to see the tanker had been detached, watched as the tractor fell away from its load. The tanker had taken on a list towards its front end but had been halted by a pair of prop legs that had been lazily left part way down. Tom expected them to not be firm in this position, but they did not give way. The tanker stopped at a 20 degree angle but otherwise undamaged; its contents still constrained securely inside.

The British team was the quickest to react. They pressed forward to capture the missionaries before they could recover. Will was too preoccupied with the wound to his forearm, the only pressure he offered was the digital sort directly on his wound. The other man had been closer to the grenade still stunned he was speedily unarmed. The pilot, who had been the closest to the RPG explosion, looked none the worse for wear but had evidently been hired as a non-combatant and offered no resistance.

Will was swiftly plastic-tie handcuffed with his hands in front of his body in deference to his wound. The others were both thrust roughly to the floor, handcuffed from behind.

Tom was not involved in the arrest and left the team to their work as he hurried across towards to where the two locals had tried to escape in the direction of the buildings. He walked swiftly past the first who was clearly dead.

He followed the trail of blood to where the other had finally given up his efforts to escape. The injury and the effort had so exercised the fellow's mind that there had been insufficient bandwidth in his brain to consider releasing his grip on the consignment papers; the reason for the earlier argument was still clutched and crumpled in his hand. Tom prised them loose.

Quickly scanning the impenetrable Arabic he concentrated on the consignment address. And there it was – 'TTR'. Its origin was the Tamegroute Tyndale Retreat.

As he turned to make this fact known he caught the flash of a second floor window being thrown open. His first thought was that it was the fourth missionary preparing to shoot and he shouted a warning to Brain and his team before taking cover. This proved truly unfortunate as instead of firing the man emptied a a large carton of insects out of the window, Tom was completely engulfed by the falling swarm.

One of Brain's team heard the shout and fired at the man in the window who fell back inside still clutching the empty box.

Tom's eyes had closed instinctively but several of the insects made it into his open mouth and he spluttered these out before running his tongue around his teeth searching for any others that might be lurking. He brushed some from his face and on examination saw that they were large aphids, some beginning to take wing. They were not biting him so he relaxed and carried on removing them from his hair and clothes.

Two of Brain's team clattered past him to go into the building to deal with the final individual. Brain arrived by Tom's side and pulled out an aerosol can. He flicked a lighter in its stream and started to burn those insects that were still in a huddle. Tom grabbed several of the aphids for later scrutiny and then joined Brain in swatting and stamping on those that remained alive.

The inside of her head was buzzing. Stevie could feel the procedure, a slow repetitive process that had been building in strength. It felt as if the process latched on to a thought that Marsha had planted in her mind and then suddenly it was as if Marsha was physically there. From each nexus she then insistently set out to weave a new set of thoughts and experiences around that point. Any resistance Stevie presented was challenged with an argument that her beliefs were the superior, were right.

She felt she had acquired a second subconscious mind. She knew her subconscious was always there, although she was only really became aware of it when a surprising thought leapt unbidden into her mind unexpectedly, from somewhere deep inside her. Occasionally it felt like a background narrator to her life, stepping up to question her motivations and goals.

That was similar to what was happening right now. Now there was a lively internal debate with two voices, two minds, both fighting for her beliefs, her knowledge base, her sanity.

Stevie recalled the doubts for her sanity that others and she herself had raised when she had become so withdrawn as a child. The therapy sessions she had been subjected to had probed and pressed at her just as Marsha was doing right now. Back then she could shut them out, block her ears, close her mind to them. Now there was nowhere for her to hide.

She was becoming increasingly unsure as to which of the thoughts were indeed her own and which were Marsha's invading ideas. Just where did one start and another finish? She was losing her clarity, her visibility, her sanity. As things progressed she found one criterion that she could use. She could discern a tone, a kind of timbre to the internal voice, which was different to these intrusive items. This was because the thought was coming through in another voice - Marsha's!

She began to realise that this was most apparent when the notions were strongly opposed to her own value judgments. It was because they were rubbing up against and erasing her own. Her fear was that perhaps there were other ideas that were insidiously slipping through beneath her guard, insinuating their way into her mind without encountering resistance. She felt helpless, slowly sinking as she became overwhelmed; it was as if she was that vulnerable child once again.

That realisation sparked her imagination and she was right back in the school chapel, once again kneeling at the altar rail. It was obviously a dream because she was watching as if from an out-of-body point of view, looking down on the scene from over her own shoulder. She could see her younger self imploring the plaster figure to have purpose. As the observer she clenched her eyes tightly, trying to recover that more innocent time, trying to recapture the state of her young mind as it had been back then. Back in a time before Marsha, a time when she was free from Marsha's thoughts.

And suddenly there it was. She was back in her own body. Her eyes felt clearer and fresher. Her senses sharper. She felt as if her eyes were opened fully for the first time since childhood. She looked up and was immediately in rapture as a beam of moonlight suddenly lanced across the chapel. It was shaped and swirled by the effects of the stained glass window as it washed across the statue of Perpetua. An unnatural rainbow of colours enlivened the simple figurine.

Perpetua was there with her again. The young saint turned and looked down upon Stevie. She smiled, such a beautiful smile. A joy flushed through Stevie. After years of doubt and countless times when she dismissed her vision as childhood fancy, now she knew she had not been deluded. It had happened! And she could resolve the other internal doubt she had held across all the years, it was definitely not her mother before her, but Saint Perpetua herself. There was the smile she had yearned for down the many years. It was real! Perpetua's lips moved and Stevie clearly heard her say 'Pax tecum'.

Where was the peace that had been promised to her as a child with these words? The words had led to abuse back then; they had certainly not been a precursor of peace in her childhood. Was this brief interlude of peace to be just that - brief? Her mind was being remorselessly assaulted from all sides; but worse it was from the inside.

With her sudden wave of despair Saint Perpetua disappeared and she was back in that horrible room, with that awful priest. The man had a bad smell about him, what Stevie could recognise now as an extreme case of halitosis and body odour. His hair was lank and abundant with dandruff. When he made her do those dreadful things to him he grew excited and the smell became even worse. Still to this day the stench of rank sweat made her heave.

At the time it had essentially been a series of physical assaults. Much of the memory of the mechanics itself had faded; but the mental scars still remained. There was this adult, a man respected by other adults, revered by the nuns at the convent, a stalwart of her and her mother's religion. Everything suggested he could not do wrong, could not be wrong. Every week his words from the pulpit had such authority, such solemnity, he made his words sound like Holy Writ in that room too.

Somewhere deep inside her she did find the resource to recognise it was wrong. Her belief had been bolstered and yet undermined by the memory of the Saint's visitation. If Perpetua had smiled upon her then surely she would not let any harm befall her? The doubts always crept back at night. The disclosing of the visitation to that silly young nun had led her directly into the clutches of the priest. Was this in fact what the saint had intended? Was this her own version of martyrdom? Was it equivalent to Perpetua being gored by a bull?

Back in her childhood after many low moments, suicide had seemed the only course but then she had realised there was another solution. She learned to handle her feelings by building a wall around the experiences; she set up a mental barrier that the priest's actions and words could not penetrate. No matter how he behaved it was all excluded, placed elsewhere, somehow thrust deeply into a far recess of her mind. She spent time accomplishing this, the years of building and bolstering this barrier had made her stout of mind.

Now it came to her. That was the solution! That was how she could find the promised peace. She just had to re-establish the same barrier that had helped her survive as a child. That must surely have been Perpetua's intention. She had to rebuild the internal wall in order to achieve her peace. She needed to identify all these invading thoughts and experiences, press them deep behind the barrier, lock it away just as securely as those humanzees had been in TTR!

# Chapter 73 - *Double-T R, Morocco*

Daniel Lehri, the canon at TTR, was becoming frantic. Having previously wanted them both gone, now he was eager to reach either Samuel or Marsha.

He had learnt that the Patriarch was not to be disturbed at any cost. He was apparently contemplating the next stages and was secured away deep within a secret location.

Dr Davenport was apparently undergoing some procedure. He had no idea that she had been sick, but guessed they would never have informed him if that had been the case. Whatever was the matter with her, he had been advised it would take some time before she might be approached.

And then there was Will Patterson's disappearance. He had been in regular contact since he had been sent sufficient material for the test in Sidi el Hassan. All reports had been entirely positive until suddenly there were no reports. What had happened? Was the material the cause of their sudden silence? Had they been killed by the material? Had they been arrested?

Chris, the local gNOS leader, had been tugging on all their Moroccan contacts in an attempt to establish quite what might be going on over there. Will and his team certainly had not been taken by the authorities or they would have learnt of this very quickly. He concluded they needed to send a team across there to get some intel; however it would take time to arrange this.

Something had clearly gone wrong and Chris concluded that the retreat was therefore to be considered under threat. The instructions were quite clear in such circumstances. He had to close down TTR and prepare to defend it against any attempt to enter.

Daniel also concluded that he had no choice but to consider the reality of the threat. He broke open the package that was supplied to the canons at each of the retreats and began to read the instructions that had been prepared for just this sort of eventuality.

The first principles were laid out. He must prepare those within the retreat and he now had the software that would accelerate a programme of group sessions to do just that. He instructed one of his team to start the process.

The children and infants were all to be secured in the underground shelter beneath the main complex building. There had been concern on some of the parents' faces and quite a few tears and histrionics from the children but this was completed without undue delay.

The warehousing and laboratories suddenly sported heavily-armed guard details and fire teams stood by at various key locations to ensure that what they had, they held.

Daniel followed each of the steps while personally still privately doubting, or was it hoping, that they would yet prove unnecessary. No harm done. It was a useful drill; such a circumstance might well have to be met in the future.

What was a relief was that the group sessions were occupying the bulk of those in the retreat, keeping them from deluging Daniel with questions or concerns; they were engrossed in the screened sessions and therefore perfectly compliant and unaware of the preparations that were happening all around them.

Daniel had thought he knew every nook and nuance of his retreat, that was his job, but now he came to a section that revealed preparations of which he had been completely unaware. This phase of his instructions was disturbing. They were spelled out in such a matter of fact and efficient way that he found himself chilled and yet thrilled that the Order had the presence of mind to have considered all of this. He felt a frisson of excitement that he was to be the one entrusted to follow this course of action, the only one trusted with this special knowledge.

Sir Joseph acted rapidly on the information uncovered at Kenitra. He was delighted he had kept the locals advised of the original plans as he was now fully able to follow through and contact the Moroccan special services with the *Marine Royale Marocaine*. They had agreed to allocate him three teams in support of his own for the incursion.

The Moroccan team had scrambled and arrived with Brain and his team at the airfield where they took possession of the tanker and discussed their next tactics. All were agreed that they had to stop the production of any more of this material. They had no idea if all the retreats were manufacturing it; but they had clear evidence that TTR was, and it had to be halted!

Tom had seen only the inside of the hospital at the retreat and had only vague recollections of their escape across the compound. Sir Joseph had countered this lack of knowledge by sending Hannah and Dieter out to join them at the airfield. He had foreseen the potential for this escalation and had moved them over to Gibraltar just in case.

Now armed with some current satellite images of the retreat, some brusque questioning of Will and his team, plus the specific site information that Dieter and Hannah could provide, they had worked up a strategy. The locals had sourced the required transportation and logistical support, the necessary armaments and munitions and they were now attending a final briefing.

The local team's officer, Younès Kaddur, commented right away that because the retreat used just one main entry and exit point they would be less prepared and therefore vulnerable to attacks from other directions.

Tom warned, 'These people are smart. They've had plenty of time to prepare for this, so their use of electronic and other measures around the perimeter should not be ruled out. Don't forget that our intelligence estimates that 1,000 of the full complement of 12,000 will be gNOS, and they are fully trained and presumably well-armed.'

Brain agreed with the need for a cautious approach, 'They have set the theatre of operation, not us. They must have expected an assault at some stage so we have to assume they will be completely prepared for us. Don't forget that there are women and children in there. Neither of our governments will be content if any of them get hurt in the operation.'

Younès became alarmed, 'We few can't mount an assault against a thousand armed combatants! I'm not sure even if I would be granted the resources to mount such an attack within our own borders.'

Brain was quick to reassure, 'We are not planning to take the retreat. We just want a surgical incursion that destroys their ability to produce these famine materials and perhaps slow up any other plans they might have up their sleeves.'

Tom pointed at the satellite photos and summarised, 'Look, we believe this building is the manufacturing facility for the chemicals. We need to take it out while not damaging the power plant beside it.'

Brain smiled, 'Hark at him! He'll be adding "with extreme prejudice" next! You can leave the soldiering to us; it's you, Dieter and Hannah who have the tough job to do. While we are attacking you have to get into those labs. We agreed that we can't just 'take them out' because of those blessed humanzees.'

'And Stevie, remember she may well be there too!'

'We've agreed that you have your chance to go look for Stevie provided that Dieter and Hannah concentrate on finding the virus and phylloxera facility and help us to destroy it.'

Daniel was waiting for news back from the team that had been dispatched to the airfield. Their report was now long overdue and he had to accept that the retreat must be compromised in some way. This was no longer a drill.

He still had no means of talking to any of the heads of the organisation. The Patriarch was off in the wilderness somewhere contemplating higher things, that Davenport woman was the only person at BiCogNaIT who mattered and she was incommunicado, Trajan as the head of gNOS was with Shepherd, the two Mission heads Dom and now Will must both have been taken somehow.

One thing that was clear from the instructions was that he should not make or take any communication from other retreats. The fear was that these could be false messages designed to undermine him, trick him into dismissing the threat that existed.

He issued the next set of software for use with the group sessions. The process of these had been increased substantially and now a communal session took place every hour. The messaging was stark. There were extreme evils out there in the world that they had been spared from. Those false prophets were still abroad and they were going to come to damage their peace, to threaten their salvation.

The gNOS team was spared this conditioning. Instead they attended their own sessions that were designed to raise the tempo, to heat up their blood, to get them lusting for action. They were running drills that tested their speed of decision making, their physical fitness to get to a hot spot fast and be fully ready to make quick killing forays upon arrival. They had been psyched up and were now itching for someone to try to invade the retreat!

Daniel alone was spared any conditioning. The canon at the retreat was the executive who would unharness the two groups when it was deemed appropriate. It was clear from his instructions that the current situation had not been envisioned. It had been expected that he would be acting upon a decision made by the Patriarch. Where was he? What should Daniel do in his absence?

They went in at 3:00 am. First they jammed all communications and the incursions were all carried out by helicopter, having concluded that the potential for landmines or other traps outside the perimeter was just far too likely. Within the compound the Order had its own residents, cattle and so on; surely they would not dare to lay mines inside?

A helicopter gunship gave them an early wake-up call as it shot two air-to-ground missiles to take out the main gate. The only ground force used had yomped a full platoon down the centre of the entrance road walking safely behind two soldiers equipped with mine detectors. Four mortars were used to lay smoke inside the compound and defensive positions were taken on either side of the road to fire on any hostiles emerging from the chaos.

Before the missiles had even hit the gates the gunship had fired live rounds across the top of the compound in two prepared directions. The plan was to spread panic while not hitting the three helicopters that flew in from the other side to achieve their real objective.

The first went directly to the manufacturing facility. Ably backed by three from the Moroccan forces, James and a colleague had the simplest objective. While the Moroccan's laid down covering fire, James was to get inside the facility and set charges that later would be set off remotely. The gNOS guards located at this facility had been drawn towards the front gate, trying to make out what was happening through the smoke. If the gNOS men had turned back to the facility then they would have been shot, but they wandered off towards the gate and there was therefore no point in drawing attention back to what they were doing.

The second helicopter dropped Brain and a larger team to clear the area at the rear of the laboratory. One part of the group was then deployed to hold this ground while the other unit penetrated the building. This was achieved with speed and again no defence was encountered which allowed the third helicopter to land Tom, Hannah and Dieter to virtually step off the aircraft onto the ground before it clattered up and out to safety. The defence unit laid down smoke as soon as it had disappeared. Each of those on the ground was equipped with infrared goggles so would have no difficulty defending their position in the mist.

Tom opened the rear door to see along the corridor there were several technicians face down with plastic ties attached to their hands. The main door to the laboratory was ajar and Brain was beckoning him forward.

They entered the lab and turned to confront the airlock door that had been one of their objectives; it too was open. Hannah led Tom and Dieter into the airlock and performed the procedure to get them inside the humanzee compound. While they were heavily isolated inside the humanzees had heard the explosions and the shooting and so were all very jittery, cowering away from the door, looking anxious.

Hannah stepped forward and signed for them to relax and that they were there to help them.

The matriarch, who had been standing securely behind a number of the larger males, stepped forward now and signed, 'I know you. Where you been? What you want?'

'Later. Now I help you escape here.'

'Sound bad out there. In here safe.'

Tom looked around at the residents. They seemed a gentle group, no sign of their being the ultimate soldiers that Davenport had sold to the DoD. There were no humans that he could see. He called to Hannah, 'Ask them if they've seen Stevie'

'How would they know who she was? She only came here the once and was not introduced.'

'She interacted with them, went in to one of their cells, played darts. It's likely she was the only one who would have done so?'

Hannah tried to explain. The matriarch recognised the description but said she had seen the girl only once.

She was getting restless, 'Where go if leave here?'

Hannah signed, 'Must go. Your babies not die, killed. Must go.'

Now the young males started to look aggressive, showing their teeth at this comment. Family was everything to them and they had been losing too many babies without any sign of illness. They had sensed that something bad had been happening.

Tom left Hannah and Dieter to it. He could do nothing there and he wanted to try to reach the Anglo's dormitory. It had not been an agreed objective but he knew Brain would be preoccupied with finding and destroying the virus and phylloxera breeding facilities. Anyway it was not too far away.

He slipped back along the corridor and out through the back door. He nodded to Brain's man who was on guard and confidently strode off into the smoke as if he had every right to do so.

He put on his set of infrareds. It was strange to see everything by its heat source rather than normal vision but he had memorised the map of the place and knew which way to go. The smoke was acrid and irritated his nose and his throat when he rather unwisely opened his mouth to increase the airflow to his lungs; he all but started to cough. Why hadn't he borrowed a gas mask too?

Ahead he saw the dorms. He had been looking in all directions and so far after passing the cordon set up at the rear of the laboratory he had seen no-one else. He reached the dormitory and peered in through a window like some peeping tom but he could see no human heat signatures inside. Where was everyone?

He turned between two buildings and there they all were, sitting in groups and rows before a large communal screen. He eased off the goggles in an effort to see more clearly as he could not believe they would all be passively sitting without even being able to see the screen, but they were! The smoke completely encompassed them and they would not have been able to see each other from just three or four paces away, yet still they sat engrossed in the audio part of the message.

It was Shepherd's voice. Was it a live broadcast from elsewhere? No, they were jamming all transmissions. So it was probably a recording, or was he actually there?

Tom listened in to his saccharin tones as he walked the lines looking for Stevie. 'My Perfects this is the moment we have all planned and worked towards. We cannot be led astray by the false prophets at this eleventh hour. The next two seals will be opened soon - the fifth seal that will raise the martyrs from their graves and the sixth seal that will redeem the 144,000, those of us securely in the retreats...'

Tom broke away from the mellifluous words that to him sounded preposterous. He was thinking, 'These are grown adults. How can they not see what that man is doing to them? He's the serpent hissing in their ears for them to walk away from what they know as right and proper.'

He had not intended to press on any further; he needed to be sure to be back at the rear of the laboratory for the extraction. He had to know if Stevie was there. He decided to walk to the main building where Stevie had once told him Shepherd's personal quarters were to be found. He could see two guards ahead. They were some way from the door of the complex and peering towards the front of the retreat, clearly they were wondering what was happening over there through the smoke.

Tom looked at his watch, 3:08. Could eight minutes have passed already? Incredible! He had only seven minutes to locate Stevie. He sidled up to the door not needing to be too quiet as the noise the gunships were making was formidable. He slipped off the goggles and prepared to enter.

As he reached it the door sprang open and Daniel Lehri emerged to face him.

'You! Guards, get over here and take care of this man.'

Two men rushed back and pushed Tom forcibly to the ground.

'Why can I reach no-one on the radio?'

'They're jamming our frequencies.'

'So where's Chris?'

'He'll be up near the gate where they're taking all the gunfire.'

'No-one is taking the gunfire. They are firing over our heads to confuse everyone. You, get down there and get Chris for me. You, go and get the industrial blowers from across at the power plant. Let's see if we can disperse some of this smoke.'

'What about the prisoner?'

Daniel unholstered his pistol, 'I can handle him.'

The two guards having gone, Daniel kicked Tom, 'Get up, against the wall, hands on your head. Now what are you trying to achieve by coming back here?'

'I've come for Stevie!'

'She's not here, so you've had a wasted journey. What's happened to Will Patterson and the others?'

'They were eaten by your phylloxera before they could release your toxins.'

'Well, it's been a wasted journey for you, your last.' He raised the pistol and Tom watched his finger tightening on the trigger. Then suddenly the retreat's Canon disappeared.

Tom slipped the infrareds back on and only then could he see the distinctive form of a humanzee crouched over Lehri. Evidently the humanzee had cannoned into him and propelled him into the smoke. Tom watched as he then finished the man with a few blows and scuttled off.

He looked around and saw a whole troop of the humanzees quartering the area; presumably their vision in the smoke was better than that of humans. He believed Daniel when he had said that Stevie was not there, and decided to make his way back to the laboratory. Through the infrareds he watched tableau after tableau unfold as the very efficient humanzees moved as a group, overpowering the retreat's guards as they pressed on.

However they gave a wide berth to the large group still sitting before the communal screen unaware of everything going on around them as they listened intently to Shepherd's words.

'… we must be prepared to stand against the false prophets, not allow them to infect our thinking, our future…'

He got back to the rear of the laboratory in good time and had not been missed. The helicopters took it in turn to come in and the whole crew was evacuated from the site unharmed.

### Kénitra, Morocco

Sir Joseph was on loudspeaker from Brain's phone. 'I've just finished having my ears chewed off by the Foreign Secretary. I need a full report of what you did down at Tamegroute. And I need it right now.'

Brain answered for them, 'We did no more and no less than we planned. James and his file went directly to the manufacturing facility and laid charges which we detonated from outside the retreat while in the air. These were relatively small charges placed strategically to destroy the plant technically and not obliterate it. With Hannah's help we destroyed the phylloxera stocks, the strain and all records and equipment associated with them. Oh, and she did insist on releasing the humanzees. They were told to get out of the retreat and hide out in the bush.'

'You are quite sure that the manufacturing facility was producing the famine chemicals?'

'Everything suggested that was the case. Why?'

'This morning's satellite pass has some pretty disturbing images. It appears all the residents of the retreat are dead. It's like Jonestown all over again, only a dozen times worse. In Tomana it was fewer than a thousand who died, here all twelve thousand look to be dead.'

Tom commented, 'I did see many of them gathered in front of a screen receiving some 'end of days' stuff from Shepherd. I thought he's all about extending life not getting them all to poison themselves in homage to Jim Jones.'

'Can you begin to imagine the paperwork involved in this? Twelve thousand people from all over the world. You'd better believe that the Foreign Secretary is not best pleased with this morning's work.'

Tom was thinking about Stevie. If they were to prove to be a suicidal cult then this was not a good omen. 'Sir Joseph, perhaps we need to warn the authorities at the other retreat locations that any incursions could trigger the same sort of reaction. We need to go for Shepherd and his leading lights rather than attack the retreats.'

Sir Joseph was as angry as Tom had ever heard him. Typically smooth and almost oily, the man normally oozed self-assuredness and a complete belief in his own decisions.

He grumbled, 'I have to get off to a meeting with the Foreign Secretary and the Professor. Apparently he has some ideas about these people that I need to hear. Leave Tamegroute to the consular team. Stay away. In fact hang fire there and prepare your written reports, individually please. I don't want any Aesop fables. I'll come back to you after this meeting.'

# Chapter 74 - *Lalibela, Ethiopia*

'I guess it's their fabled, inexhaustible supply of long distance runners or maybe their famine.' Trajan was replying to Shepherd's query about what he had known of Ethiopia before arriving here for his first trip.

Shepherd was strolling with his security boss across difficult terrain. It was his regular morning constitutional, but that particular morning he had lost all his bounce. Trajan's leg was almost fully repaired but he was happy to stay at the older man's speed. The gNOS chief could see that Shepherd's pace was slower than normal, he had been badly affected by the recent turn of events.

They were preceded on the track by two gNOS guards who were fifty or more metres ahead, perhaps another eighty metres behind them was another pair of his security detail. Shepherd was completely unaware that a further four had been deployed for the morning event. It was Marsha who had insisted that the Patriarch was not put at any risk at that sensitive time.

Each of the group was dressed in local clothing so their presence would not be remarked upon. This had the added benefit that sidearms were more easily concealed.

'You're right. That's what most Americans would come up with, but the famine was way back in the 1980s and it has nothing to do with the way they are today. Ethiopia is a proud nation that boasts a strong history, and a very long one. In truth it is something of an elder statesman in country terms, one of the world's very oldest nation states.'

Trajan recognised that the old man needed diversion, a conversation that would be on anything other than recent problems. He wanted to keep him relaxed and nothing relaxed the Patriarch more than letting him pontificate.

Trajan prompted him to continue, 'I guess I think of all African nations as being needy.'

The old man's head came up as he warmed to his subject. 'Far from it in this case. Ethiopia has been one of the fastest growing economies in the world for the best part of a decade.'

'What is it that the country makes then?

'Like many its wealth is mostly based upon mineral resources but then there is also a ready supply of water, what they call their 'white oil'. And then there's the 'black gold' or coffee; coffee was first cultivated here in Ethiopia.'

Trajan commented, 'I was a little surprised to see that many of the major pan-African organisations are based here, operations like the African Union and the United Nations Economic Commission for Africa.'

Shepherd had no time for these organisations or their nations; he planned that both would soon be eliminated. 'Much more significantly it was here in Ethiopia that some of the oldest hominid remains were discovered. In the 1970s in Ethiopia's Afar region a group of anthropologists found half of a particularly ancient skeleton, the hominid known as Lucy.'

'Lucy?'

'They quickly established that the skeleton was a female. The formal name they gave it was *Australopithecus afarensis* which literally means the 'southern ape of Afar'. It was while they were back in camp studying the find that a Beatles number came on the radio, "Lucy in the sky with diamonds"; so they called her 'Lucy' and she became world famous.

'Lucy was built something like a chimpanzee, actually somewhat more like one of Marsha's bonobos. Her knees and pelvis showed that she must have walked upright for much of the time. They carbon dated her and found she lived over three million years ago; at the time that meant she was the oldest hominid find.'

Trajan could see Shepherd was shaking off his depression and didn't want him slipping back. 'When you look around at our fellow man it's not difficult to work out where we came from!'

'Precisely. The human line and that of the chimpanzees had a parting of the ways around seven to eight million years ago. Our DNA research shows it wasn't any sort of clean break; it's clear that the two species continued to intermingle for a long time thereafter.'

'I guess needs must, as long as I wasn't left with the ugly one!'

Shepherd gave him a quizzical look at this, but pressed on. 'When I asked Marsha and her team to collate all of our and any others' genographic research she was able to backtrack the spread of humanity around the globe from our very earliest days. She confirmed the conclusions of others and proved that every single modern human could be traced back along the ancient trading and migration routes. Her research and fossil records reaching back almost six million years show that this country can confidently make the claim to be the original cradle of humanity.'

Trajan laughed aloud, 'So what you're saying is that Marsha found that all roads don't lead to Rome. In fact they all started out from Ethiopia?'

Shepherd smiled, but he had a more important observation. 'Don't you see though that if Ethiopia was the modern human "ground zero" then it must have been here where the genetic quantum leap took place. It must have been here where the alterations were first made to the primates that had previously evolved naturally upon our planet.'

Today he had relished the physical exercise, giving him a chance to think through the next steps he would define for the Order, how they might take things forward. Given the series of set-backs of recent weeks, he found himself dwelling more on the past than the future.

He could no longer stop himself saying what he was thinking. 'Tell me Trajan, how can we have got it so wrong? First that ape running around London, then the break-ins at Dublin and San Francisco. Now the Sidi el Hassan test has been frustrated and I can't quite believe that Tamegroute has fallen too!'

His words made Trajan's injury flare up and his leg hurt afresh. 'It seems to have been following the taking of Dom. He must have given them the intel for the raids.'

'And now Will has gone too. Mission has virtually been eliminated as a force. Where did it all start to go wrong?'

Shepherd answered his own question. 'It was probably when I decided not to leave that goddamned Tom Carter to die by the side of the road back in Tamegroute.'

He was thinking that actually it was the price he paid for his hubris in trying to convert the pundit to the beliefs of the Order, but he said aloud. 'Was it just a horrible coincidence that Marsha also selected Stevie, Tom's love-interest, to become her receptacle?'

Trajan was happy that the direction of the conversation was not turning his way. 'It does seem that we inadvertently stirred up a hornets' nest in brushing up against this particular couple.'

'Two insignificant individuals derailing all that we built!' Samuel knew it was far too late for regrets. He had to move on, press ahead.

Samuel was pleased that at least he had enough caution to have withheld one of his collected serpent references from Tom. Even back then he realised that his interest in Ethiopia had to be kept a very close secret. The particular snake reference. that he had chosen not to mention. was from the time when Ethiopians ruled Egypt. They had formed its $25^{th}$ dynasty at around 750 – 650 BCE and it was one of the dynasty's pharaohs, *Taharqa*, who had worn a crown that bore two snakes. Historians suggest that this was to depict the fact that he ruled both Egypt and Ethiopia, but Shepherd knew better.

Well before that time Ethiopia had been referred to by the ancient Egyptians as 'Punt', a region that they had given the name of *Ta Netjeru*, or the 'land of the Gods'. To Shepherd this just proved that this birthplace of humanity must have been visited by our genetic creators.

Further research had indicated that some of the early peoples living in Ethiopia had been extremely advanced in agricultural terms. They were certainly very advanced in digging deep wells, using stone to construct complex irrigation schemes designed to operate both above and below ground. Clearly they must have learnt of these techniques from somewhere, but where? Surely it had to be from an external source; but who on earth was there at that time who might have taught them these techniques?

Before the $5^{th}$ century BCE Ethiopians also developed some of the earliest astronomical devices. They had erected megaliths for use as simple calendars a thousand years before those at Stonehenge.

For all these reasons it sounded to him that this country was very much the land of the Gods, the place of re-creation!

The Professor had been working through his hastily acquired Bible and researching all they had unearthed about the Perpetua Order. He was now ready to share his thoughts with the Foreign Secretary and her invited audience.

'I have to start by saying that theirs is clearly a very confused credo. They present themselves essentially as a Christian organisation, and they do use the Bible and the very early Church for many of their central ideas, but then you need to rationalise this with their more outlandish genetic leanings - alien genetic interference, brain dumps, immortality and the like.'

Sir Joseph snapped, 'Clearly they are just off their trolley and we shouldn't be wasting time considering their craziness, but instead hasten to arrest or stop them permanently.'

The Foreign Secretary commented, 'Isn't the usual advice to humour a madman so you understand where he is coming from; only then are you able to deal with the matter more accurately.'

The Professor proceeded, 'I looked for a link between these two otherwise apparently unconnected strands. It turns out that Revelations may be the thing.'

Sir Joseph muttered under his breath. 'Could it be all the stuff about the four horsemen that gave it away?'

'This New Testament book was originally called the 'Apocalypse of John'; the word apocalypse literally means an unveiling. The whole book is pretty impenetrable in many ways and itself is in much need of some unveiling. It's so obtuse that it permits any charlatan to read into it whatever he might wish to see there.'

Sir Joseph was fearful that this was going to be one of the Professor's habitual long academic diatribes and attempted to move things along. 'If that is the case then let's not waste any more time on their interpretation. Can we cut to the real issue which is where we might be able to find them?'

The Foreign Secretary gave what Sir Joseph often privately described as one of her 'Paddington Bear stares' as she cautioned him. 'This is my meeting and the Professor has been asked to give us the background leading to any conclusions he may have reached.'

The Professor nodded and continued. 'Many dismissed the book as the wanderings of a theologian rather than Holy Writ, but its parallels with the Old Testament book Daniel are probably what kept it in most versions of the Bible. From the information we have amassed on the Perpetua Order, theirs is a Gnostic or Kabbalistic interpretation of Revelations.'

Sir Joseph grumbled, 'The Kabal - isn't that what Madonna and other self-obsessed celebrities waste their time and money on?'

The Professor nodded but was unwilling to be sidetracked by the comment, 'These people see the Revelations as full of spiritual symbolism. It was written to seven early churches and refers to seven seals, and they consider this to be analogous to the seven chakras, or spiritual centres. They also maintain it has other significances in physiology, which leads us back to genetics. In this area they suggest the twenty-four elders mentioned in Revelations 4.4 relate to the twelve pairs of cranial nerves that emerge from our brain stem.'

Now it was the Foreign Secretary who was dubious, 'Seven and twelve are numbers that regularly pop up everywhere in history, folklore, fiction. What makes this occurrence compelling enough for them to credit it?'

'Ah, that's the joy of religion over science! Because it is based on mystery and faith, it doesn't have to be logical. While these numbers are frequently significant in all walks of life, they would suggest that this is in itself notable because they seldom appear in nature. Regardless of that, they are convinced and they suggest that developing your knowledge of these spiritual matters will lead to unravelling layers of understanding.'

Sir Joseph was getting restless again, 'Where does this all this take us?'

'Tell me, do you need to be somewhere else? Is there anything more pressing on your desk?' The Foreign Secretary was getting angry. She nodded to the Professor to proceed.

'Don't you see that Revelations with its apparent symbology, all these stories about plagues, sores on the body, infertility, famine – this is all the stuff of genetics. I believe this is where their beliefs in religion and genetics converge. We managed to download from captured hard drives some of their secret gospels and this is what they suggest.'

Sir Joseph said good-naturedly, 'Reworking what my old chief used to say "Don't bring me parables, give me salvation!"'

'Given you are in some sort of hurry, let me move on to the other major focus. A lot of what they have been up to is more about history and DNA - their grave-robbing and Gene Genie shops. What is that all about?'

'Isn't that how they selected their members?'

'That doesn't explain the theft of relics that this Berkeley character presided over. They are inordinately interested in old DNA, especially any sanctified DNA I believe they are backtracking DNA, seeking out the genetic big bang, the singularity.'

The Foreign Secretary queried, 'I didn't understand Stephen Hawking when he wrote about singularities in his book.'

Sir Joseph smiled, 'Multiple singularities. That's like asking why there's only one Monopolies Commission.'

'They are backtracking to find the moment when they believe aliens meddled with our development...' The Professor paused theatrically, '...and that will inevitably take them to Ethiopia.'

# Chapter 76 - *Lalibela, Ethiopia*

Shepherd's attraction to Ethiopia was not just its status as the human DNA ground-zero; religions too had conspired to make it an important nexus.

Ethiopia had been a very early adopter of Christianity. The religion had not been brought here by marauding missionaries from Europe; it had instead sprung directly from the Holy Land. Ethiopia was involved right from the very outset of the early Church. The Ethiopian king converted and declared the country a Christian state during the 4th century CE. Today almost two-thirds of the population is Christian, mostly Ethiopian Orthodox.

Ethiopia was also involved in the inception of Islam. It was the site of the first migration; the prophet Mohammed had counselled a group of early Muslims that this was where they should go to avoid persecution by the then rulers in Mecca. The country is home to Harar which has over a hundred mosques, as many shrines and is the fourth holiest city of Islam.

Judaism too has strong connections. Shepherd was surprised to learn that the original Ark of the Covenant had not been lost as Indiana Jones and many other fictional characters down the years had suggested. It could be found today within the ancient capital of Ethiopia at Axum, having been taken there from the Holy Land and safely secured in the church of St Mary at Zion.

Shepherd had absolutely no time for the fourth religion said to have derived directly from Ethiopia. He could not begin to understand the Rastafarians and their belief that Haile Selassie was Jesus and that Ethiopia was Zion. Haile Selassie himself dismissed this thinking; and he had been a strict Ethiopian Orthodox Christian.

Shepherd believed the country to be a very important island of Christianity that was set adrift right in the middle of the vast ocean that was Islam. It stood firm against the trends of the region, maintaining a brilliant bastion of the true Faith; this surely could be no accident? Ethiopia beckoned him.

Tom was rather less impressed as he arrived in Addis Ababa. Inevitably he had been reading up on his destination and focused on its more recent history, of the Italian occupation and the founding of Italian East Africa after the mustard gassing of almost a million Abyssinians.

Perhaps his negative mood was influenced as much by his other background reading on genographics. He was realising, perhaps a tad late in the process, that this subject might have an impact on his book; delays for large rewrites beckoned if this was the case. He was having to consume material on the subject during his journey.

He was reading about 'snips', SNPs or single nucleotide polymorphisms, minor variations in DNA used to backtrack human migrations. Research to date clearly showed that the human race walked out of Africa from near Addis Ababa, travelling first to central Asia and then splitting up, some turning left into Europe and others right to travel down into Asia.

The research revealed some interesting anomalies but he was frustrated to find that the numbers and breadth of research did not help with his quest to confirm his Sumerian-Carthaginian conclusions.

His quest was driven by the fear that data might exist that completely confounded his book's theories? He did not need the professional opprobrium that would follow from that.

The really frustrating issue was that the answer which would resolve this was probably in Shepherd and Davenport's huge DNA database. Yet his reason for being there was to damage or destroy it!

Further annoyance resulted from learning there was no time to visit the Ethiopian National Museum where he had wanted to see 'Lucy' for himself. Instead they were forced to leave immediately, though the bustling traffic in the city did its best to detain them much longer than planned.

So it was in grumpy mood that he found himself travelling to a place identified using a combination of Mark Elliott's electronic capabilities and data that Dieter managed to pluck from the Order's network. They were headed for Lalibela.


Having accepted he had been beckoned for a purpose to Ethiopia, Shepherd knew deep in his heart that something else had directed him specifically to seek out the Ethiopian town of Lalibela. He could not have explained how or why. However an absolute faith in his instincts was strong enough for him to take it as a significant and powerful inspiration.

Lalibela was no mystery location; it contained what many heralded as 'the eighth wonder of the world' - its series of impressive rock-hewn churches. The area was named after King Lalibela who had followed in his ancestors' footprints and visited Jerusalem.

The Queen of Sheba had been one of those illustrious ancestors. She had been drawn to the Holy City and the court of King Solomon. Like a moth to his bright light she had journeyed to experience his reputed wisdom. She had returned 'with child', reputedly fathered in rape by Solomon.

That child grew to become king who in his turn had been drawn to visit the Holy Land, only to find Jerusalem under threat. It was he who had returned with the original Ark of the Covenant to keep it safe from unbelievers.

At the time of King Lalibela, Jerusalem was under threat yet again. He despaired when the city was captured by Muslims and set about transforming his own capital to create a 'second Jerusalem', even the main river became known as the River Jordan.

Shepherd was transfixed when he first arrived in Lalibela. The town was quite isolated; lacking most of the modern conveniences, it looked and felt biblical. This was a fitting place for him to be based as he led his Order into its end-game, and on towards salvation.

Lalibela's rock-hewn churches had self-evidently been hard won from the rock by hammer and chisel, though local folklore suggested that angels had come each night to augment the human effort. A number of the churches had been hewn from a single piece of rock, others fabricated from natural clefts or existing caves; all were interconnected by a complex network of tunnels. Implausibly perched high on the mountains, the builders had found natural springs deep within the rocks which they harnessed to provide wells beside the monolithic churches.

While he instinctively drew the line at an angelic workforce, Shepherd did believe that these churches and their artesian techniques revealed a special knowledge. This was further evidence of coaching received from another intellect, an alien intellect that would have been godlike to the simple locals of the time.

The liturgy of the Ethiopian Orthodox Church was conducted in an ancient language called *Ge'ez*, the Ethiopian Bible containing a total of eighty-one books including a number not included in 'western' versions.

Shepherd's interest had been drawn to the book of *1 Enoch* which had only been handed down in the Ge'ez kanguage, though the more recent Qumran discoveries, the so-called Dead Sea Scrolls, had also provided eleven fragments from *1 Enoch* expressed in Aramaic.

Enoch the man was from a very early time. Described in the book of Genesis as having 'walked with God', he was the father of Methuselah and the great grandfather of Noah. The opening sentence of *1 Enoch* is claimed to be the first and therefore the oldest sentence written in any human language! Parts of the book date back to 300 BCE yet it is generally agreed that its contents were influential in New Testament thinking.

It was not only *1 Enoch*'s age but its message that was a beacon for Shepherd. Enoch talked of fallen angels, of couplings between these angels and humans; it provided a first approach to establishing an astronomical set of rules and it also introduced the concept of the 'End of Days'.

Shepherd learned that Enoch underwent an epiphany, when he was given insight and knowledge by the sons of God. He talked of the fallen angels as 'Watchers', writing that they came during the time of his father that they were fugitives from some far off place. Each of these two hundred fallen angels had a name ending in '–el', as do Gabriel and Michael - the suffix indicating 'God' or 'of God'. One of these, named Gadrel, is said in *1 Enoch* to have been the angel who tempted Eve!

Shepherd pondered, 'Was this Gadrel truly an angel or a serpent?' These Watchers who came to earth were not described as winged; they had no halos, none of the angelic attributes that we expect today. But they were quite keen to mate with human females who subsequently 'bore great giants'. These Watchers were also said to have taught humans the use of metals to make weapons and armour, or bracelets and ornaments. They even introduced the notion of cosmetics to womankind.

Yet these angels were not considered beneficial. According to Enoch's *Book of Watchers* it was their presence and influence that led directly to the Great Flood which was a purge or judgment, something that was forewarned to his great grandson, Noah. Noah was told not only how to survive but also of the importance of saving all seeds and life forms within his ark.

Shepherd considered, 'Once more, a genetics concept from a time when the notion was not possible at that stage of their development.'

Shepherd explained all this to Trajan on their walks, 'Here in *1 Enoch* it is all laid out for us; there can be no doubt. A visit from some non-earthly beings meddled with our genes. They brought new knowledge, and clearly they must have understood DNA and other scientific principles.'

So far as he was concerned, 'These Watchers were clearly our "creators". They also helped Enoch to forecast the Great Flood, and they must have briefed him on setting out the basis of the 'End of Days''.

He was definitely in the right place!

Tom was reading up on Lalibela too, a place that had meant nothing to him. The fact that he had never heard of the place was tempered by his recalling that this had been the case with Tamegroute which was now etched into his psyche for ever. Would this place end up in the same category? Would Stevie be there?

Lalibela's largest church, *Bet Medhane Alem*, the House of the Redeemer of the World, was home to the famous Lalibela Cross, a solid gold crucifix used to bless and heal the congregation or any pilgrims. During these ceremonies the old priests looked on while leaning heavily upon their staffs of office. Staffs – the other part of Shepherd's symbology!

His interest was piqued when he learned that another church, *Bet Maryham*, contained a stele inscribed by King Lalibela explaining the secrets used in the construction process of the churches. Lalibela's stele was however reported to be constantly covered by cloths so only chosen priests could study the information. Tom would really like to take any chance to look at that while he was there.

The Monastery of *Nakuta La'ab* was sited a few kilometres outside Lalibela, securely on the tourist route and if anything rather too easily reached. The monastery was named after Lalibela's nephew and successor.

The simple 13th century church was dramatically located in a hollowed out cave, looking very much at risk of being crushed by the threatening overhang, or at least eroded by the constant flow of water running down and through the rock into the church. A natural disaster had led to its rebuilding back in the 19th century CE.

The local priests and nuns have earned an obliging reputation, quick to prompt contributions by readily showing their treasures which include crowns, regalia and ancient illustrated vellum bibles, or simply in return for providing a drink of the holy waters. Nearby villages too see the monastery as a 'nice little earner'. Young children haunt tourists offering to become guides; women with babies slung across their hips beg persistently.

It was simplicity itself therefore for the Mission team, despite its recent setbacks, to take possession of the church without meeting any sort of resistance. The loss of Dom and Will had either left them without originality, or perhaps they saw no reason to change their approach; once again they posed as a UN team securing a local disaster. The local guides and beggars were not very good at understanding the word 'no', but the UN barriers backed by guns pressed the point persuasively; the formal tour guides simply rerouted their charges to visit *Asheton Maryam* instead.

Shepherd immediately took over the church as a base, getting vicarious pleasure from the stark and spartan style of living within it. He considered it his personal forty days in the wilderness.

However the gNOS team did not share his commitment. Instead they erected tents and other temporary buildings in a protective array around the monastery site. These were heavily camouflaged to minimise the evidence of their presence and to minimise satellite visibility. They waited on the old man's needs and upon his next decisions.


Sir Joseph had sought the support of the Ethiopian National Defence Force and specifically the Federal Police Force but British-Ethiopian relationships were not that strong given the recent kidnapping of several Brits with diplomatic connections. They were said to have been visiting an ancient Dalol salt mine in the Afar region, but this had placed them inside the sensitive Eritrea border area.

The ENDF was somewhat preoccupied with its other duties, supplying peacekeeping forces in Liberia and Darfur while having to maintain control of a less than peaceful home front. The police were a little more helpful but only in the supply of local maps and information.

The real data and support came via Mark Elliott who was able to call upon the US Navy resources currently sitting off the Arabian Peninsula, preparing for their next stint in the Arabian Gulf. He also found ready support from those deployed to combat the rising threat of Somali pirates to the merchant shipping in the area. They were delighted to find something more positive on which they could hone their skills.

Mark had identified and monitored Trajan's communication with the various retreats and once these had been pinpointed it was pretty painstaking stuff, but relatively straightforward, to identify *Nakuta La'ab* as the source. Satellite passes were organised and the makeshift camp identified; the Federal

Police were able to confirm that this was a new encampment and Tom and the team were directed there.

Mark had managed to conjure up an MQ-1 Predator from the anti-piracy team. The Predator was a drone, an unmanned aircraft system. Flown at medium altitude its ground-based pilot could keep it on station for long periods while two sensor operators applied its cameras to get full motion video by day or infrared at night. The Predator was flown unarmed; it was perfectly capable of carrying two Hellfire anti-tank missiles but there was absolutely no way the USA or the British Foreign Secretary would sanction any such sacrilege of this holy site.

Tom attended the briefing following receipt of the Predator results or 'product' as they termed it. He was disappointed to learn that not a single woman had been identified by the image interpreters; the intelligence report estimated the numbers distinguished as fewer than twenty males. Where was Stevie then? And where was Davenport? Would he have to scour every one of the retreats to find them? He feared the Foreign Secretary would lose resolve if this were to be the case.

Brain and his team discussed at length how best to take the monastery but it appeared it would be much easier to defend than to attack. The Predator sorties had revealed that Shepherd took a daily promenade around the area and this was judged the best time for any planned assault; go for the preacher rather than his base. Shepherd, or more likely Trajan, varied the route each day so they would have to be flexible and quick in setting their ambush.

The day before the planned assault the British team deployed along one of the routes to try out their approach and Tom convinced them that he could and should be part of the exercise. They had yomped across the rough terrain in the early hours and he was shown how to select a natural gully and use the local vegetation with the aid of camouflage netting to conceal his position.

He was surprised to learn how excruciatingly painful it could be to spend hours without moving. At first he had enjoyed the unique experience. He could not remember intentionally staying still for any length of time since playing statues at birthday parties in his childhood, and that had to be way before his twin William's drowning.

He had feared it would be the heat that would bother him but that factor did not come into play as muscular discomfort took all his attention. He had been in some uncomfortable expeditions, particularly on digs, but he had seldom had to kneel on rock before. He did not want the others to see him as weak and he persevered through the long morning on the assumption that with time he would reach a point where he would become comfortable; but he never did.

At a point when he felt he could bear it no longer he saw them coming. Two of the gNOS men were picking their way along the track; and they would be coming within thirty metres of his position. Now he finally got his agony under some sort of control.

The two passed without any conversation and next Tom could see the preacher picking his solitary way towards him. When Shepherd was a few paces from his position Tom could not resist the opportunity.

'Samuel Shepherd, we need to talk. It's Tom Carter!' Having shouted this from cover he stood up to close the gap between them. His leg spasmed and he fell forward just as a shot rang out from the guards who were racing up from behind Shepherd. When he thought back to this moment, which he would do for some time, Tom could never conclude whether the spasm had saved his life or the guard's running had made him wildly inaccurate.

Shepherd ran towards him, waving his arms and shouting, 'No, don't shoot. It's OK!'

Tom had been hugging the floor since the shot, now he cautiously raised his head looking up at Shepherd who was dressed once again in ethnic garb.

'What have you done with Stevie?'

All four guards came running to the Leader's side and frisked Tom for any weapon. He could now see that there were two more guards out at the flanks of their position who had bobbed up to see what was happening.

'Young man, you need to forget her. Stevie as you knew her has gone. She has been enhanced.'

'She didn't need any enhancing. Just what have you done?'

'You have to appreciate what is happening. We are entering the End of Days and we all have to be prepared to grow, to change to meet our new situation.'

'Where is she?'

'I have given a lot of thought to you and her in recent days. At first I thought it was just kismet that you kept blundering in to spoil my years of planning, but I think there is no such thing as coincidence. You and she are meant to be a full part of all this. My instinct to talk with you in Tamegroute was right. I need you to understand and appreciate all we are doing. Come back to the monastery with me and I will explain everything…'

One of the guards butted in, 'Sir, we need to know if he is alone. How did he get here? Are others coming?'

Tom was quick to reassure them, 'I am alone. I came here for Stephanie Tasker!'

The old man agreed that to serve all purposes they should get back to the safety of the monastery. He insisted that Tom walked with him and the guards fell into their lead and point pairs again, allowing the distance to open up between the three groups.

Shepherd was talking but Tom took little in. He was wondering when Brain would strike. Surely he would not want to wait until they got back to the monastery.

'Have you followed the information I gave you? I would imagine it took your manuscript in many new directions?'

'I can't deny that it was all very intriguing…'

Tom heard a muffled noise behind him, but before he could turn he saw the pair up ahead being taken out by members of Brain's team. One was neatly and accurately stabbed so that he crumpled to the ground like a pile of old clothing. The other was much quicker to react and he and his attacker rolled on the ground, locked together trying for an advantage. The first assailant having silenced his target stood beside the pair for a few seconds until he saw an opportunity to land a vicious kick in the gNOS man's ribs; that was sufficient for the other Brit to prevail.

Tom swung to look behind him and saw the two there had already been dealt with. He started to shout that there were two flanking guards but saw two Brits sauntering in from those locations and saved his breath. It all happened in less than a minute. They had Shepherd captive.

Brain rushed them back to Addis Ababa where Sir Joseph had arranged for them to exit under a diplomatic smoke screen. Leaving a small team behind to liaise with Mark and his surveillance capabilities, Brain and the spy chief had chosen not to assault the main group at the monastery, in the hope that perhaps Trajan Milos might move off and lead them to the Davenport woman.

# Chapter 77 - *Selçuk, Turkey*

The process had been underway now for many days and Marsha was becoming distraught that they were making such slow progress. Stevie had not suffered the deterioration which some of the earlier experiments had shown, but she was not being overtaken by Marsha's wills and thoughts either.

Now a new fear started to kick in. Perhaps an extended exposure to the drugs might start to have some other deleterious effects on Stevie. Marsha was having to weigh that risk against her desire to complete the process.

She concluded that she needed to stop the current approach and give Stevie a little time to recover from her ordeal. Then perhaps she might try the deep-rooted conditioning she had applied at Tamegroute to order Stevie to relax and to accept the brain download. She thought it too dangerous to try it when she and Stevie were wired up directly together.

She could not help but admire the capabilities of this young woman; no previous subject had come close to holding up against the process. Worse still, there had been two occasions when she had sensed that Stevie was reaching out across the connection to plant her own thoughts into Marsha's mind. That should not even be possible!

Unhooked, Marsha was able now to reconnect herself to the outside world and learn how badly things had gone while she was trying to assert her will and her mind on Stevie. The test of her material for the famine had been thwarted. Tamegroute and all its residents had been lost, and apparently Trajan was waiting for her in her office to explain how Samuel had been taken too!

It was as though she had been one of the seven sleepers. What she had thought was just a few days now appeared to have amassed a millennium's worth of mishaps. The moment she had turned her attention to resolving her own future everything had fallen apart.

Why could no-one be trusted to see through anything she set them to do? Men were so pathetic - too much testosterone and not enough judgment or commitment!

And here was Trajan, testosterone personified. The man really rated himself as some sort of super stud soldier and yet he had let a word warrior, a celebrity oceanographer, spirit away his vital charge. Where was his samurai code, his bushido sense of duty, that meant he should fall on his sword at such disgrace?

'Just what use are you? What was gNOS for if it couldn't protect our retreats or our Patriarch? Get out of my sight while I consider what we should do next'

'Shepherd put himself at risk for just that reason. He insisted that he needed these walks to make his decision as to what we should do next.'

'Just go!'

Mark Elliott was able to track Trajan from Ethiopia all the way here without needing to draw on any really high tech resources. The man had behaved like a whipped dog running for home, or rather limping because the recent setbacks appeared to have exacerbated his injury.

He and his team had lost the Leader and therefore lost the plot. They gathered up their personal things, abandoning any attempt at stealth or security as they travelled to Turkey on a series of flights.

Taking scheduled aircraft they had of course to forego carrying any weapons. For this reason Mark had strongly proposed taking them down before they could rearm themselves but Sir Joseph had his way and insisted they be allowed to complete their journey.

As it became apparent their destination was Turkey there was a general relaxation on all sides as this was a country in which both the UK and USA held more sway. Sir Joseph argued who else could they be headed for but for Marsha Davenport? Tom was completely behind this plan too as he firmly believed Stevie would be found wherever Marsha was hiding.

Marsha was called to Stevie's bedside as soon as she woke; no-one was allowed to talk with her before Marsha got there.

'How are you feeling?'

'Fine, what happened to me? Did I have an accident? No-one here wants to tell me.'

'No, not an accident. You have just been undergoing a minor procedure.' Marsha looked deep into her eyes, 'Where were you born?'

Stevie was surprised to hear herself start to say Gettysburg, Pennsylvania. What came out was, 'Getty... uh, Richmond in Surrey.'

Marsha quickly asked, 'How old are you?'

'Forty.., thirty...' Stevie was confused by her stumbled response; she also felt a wave of nausea, a deep feeling of depression. She was unaware the reason for this was her confronting the barrier in her mind and this was all too reminiscent of her terrible time of abuse.

Marsha was confused too. It was evident that some of the brain transfer had been achieved but somehow Stevie was fighting it, still able to access her original memories, her life history and not that of Marsha's that they had been busy inserting.

Stevie asked, 'What has happened to me? Why am I confused about straightforward facts? Have I had some sort of stroke?'

'No, you are perfectly fit and healthy. What was your first dog called?'

'Benjy.' Stevie was now extremely disturbed. She had never had a dog, never wanted one, so where did she come up with that name? More interestingly, why did she come up with a name for s non-existent pet?

Marsha could see that the questions were upsetting Stevie so changed tack.

'We have so much we can do, so much to achieve together. I wish you could appreciate that and not fight me so.'

The words were clearly heartfelt and Stevie gave an unguarded reply. 'I was very keen to come and work with you. I appreciate your genius. My only concern is that you lack compassion in quite a few areas. That's my worry about you, but the Order and Samuel Shepherd is an entirely different thing. I really don't understand why you have allowed him to control you with his special brand of religion.'

Marsha laughed, 'You think he controls me? You think his religion is his? He was a mish-mash of happy-clappy evangelical claptrap before I got hold of him. He's my front man, don't you get it?'

'I don't understand?'

'This world is still largely run by men so I had to use one to get where I wanted to be. Once we get there then we won't really need them ever again. Not for procreation and not for screwing up the world either. We'll still keep some for ornament and for sex, use their extra bulk, their bovine qualities, to do our bidding, but we won't need them!'

'I'm confused. You were a Perfect; you were involved in all the conditioning, the genetic research and development. His was the dream, his the route to Salvation.'

'It was I who found the ancient scrolls that gave us the special knowledge, I who discovered the DNA coding. But you should know all this. What are the three triplets that code for Leucine?'

'There are five CTC, CTG, CTT. TTA and TTG.' Stevie said this with a look of shock on her face.

'And what is RecLOH?'

Stevie automatically replied, 'Recombinational loss of heterozygosity.'

'Which means?'

'It's one of the means our bodies use to slow gene degradation; it refers to the Y chromosome's ability to do gene conversion using palindromic bases. The same process operates in bonobos too.' To Stevie it felt there was a ventriloquist let loose on her. Where was this coming from?

'You see, if you scan your mind you will find that you know much of what I know. You will see what I have done to get us to where we are today. No mere man could have achieved all this, it takes a woman. We develop faster, peak much later. We're brighter and earn more degrees than men. Just consider that our creator made the first man out of clay, but needed much more sophisticated material to create a woman.

'The serpent had to use its guile to encourage Eve to eat the apple, while Adam just had to be told to do so. We are the ones who create and rear the offspring. The Virgin had a child without a man, but God with his ineffable power has never made a child with a man and no woman.'

Stevie had no idea what to say to this; besides she had her own internal battle going on, wondering where these apparently random comments were coming from.

'I am the real power behind Samuel's throne, the true architect of the Order. You need to understand that it's always easier to wield power from the sidelines, keeping well out of the firing line. Who do you think it was who named the Order for a female saint? Why do you think I recruited only female Anglo Apostles? It's also why we are based here in this 'holy of holies of femininity'.'

Brain received the latest reports from his scouts. They had spent the previous night gathering as much intel as possible on the facility which was located a little way up the road. They had also tried to come up with some idea as to its complement of guards and other personnel.

Tom admired the manner in which they reported; the language used was a shorthand that while explicable to him would never have formed part of his lexicon. They talked of cover, firing points, defensive locations, high vulnerability points, best forms of access and egress, fall back positions and they fleshed out the distances between each of these locations. They briefed tersely though thoroughly on all aspects of the laboratory facility, how it was backed up by a linked and well-appointed residential block. It had been night when they made their approach, they estimated the staffing at around fifty personnel in total, a dozen or so in security and the rest being the laboratory crew.

Between them they sketched out their best guestimate of the general arrangement of the buildings. All of this was with no assumptions as to strategy; it was Brain's task to assimilate what information was available and then define how they might best set about taking control of the facility. He concluded that success would be as much about the when as the how.

Brain looked across at Tom as he told his team, 'There's a high probability that Stevie Tasker is in there so we need to be surgical in our approach. There's no place for any hose and hope.'

Tom flashed a look of thanks.

Brain continued, 'We'll go in at oh-four-hundred. One group will attack the residential block with smoke and thunderflashes, maximum noise and confusion.' He pointed at the map. 'Assuming they do emerge from here we will maintain that noise and confusion to herd them across to here where we will take down any who have guns and appear prepared to use them. Others we will need to cuff and subdue.'

He would be the leader of this team and he designated those who would be with him for that part of the task.

'We are assuming that at that time the laboratory will be quiet, so the rest of you and Mr Carter will need to take out the guards and secure the laboratory. Go for you will be thirty seconds after all hell breaks loose at the res-block.

With luck the guards will rush out and make your task easier.' He saw a few of that team looking a wee bit crestfallen. 'I promise you if the humanzees are loose in there then this will be no walk in the park. They're strong and you really don't want to get close up and personal with the females.'

Several obviously knew of his encounter in London and broke into broad smiles.

Marsha's meeting with Stevie had reassured her, for it seemed that Marsha's thoughts and experiences that did not clash with those of Stevie's had been assimilated. She decided to mount another assault on the stubborn kernel of what remained. They were back in the lab, Stevie once again drugged into quiescence and the brain transfer equipment connected and started up.

Many hours had passed while the equipment showed the immense patience that only inanimate electronics can achieve. It searched for the implanted nodes from Marsha's conversations with Stevie and worked from these to overwrite the inherent data that it was gathering from the donor mind.

Stevie appeared to be passively accepting the process but unbeknown to Marsha she had developed two further defences to these assaults.

The first approach she thought of as 'joy bursts'. Apparently the date-rape drug did nothing to interfere with her use of positive emotions; in fact if anything it encouraged them. Whenever she detected any intrusion she filled her mind with happy memories, trying to overwhelm the chemical action with one of her own.

Marsha had explained something of her approach, but now it also formed part of Stevie's memory, part of what she had received from the procedure. She could now fully appreciate that the hippocampus could hold only half a dozen thoughts simultaneously; and then for a maximum of thirty seconds. She understood how the route to her long-term memories was through the hippocampus too. So her theory for this first defence was based upon her choosing to bombard her short-term memory with as many joy bursts as she could muster, seeking to overload the hippocampus and allow nowhere for the implanted material to gain a foothold or access to her memories.

Her second defence had been triggered from her comment a day or so ago about having a soft spot for the epsilons in 'Brave New World'. She had developed the feeling upon first reading the book. Now the fictional concept had found a concrete form in the humanzees, so this mid-term thought had not yet faded away.

One of Stevie's innate skills had always been to see connections between seemingly unrelated subjects. She did precisely this now. She cross referenced this recent thought with a newly-implanted memory from Marsha. It was an obscure reference to epsilon cells present in the pancreas. Her mind immediately applied her skill and made a connection that brought the two items to the front of her mind and, from there, sought out a third.

The first implanted memory told her that the epsilon cells and others found in the lining of the stomach were there to produce a hormone called ghrelin. This hormone builds up when we become hungry and is an important prompt to get us to eat; then another, called leptin, kicks in to tell us when we are full; at least that's the normal process. Ghrelin, she now knew from another piece of implanted knowledge, also stimulates the superior olivary nucleus, a part of the brain that handles hearing tasks.

Stevie therefore had decided to take no food. For almost thirty-six hours she had been stashing it in her bed to hide later. It was the olivary nucleus that was assaulted by Marsha's binaural beat and she had concluded that higher than normal levels of ghrelin would somehow interfere with the technique.

She was holding her own against the process, interfering with Marsha's plans, and when they did get through she thrust any unwelcome thoughts deep behind her barrier. But how long was she going to be able to hold out?

There were just a few desultory low-powered lights around the residential block, dimly illuminating any corridors and landings. At precisely 4am this changed.

On one side of the block there was mayhem. First came the sound of breaking glass which was followed by the noise of thunderflashes and smoke canisters exploding inside the building – all designed to bewilder and panic.

Many had been deeply asleep and would have been confused by the sound of windows being breached, but with the short fuses on the thunderflashes and smoke canisters they were still not fully awake when the noise, light and smoke combined to have them rushing away from the source. Few had the wit to grab weapons, they fled.

The placing of the explosions had done its job. Everyone made for the far exit emerging still not fully awake to an area starkly illuminated by sodium flares. Beyond the brightly lit arena they could see nothing.

One of the more sharply-witted residents raised a handgun to shoot out what he assumed were floodlights, but his arm never reached the horizontal. A headshot threw him to the floor where the other residents swiftly joined him. Most put hands over their heads in an attempt to show no aggression and offer no target. When no further shots rang out some raised their heads to peer out beyond the lighted area. A couple of shots were fired and they rapidly dropped to the ground again.

Two pairs from Brain's team moved through the residents applying plastic handcuffs while the others stood guard. Brain and James, seeing all was in hand, took off their shaded glasses and after allowing a few seconds for their eyesight to regularise they entered the residence to make sure there was no one left inside.

Tom heard the fracas as it unfolded across at the residential block. He just hoped that if Stevie was there that she was not harmed. Do please let her be here. He could not bear the thought that he might have to work his way through all the Order's locations to reach her.

Brain had assessed correctly. The noise had drawn out the guards and they had easily been disarmed and secured. Tom was the third person to enter the labs; they entered cautiously expecting to meet more resistance inside.

The four Brits with him efficiently checked each side door; working as a team as they leapfrogged each other to ensure each room was clear. Tom had a handgun but it still felt extremely unnatural to him. It was heavy in his hand and on his heart. Yes, he had killed, but no way was he rushing to find a further opportunity to do so.

The point team had just entered a room when a shot rang out. One of the men came tumbling back through the doorway, the other had taken a head shot. From his angle Tom could just see enough, no it was rather too much, to know he was dead.

The room led through to another so it was unclear whether their assailant shooting from that room or the next. While one of the team left to fetch Brain they waited to see what whoever was inside might do next.

Tom was getting bored by the inaction, 'You are surrounded. We've taken out all your colleagues, and there's no point fighting for a lost cause.'

'Hah, Mr Carter I presume. You're right. Your Stevie is a lost cause. She's right here and I'll kill her before you get your hands on her.'

Brain arrived with James and nodded to Tom to respond.

'Trajan Milos I presume?' He mockingly described him to the rest of the team. 'He's the head of the Perpetua Order's security team, gNOS. Now let me see, we have your Patriarch, Dom Berkeley and Will Patterson, all in custody, and each plucked from under your nose. We stopped your Gene Genie operation, we took out BiCogNaIT in San Francisco and we made you abandon the Dublin facility. We've stopped your famine, your retreat in Morocco is no more, and this Ephesus facility has now fallen. It will all look so very good on your CV. And how's your leg?'

'A lot better than your monkey throat will be when I get my hands around it.'

Brain urged Tom to keep up the dialogue, while he was making hand signals to his team setting out what he was about to do.

Tom continued, 'Just give it up. You know you have no hope.'

'I don't think you appreciate what's in the room behind me - a heavily drugged Stevie. Lying there she's completely vulnerable. Anyone could do anything they liked to her; she's so high she would just go along with it.'

'It'll be the last thing you ever did!'

'Don't worry I'm not your problem. You see she's being mind-fucked by Marsha. While we all stand around here chewing baccy, the Doctor is writing all her own thoughts and memories over those of Stevie. And, you're too late to stop it. You might get her body back but her mind will be gone.'

Before Brain or any of his team could react Tom burst into the room. Jumping over his fallen colleague and then naturally dropping into a crouch to minimise his profile, he had his gun thrust ahead of him as he blundered blindly into the small room.

Like too many drivers who turn to look at their passengers when talking to them, Trajan had turned to look into the room at Marsha and Stevie as he hoped his taunt was correct and the process was too far advanced to be stopped. Both Stevie and Carter had to pay for the destruction of the plans.

He lost split seconds to respond to Tom's wild attack, which was all it took for Tom to crash into him. He pressed his handgun up and under Trajan's jaw and fired. Nothing - he had forgotten to take off the safety!

He tried to reverse the gun so he could use it to club the big Serb, but Trajan recovered and smashed the gun from his hand. Rolling him onto his back, as he had threatened he closed his large hands around Tom's throat.

As the hands closed around his neck, Trajan was pulled off of him. James had entered the fight and rolled Trajan away from Tom. The two big men got to their feet and sized each other up. Circling one another each looked for an opportunity to do some damage. Brain appeared with a gun pointed at Trajan but James waved him off, he wanted this fight.

They closed and parried each other's blows. Both tried for a kick as they backed away and their legs acted to counter the other's attempt. Trajan then went for his favoured attack, the high kick followed by the kidney punch as they passed each other, but James read it and spun away from the follow-up blow.

As Trajan went on by, James launched a fierce kick to the other man's damaged leg, the one that had received a bullet in Dublin. James thought this went under the category of 'know your enemy' but Trajan bent with the blow negating much of its ferocity.

He turned favouring his other leg which was why Tom chose to shoot him in that knee. Having recovered his gun and removed the safety, he had no interest in this mano-o-mano macho stuff. He needed to get to Stevie. Trajan dropped to his knees and surmising that James and Brain could sort him out now, Tom went for the back room.

He burst into a scene from a nightmare. Two operating tables were commanding the centre of the room. Stevie on one and Marsha on the other, they were connected by a rat's nest of cables and fluid lines that disappeared into the big hoods were placed over their heads. Two technicians were cowering in the corner.

'What's being done here?' Tom demanded.

One of the technicians answered, 'It's a brain transfer.'

'Switch it off. Now!'

'You could do irreparable harm if you do that. Things need to be cycled down carefully or both of them could end up with brain damage.'

The hunger pangs were weakening Stevie's resolve. She found it increasingly tough to summon up her 'joy bursts'; they somehow dissipated within the ever present tummy rumblings. She had set off to recall some happy moment but she kept getting dragged back to the thought that she needed food.

The equipment was going about its patient task to deliver her with Marsha's innermost thoughts and memories. To Stevie it felt that Marsha was doing this willfully, that somehow she could sense her inner turmoil and was building up the pressure to overwhelm her.

The 'binaural beat' was overcoming the ghrelin, or perhaps the sustained use of it could no longer produce an effect. Stevie was using all her skills to search through the memories she had received, to look for new means of countering the effect. Perhaps if she knew how this equipment worked?

One minute she was completely on the defence, feeling as if she would shortly be overwhelmed. She was marshalling her meagre resources, summoning up her hunger to combat that infernal beat. She was struggling to play back her 'joy bursts' to overwhelm the hippocampus and maintain her internal mental barrier; and it was taking all her mental strength.

The next instant she realised she had crossed back through the equipment and was travelling through Marsha's mind. A labyrinth opened up before her. Which way should she go to make all this stop? What if this was a part of the process and that she had finally lost her battle?

She summoned up her memory of the meeting with Perpetua. This time she realised she could see beyond the altar rail. The darkness behind the statue of the saint was flooded with a technicolor light that she assumed was coming from the stained glass windows of the chapel.

The lights swirled and twinkled as she tried to make out the features that lay beyond the statue. To Stevie they illuminated routes into the recesses of Marsha's considerable mind and she realised that the colours had significance. Those at the violet end of the spectrum led to Marsha's darker thoughts and memories. Those at the other end were rosier, more reliable, and righteous.

Stevie knew that Marsha had no resistance to her prying; there was no barrier. She saw how Marsha's love for Samuel Shepherd had once been pure, but how she had become frustrated by his lack of ambition and had chosen to manipulate him. She saw with a shock how Marsha planned to invade her mind and then use her younger body to control the Patriarch even more directly. Sensed too some of the concepts that Marsha believed would develop immortality so that she might sustain herself inside Stevie's youthful body.

She progressively realised she had some sort of executive control. She could sift through the many thoughts and memories and separate the wheat from the chaff. She created a barrier within Marsha's mind and started to thrust the harmful ideas behind this new filter.

As she was doing this she was horrified at her power. No-one should be able to access another's thoughts so readily. No-one should have the right to choose what was right and wrong for another.

As she was reaching these conclusions she became aware that Marsha was rallying. She was sending horrible images and bad thoughts in an attempt to repel Stevie, to get her to leave her mind. Stevie did not believe she had the right to be there; she did not want to look at any more of Marsha's madness. For that was what she realised she was sensing - a mind with so many prejudices, so much hurt. For all her rational powers it was clear that the driving force for Marsha was her strong sense of injustice and a need for revenge against the whole world; all of which was repellent to Steve.

With the last vestiges of her mental strength Stevie tried to leave a positive message behind her. She worked at constructing her barrier across all the dark-coloured avenues.

Marsha telepathically screamed at her, 'Don't interfere! You just don't understand everything I know, everything I am working for. I don't share your sunny outlook about life. It's just a process, one that we need to manage proactively.'

'It's not a process, it's not just biology. You need to learn how to enjoy stolen moments, the sunlight reflected on a lake, the relief of a cooling evening breeze. You have to appreciate what friendship is, learn how love can overwhelm all your senses. Appreciate how growth, change and death is all part of our human experience'

'It's all just chemistry!'

It wasn't just the words that were impacting upon Stevie, all Marsha's beliefs were being thrust at her too. She couldn't help it, she became angry. She generated probably the most anger she had ever experienced before. She used all her pent-up mental energy to thrust the image of Perpetua, her sweet smiling face, into every corner of Marsha's mind.


As I told you earlier, it all needs to be cycled down carefully or both of them could end up with brain damage.'

Tom waved the gun at them, 'Well, you'd better start your pedalling. I want it cycled down now!'

The technicians crossed to the control area and began pressing buttons and turning dials. He kept his gun in sight; there was to be no doubting his objective.

It took the best part of an hour before the technicians could say they had completed the shutdown. Brain had come in during the process to announce they had secured the facility and were handing the captives over to the Turkish authorities.

Tom ordered the technicians to unhook both women from the equipment as members of Brain's team waited to arrest Marsha once she had been detached. It was Marsha who came around first but she was confused and was unable to reply to their questions. The technicians gave Tom a 'told you so' look. She appeared to have lost function.

Tom couldn't bear it. So close and yet so far! Had he lost her again?

He realised that he needed to be alone when Stevie came around, so he wheeled her trolley away. Along a corridor he found a pleasant and lightly furnished room and pushed her into it. Not knowing what he was saying he stood by her side and held her hand, keeping up a constant dialogue in an effort to bring her around. He kept repeating that she was safe, he was by her side and didn't plan on leaving it ever again.

Stevie opened her eyes, 'You're real. I thought you were just one of my joy bursts!'

'Are you OK?'

'I'm absolutely ravenous. Have you brought anything to eat?'

'Seriously, are you OK? They said that awful woman was loading her mind into your brain?'

'She was trying to do that but I managed to contain it, pretty much anyway.'

'You're really OK? You are still you?'

'Yes, silly, of course I'm me. I just have a whole series of other thoughts inside my head that are not really mine. But that's just like having read someone's autobiography I guess.'

'It must feel weird.'

'No all the weird stuff I was able to package away behind the barrier I created when I was a child when I was being abused by that awful priest. I do feel a degree of confusion though. After what has happened to me at the hands of these supposedly religious people I suppose I shouldn't be prepared to entertain religion ever again. But then there's dear Saint Perpetua who saved me when I was a child and she came to help me through this too.'

'Let's get you home.'

'That sounds good. Can we go to a restaurant first?'

# Chapter 78 - *Double-T R, Morocco*

Despite his promise to Stevie they had been separated for a little over three months. Events had rather overtaken them and they agreed they each needed to complete their own tasks to find closure from the whole terrible episode.

Now he was rushing back down this familiar road that already created too many memories for him. He wanted everything to be securely consigned to the back of his mind. He wanted her to come back with him.

Implausibly she had spent much of the last month touring the world with Dieter, Hannah - and Samuel Shepherd! They were visiting each retreat and de-conditioning the Perfects so they could either decide whether to stay on in the community or move back into general society.

One of the many things that had successfully been implanted into Stevie's mind was the control phrase that Marsha had developed with Shepherd.

Stevie was stunned when she tried it out, 'You are the Leader. The world needs your leadership.'

Shepherd had intoned in reply, 'I am the Leader. The world needs my leadership.' Then he proved to be completely compliant to Stevie's instructions!

She also knew of her own phrase, 'Perpetua chose you. Perpetua needs you.' She worked hard to expunge it because she had absolutely no idea who else might know of it. The power she had over the old man was stunning; and she really was not prepared to let someone exercise that sort of control over her.

They travelled as a team to each retreat and used the Patriarch as their authority as they turned the communities back in to the pastoral idylls that they had once resembled. The walls had come down but not before the big screens and the surveillance technology had been dismantled.

The local authorities in each location were invited to see the community and in all cases they had allowed the developments to remain despite their violent birthing and their having displaced the original residents so aggressively.

Stevie had been the one who had the drive and the ambition to plan all this and to make it work. Clearly part of this energy was derived from the mind transfer process. She had inherited some of Marsha's workaholicism, but the wisdom and the emotion were all hers.

Tom travelled to meet Shepherd after the retreats had all been rehabilitated. The old preacher had decided to retire to the retreat on the Isla del Sol. He still had a great deal of natural charisma but somehow much of the sparkle had gone; his sense of certainty of direction had been removed.

Tom took the final manuscript for his book to show to Shepherd and to advise him that he would receive an acknowledgment for the input he had provided. Shepherd was grateful but uninterested in the thought processes that he had inspired. As Tom got up to leave he met Hannah and Dieter returning to Shepherd's apartment.

She explained, 'He was a great man before Marsha Davenport messed with him. He's still a great man who deserves respect and attention.'

'Is he still as sexually voracious as before?'

Dieter smiled, 'Not since Stevie gave me his control phrase!'

Prior to the meeting, while Stevie was resolving the retreats, Tom had not only been working on his book. With the Professor he had led an ever-growing team to annex Marsha Davenport's patents, inventions and discoveries; they had corralled the DNA databases into their care. Once they felt they had grasped all of her life's work, they formulated a series of initiatives that would exploit some of her notions. Others they used instead as the basis to draft legislation and controls that would make sure that nothing like the Perpetua Order could ever emerge again.

Tom had finished his work on this and also delivered his manuscript to the publishers. Apparently Stevie had finished her work too; she had called him to meet her at Tamegroute.

It was with mixed feelings that he drove past the place where he had been shot through the throat, past where they had escaped that night through the wall. He found that the gates had not been replaced following their assault, and signs of the helicopter gunship's rockets were still there. He drove past the field through which he had been chased after acting as the diversion for Brain.

At first all his thoughts were focused on these past series of indelible memories; it was only when he reached the field that he realised it was being worked by humanzees. He drove to the centre of the complex and found a market atmosphere; hundreds of humanzees going about their business.

He pulled up in front of the main building and the door was flung wide as Stevie ran across to him and flung her arms around him. 'I missed you so much!'

'I can't believe what I'm seeing here!'

'Didn't you know? I made sure that I released and then brought all the TGs here from each of the retreats. The Moroccan Government gave me the approvals and we now have a thriving community of around eight thousand. They are so committed, so keen to build something. Let me show you around.'

Three days later Tom was leaving - without Stevie!

She was staying on at Perpetua as it had been renamed - by her of course. She was clearly committed to these creatures that were neither man nor beast, sitting somewhere between the two. With her stewardship she was ensuring that they would have the benefits of both.

He could see that she wanted to work to allow them to develop unfettered, free to express themselves, to develop their own culture. She was so driven that he believed maybe just a little too much of Marsha must have been transferred.

As he looked around he tried to shake off the concern that this might just be fiction being turned fact, the genesis of what would one day deliver the prophesy in the book *La Planète des Singes* that had inspired the 1968 film 'The Planet of the Apes.' It did not seem all that fanciful that we might end up destroying ourselves and that this new community would follow in our footprints out of Africa to inherit the earth.

He drove out that evening through the gate with his stomach knotted with what could only be described as grief - grief that he was accepting her loss to this place and these albeit inspiring and gentle creatures.

The one thing they had agreed upon was that, despite the origins of the new name for the community, the humanzees should have no religion foisted upon them.

His last sight of a humanzee was to see a couple at the side of the road looking up at the stars…

**Richard Dawkins:**
'I am against religion because it teaches us to be satisfied with not understanding the world.'

www.ingramcontent.com/pod-product-compliance
Lightning Source LLC
Chambersburg PA
CBHW071201250626
47159CB00001B/162